# THE BOOK

# Of

# BLOODBONE

## *A San Juan Islands Mystery*

## Book Nine

## By D.W. Ulsterman

**Copyright 2023**

D1737934

## The San Juan Islands Mystery Series:

-The Writer

-Dark Waters

Murder on Matia

-Rosario's Revenge

-Roche Harbor Rogue

-Turn Point Massacre

-Deadman Island

-The Truthing Tree

-The Book of Bloodbone

# San Juan Islands

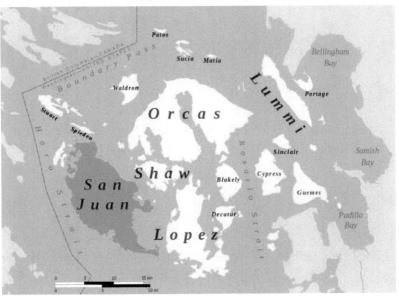

Dedicated to Wendy Cuomo.

Thank you for helping to make these books

a part of the Roche Harbor experience.

# Prologue

Running had always come easy to Jackson Ray, which meant it also afforded him the opportunity to experience that which he enjoyed above all else.

Winning.

Actually, that's not entirely accurate.

Jackson didn't enjoy winning nearly as much as he loathed losing. Not that the competition for this particular race was much to worry about. Most of the other runners were mere area locals with just a handful of exceptions. It was a charity event to help fund the restoration of some historic buildings in downtown Friday Harbor that were recently lost to a fire—one the authorities believed was arson. The group who put on the marathon fundraiser reached out to him asking if he would attend to improve the event's profile so it might raise more cash. He had a far more serious race coming up the following month in Vancouver, British Columbia so Jackson agreed, thinking the San Juan Island race could be valuable to him as a decent tune-up for the BC marathon. Besides, it was just a quick yet scenic flight in his private plane from Bellevue to the Friday Harbor airport. He would land, shake some hands, smile and nod for the selfie-seeking public, lace up his running shoes, and then easily record yet another win as well as a bit of positive publicity. He'd be back home in his high-rise Bellevue condo soaking in the hot tub by late afternoon while enjoying the company of any number of willing women harvested from his long and still growing list of lovers.

A quick check of his runner's watch confirmed that he was reaching the last few miles of the island course as he neared the same Friday Harbor business district where the race had started almost three hours earlier.

Three hours.

It was a rather appalling time, far from Jackson's best, but on this day, he assumed it would still be good enough. At forty-three he was already a marathon elder who had been competing for more than half his life while also climbing the corporate ladder at one of the world's largest aviation companies where he was now a top executive. Age and professional obligations were catching up to him though. The San Juan Island race was his first in nearly three months, one of his longest stretches of running inactivity. While he was certain to win, he knew he had much more work to do if he was to be ready for the coming race in Vancouver—a race he had won three times before. His status among the world's running elite was enough to garner appearance fees in the tens of thousands while his accumulated annual race winnings often reached six figures. While it wasn't the kind of money he made as an airline executive, it certainly contributed to a very comfortable lifestyle—one that most could only dream of living. Good-looking, thin and long-limbed, with a net worth in the millions, Jackson Ray lived a charmed life of wealth, accomplishment, and sexual conquest and he had no intention of slowing down anytime soon.

*Two miles to go*, he thought, grateful to be nearing the end. He was always tired at this point in a race but today even more so. Too much time off combined with a rather difficult twenty-six miles around the island that included several significant changes in elevation had him breathing heavily while trying to ignore the growing fatigue-heaviness in his legs and arms. He would push through it. The slap of his shoes striking the pavement brought him comfort. The sound meant he was moving and moving meant winning and for Jackson winning was the only thing that ever really mattered.

And then he was passed by Alice Cooper.

"On your left," a female voice barked out behind him.

The woman's shoulder brushed his upper arm as she sprinted ahead, the music from her headphones blaring out Cooper's "No More Mr. Nice Guy". She was youngish, perhaps thirty, five foot four or so, lean and strong yet with her feminine curves still very much intact. Her brown hair was tied in a short ponytail that bounced against her upper back as her arms and legs moved in unison like the pistons of well-tuned and powerful engine.

She was also fast.

Very fast.

Jackson's pace temporarily slowed as he processed the shock of seeing a woman suddenly in first position. Seconds ago, he was confident the nearest competitor was hundreds of yards behind him and yet there she was now increasing her lead.

Losing the race wasn't an option.

Losing that same race to a woman was unthinkable.

He would never allow it.

Jackson lowered his head slightly, dug deep, and switched gears. Sweat soaked the soft cotton band around his head and stung his eyes. He lengthened his stride, pumped his arms, caught up to the woman, and then passed her, determined to make his first-place finish as decisive as possible.

Crowds had gathered on both sides of the road by then, cheering the runners on as they sped by the Friday Harbor city limits sign that signaled only a mile or so remained until the finish line. Jackson's lungs burned as he gulped air. *Just a few minutes more,* he told himself.

"On your right."

Alice Cooper had been replaced by the band Heart bellowing "Barricuda" as the half-mile mark approached. Jackson and the woman were nearly shoulder to shoulder. When he tried to pass, she somehow found the speed and endurance to match him.

It was infuriating.

Jackson grimaced as he pushed himself to go even faster. *How is she keeping up with me?* Out of desperation he did something he hadn't done in a very long time—cheat. He jabbed his elbow out sideways, striking the woman just above her breast. She grunted and then elbowed him back.

"Don't do that again," she said sternly as she started to pull ahead.

Jackson stuck out his foot. The woman hopped over it, turned, and then shoved him hard in the chest with a strength that surprised him given her small size. They faced each other in the middle of the road as the people watching the race suddenly went quiet.

*"Really?"* the woman growled. "Is that how you want to win? By tripping me?"

"It was an accident," Jackson replied with arrogant indifference.

"Liar."

Jackson glanced behind him. Another runner was coming into view. He turned and stared down at the woman. "Get out of my way."

The woman shook her head. "You're done."

*"What?"*

"You heard me."

"Do you know who I am?"

"You're a cheater. I don't need to know any more than that."

Jackson started to step around her. "I have a race to win."

The woman grabbed his arm. "Me too."

He yanked his arm away and then took off running. "What the hell?" he gasped as he looked up to see a large raven flying no more than twenty feet directly in front of him. He glanced sideways and saw the fiery determination in the woman's eyes. "Give up." Even as he said it, he knew the answer that would follow.

"Never," the woman hissed through gritted teeth as she somehow ran even faster and started to pull away while the raven let out a croaking laugh, flapping its wings in time with the movement of the woman's arms and legs.

Jackson cursed under his breath when he realized the finish line was now just a hundred yards away. He was running out of road. He groaned loudly as he grabbed his hamstring, slowing, limping, and then stopping altogether. The woman slowed as well and then turned around to face him.

"Oh, I see. You're a cheater *and* a quitter."

Jackson glanced behind him and saw the other runner approaching. "You better get going," he gasped, "or it's going to be second place for you."

"You can't beat me, so you quit. Is it because I'm a woman?"

"I pulled a muscle."

"Stop lying and start running."

Jackson slapped the back of his thigh. "I can't."

"Don't do this. You give up like this now and you'll start to make a habit of it."

"Lady, I don't know who the hell you think you are, but I don't lose."

The runner behind them was now close enough they could hear his ragged breathing.

"Prove it," the woman said. "You and me from here to the finish line."

"A sprint?"

The woman nodded. "Yeah."

"I told you already—I can't."

"You're still lying. That's pathetic."

"And you're a mouthy bitch. Why is it so important to you that I finish the race?"

"You're supposed to be the best runner here, right?"

"So you *do* know who I am," Jackson replied. "That means you also know I'm the best here by far and I'm certainly better than you."

"I'll say it again—*prove it*. If you're as good as—"

Jackson took off running. Within seconds the woman was next to him matching him stride for stride as the crowd cheered them both on. He elbowed her. She elbowed him back. And then, despite his best efforts to prevent it from happening, she pulled ahead. It was impossible. He had never before experienced someone even more determined not to lose than him.

She crossed the finish line first.

A damn woman.

And it wasn't even close.

Jackson turned away, not wanting to see or hear the throng of people congratulating her victory. When a boy asked for his autograph, he shoved the pen away and walked off without looking back. He couldn't get off this backwoods island and return to Bellevue soon enough.

The same raven from earlier was perched on a nearby tree limb looking down at everyone. Jackson swore the bird was laughing at him.

*To hell with these islands and these people,* Jackson thought. *And to hell with that woman.* He made a promise to himself to never return.

It wasn't long, though, before he decided to break it.

# 1.

"I propose a toast." Tilda Ashland raised her wine glass. "To our own little island road runner."

"Yes indeed," Sheriff Lucas Pine said as he lifted his bottle of beer over the table they were all seated at inside of the restaurant lounge that overlooked the water near the Friday Harbor ferry terminal. "To Adele Plank, a hard-running badass who faced down twenty-six long miles and came out ahead. I imagine there were some surprised by your first-place finish but not among those of us sitting here with you right now. We not only knew you *could* do it, but we were also pretty sure you *would* do it. Now you can add marathon winner to your already impressive resume."

"Stop it," Adele replied. "It was just a race."

Suzanne 'Suze' Blatt, the longtime owner of the Friday Harbor bookstore, leaned over the table, her smile and fleshy cheeks pushing up against her thick glasses. "A race that raised almost thirty thousand dollars at last count. That'll go a long way toward helping those who lost their businesses to the fire."

"And don't forget Roland promised to personally match the final amount," Tilda said. "So the actual number raised today is at least sixty thousand."

Lucas looked around the room. "Speaking of Roland where is he?" He tipped his beer back and then set it down. "Not shirking his financial obligations, I hope."

"He's visiting his grandmother over on Shaw Island," Adele answered.

"Mother Mary Ophelia." Tilda's eyes warmed when she said the name. "I haven't seen her for some time. How is she doing?"

"Fine, I think. She's getting older of course."

Tilda arched a brow. "Aren't we all."

"I would have thought Roland would be back by now though." Adele took out her phone. "I'll send him a text telling him to get his little butt over here."

Lucas raised his nearly empty beer. He was off duty and enjoying that rare occasion when he allowed himself time to relax and enjoy a nice beer buzz in public. "To Roland's little butt."

Suze giggled as her already ruddy cheeks reddened further. "It *is* a rather nice backside."

"Nope." Lucas shook his head and scowled. "We are *not* going there."

Tilda pointed at him. "You started it, Sheriff."

"And I'm taking it back—all of it. The next one of you who mentions Roland's ass spends the night in jail."

"Are you talking about my ass again?" Roland stood directly behind Lucas. He placed his hands on the sheriff's broad shoulders and gave them a playful squeeze. "I always knew you were a fan, big guy."

Adele sprang from her seat, wrapped her arms around Roland, and hugged him tight.

He pulled away and smiled down at her, his eyes twinkling. "It seems someone is having a good time. How much have you had to drink already?"

"I'm just getting started." Adele stood up on her toes and nibbled Roland's earlobe. He still smelled of the sea from his trip by boat over to Shaw Island. "I missed you," she whispered. Then she stepped back. "Is Ophelia okay?"

Roland looked away.

"What is it?"

"Nothing." Roland smiled but in his eyes a hint of sadness remained. "You actually won the race."

Adele nodded. "I did."

"That's impressive. Wasn't there some big-shot runner here as well?"

"Jackson Ray."

"Yea, that's the one." Roland grunted. "Adele Plank, you never cease to amaze."

Adele thought he might lean down and kiss her. She wanted him to. It had been far too long since they had shared a bed. Their relationship had remained respectfully distant since the recent Truthing Tree mystery—a distance that left Adele increasingly hungry for his company.

Roland didn't kiss her though. Instead, he motioned for her to take a seat and then he sat across from her and declared to everyone else in the lounge that their drinks for the remainder of the evening were on him, an act which was greeted by a raucous round of grateful, alcohol-fueled applause. Adele spied him over the brim of her glass, taking in his simultaneously delicate yet masculine features. Roland Soros was a pretty man, but time had also more recently imprinted a rough edge onto him, which Adele found intoxicating. She also knew that underneath the tailored clothing was a body that was every bit as firm and tight as her own. The newly emerging silver hair near his temples only increased his overall attractiveness, lending him an air of one who was experienced and knowledgeable beyond his years.

"You're staring," Tilda whispered as she leaned in close.

"I know," Adele replied.

"Are you two in a good place?"

"We're fine."

"Still reading Bloodbone's book?"

Adele shook her head. "I stopped."

"Why?"

"There was so much work to do with the newspaper after the fire, covering the investigation, and then getting ready for the race, I figured I should put it on the backburner so I could fully focus on the job in front of me."

"And now?"

Adele hoped she was successfully hiding her annoyance at Tilda's repeated questions. She didn't want to dampen the evening's good spirits. "I'll start reading it again soon."

"You seemed so anxious to read it before that—"

"I just told you I'll get back to it."

Tilda drank the last of her wine and then motioned the wait staff that she wanted a refill. "I didn't mean to intrude."

"Sure you did."

"Okay, perhaps a little." Tilda put her hand over Adele's. "I apologize."

Adele smiled. "No need. I was being overly sensitive."

Again, Tilda leaned in close. "He's looking so much like his grandfather Charles these days. It really is uncanny."

"It suits him," Adele replied. "He wears it well."

"That he does." Tilda sipped from her just refilled glass.

"What are you two ladies whispering about?" Lucas asked.

"We were just wondering what song you'll be singing tonight," Adele answered.

Lucas frowned. *"Singing? Tonight?* I don't think so."

Roland chuckled. "C'mon now, golden boy, don't deny your adoring public."

"I didn't know you sang," Suze said.

"That's because I don't," Lucas replied. "Not anymore."

Suze pushed her glasses up. "Do they still do karaoke here?"

"I believe so," Roland replied. "I know the machine is still up there. Besides, I own the building. If Lucas really wants to sing, I'll make it happen."

Lucas asked for another beer and then pointed at Roland. *"You're* the singer, remember?"

"That's right," Tilda said. "Your housewarming party back at Roche. You sang and Lucas played guitar. My goodness that already seems like a lifetime ago."

Adele nodded. "I know what you mean." She locked eyes with Roland. "That was a good night."

Roland gave her a knowing grin. "Yes, it was." He nodded to someone behind the bar and seconds later the lounge lights dimmed except for those directly above the small stage in the corner of the room. "It's showtime, Sheriff."

"That's not going to happen," Lucas replied. "I just want to sit here, drink a few more beers, and then walk back home."

Roland stood, raised his hands, and asked for everyone's attention. "In celebration of Adele's remarkable victory at today's race our beloved and fearless sheriff here would like to sing a song in her honor." The people around them clapped and stomped their feet. Roland looked down at Lucas. "You have an election coming up next year, Sheriff. Consider this an early start to your campaign efforts. I mean, c'mon—who doesn't love a singing lawman?"

Lucas sighed. "You are such an asshole." He set his beer down. "I tell you what. I'll sing one and then you'll do the same."

"Listen to your public," Roland said. "They just want to hear from you."

"Me first and then you. That's the deal."

Tilda joined in on the clapping. "That sounds fair, Roland. That way you *both* get to entertain us."

Roland nodded. "Fine." He held his arm out toward the stage. "After you, golden boy."

Lucas grabbed his beer, finished it off, and slammed the empty bottle down onto the table. "You asked for it." He walked to the stage and then kept his back to the crowd while telling the staff his song of choice.

"What's he going to sing?" Suze asked.

"No idea," Adele answered with a shrug.

Lucas, his back still to the room, spread his arms out at his side. He then slowly curled them inward and flexed as the muscles threatened to rip apart the sleeves of his shirt.

Suze's eyes widened as she sipped from her glass of pink champagne and then licked her lips. "Oh my."

Women howled lustily when Lucas spun around and started singing to the music of Bob Marley's "Bad Boys". The whistling and howling continued. Lucas appeared oversized for the little stage, but he made it work, turning, pointing, flexing some more, and doing his best to follow along to the scrolling lyrics. What he lacked in tone he made up for in effort. When the song ended, he pointed at Roland. "Your turn."

Roland got up slowly and lifted his empty glass high above his head. "Sure, I'll sing for you tonight, but you all have to do one thing for me first. Bartender, shots of your best whiskey for everyone. Drink it down and then I sing."

Glasses were filled. The whiskey was drunk. Even Suze managed to get hers down though it made her cough and sputter. "Alright then," Roland said, satisfied. "Here goes something."

Adele watched him closely as he went to the stage. While everyone else might have thought he was merely having a good time she sensed something else was going on within him— something sad and almost manic. A quick glance sideways allowed her to catch Tilda staring at her while she stared at him. She ignored Tilda and returned to focusing fully on Roland. He rolled up the sleeves of his crisp white dress shirt to reveal his tan forearms and then he motioned to have another glass of whiskey brought over to him. When it arrived, he took a sip while looking out at the others in the room. He asked that the lights be turned down a bit and then he stood there, whiskey in one hand, microphone in the other, seemingly watching and waiting for something.

"What's he doing?" Suze whispered.

Adele was so focused on Roland she hardly heard the question.

"Some of you in here might be old enough to remember my grandfather, Charles Soros," Roland said as he set the whiskey down and then ran a hand through his thick hair. "After my mother and father were killed in a car accident my grandparents took me in and raised me, making these islands my permanent home. Charles was a complicated man: mysterious, intimidating, strong-willed, a genuine force of nature. There were those who feared him and those who respected him, but he didn't really care either way. I admired him for that. My grandfather did his thing regardless and woe to anyone who got in his way. Isn't that right, Tilda?"

Tilda raised her glass and nodded.

"I have no clue if I'll ever be capable of filling his shoes," Roland continued, "or if I should even try. Like I said, he was complicated. The older I get the more I realize how complicated life is too—how the act of living can be so tough sometimes. It gives and it takes and it..." He sighed, and his voice lowered. "I don't know." He reached down for his whiskey and took a sip from it. "Anyways, my grandfather loved listening to Sinatra. He listened to a lot of music, but Sinatra was always his North Star that guided him back to the place he was meant to be—here, on the islands. It was a side of him most never saw. He would sit in his favorite chair underneath the lamp at home in his study, drink in one hand, cigarette in the other, eyes closed, playing his Sinatra records over and over again. I knew never to interrupt his Sinatra time, but sometimes I'd spy on him while the music played and wonder what might be going through his head when he did. This song I'm going to attempt for all of you tonight might very well have been my grandfather's favorite and I think I know why. It just, well, it reflects his vibe, you know? Peel away the hard-nosed businessman and at his core my grandfather was a melancholy romantic who would have spent his last penny to have just a little more time with the one he loved most."

Roland looked up and then out at the audience of islanders. "There's not a one of you in here who doesn't know something of how that feels."

The soft plink of a piano started to play. Roland stared into his whiskey glass as he sang of it being a quarter to three. It was the opening line to "One for My Baby". By the next verse his voice gathered strength, filling the lounge while the people there watched and listened.

"He does a rather nice attempt at Sinatra," Tilda said. "Have you heard him sing this before?"

Adele shook her head. She wondered who or what Roland was thinking about as he sang. She wanted him to look at her so she could see into his eyes, but he kept his head down, focusing on the whiskey in his hand. Finally, when he crooned about wanting to say a lot but having to stick to a code he looked up and then directly at Adele, his voice cracking—not enough for others to notice, but she did.

He was in pain. The reason why remained unknown.

Suze dabbed a tear away with the back of her hand as she sang along. "He's really good."

Even Lucas appeared to be impressed. He sat still and quiet and then leaned toward Adele. "Is he dealing with something?"

"Who isn't?" Adele replied.

"I'm serious. Don't forget, I've known Roland for most of my life. I've seen him at his best, his worst, and all the space in between. It sure seems like something is bothering him."

"Maybe."

"Do you want me to ask him?"

Adele snapped her head to the side. "No."

"Why not?"

"I'll do it."

Lucas shrugged. "Okay. I'll stay out of it."

"I appreciate that."

"Maybe I should be asking if something is bothering *you*."

"I'm fine."

"You sure about that?"

"That's enough, Sheriff," Tilda said. "Be quiet and let her enjoy the song."

Adele was grateful for Tilda's intervention. She wanted to focus on Roland, not be forced to answer questions about what might or might not be troubling him.

Roland's voice lowered to a near whisper as he sang of his hope that people didn't mind his bending their ear and then declaring he would make good on the song's promise of having one more for the road. He raised his glass to his lips, swallowed the last of the whiskey, and then gave the room a little half smile that made him appear almost shy. "Please get home safe everyone," he said right before stepping off the stage, zigzagging between all the tables, and then walking outside.

"I'll be right back." Adele got up and followed Roland out. She found him standing on the sidewalk with his back to her. It was a warm evening bathed in the light of a nearly full moon. "Hey."

"Hey," Roland replied without turning around.

"Is everything okay?"

"No."

Adele stood next to him and tried to see his face, but he turned his head away. "What is it?"

"There's never enough time."

"Look at me." Adele touched his upper arm.

Roland glanced down at her. "I'll be fine."

"You just said you weren't okay."

"No, you asked if everything was okay. This isn't about me."

"What's going on?"

"I can't say. Not yet."

Adele was frustrated by Roland's secretiveness, but she made sure not to show it because she wanted to keep him talking. "Why not?"

"I gave my word."

"To whom?"

Roland shook his head. "I can't tell you that."

"This is stupid. If something was bothering me, you'd want to know what it was."

"You're right." He straightened his shoulders and forced a smile. "I'm really sorry I wasn't here to see you run your race."

"I don't care about that." Adele put her arms around his lower back and pulled him toward her. "Are we good?" The question felt empty. The fracture that had developed between them at the end of their quest for the Truthing Tree and the discovery of Bloodbone's journal still remained.

Roland brushed Adele's cheek with his thumb. "I'm not sure I know what good is anymore. Everything is changing." He held her face in his hands. "Have you been reading Bloodbone's book?"

Adele stepped back and shook her head. "I stopped."

"Why?"

"It's hard to explain."

Roland shrugged. "Try me."

"I started to read it."

"Uh-huh."

Adele swallowed hard, suddenly reliving the moment when she first read from the journal's pages. "It made me feel different."

"Different good or different bad?"

"I'm not sure."

"And then you stopped reading it."

"Yeah."

"Why?"

"You know, I came out here thinking *I'd* be the one asking the questions, not you."

Roland's eyes sparkled when he smiled. "And yet here we are, like it has always been for some time now—you and me."

It was a flash of the old Roland, the one Adele had come to realize was as irresistible as gravity. "You and me then, you and me now, but what about you and me forever?"

"Stop deflecting." Roland's eyes narrowed. "Tell me why you stopped reading Bloodbone's journal."

"It really is hard to explain."

"Go on." Roland ran his fingers down Adele's upper arm. "It's okay."

"I'm not sure it is."

"Because reading it made you feel different."

"Yes. I didn't like it because I felt like I was losing myself."

Roland cocked his head but said nothing.

"Like the old me was being replaced by someone else."

"Huh." Roland scowled. "I can understand why that would be unsettling."

"You do?"

"Sure. Here's the thing though."

"What?"

"I still think you should read it."

"Why?"

Roland took a deep breath. "It's important. I don't necessarily know *why* it's important but I'm sure it is. You spent a lot of time and effort to find it—we all did."

"I know."

"Marcus Snell died helping you to find it."

Adele's jaw clenched. *"I know."* The recent shooting death of the former San Juan County health director continued to haunt her.

"I didn't mean to upset you." Roland looked away. "I understand when you say you feel like you're losing yourself. I said something similar to you not so long ago in Roche Harbor."

"I remember."

"But I've come to embrace that change. It took some time, but now I figure why try to hold on to who I was when it has become so obvious it's time for me to continue moving forward with who I'm meant to be. Perhaps it's the same for you. I know that you won today's race but even you can't outrun your destiny."

"That's a big part of what is scaring me," Adele replied.

"I didn't think anything could scare you these days."

"I'm not so tough."

"Yes, you are." Roland looked away again. "I have a proposition."

Adele's brows lifted. "Oh?"

"Make reading Bloodbone's journal your top priority while I deal with what needs to be done on my end."

"You mean we give each other the time and space to take care of both those things?"

Roland nodded. "Exactly. Will you promise me you'll finish reading it?"

"If you promise to tell me what it is you need to take care of."

"Soon."

"Promise?"

"You have my word, Adele. Hopefully that still means something to you."

"Of course it does."

"Good."

"Do you have doubts about where you and I stand regarding our relationship?"

"You don't?"

Adele was about to say no but then realized she'd be lying. She paused, pursed her lips, and then shrugged. "I suppose I do have some concerns."

Roland nodded. "Me too. Like you said, so much is changing with us. We're not the people we used to be." When Adele started to reply, Roland cut her off. "And that's okay. We should be evolving. Wasn't it Bob Dylan who said that those not busy being born are busy dying?"

"Something like that."

"Well, there you go. We're busy being born, Adele. That doesn't mean we can't go through these changes together, though, and then both come out stronger for it."

"It's been a while."

"A while for what?" When Adele smirked, Roland's thin smile let her know he understood. "Ah, *that*. I'm glad I'm not the only one who has been missing us being together. It'll happen again when the time is right."

"Yeah?"

Roland nodded as he stared into Adele's eyes. "Yeah."

"What if we both lose ourselves to whatever future is unfolding before us?"

"We won't."

"How can you be so sure about that?"

"Because wherever you might lose yourself, I won't stop looking until I find you."

"Do you mean that literally or figuratively?"

"Does it matter?"

Adele shook her head. "I suppose not."

"Are you still afraid to read Bloodbone's journal?"

"I am. And not just because I feel it pulling me toward some place I might not want to go, but also because I think I was meant to find it long before I started looking. It makes me wonder if everything that has happened since I came to the islands. . ." Adele's voice trailed off.

"Was for a very specific reason."

"Yes." Adele's eyes widened. "That's *exactly* it and I'm not sure I like it. I can't help but wonder if I've been in control of any of this."

"You think Bloodbone might be manipulating the situation?"

"It has certainly crossed my mind."

"And there's still no sign of him?"

"It's like he's vanished into thin air," Adele replied. "It's been over a year since anyone has seen or heard from him."

"All the more reason you should be reading his journal don't you think?"

"I know you're right about that."

"It's not about being right or wrong. It's about doing what needs to be done—you need to read it."

"I will." Adele smiled. "Thanks for the pep talk."

"My pleasure."

"And the Sinatra song—you sounded great. Can I ask what you were thinking about while you were singing it?"

"Life," Roland answered.

"Yours?"

"Among others. At the end of the day, we're all just hoping for one more for the road, aren't we? Speaking of the road, when is Fin due back from Ireland?"

"Next month."

"And when he returns, he plans to stick around for good?"

"That's what he said. Are you okay with that?"

Roland shrugged. "Fin? Sure. I like the guy well enough and he seems to fit this place."

"I think so too."

"Where will he stay?"

"Tilda said he can have a room at the hotel for as long as he needs."

"She seems to enjoy his company even more than you."

From inside the lounge came the wailing of a woman attempting to sing Madonna's "Like a Virgin". Her voice reminded Adele of the sound a cat makes when you accidentally step on its tail.

Roland winced. "Looks like we got out of there just in time." He turned toward the road. "I should be getting home. Do you need a ride back to Roche? My car is parked up on the hill."

"Tilda has a shuttle picking us up in about an hour. I'll stick around inside with her until then."

"You sure?"

Roland's brow arched after he made the implied offer of Adele staying the night with him. She quickly considered it. Part of her certainly wanted to, but she pushed that moment of lust aside in favor of better judgement, knowing that now wasn't the time for such potential complications. "Don't you try to tempt me, Mr. Soros."

The screeching rendition of "Like a Virgin" reached its climax inside the lounge. Roland rubbed some of Adele's hair between his fingers. "I can't help it. I won't ever stop trying to tempt you, Ms. Plank."

Adele put her hand over Roland's. "I can live with that."

"The real question," Roland said, "is can you live *without* it?"

"If it's alright with you I'd rather not have to find out."

Roland leaned back and smiled. "Deal." He turned to walk away, but Adele held tightly to his arm and then pulled him close. "Is something wrong?" he asked.

"It's been too long since we really kissed each other."

"Has it?"

Adele nodded.

"What do you propose we do about—"

Before Roland could finish Adele placed her hands behind his head and pressed her lips against his while his hands ran down the length of her back and then squeezed her hips. When she withdrew, they were both breathing heavily.

"How was that?" he asked.

"It'll do—for now." This time Adele let him go. He turned away slowly, looked back once, and then walked into the night.

The music inside played on, but Adele's thoughts were already somewhere else.

The Book of Bloodbone was waiting, the contents of its pages demanding to finally be known regardless of the cost to who she was or who she might yet be.

Adele knew Roland was right.

There would be no more putting it off.

It had to be read.

# 2.

*Take by force what was not given.*

*Sell the strong into slavery.*

*Kill the weak who are unable to provide.*


*That was the way of my kind. My father was Haida from the north. My mother's tribe was never told to me because Father declared it didn't matter—they were a weaker people unworthy of memory. He was part of a war party that destroyed her village and took her first as slave and then later as wife. It was from that union by force that I came into this world. The act of my birth killed my mother and so left me to learn my place under the unyielding hand of a fearsome warrior father.*

*Our home was on the northernmost shores of what was by then called Vancouver Island. I grew tall, taller than any other I knew, and by the age of twelve I towered over my father. Yet despite my great size and strength, I still lived in awe of his frightening ferocity until he died of a wasting disease that decimated our village in the winter and spring of my nineteenth year. Some of those who survived returned to the ancestral Haida territories to the north while others, including myself, chose to venture south where, we were told, a near endless supply of potential slaves and riches were there for the taking.*

*We were not many, but we were strong and soon our weapons dripped the blood of those who inhabited the Salish Sea lands to the south. They died as we quenched our thirst for conquest and I became a monstrous tale told to children—a thing that would come for them should they misbehave. The nightmare of blood and bone they called me, and Bloodbone I was forever more. The unfortunate few who dared challenge me met a swift and brutal end. Even the white men who began to place their claims upon our lands feared my wrath.*

*Except for one.*

*He was a capable Russian trapper named Asav and for a bit of gold or a night with a comely slave he would help to guide us through those lands we knew so little of. This went on for weeks and then months as we continued to make our way further south.*

*Asav was devious, even by the white man's standards. We called him the bearded fox. He avoided serious conflict like darkness avoids the light, yet repeatedly we found ourselves doing his bidding, so adept he was at whispering suggestions without others realizing he was doing so. It was Asav who first advised we make our way to the islands of San Juan where we could earn fortunes selling into slavery the more peaceful tribes that seasonally inhabited those generous shores. And so we did, leaving a long trail of death and destruction behind us.*

*True to Asav's promise, our arrival in the islands was greeted with a cautious friendliness from the inhabitants of Tsuhl-whee'k-seeng, which was later renamed Eastsound by the white settlers who would soon dominate the region.*

*They took us in, provided us food and drink and a place to lay our heads. We were weary of war and found the islands a welcome respite. Within weeks some of my people took wives even though Asav warned them not to, fearing that further familiarity with the local tribes would endanger our original intent to make slaves of the most valuable among them.*

*It was during the second pleasant summer month of our stay on the island of Hull, later to be renamed Orcas in the year of 1847, that I was summoned by one of the Lummi described as the oldest and wisest among them. It was said he had journeyed from the mainland to the great longhouse of Tsuhl-whee'k-seeng for as many summers as there were pebbles on a beach. His given name was Goliah Kwult-she, but most knew him as Old Raven. While many mainland Lummi chiefs had come and gone, it was said that Old Raven and his island summer haven had always been.*

*I arrived within the longhouse and was escorted to the back where Old Raven sat propped up against the wall under layers of blankets. He was a shrunken thing, little more than parchment skin and wisps of white hair, barely able to see or speak, yet even then I recognized there was great power in him. His milky eyes strained to make out my features as he motioned with bone-thin fingers for me to come closer.*

*"Sit." His voice was the sound of water retreating over sand and stone. "I have waited so long and now, finally, the greatest warrior of the Haida has come as promised."*

*"Who promised this to you?" I asked.*

*Old Raven smiled. "The wind. The sea. The earth. Those are the true voices of the Great Ones."*

*My heart remained hard and my insolence and arrogance still consumed what little remained of my better nature. "I have come to conquer your people—to enslave the strong and to kill the weak."*

*"I know," Old Raven said.*

*"Do you not fear me because of this?"*

*"What is to be is already done."*

*"Have you not heard of Bloodbone? My reputation—"*

*"Is well deserved, I am sure."*

*"For good reason. I kill. I subjugate. I take what I want from those unwilling to give as my father taught me and his father before him."*

*"True."*

*"Then why would you believe I am the one you have been waiting for?"*

*"Those things you have done make you the worthiest among us for the white darkness that is already here. If this sacred place is to survive it will need the protection of one such as you." Old Raven pushed away his blankets and asked that I help him to stand. His legs were unsteady, his back bent, and he weighed no more than a dry winter leaf. A brilliant stone crystal lay against the center of his sunken chest. Another who stood nearby wrapped him in a sea lion pelt and then Old Raven shuffled out of the longhouse and stood smiling under the warm summer light while pointing to a dark outcrop of land that disappeared into the sea. "When this day's sun completes its journey into the endless sky, I shall be buried there among my ancestors."*

"I don't understand."

Old Raven looked up at me. "I speak of death, something you most certainly do understand. I am tired. At long last my time in this world gives way to another."

"Who?"

"You, the one they call Bloodbone, but I shall declare you . . . Karl."

I laughed. The name was absurd.

"If you are to navigate the coming white man's world," Old Raven continued, "then you must do so with a white man's name."

"I bend to the will of no man—white or other."

"Navigating is not bending, Karl Bloodbone."

"That is not my name."

"It is said. It is done."

My frustration turned dangerously toward outright anger. "You have no power over me."

"Hold out your hand."

I refused, startled by how easily this ancient little shadow of a man suddenly stirred fear within me.

"Your hand," Old Raven repeated. "Open it."

I obeyed.

Old Raven dropped the crystal into my palm. "Close it."

Again, I obeyed.

When Old Raven sighed, a dry rattle shook his chest. "Do you feel it?" he whispered.

*"A heartbeat," I replied.*

*"Yes." He smiled. "The heartbeat of this place that was born long before the mountains were young."*

*When I attempted to return the crystal to Old Raven, he refused it. Just then Asav walked up to us. "As agreed?"*

*Old Raven nodded. "The crystal is now his. The new beginning is upon us."*

*Asav's eyes narrowed. "As agreed then," he growled. "Where is my gold?"*

*"My word is good, white man." Old Raven reached into the folds of the sea lion pelt, withdrew a leather satchel and then dropped it into Asav's outstretched hand. "See?"*

*Asav poured the satchel's contents into his hand—ten gold coins. He looked up and smiled. "Very good."*

*Realization struck. I grabbed Asav by the throat. "You brought me to this place for your own gain."*

*"His idea," Asav gasped as he pointed to Old Raven. "I was here three summers ago and he asked about a Haida warrior who stood as tall as a tree. I promised to deliver you to him—for a fee."*

*"Is this true?" I bellowed.*

*Old Raven nodded. "It is."*

*I squeezed Asav's throat harder. "I should kill you for your deception." Asav gripped my wrist with both his hands but could not free himself from my grasp. To me his strength was that of a child.*

*"This is to be my day of death not his," Old Raven said. "Release him."*

*Asav dug his fingernails into my skin. "Listen to your elders."*

*"I told you," I said. "I bend to no man."*

*Old Raven shrugged. "Then perhaps this day of death will not be mine alone." From the surrounding forest emerged a long row of forty Lummi warriors. "They will fight to the last. You will die as will your Haida brothers. Or you will lead them all for the good of the islands into the next age where they might grow old and fat with wives that bear them many children along the way."*

*I let Asav go. He dropped to the ground gasping for breath. "Why care about the well-being of one such as this?"*

*"From this new beginning to its distant conclusion, Karl Bloodbone, there are parts yet to be played—including his."*

*"What parts do you speak of?"*

*"The lives of important people, men and women, with contributions both great and small."*

*"All are small next to me."*

*"You speak with the false authority of youth. You will not be so young for long and then you shall better understand these things I share with you now."*

*Asav was back on his feet. He held a knife in one hand and the satchel of gold in the other as he stared up at me. "Big or not your guts would spill all the same." He used the tip of the knife to point at Old Raven. "Any more of those crystals to be found around here?"*

*I stepped between them.*

"No need for that," Asav said. He sheathed his knife. "We're friends after all."

A procession of Lummi made their way toward the outcrop of land Old Raven had pointed out earlier. Two near the middle of the line carried a large woven basket. "Ah," Old Raven said. "The long rest awaits me." He reached up and placed his arm over mine. "Would you please help me to get down there?"

I led him to the shore and made certain he didn't fall. The way was slow as he tired easily. The basket had already been placed into a shallow hole that was dug into the earth.

Old Raven turned and faced the large gathering behind him. One by one the Lummis came forward to hug and kiss him and thank him for his wisdom. By the time the last had done so the sun was barely visible over the horizon. "The crystal," Old Raven said. "Let them see." When I bent low to allow him to place it around my neck, the Lummis murmured loudly among themselves.

I spied Asav standing at the back of the group staring at the crystal I now wore, his eyes shining with the light of obsession. Old Raven tugged on my tunic. "The names of the others I spoke of, I will never meet them for they are from a time long past my own, but before I go let me tell them to you." He was exhausted and barely able to stand. I crouched down so he could whisper into my ear.

The Lummis unleashed a chorus of cries and chants as Old Raven was wrapped in a thick blanket and then lowered into the hole with his head facing west. He stared up at us from that narrow little indentation in the earth and smiled. The tide was going out as the last remnants of sun clung to the shore. Old Raven's eyes closed. He gasped once and *then no more. Rocks were placed over the hole and, soon after, the Lummis returned to the longhouse where they sang and feasted in Old Raven's honor.*

*Later that night, I recounted the strange names Old Raven had whispered to me and many years later I wrote those names down in this book. I have yet to know any of these people, but Asav assures me I will. Over time, as the sharper edges of my reckless youth gave way to what I hoped was experience and understanding, he became a trusted adviser who helped to shoulder the responsibility Old Raven left to me—a responsibility I continue to struggle to fully comprehend.*

*And so, even now, I wait and watch and prepare for those who have yet to reveal themselves to me. Are they to be friend or foe and in the end will it even matter?*

*Their names are as follows:*

*John McMillin*

*Robert Moran*

*Samantha Ashland*

*Dylan Bowman*

*Charles Soros*

*Edmund Pine*

*Delroy Hicks*

*And perhaps the most important name of all, though I know not yet why:*

*Adele Plank*

After rereading the first part of Bloodbone's journal Adele closed it, turned her head, and looked out through one of the sailboat's portholes. It was a rainy Roche Harbor morning. She had been up for the last hour gathering up the courage to do what she had promised Roland she would—read the book. Unfortunately, the very same sense of dislocation that had struck her when she first started to read it was back even stronger than before. She took in a few slow, deep breaths and folded her hands in front of her.

*If I finish this,* she thought, *I won't ever be the same.*

The question that remained unanswered was if it was worth it. Adele sat listening to the rain pelting the top of the sailboat. She hadn't yet taken a shower or had her morning coffee so she decided then that the book could wait. Perhaps some clean clothes and caffeine courage were what was required to keep reading.

At least she hoped so.

A half-hour later, Adele was back sitting at the table with the book and a cup of coffee in front of her. She was clean, freshly dressed, and feeling more like her usual self. The book was opened. She continued to read.

*Asav disappeared for the remainder of the summer, not returning until the days grew short and winter's breath hinted at the colder days to come. He looked the same, but he wasn't. His eyes bled greed and his mouth had turned cruel.*

*"Look here," he said as he held up a crystal similar to the one Old Raven had given to me. "I found it deep in the mountain called Turtleback where the earth is alive with the power of this place."*

*"You should not have taken it," I replied.*

*Asav spit his words at me. "Who are you to dictate what I can and cannot do? Was it not me who brought you here? Was it not me who introduced you to Old Raven? I deserve your gratitude not your judgment."*

*"You should return it."*

*"No."*

*I stood and towered over him. "If you won't then I will."*

*Asav stepped back. "You have far greater concerns than this crystal."*

*"Oh?"*

*"More white men are coming. They travel here now from the mainland."*

*"And you know this how?"*

*"I saw their ship from a lookout near the top of the mountain."*

*"How many?" I asked.*

*"The ship is likely to be carrying three or four dozen of them."*

*"That is not so many."*

*"It is if they are armed and their intent is to take these lands from you."*

*"These lands are not mine," I replied. "The islands belong to everyone. They would be taking that which is not mine to keep or to give."*

*Asav's contemptuous laughter filled my ears. "Keep telling yourself that. My guess is those white men have a very different perspective on how ownership works. Make no mistake, trouble is coming. You owe it to the tribe to let them know so they at least have the opportunity to decide if they wish to stay or leave."*

*I noted how the crystal in Asav's hand winked dark when the light from outside the longhouse caught it. It was the opposite of the crystal given to me by Old Raven, which absorbed light and then reflected it back. It was as if his crystal had a black heart beating inside of it.*

*"Did you hear me?" Asav said. "Tell the tribe about the white men who are coming."*

*"I will," I replied.*

*"When?"*

*"Now." I moved past him and stepped outside into the welcome warmth of the island sun. The waters beyond our village were calm, the air crisp and clean, and the skies above us clear. This was our home but now that home was threatened by the white man's intrusion. I would do as Asav suggested and let them know of the danger. Many chose to leave, returning to lands in the north. Those who stayed wanted to fight—a fight Asav strongly encouraged. He was openly confused by my reluctance to do so and that confusion soon turned to outright hostility.*

*"What has happened to you?" he would bellow. "You killed so many so easily before. Why is it any different now?"*

*"I am no longer that monster," I replied. This conflict between us raged for days. Asav demanded action. I ruled that those of us still living in the village would remain patient. It was my hope the ship would eventually leave and so too would the threat of violence. The ship was anchored in what would later be known as Deer Harbor, which was half a day's walk from our village. Over and over Asav would demand we strike them first and again and again I refused.*

*And then the white man arrived at our village and death followed soon after.*

*It was the ship's captain and ten of his crew. They had marched across the island from Deer Harbor and brought with them gifts of worthless trinkets. The captain marveled at my size. He was friendly enough, an older man short of stature with remnants of white hair that did little to cover his age-spotted scalp. His crew were young, strong, clearly capable, and heavily armed.*

*In private Asav again urged me to eliminate them, suggesting a surprise attack on their Deer Harbor encampment. I declined. He argued. And so it went between us for several more days until the captain and his men returned one afternoon, demanding to be shown the location where more crystals like the ones Asav and I wore, could be found. When I declined the request, the captain's earlier friendliness quickly devolved into aggressive determination that I be made to comply. His men aimed their weapons at me. My tribe predictably then did the same to them.*

*It was a standoff.*

*"I don't wish to hurt any of you," the captain said.*

*"Then don't," I replied.*

*"Show us where we can find more of those crystals, and we'll be on our way."*

*I shook my head. "No."*

*The captain pointed to Asav. "Then your Russian friend will."*

*Asav grinned. "For a price."*

*I grabbed the front of his tunic. "You are not to negotiate with these men."*

*"Or what?" Asav hissed. "You have no power over my choices. I am not a member of your tribe."*

*"It is unwise to keep reminding me of that."*

*"I tell you what," the captain said. "I'll give you until tomorrow to agree to show us. We're not just taking the crystals—you'll be compensated. This time tomorrow I'll be back here with all of my men. Is that understood?"*

*The threat was clear. If I refused there would be war.*

*"See?" Asav said after the white men left our village. "It's either them or us."*

*I looked down at him. "Us? Didn't you just tell me you're not a member of this tribe?"*

*"You know what I mean."*

*The only thing I knew for certain was that Asav couldn't be trusted.*

*"We should attack them tonight," he continued. "Let us turn the waters red with their blood and be done with it."*

*"And what of our blood, Asav? Why are you so willing to see it spilled as well?"*

*"All life is risk."*

*"The lives of others are not mine to give up so easily."*

*"You speak like an old man who has grown afraid of the dark."*

*I looked down on him and made certain to capture his eyes in my own. "That is not always fear, Asav, but wisdom. You would do well to know the difference or old age is something you will never experience."*

*"You were once a man of action, a slayer of enemies. It was your namesake—Bloodbone. Now? All you offer are words and more words."*

*A terrible cry was unleashed from deep within the woods that surrounded our village. I ran toward the sound while others among my tribe did the same including Asav who ran alongside me. At the base of a large tree were two bodies. The first was a woman, her throat slashed, her clothes torn, and her legs open. Next to her was her newborn child, its skull crushed by the blood-spattered stone that lay next to it.*

*Asav pointed at the corpses. "Look at what the white men have done. A mother raped and murdered and her child's life taken as well. Yet you seek some sort of peace with those men. You would make victims of us all."*

*I knelt down and felt the woman's body and found it cold and stiff. She had already been dead for hours. The tribe gathered behind me, their shocked murmurs quickly turning to seething rage. They demanded revenge. I understood their anger for I felt it every bit as deeply as they did, but I also knew that such anger, if allowed to overcome reason, could just as quickly be the cause of our own demise.*

*"We march on their camp tonight," Asav shouted. "None of them shall live to see another day."*

*The tribe raised their fists and shouted their agreement and then they grew quiet as they looked to me and awaited my response.*

*"Do not deny them this," Asav whispered.*

*I felt the eyes of my people burning into me. There were more of us than the white men, but they had guns and we did not. Many would die on both sides and yet a terrible wrong had been committed. Doing nothing was never a consideration. I sighed and then nodded. "Begin the preparations," I said. "Tonight, we go to war."*

*Asav beamed as he slapped my shoulder. "Well done. This will be a great victory for you and your people."*

*Even then I sensed some version of betrayal. Asav was manipulating me. I knew not how or why, but I was certain of it. Lacking the proof and with two of my tribe already dead and the rest understandably hungry for retribution, I felt I had no choice but to proceed with the planned attack on the white men's encampment.*

*I was such a fool.*

# 3.

Adele closed the journal. She got up, placed her coffee cup in the sink and then stepped outside to find the clouds and rain had been pushed out by the sun. The Roche Harbor docks were already bustling with tourists walking around while marveling at the multi-million-dollar yachts that occupied many of the marina slips. The air was still and the surrounding waters like glass.

*"Look here," he said as he held up a crystal similar to the one Old Raven had given to me. "I found it deep in the mountain called Turtleback where the earth is alive with the power of this place."*

So Asav had said to Bloodbone centuries ago. Adele turned to look in the direction of Orcas Island and Turtleback Mountain. She knew the cave Asav spoke of, having discovered it years ago when she was first looking for Bloodbone. She had returned there more recently to try to find him again but only went ten or so feet inside because of the swarm of bats that had greeted her during her first visit there, an experience she had no interest in repeating.

*Sooner or later, I'm going to have to go back into that cave,* she thought.

Adele started to step onto her sailboat when she spied Roland leaving the harbor on the large dinghy that served his beautiful Burger yacht that remained a proud fixture of the resort.

He had already reached open water and was turning east into nearby Spieden Passage. She wondered if he was on his way to Shaw Island again to see Mother Mary Ophelia. *Two trips there in as many days,* she wondered. *That's unusual.* She thought of jumping into her powerboat that she kept tied up alongside the sailboat and following him but decided against it. The last thing their relationship needed at the moment was her being caught spying on him.

As always, Tilda's Roche Harbor Hotel stood watch at the back of the resort. Adele considered stopping in for a quick visit but knew Tilda would inevitably ask how her reading of Bloodbone's journal was going and she didn't feel like answering those kinds of questions just yet. She bent down and touched her toes, trying to loosen leg muscles that remained sore from yesterday's marathon.

A pair of sea otters played at the end of the dock, rolling in the water and then swimming happily on their backs as they appeared to smile up at the blue skies above them. Footsteps approached Adele from behind. She turned to find a college-aged, blonde-haired woman walking up to her while holding a small white bag. Her shirt indicated she was a member of the resort's seasonal staff.

"Ms. Plank?" The young woman's voice, like her face, was cheerfully pleasant.

"Yes?" Adele answered.

The woman handed her the bag. "Ms. Ashland asked that I drop this off with you. She thought you might be too busy to stop in at the hotel for breakfast, so she wanted to make sure you had a snack to help you with your reading assignment."

Inside the bag were two freshly baked donuts from the resort's popular dockside restaurant. "Thank you," Adele said.

The woman flashed a bright smile. "You bet."

"And please tell Tilda thank you for me as well."

"Can I get you anything else?"

"I'm good."

She started to turn away but then stopped while fidgeting with the hem of her shorts.

"What is it?" Adele asked her.

The woman cleared her throat. "I'm a big fan of your articles. I read them all the time back in college."

"Thanks."

"The message Ms. Ashland sent with me."

"Uh-huh."

"The reading assignment. I was wondering, I don't mean to pry, but are you reading something for another article?"

"I don't think so."

The woman appeared disappointed. "Oh. I'm sorry. It was a stupid thing to ask and I shouldn't be bothering you like this."

Adele smiled. "It's okay, Sky."

"How did you know my name?"

Adele pointed at the tag.

Sky looked down at the front of her shirt and then up at Adele, her cheeks red with embarrassment. "Duh. I'm such an idiot sometimes."

"Can I ask you a question?"

"Sure." Sky's brows lifted. "What is it?"

"Why do you want to know what I'm reading?"

Sky shifted on her feet. "I was being stupid. I'm sorry."

"You really should stop putting yourself down so much. There's nothing wrong with asking questions. I do it all the time. Asking questions and then trying to figure out the answers is pretty much the model for how I live my life."

"Your life is awesome."

"Awesome? I don't know about that. Interesting, sure, sometimes. What year are you?"

"I'll be starting my junior year at Washington State in the fall."

"And what's your major?"

"Journalism."

"Ah," Adele said. "Now I get it."

"Your story about the writer, Decklan Stone, and how he found his wife still alive after all those years, it was amazing. And then the thing with the poor sea lion that was being experimented on by that crooked Professor Khan, I mean you actually get to make a difference in the world, Ms. Plank."

"Call me Adele."

"One of the reasons I took this job was so I might have a chance to meet you and now it's actually happening. I'm sort of freaking out right now. I mean seriously—you're standing right here in front of me."

"Please don't freak out, Sky." Adele held up the bag of donuts. "At least not until after I get some empty calories in me first."

"Did you really win the island marathon yesterday?"

Adele nodded. "I did."

"Is there anything you *can't* do?"

"Believe me, there are plenty of things I can't do. I have a lot of help around here—people I can count on."

"Like the sheriff."

"Yes, he's one of my closest friends."

"He's so fricking hot. All the dock girls start buzzing when he stops by. I mean that body—my goodness."

Adele chuckled. "He does keep himself fit."

"And you're friends with Ms. Ashland."

"I am."

"She sorta scares me."

"Tilda has that effect on most people, but underneath the tough exterior is a really beautiful soul."

Sky looked up and squinted at the sun. "This really is a special place, isn't it?"

"No doubt," Adele replied.

"Magical." Sky stared into Adele's eyes. "I feel that magic when I read your articles."

"Thank you."

"Well, I should let you get back to whatever you were doing, Ms. Plank."

"Adele."

"Oh, Adele, right—sorry."

"Don't be so quick to apologize."

Sky scowled. "What?"

"Would you like some free advice?"

"From you?"

"Sure."

"Of course I would."

"You'll be graduating with your degree in another year or so, right?"

"Uh-huh."

"And after that you'll be trying to find your place in the world."

"That's the plan."

"That same world will try to box you in," Adele said. "People will want to label you, to minimize you, to make you conform to their version of you."

"Because I'm a woman?"

"Partly, but mostly because that's what society does more and more these days. Everyone and everything are supposed to have a label and then you're made to not deviate from those expectations. Instead of wasting time trying to live up to what others want, spend that time learning what is actually best for you. Be your own person, Sky. See this world for what it truly is by looking at it through your own eyes and don't *ever* apologize for doing so. As much as you might think I have all the answers, I'm telling you I don't. I'm learning something new all the time—mostly about myself. I hope to keep learning like that until the day I die. It doesn't matter if you're a journalist or a window washer—unless you know the truth about who you are and who you want to be you'll always be a slave to the perceptions of others and that's a prison from which real happiness can never survive and flourish."

Sky stood there blinking with her mouth hanging open. "Wow," she eventually mumbled. "That was some heavy subject matter you just unloaded on me." Her brow furrowed as she sighed. "Thanks. What you said really means a lot—especially coming from you."

"My words don't mean any more than anyone else's."

"Yes, they do. You're what I hope to be someday. For someone like me your words mean everything."

"You're required to do an internship next year as part of your journalism program, right?"

Sky nodded.

"Do you have anything lined up for that yet?"

"No. I won't start applying until winter quarter."

"I tell you what, if you're able to make it back out to the islands next year you have an open invitation to intern with my newspaper—and we'll pay you. I hate the idea of having someone work for nothing."

Sky's eyes widened. *"Seriously?"*

"Yeah."

"I don't know what to say." Sky looked like she might cry. "I just came here to give you some donuts and now you're offering me an internship. That's amazing. Thank you so much."

"I'll let you in on a little secret about how things work here in Roche Harbor."

Sky cocked her head.

Adele pointed at the hotel. "Almost nothing happens without Tilda either letting it happen or making it happen. I'm pretty sure this was an example of the latter. She sees potential in you, figured I would see the same, and that your donut delivery had a reasonable chance of turning into something more."

"I guess I should be thanking her as well then."

"It certainly wouldn't hurt."

"Thank you again, Ms. Plank."

"It's Adele, remember?""

Sky's smile was warm and her gratitude sincere. "Right—Adele."

"Enjoy your summer here. I'm betting you won't ever forget it."

"I know I won't. I'll be in touch early next year about that internship. Please don't forget."

"I won't. I'm looking forward to it." Adele watched Sky walk away, remembering that it wasn't so long ago that she was the young and idealistic college student coming to the islands for the first time. Looking back now it felt like it had all happened in the blink of an eye.

*"There's never enough time."*

Those were Roland's words spoken to Adele last night in Friday Harbor when it was so clear to her that something was troubling him. She was certain he would let her know what it was eventually when he was ready.

Until then she had more reading to do and fresh donuts to enjoy.

# 4.

*We killed them all.*

*Asav was especially enthusiastic to see blood spilled that night.*

*I took no pleasure in the many lives ended. The shouts that quickly turned to screams, the gunfire, the blades sinking into soft flesh, the ground that turned crimson, it was all a revoltingly terrible mistake. Those white men did not deserve the brutal end that visited them under cover of darkness.*

*Seven of my own people lay dead as well. Another five were likely to die soon from their injuries and four more would require weeks to recover. Within days half of those who had survived left the island for the supposed safety of the northern lands. More were likely to follow until eventually only Asav and I would remain.*

*"They'll return," Asav said as we sat together around the fire inside of the longhouse. "But until then their absence gives us time to search for more of those crystals inside the mountain."*

*"Those are not yours to take," I warned.*

*"So you keep telling me."*

*I watched the bodies being strapped across a line of canoes that sat in the water waiting to take them to a little remote island along the north shore of nearby West Sound that would one day be known as Skull Island. It was Asav's idea to put them there, thinking they wouldn't be found should someone show up looking for the captain and his crew. When I asked him what should be done with their ship, Asav smiled. "After we remove any valuables aboard, we burn it until there is no evidence it was ever here at all."*

*"It appears you have thought of everything."*

*Asav looked up. "That is why I am so valuable to you. If you wish to keep your people and these islands safe, then you need me to help."*

*"And why is that?"*

*"I know how the white man thinks."*

*"Because you are one."*

*Asav squeezed the crystal that now hung around his neck with fingers still stained by the blood of the men he recently killed. "You and I are not so different."*

*"We are nothing alike and you will not be returning to the mountain cave to take that which is not yours. Do not test me."*

*Asav cursed in Russian and then laughed. "These islands have changed you, my friend."*

*"I hope that to be true."*

*"Why? What was so wrong with the man you were before?"*

*"My purpose is no longer to destroy but to protect and nurture."*

*Asav laughed again. "That old sack of skin and bones who gifted you that crystal really got into your head didn't he? What's the name he gave you? Karl, was it?" He nodded. "I suppose Karl suits you now because Bloodbone sure as hell doesn't."*

*"Your opinion of me means nothing."*

*"No?"*

*"I am discovering my own truth."*

*Asav pointed to the dead bodies strapped to the canoes. "That truth helped us to kill those men. Don't run from who you are—embrace it. You are a fearsome warrior who has taken countless lives because you can. There is no shame in that. There is only power and in this life, power is everything."*

*"I will not be a slave to your perceptions of who I should be for that would be a prison from which real happiness can never survive or flourish."*


Adele sat up straight while staring down at the words she had just read. She had spoken almost the exact same thing to Sky earlier. *But I never read those words before,* she thought. *How would I have known to say them now?* She wanted to believe it was coincidence but knew better.

Something more was going on.

Much more.

Bloodbone's story continued.


*"Happiness?" Asav sneered. "Gold in my pockets and warm flesh to share a bed with—those are what helps to make this miserable existence of ours bearable."*

*"What of your spirit?" I asked him. "And the spirits of your ancestors and the world beyond this one?"*

*"There is no world beyond here. No spirits. No souls. There is only right now and then there is nothing."*

*"You are wrong about that."*

*"I suppose sooner or later we'll both find out who is right and who is wrong."*

*"There is darkness in you, Asav."*

*"There is darkness in every man—yourself included."*

*"True."*

*"Ah!" Asav grinned as he stood. "We finally found something to agree on." When he left, I felt a sense of relief, like some great weight was lifted from me. So it would remain between us, our differences further magnified by the passage of so much time.*

*Later that evening, Old Raven visited me in a dream as I lay on my back wrapped in furs while trying to forget the images and sounds of the killings that took place earlier.*

*His face was partially hidden in shadow, but the eyes shone like black ice as he stared down at me.*

*"This is to be your only warning," he said. "Never again."*

*"Never again?" I replied. "I don't understand."*

*"Never again are you to take a life by your own hand or to directly intervene in events that have yet to unfold. To do so is to terminate the agreement between yourself and the islands."*

*"What agreement?"*

*Old Raven pointed at the crystal he had given me. "My time was then. Your time is now."*

*I tried to sit up but couldn't move.*

*"This longhouse you now sleep in," Old Raven continued, "was built more than two hundred summers ago when I was still a boy."*

*"You have witnessed more than two hundred summers? That isn't possible."*

*Old Raven's mouth widened into a toothless smile. "Here all things are possible."*

*"Again, I don't understand."*

*"You will."*

*"Why am I forbidden from direct intervention?"*

*"Because that is the way it has always been for those like us. Are you familiar with the Christian concept of free will?"*

*I nodded.*

*"Then that is an example for you to follow. The people of these islands, for better or worse, must be allowed to seek out destinies of their own choosing. If you were to use the knowledge you will accumulate over time to directly manipulate future events, that future will have been corrupted by your hand. This is not allowed."*

*"Who doesn't allow it?"*

*"The islands."*

*Though my confusion remained I no longer bothered to share it with Old Raven. Instead, I lay there still and quiet, waiting for him to continue. He gave me an approving nod.*

*"Good."*

*"What is good?" I asked.*

*"You are learning to watch and to listen," he answered.*

*"What is my purpose here?"*

*"You are to be the protector of the islands."*

*"Like you were?"*

*"Yes and no. Each must find their own unique path and yours has yet to be taken."*

*"And what of the white men who will continue to come here? What am I to do about them?"*

*"Nothing."*

*"Is it not my purpose to protect the islands from them?"*

*Old Raven shook his head. "No. Think of the white man as you would the rising and retreating of the tide—there is nothing to be done to stop it. The trick is to find ways to live in harmony with that inevitability."*

*"But won't they eventually take everything from this place?"*

*"Some will try."*

*"Like Asav."*

*"The islands believe he has a purpose."*

*I frowned as I again tried to sit up. "Purpose? Asav? His purpose will never extend beyond his own greed."*

*"All will be revealed eventually."*

*"When?"*

*"I do not know."*

*"You speak of the islands as if they are living things."*

*Old Raven bent down until his face was inches from mine. I could smell the earth and saltwater on him and his breath was the whisper of days long ago. "Because they are. The life force here is ancient and powerful. I know you feel it."*

*"I feel something but know not what it is."*

*"In time you will." Old Raven drew back until his features were hidden in shadow and only his glimmering eyes could be seen. "What do you know of the white spirit bear?"*

*"Only the stories told to me when I was a child. That a white bear was meant to be a reminder of the passage of time."*

"It is that and so much more. The white spirit bear was a thing of great power and a traveler of time and space, especially to those undiscovered corners of the earth where remnants of the magic of the ancients remained. One such bear is said to have found these islands when the world was still young."

"I do not believe in such foolish tales."

Old Raven's eyes sparked like the embers of a fire. "There is no need for you to believe in them because they believe in you. Merely saying you do not believe does not make it so. One may claim not to believe in good or evil, but both exist the same as life and death or the earth and the sun. Too often people use a lack of belief to excuse what is actually a lack of understanding."

"I was not making excuses. I am my own man free to choose how I see myself and the world I live in."

"Were you your own man when you recently chose to kill or was that done at the request of your Russian friend?"

"Asav is no friend."

"And yet you continue to listen to his counsel."

"You are the one who made a deal with him to bring me here."

"As I said, he has a part to play."

The weight that had been holding me down under the blankets was suddenly lifted. I stood and towered over Old Raven, yet despite the great difference in size between us, it was I who feared him. "You're not real. This is a dream, a vision, an imagining."

*Old Raven chuckled. "Make up your mind, Karl."*

*"I am Bloodbone."*

*"Yes, Karl Bloodbone—protector of the islands."*

*I moved past him and stepped out of the longhouse and into the night where a star-scattered sky greeted me. The air was warm and heavy. In the distance I heard waves gently kissing the sand and pebble shore where a large madrone tree's branches reached out over the water. It was a place I returned to often during the seemingly unending days, weeks, and years that followed that night. I thought then of fleeing and rejoining my original tribe far to the north.*

*"You cannot run from your destiny," Old Raven croaked from inside the longhouse. "No more than you could run from the wind at your back."*

*I sighed, knowing he was right. My fists clenched. "I am Bloodbone." The words sounded foolish, desperate, and weak.*

*"You are already so much more than that."*

*The crystal felt warm against my chest. I glanced down at it and then spun around, prepared to confront Old Raven and his plans to control my future, but he was no longer there, making me question if he had been there at all.*

*Looming high above the fir trees that stood watch over the longhouse was Turtleback Mountain. I noted how the moonlight that illuminated its peak was the exact same color as the crystal around my neck. The mountain beckoned me—a gentle tug that was becoming more forceful, urgent, and demanding.*

*A journey into the mountain had to be taken.*

*I would leave at first light.*


Adele marked the page and then closed the journal. She looked out through the porthole and was shocked to discover that morning had already turned to afternoon. *I've been reading for hours,* she thought. It didn't seem possible and yet her phone confirmed the time. Her head cocked at the sound of footsteps and soft whistling. A familiar pair of shoes passed by the porthole—Roland's shoes. She waited for him to knock on the side of the sailboat, but he kept walking.

"Hey," Adele shouted as she scrambled out of the sailboat and onto the dock. "No hello for me?"

Roland stopped with his back to her while keeping his hands shoved into the side pockets of his jacket. "I didn't think you were home," he mumbled, his voice unusually low and soft.

"I saw you leaving this morning."

There was no reply.

"Did you go to Shaw again to see Ophelia?"

Roland's shoulders straightened and his head tilted upward. "Yeah."

Adele's mouth went dry as she sensed bad news was coming. She cleared her throat. "What is it?"

"I'm truly an orphan you know."

"Roland, please tell me what's going on."

"I lost my parents, my grandparents, and now. . ."

"Roland," Adele said as she reached out to touch his shoulder.

He turned around looking every inch the smartly dressed island-casual businessman. Even his hair was its usual perfection despite the boat ride to Shaw and back. The eyes told a different story though. They swirled with the same pain and confusion Adele had seen in them earlier, but now even more so. His jaw clenched as he scowled while looking down at his feet. She knew what he was about to say, but that knowing made the words no less jarring to hear.

Roland looked up. "Ophelia is dying."

# 5.

"You can talk to me if you feel like it or we can just sit here together." Adele reached across the little galley table inside of her sailboat and patted the top of Roland's hand. "Whatever you want."

Roland sipped his coffee, sighed, and then gave Adele's hand a light squeeze. "Thanks." He leaned back, closed his eyes, and rolled his head from side to side. "I promised her I wouldn't tell anyone, but time is running out. People should know so they have a chance to say their goodbyes."

"What's wrong with her?"

"It's something called Rasmussen's encephalitis and she's suffering from an especially rare and aggressive form. It causes inflammation in parts of the brain that leads to strokes that get progressively worse. I flew a specialist from Seattle out to Shaw last week to examine her. He said it's likely she suffered her first stroke about a month or two ago and she's had multiple ones since then. He suspects her brain is covered in lesions. She can't get out of bed; her vision is getting worse; sometimes it's hard for her to speak and it won't be long before she can no longer swallow food or drink."

"There's no treatment?"

Roland shook his head. "Not really. The only option is to remove the already damaged parts of her brain, which would then leave her in a permanent coma."

"My God."

"Yeah, it's grim. Besides, Ophelia told me she's not leaving the islands. I offered to transport her to anywhere that could give her the best possible care, but she refused."

"I respect her determination to die on her own terms."

Roland flinched when Adele said the word die. "I know I shouldn't be so shocked. She's well into her eighties after all, but I just thought there would be more time for us to be our own unique little version of a family, you know? She seemed like one of those people who would just go on living forever."

"I'm so sorry, Roland."

"I have a favor to ask."

"Name it."

"Come with me to Shaw tomorrow morning. I know you're busy with Bloodbone's journal, but I hoped that just a few hours or so wouldn't be too much of a hassle for you."

"Done," Adele said. "Not a problem."

"You sure?"

"Absolutely."

"I have to warn you, she's looking pretty rough. I think that's part of the reason why she doesn't want anyone besides me to see her."

Adele was caught off guard by the arrival of tears that left wet tracks down her cheeks. "Poor Ophelia."

Roland brushed away his own tears. "I wouldn't have known about my connection to her if not for you. I won't ever forget that."

The compliment made Adele want to cry even more as the realization that Mother Mary Ophelia would soon be gone suddenly hit her hard. "We've been through a lot together and I'm here for you now, Roland. No matter what, I always will be."

"Do you remember the first time we saw each other?"

Adele smiled. "I do. It was a county council meeting. You stood up to make a comment looking like the island edition of Richie Rich and I was wondering what you were all about."

"The island edition of Richie Rich?" Roland shook his head. "Not exactly the image I want to project."

"You seemed so serious and confident, but, even then, I sensed your bad boy side."

"Oh? You like the bad boys huh?"

"Not necessarily. My likes and dislikes have always been on a case-by-case basis."

"If I recall correctly, you were giving Lucas a pretty hard look as well in those days."

"What do you mean *in those days*? I still enjoy checking out that hard body scenery of his."

Roland shook his finger. "Watch it."

"Believe me, I'm watching it. I'm watching *all* of it."

"Are we still talking about Lucas?"

Adele chuckled. "You tell me."

"Didn't you two take a bath together once?"

"We most certainly did not."

Roland frowned as he scratched his head. "Really? Because I seem to recall—"

"He fell asleep in the bathtub and I helped to get him out."

"That's right—you got to see the golden boy in all his natural glory."

"I suppose you could put it that way." Roland's devious little grin made Adele's heart flutter.

*"Well?"* he asked.

Her eyes narrowed. "Well, *what?*"

"You know what."

Adele blushed. "Nope—not going there."

"It's nice to see I can still manage to embarrass you."

"Besides, it's not a fair question."

"Why is that?"

"The water was cold."

"The water was. . ." Roland paused and then his brows lifted. "Ah, yes, the great enemy of insecure men the world over—cold water."

Adele shrugged. "Frankly I don't know how you all walk around with those temperamental little things."

"Hey now, go easy on the use of the adjective *little.*"

"If the adjective fits. . ."

Roland laughed. Then he went quiet, his shoulders slumped, and he sighed. "I appreciate you trying to take my mind off of what is going on with Ophelia." He turned his head and looked through one of the portholes. "I think I'm going to go for a walk."

"Mind if I tag along?" Adele asked.

"I'd like that."

"Are you sure? Because if you want to be alone, I understand."

"I don't want to be alone."

Adele nodded. "Okay, I'm ready when you are."

They stepped outside together. The sun peeked out between mounds of slow-moving clouds while a firm breeze blew across the marina.

Adele turned toward Roland. "Where to?"

"I was thinking we could head out to White Point. There's a nice lookout there with views of Horseshoe Bay."

"Sure. I run out that way all the time."

Once beyond the resort they walked side by side for some time without talking. Roland reached down and took Adele's hand. She looked up and smiled at him while he continued to stare straight ahead. Tall trees surrounded them on both sides of the road.

"She's been talking about my grandfather a lot."

"Ophelia?" Adele asked, happy that it was Roland who finally broke the silence.

He nodded. "Sometimes she does it when she's lucid and other times when she's drifting into and out of sleep. I've even overheard her having these lengthy conversations with him as if he's right there in the room with her. Last week, she was sitting in bed telling me about how when Charles would visit her at the monastery; she'd usually come across him leaning against the entrance to his cabin there with his hands in his pockets, his tie loose around his neck, shirt tails hanging out, just watching and waiting for her to find him and when she did he'd give her what she described as his half-a-smile and then he'd say, 'What's up, kid?' Nearly every time he showed up those were the first words out of his mouth when he saw her. Ophelia had this big smile when she told me about that. I could almost see the years fade from her features and glimpse the much younger woman she once was. She really loved him you know. With all her heart. It must have been tough in the end when he chose to remain married to my grandmother."

"It certainly sounds complicated."

"They weren't together for very long, but it clearly was a very intense time for the both of them."

"Do you think she has any regrets?"

Roland glanced upward at the sound of seagulls passing overhead. "No. She seems to be at peace with it and I think she's been that way for a while. She did admit to me that she never stopped loving him and that it took her some time to get over the news of his death all those years ago."

"Ophelia is a strong woman. I imagine going through something like that only made her more so."

"You're probably right about that." Roland's brow furrowed. "Today wasn't one of her good days though."

"What happened?"

"There was a moment, not more than five seconds or so, when she looked right into my eyes and called me Charles while caressing my face. Then she leaned back, confused at first and then embarrassed which made me feel terrible. I told her it was okay, but she started to cry as she apologized while also saying that I looked and sounded so much like him. She called it eerie how alike we were." Roland suddenly stopped and turned. "I'm sorry. I've been going on and on about myself."

"It's fine," Adele replied, "especially given what you've been dealing with."

"I noticed Bloodbone's journal on your table. How's that going?"

"Interesting."

"Interesting good or interesting bad?"

"I'm not sure yet."

"Ophelia asked about him as well." Roland almost smiled. "She joked how it wasn't fair that Bloodbone was already old when she was still young and yet it looks like he'll manage to somehow outlive her."

"That's if he's actually still alive."

"She said he is—she's certain of it."

"How would she know?"

"Maybe you can ask her that yourself when you see her tomorrow."

They started walking again.

"Yeah," Adele replied. "Maybe."

The tops of the trees started to sway as the wind picked up. Darker clouds gathered and the air was heavy with the promise of coming rain.

"Any plans for dinner?" Roland asked.

"Just whatever I manage to scrounge up in between reading more of Bloodbone's journal."

"How about I cook you up something later and bring it to you?"

"Like what?"

"A BLT?"

"Sounds good."

"Around six?"

Adele squeezed Roland's hand. "Perfect."

The first fat drops of rain began to fall. Roland pulled Adele close. "I better get you back before you end up soaked."

Adele ran her fingers through his already damp hair. "I don't mind getting a little wet." She kissed his cheek. "Thank you for letting me know about Ophelia."

"I figured if I told anyone it had to be you."

"Why is that?"

"Who else would it be? I know we've had our less-than-ideal moments, but I trust you completely. Hell, I trust you with my life."

Adele kissed him again—this time on the lips.

Roland kissed her back, gently at first, and then with greater urgency. They stood facing each other like that for some time, saying nothing, their foreheads pressed together, as rain fell around them.

Far above the road, deep within the branches of a tall evergreen tree, a pair of midnight eyes secretly watched.

# 6.

*I wasn't certain if I found the cave on Turtleback Mountain or if it found me.*

*After hours of wandering the mountainside without result I was prepared to give up and demand from Asav that he show me its location. As I stood in a narrow valley looking up at a line of trees a swirling blur of darkness caught my attention. It was late afternoon by then and the sun hung low in the western sky. More bits of darkness followed, fluttering about in between the tree branches and then out across the tall grass valley and beyond.*

*Bats.*

*Thousands of them.*

*Their presence signaled the cave was close.*

*I walked slowly through the trees while searching for the opening into the mountain. The earth was dry, the smell of pine needles strong, and the air unusually still. By the time I located the cave entrance the mountain was covered in shadow as day gave way to night. I decided to make camp in the valley and wait until morning to investigate further.*

*Right before full darkness descended, I gathered wood for a fire and found myself enjoying the peaceful solitude that was a welcome contrast to the prior evening's violence. I sat by the fire with my arms around my bent knees, looking up at the blanket of winking stars above me. Occasionally I would hear the high-pitched chirp of a bat and the flutter of leather wings passing over my head and wondered how many generations of the creatures had made their home in the mountain cave. Was it hundreds? Thousands? Or perhaps it was not nearly so many because they enjoyed unusually long lives as Old Raven had due to their proximity to whatever power resided within the mountain's interior.*

*And then my solitude was interrupted.*

*Asav strode through the tall grass toward the fire and then sat down across from me. "I figured I'd find you here," he said. "I also thought you might want some company."*

*I fondled the hilt of the dagger that hung from my belt while imagining how easy it would be to get up, grab Asav by the scruff of his neck, pull his head back, and slit his throat from one ear to the other. Then the imagining quickly became serious contemplation. I stared at him, wondering if the slain mother and child found in the woods were victims of his manipulations. My instincts said yes.*

*Asav unsheathed his own blade and then proceeded to casually pick his teeth with it. "Cooked a little deer over the fire back at camp. I didn't think to bring any with me. I apologize." He frowned. "I don't recall you being a mute. Why so quiet?"*

*I tossed a limb into the fire. Sparks shot up, swirled over our heads, and were then swallowed by darkness.*

*"Don't be rude, Karl." Asav spit into the fire, making it hiss. "Good riddance to those white men."*

*"You're a white man the same as them."*

*Asav grunted. "So you keep reminding me. The same as them you say? No, you're wrong about that. I'm Asav. I haven't lived in the world of the white man for a very long time."*

*"Why are you here?"*

*Asav's head lowered slightly. "I could ask you the same."*

*"You know why."*

*"Did you find it?"*

*I didn't answer.*

*Asav pointed at me with his knife. "Yes, I believe you did. I can smell the bat shit on you from here." He leaned forward until his face was illuminated by the fire's warm glow. "I found it first."*

*"Are you claiming the cave as your own?"*

*Asav's eyes narrowed, giving him the appearance of an especially devious, bearded pig. "I'm within my rights to do so." The pink tip of his tongue poked out between his lips as he slowly ran his thumb along the edge of his blade. "But I'm also a generous man."*

*I straightened. "Generous?"*

*"I am willing to share the contents of the cave with you."*

*"The cave is neither of ours to share."*

*Asav gritted his teeth. "It's mine."*

*"No." I shook my head. "It is not."*

*The fire's flames grew hotter between us as it crackled and popped. Asav glared at the crystal around my neck. "That came from the cave."*

*"Perhaps."*

*He held up his own crystal. "The same as this one."*

*"Mine was given. Yours was taken."*

*"In order to give someone must first take."*

*"See?" I shrugged. "You speak like a white man because you are one—always obsessed with having more. Why is the cave so important to you?"*

*Asav went to answer but then his face tightened. He grimaced while looking into the fire. "It's not so easy to explain." He looked up. "It is important because it's supposed to be important."*

*"Why?"*

*"Stop asking me that, you red-skinned bastard. I cannot explain what I don't fully understand. Something is going on in that cave. Something different—something powerful."*

*"All the more reason why we cannot claim it as our own. The cave belongs to the islands."*

*"These islands belong to those who control them and right now that is us."*

*"You can no more control these islands than fly among the stars in the sky."*

*Asav pointed upward. "Someday men WILL fly among those stars, my friend. Do we not sail upon the sea? The stars will be no different."*

*"Why are you here?"*

*"Because you are. We came to these islands together."* *Asav picked up a stick and poked at the fire. "Do you recall when we first met?"*

*"No." It was an honest answer. I had no memory of meeting Asav. He just appeared and then never left.*

*"Well, I certainly remember the first time I saw you. It was the battle at the spit."*

*"Against the Semiahmoo tribe to the north."*

*Asav nodded. "Yes. I was camped out in the woods on the hillside just to the south of the spit when your war party approached from the water. I watched you step ashore, this giant nightmarish thing that cut through the Semiahmoo like my blade would carve through sand. They were nearly three hundred strong, but it didn't matter. Within an hour you and your warriors had taken control of the spit and its longhouses after the Semiahmoo fled to the east."*

*"We spent a winter there feeding off of the smoked salmon they had left behind."*

*"An enjoyable winter that was."*

*"You began trading with some of my men."*

"That's right," Asav replied, "but my focus was always on you."

"Why?"

"The power you showed when you took the spit made clear you were a man meant for great things and I wanted to be a part of it."

"You thought I might help you to line your pockets, like some wretched creature scavenging the scraps left by the bear."

Asav's face darkened. "I am no wretched creature and am more than capable of creating my own opportunities."

"Like the opportunity to have Old Raven pay you in gold to bring me here?"

"I merely helped you to be where you were meant to be."

"Are you so arrogant as to think that you would know where that is before I would?"

Asav's smile was a cold contrast to the fire's warmth. "I know what I know."

"Come morning I walk into the cave alone."

"Fine. I shall wait for you here."

"There is no need for you to wait. You can return to the village."

"I'll wait." Asav stroked his beard. "You should also know that there is a part of the cave I did not venture into. It would be easy to miss if one didn't know where to look."

"Go on."

"Ah," Asav said. "Now you wish to know what I know."

I waited for him to satisfy his need to gloat.

"Most of the bats roost directly above a mass of crystals that appear to be growing out of the cave floor," he continued. "Your size will require you to stoop so it will likely be slow going for you. There will be no need for a torch—the crystals illuminate most of the cave much like a lantern would. The light they give off appears to come from somewhere deep in the earth. The cave goes beyond this place though. Keep to the right until you come to another opening. The way forward is even lower here, but at least there are no bats."

"What is in this other cave?"

"I do not know."

"You didn't investigate when you were there last?"

"Not more than a few feet. Truth be told, I lost my nerve. The way the cave ceiling and walls shift, all of those furry winged bodies and countless pairs of eyes looking down at me, it was quite unsettling." Asav held up his crystal. "Once I had this there was no need for me to remain in that place any longer. I was anxious to breathe fresh air again. The smell in the cave is . . . unpleasant."

By then the fire was burning low. Asav lay down with his hands behind his head. I remained sitting up, wanting to keep my eyes on him, wondering if he might be planning to stick his dagger in me while I slept. Once more I thought of killing him but was reminded of Old Raven's warning that I should never engage in such an act again or risk the wrath of the islands.

*"Tell me something, Karl."*

*"What?" I replied.*

*"Were you and I ever truly friends?"*

*My reply was immediate. "No."*

*Asav propped himself up on his elbows. "No?"*

*"No."*

*"I considered you, if not a friend, at least an ally."*

*"You are an acquaintance."*

*"Nothing more?"*

*"Nothing more," I answered.*

*It was then I glimpsed hatred burn within Asav's eyes. It was only a second or two at most, but the fire gave off just enough light that I saw it clearly. I knew there would be an unavoidable reckoning between us someday. He fingered the crystal that rested against his chest. "Pity. I like to think we make a good team."*

*"You are welcome to think whatever you want."*

*"Your people are leaving the islands. Soon all of them will be gone. Do you intend to follow them north?"*

*I had no intention of ever leaving the islands again but didn't wish to share that with him. "I do not know," I said with attempted indifference.*

*"I'm staying." Asav continued to press the crystal between his fingers. "I like it here."*

*"What of your homeland?"*

*"Russia? The czars can have it. On these islands all men are free to seek their fortunes."*

*A white moth fluttered just beyond the reach of the fire's warmth. Asav tried to snatch it out of the air, but the moth avoided his grasp and continued swirling around us. It rose, dropped, then rose again, a speck of madly twirling white.*

*And then something remarkable happened not once but twice.*

*A bat flew over our heads close enough that I could count the rows of tiny razor teeth in its open mouth. Asav cried out and scooted backwards as the bat bit down on the moth.*

*Time slowed.*

*As impossible as that might sound it is true. I watched the beating of the bat's wings while it circled around the fire and heard the moth's cry of pain as its body was crushed between the jaws of its dark predator.*

*Asav shouted again.*

*A white face shot out of the gloom, its glowing eyes fixed upon the bat and its prey. The great bird paused midair with its talons extended out in front of it, wings beating within the fire's swirling smoke. The bat, sensing death's arrival, attempted to flee. It was fast, but the owl's attack was faster. Talons sunk deep into the bat's flesh, yanking it out of the air like one might pick a flower. As quickly as the owl had appeared it just as quickly returned to the darkness.*

*Asav sat cross-legged, mouth hanging open, one hand on his crystal and the other caressing the hilt of his knife. "I wouldn't ever believe it if I hadn't seen it with my own eyes," he whispered.*

*I remained quiet even as the image of the white owl repeatedly played out in my mind. Was it a message? Perhaps a foretelling of some still unknown future? The answers, if any, were well beyond my knowledge at the time. There was nothing more to do but to continue watching Asav while awaiting daylight's gradual return.*

*The fire burned out until only ash remnants remained.*

*Asav slept.*

*I did not.*

# 7.

Adele woke with the side of her face resting against the top of the galley table in a puddle of drool. She sat up, wiped her mouth with the back of her hand, rubbed her eyes, and yawned. It was just past seven in the morning. Bloodbone's book sat open next to her. She closed it, pushed it against the wall, and then stood. The crumbs of the sandwich Roland had dropped off to her the night before lay in the sink on a plate. They had agreed to meet at her sailboat at nine that morning and head out by boat for their visit with Ophelia on Shaw Island.

She paused next to the table, looked down, and then pulled Bloodbone's journal toward her, recalling something she read earlier that she didn't want to forget. *There,* she thought, tapping a page. *When Old Raven told him he wasn't allowed to interfere.*

Adele reread the passage:

*"Never again are you to take a life by your own hand or to directly intervene in events that have yet to unfold. To do so is to terminate the agreement between yourself and the islands."*

During that terrible conflict years earlier when Adele had been kept hostage in the concrete cellar of the Turn Point Lighthouse, shortly after Brixton Bannister had sacrificed himself on the cliffs so that she could escape, Bloodbone had emerged from under a tree right before Liya Vasa was about to shoot her. Adele closed her eyes and replayed that moment when Bloodbone had wrapped his massive hands around Liya's head and then snapped her neck as easily as one would break a twig.

That time at Turn Point had cost Adele her unborn child. Adele now wondered if it had also cost Bloodbone his life. Certainly, what he did for her was an act of direct intervention via a life taken by his own hand. The timing of his subsequent disappearance would seem to confirm this link to Old Raven's long-ago decree.

*He might have given up everything to protect me.*

Adele turned more pages until she came to Asav's description of the secondary cave inside of Turtleback Mountain:

*"There will be no need for a torch—the crystals illuminate most of the cave much like a lantern would. The light they give off appears to come from somewhere deep in the earth. The cave goes beyond this place though. Keep to the right until you come to another opening. The way forward is even lower here but at least there are no bats."*

She took a photo of the entry with her phone, closed the journal, got the coffee brewing, and then jumped into the shower. Thirty minutes later she was dressed and enjoying her morning cup while walking the docks. It was a perfect Roche Harbor morning— clear and crisp and surrounded by calm waters. The summer season resort staff were already at work, checking in on the marina guests and making sure the facilities were ready to greet another day.

*What's Lucas doing here?* Adele thought as he walked down the entrance ramp. He waved. She waved back and then noted how some of the female staff, including Sky, were watching wide-eyed as he passed them.

"You're so fricking hot."

Lucas scowled. "Huh?"

Adele chuckled. "Never mind." She turned at the sound of someone clearing their throat behind her.

"Good morning, Ms. Plank," Sky said as her eyes lingered on Lucas. Despite the brisk morning temperature, she was wearing short tan shorts which showed off a pair of impressively shapely legs.

"It's Adele."

"Right." Sky nodded. "Sorry."

Adele tilted her head toward Lucas. "This is Sheriff Pine."

When Sky smiled, her lips pressed tightly against her teeth like she had just stuck her finger into a light socket. "Hello, Sheriff Pine."

"Hi there." Lucas stepped forward and stuck out his hand.

Sky stared down at it, shook it a few times, paused, and then kept on shaking.

"Ma'am," Lucas said. "Do you mind if I have my hand back?"

"Hand?" Sky looked up. "Oh!" She snatched her own hand away. "That's the first handshake I've done in like forever. These days we just, you know, text each other with a bunch of emojis or something."

Lucas gave Adele a quick glance that let her know he thought Sky might be a few fries short of a Happy Meal. "I don't do emojis," he said. "I'm more of a tell it to your face type."

When Sky smiled, she also let out an odd, low-throated groan. "Of course. You're the sheriff. That's serious work—important work. Helping to keep us all safe and everything. I mean really. You make it look so easy, but I know it's not. There's a lot of weirdos out there, so, yeah, what you do is really important for, like, law and order and stuff."

Adele decided it was time to save the poor girl any further embarrassment by sending her on her way. "Sky, did you need something?"

"No."

"Then why are you here?"

Sky blinked like she was waking up from a dream. "Uh, to see if you needed anything."

"I don't."

"Sheriff Pine, do *you* need something?" As soon as she asked Sky's cheeks turned a deep red.

Lucas straightened as he laughed which pushed the buttons of his tight-fitting shirt that left so little to the imagination regarding his remarkably well-sculpted chest, nearly to the breaking point. "I'm fine."

"Okay," Sky muttered, her shoulders slumped in defeat. She started to walk away but then turned around, her expression suddenly very determined. "Here's the thing."

Adele and Lucas both waited.

"I want to get to know you better," Sky continued.

"Me?" Lucas replied.

Adele elbowed him in the side. "Who else?"

Lucas shrugged. "These days it could be anybody."

"Yes," Sky answered. "I mean you."

*Good for her,* Adele thought, impressed by Sky's surprising assertiveness despite her comically awkward first impression.

"Get to know me better how?"

Sky dipped her head slightly and her knowing smile was the perfect balance of innocence and seduction. "That's up to you." When Lucas went to answer, she cut him off. "Just to let you know, this is the first time I've ever really put myself out there like this so if I'm coming off sounding like an idiot, or some stupid kid, well, I guess that's to be expected. I've only had one serious boyfriend before, but that ended last year. His name was Jay. We started dating in high school. He wasn't bad or anything—we just sort of grew apart. He went to one college; I went to another, and the long-distance thing didn't work out." She shrugged. "It was probably for the best." Then she looked Lucas up and down. "And he sure didn't look anything like you. Heck, I didn't think men *could* look like you except in the movies or something. Seeing you up close right now makes me feel like I'm seeing a real man for the first time."

It took some effort for Adele to keep from smiling too much. "You hear that, Sheriff? You're the first *real* man Sky has ever seen. Talk about a lot of pressure. Do you think you're up for it?"

"Shut up," Lucas whispered out of the corner of his mouth.

"Piece of advice," Adele said to Sky. "Get him drunk and then wait for him to take a bath. That's when you'll have your chance to *really* get to know him."

"Don't listen to her," Lucas growled.

"I don't know about a bath," Sky replied, "but I'm open to a midnight swim in the resort pool. I'll bring the champagne."

"Alcoholic beverages aren't allowed in the pool."

Adele rolled her eyes. "Oh my gosh, Lucas. Don't be such a stickler for the rules."

Sky shrugged. "I won't tell if you won't, Sheriff."

It was Lucas's turn to appear overly awkward. "Uh, I'll have to get back to you on that. For now, I need to speak privately with Ms. Plank."

"Sure," Sky said. "No pressure. I'll just be hard at work obsessing over you until I hear back." She stuck out her hand. "It really was nice to finally meet you in person. I've been wanting to since I first laid eyes on you, but I kept chickening out."

Adele caught Lucas giving Sky a quick and appreciative sideways glance at her backside as she walked away. "I never took you for a dirty old man," she said.

"Stop it."

"You should be flattered. She's very attractive."

"And young."

"She's not *that* young."

"Thanks for bringing up the time you found me passed out in the bathtub by the way."

Adele actually did feel a little bad about that. Joking about it with Roland was one thing, but with a stranger it was an entirely different matter. "You're right. I'm sorry. I was just trying to break the ice a bit."

"I don't need you breaking any ice or trying to set me up with someone."

"Speaking of which, why are you here? I assume it wasn't just to say hello."

"No, it's not. I had a conversation last night with my Interpol contact."

"And?"

"After what happened at Turn Point, I had requested that he continue to notify me of any unusual activity regarding the Vasa organization. He let me know that Arthur Olegovich is suspected of having recently flown into County Cork, Ireland."

"Fin."

Lucas nodded. "Exactly."

"Is he in danger?"

"There's nothing yet to indicate he is. Interpol alerted local law enforcement there and I texted Fin myself."

"What did he say?"

"I haven't heard back yet."

"How long ago did you text him?"

"Just this morning. Give it time."

"That's easier said than done, Lucas, with Vlad Vasa's right-hand man suddenly poking around Fin's backyard for some reason."

"The two things could be totally unrelated."

"You and I both know that's not likely."

Lucas sighed. "Yeah." He folded his arms across his chest. "Fin's a capable guy, though, and he's with his people there. He'll be fine."

"You hear anything, *anything at all,* I want to know about it."

"Of course."

"By the way, how is work going?" It was far from a casual question. Lucas had been scrambling once again to repair a department ripped apart by death and scandal that were the casualties of Vlad Vasa's manipulations. Lucas's longtime receptionist, Samantha Boyler, and his most recently hired deputy, Shane Eagon, were killed soon after being implicated in dealings with the Russians.

"All I can say is thank God Gunther delayed his move south so he could continue helping us out on a part-time basis by keeping an eye on things over on Lopez Island. He's old and cranky, though, and his heart isn't into it."

Gunther Fox had retired as a deputy sheriff but was now assisting Lucas and his only other full-time deputy, Chancee Smith, who spent most of her time at the Orcas Island substation, until Lucas could fill the vacancy left by Eagon's death.

"I'm running around like crazy trying to keep up with the workload while at the same time knowing full well the county council might just decide that there's no need to spend the money on another deputy if it seems I'm capable of handling it all myself. I'm damned if I do and I'm damned if I don't."

"Who's handling the reception desk?"

Lucas scowled. "Me."

"You're the county sheriff *and* you're handling reception duties for the department?"

"Yup."

"Do you want the newspaper to apply some pressure to get the council to move more quickly in getting you some replacements?"

"Thanks for the offer, but it's not time for that yet. I don't want to be pissing anyone off if I don't have to. Besides, it's not the council's fault. The positions are posted and the funding, for now, is there."

"Then what's the problem?"

"Getting qualified people to apply. It seems like nobody wants to work these days."

"It'll happen."

"I hope so because I'm running on empty." Lucas checked his watch. "What are you up to?"

"Heading over to Shaw with Roland soon," Adele replied.

"For a story?"

"No, just a visit with Mother Mary Ophelia."

"Is she okay?"

This was what Adele wanted to avoid—lying to others about Ophelia's condition. She paused, trying to come up with a reply that would keep her word to Roland about not telling anyone else while also not deceiving Lucas.

"No worries," he said. "Tell me about it when you're ready."

Adele was relieved and grateful to have been let off easy. She knew Lucas had good instincts and likely already sensed something was wrong, but he was also giving Roland and her the space they needed to deal with it in in their own way. "Don't forget to tell me about any news regarding Fin."

"I won't."

"And Lucas..."

"Yeah?"

"Don't be afraid to take a chance on getting to know someone better."

"She's too young for me, Adele."

"And you're much too good of a guy to be going through life alone."

"I'm not alone." Lucas pointed at Adele. "I've got you, right?"

"Sure but—"

"That's good enough for now. My plate is plenty full."

"You keep saying that, but sooner or later you're going to look around and realize a whole lot of time has gone by—time you can't ever get back."

"I shouldn't have to remind you that the last girlfriend I had didn't end well."

Sandra Penny, Roland's former bank vice president and Lucas's one-time love interest, was yet another fatal casualty in the ongoing conflict with the Russians. Adele didn't mean to poke what was likely a still painful wound for Lucas, yet she also wondered if he might be using Sandra's demise as an excuse to avoid risking getting hurt again.

"Don't allow past pain to take away a chance at future happiness."

"I didn't come here for a therapy session, Adele. Do you want me to try to make you tell me why you're *really* going to Shaw Island with Roland?"

Adele held her hands up in front of her. "Fair enough."

"Look, I know you're just trying to look out for me, but I really am doing okay. Work is about all I have time for. Besides, I'm not exactly in the right frame of mind to be boyfriend material right now."

"I get it—end of discussion."

"Thanks."

Adele watched Lucas leave and then drank the last of her coffee. Roland would be here soon and then it was off to Shaw to see Mother Mary Ophelia.

She prayed it wouldn't be for the last time.

# 8.

Adele had experienced a multitude of difficult moments in recent years that had helped to develop a toughness that she now believed would allow her to face potential future adversity that might overwhelm others. Yet, despite that toughness, even she was left stunned by the sight of Ophelia and the disease that was so cruelly ravaging her mind and body.

"She's sleeping," Roland whispered.

The other nuns in the monastery, wanting to give them their privacy, had retreated from Ophelia's room like scurrying crows upon Roland and Adele's arrival. Adele noted the strain on their faces though. Ophelia had called the Shaw Island monastery her home for longer than any other nun in its history and she was also the oldest among them. Her tenacity and wisdom were highly valued among the other residents there, so much so that even the Seattle archbishop had recently reached out to inquire about her condition.

"She's lost so much weight and she didn't have much to spare to begin with."

Roland grimaced. "She hardly eats or drinks now. Swallowing is becoming difficult."

"What about intravenously?" Adele asked.

"She refused it."

"Why?"

Ophelia's sunken eyes opened as her head turned slowly toward Adele and Roland. "Because if this is my time then so be it," she croaked in a voice that was uncharacteristically weak and garbled, like her tongue was too big for her mouth. Her eyes narrowed as they focused on Adele. "What are *you* doing here?"

"I invited her to come," Roland replied.

"Why?"

"She's your friend."

Ophelia frowned. "I didn't ask you to bring her here."

"It was my decision."

"Not like this."

Roland let go of Adele's hand and moved toward the bed. "What do you mean?"

"I don't want others seeing me like this. Why is that so hard to understand?"

"I wanted to come," Adele said. "For both you and Roland."

Ophelia's eyes closed. "You Soros men—always trying to control everything."

Roland stood at the end of the bed and looked down. "Grandma."

That single word clearly meant a great deal to Ophelia. Her frown retreated like mist under a warm sun. She smiled and nodded. "My grandson."

"You shouldn't deny others their chance to see you," Roland continued.

"Let them remember me for what I was. Not like I am now—a barely living scrap of nothing."

Roland's tone took on an edge of frustration. "Stop talking like that."

"I'll talk however I damn well please. I'm the one dying."

"You would actually deny Adele a chance to talk with you again?"

Ophelia turned her face away. "She's been through enough," she murmured. "I don't want to be the cause of more pain for her."

"Pain would be if I couldn't see you again," Adele said. "I *want* to be here."

"Have you found him?"

"Bloodbone?"

Ophelia nodded.

"Not yet," Adele answered.

"He still lives. I know he does."

"How?"

Ophelia looked directly at Adele with eyes that still flickered with the fiery determination that she had long been known for. "I can sense it." She smiled. "As can you. That's why you haven't stopped looking." She raised a trembling hand. "Roland, please sit me up."

Roland flinched. "What?"

"Help me up," Ophelia growled, sounding more like her old self.

"I don't think that's a very good—"

"Boy, I wasn't asking for your opinion." Ophelia lifted both arms. "I want to sit and talk not lie on my back like a corpse. I'll have plenty of time to do that soon enough."

Roland put his arms around Ophelia's upper body and then sat her up against several pillows that he stacked behind her. "How's that?"

"Much better," Ophelia answered as she pointed to the door. "Now get out."

"Huh?"

"You brought Adele here and now I wish to speak with her in private."

"Oh," Roland replied. "Of course." He turned toward Adele. "I guess I'll leave you to it."

"Grandson," Ophelia called out. "Thank you for bringing her. I know I told you not to tell anyone what was going on with me, but now I'm glad she's here. We have much to discuss."

"If you need anything, I'll be right outside," Roland said. "Take all the time you want." He nodded to Adele and then walked out, closing the door behind him.

Ophelia patted the mattress. "Come here, child, and let me get a proper look at you."

Adele sat on the edge of the bed and then tried not to let her sadness over Ophelia's emaciated appearance show.

"How is Roland holding up? Please be honest. He was nearly inconsolable when I first told him about my condition."

"He's understandably upset but seems to be managing," Adele answered.

"That's good. His grandfather Charles was the same. After the initial shock of bad news, he had a real knack for compartmentalizing his emotions and getting on with whatever needed to be done."

Adele took Ophelia's bony hand. The paper-thin skin was shockingly dry and her forearm was covered in purplish bruises. Her once long and lustrous hair was now a scraggly nest that was nearly the same hue as the odd yellow-white color of her face and her dehydrated lips were badly cracked. "Can I get you anything?"

"A little conversation would be wonderful. I love Roland dearly, but it's nice to be able to talk to another woman from time to time. How are you two doing?"

"It's been different lately but, overall, I'd say we're doing okay all things considered."

"Don't give up on what you two have. Take it from someone who learned the hard way—a love like yours is always worth fighting for."

"I don't give up easily."

Ophelia smiled. "Keep it that way."

"I intend to."

"And what of Fin?"

"He's back in Ireland."

"For good?"

Adele shook her head. "No, he should be returning soon."

"He's a good fit for these islands don't you think?"

"I do."

"How about Tilda?"

"She sends her regards."

Ophelia scowled. "She knows about my illness?"

"No, your name came up and she remarked how it had been too long since she had last seen you. I believe Roland has honored your request not to let others know what's going on."

"With the exception of you, of course."

"Is that a problem?"

"Not at all. As I told Roland, I'm glad you're here, but for now could the both of you please not tell anyone else?"

"Of course, but for how long?"

"I don't know." Ophelia looked down at the red-and-white crochet blanket that covered her. "Did you finish reading Bloodbone's journal?"

"I just started. Actually, I started before but then stopped and now I'm back at it for real."

"How is it? Learning anything new?"

"It's definitely interesting."

"Don't want to talk about it, eh?"

"I don't mind. It's just that, well, it's hard to explain how it makes me feel when I'm reading it."

"Any mention of Charles in the journal yet? Those two were thick as thieves back in the day."

"That's the thing. I'm still years away before reaching Charles Soros's time period."

Ophelia grunted as she leaned back against the pillows. "The unanswered question that I've long contemplated while others chose to ignore it. How does one live so long? Charles' time period, as you put it, was many years ago. Is Bloodbone flesh and blood like us or could he actually be something else?" She pointed to the crystal around Adele's neck. "Are those stones the key to something that exists beyond the realm of normal understanding?"

"He wrote that the islands are alive and that a great power exists within them."

"Did he now?" Ophelia leaned forward. "And what does your reporter's mind believe?"

"You first," Adele replied.

"As you well know, Bloodbone and I had a rather contentious history when he was playing the part of some hippie guru and allowing all of those ridiculous New Age sycophants to descend upon Orcas Island. What I don't think I told you is that Roland's grandfather was adamant I let Bloodbone be. As I said— thick as thieves those two. Anyways, I ignored his demands on that particular subject and continued to do what I thought was necessary to shut Bloodbone down."

"You actually told Charles no?"

Ophelia beamed. "I certainly did. The thing of it is, as mad as that made him at the time, I could tell he respected it as well. He wasn't accustomed to not getting his way, and at least with me, I think he kind of liked it."

"Roland was the same," Adele said. "He tried to control me at first and then when he realized he couldn't, it seems that's when our relationship turned into something much deeper and more meaningful."

"Nothing like a bit of push and pull to keep things interesting." Ophelia turned her head, coughed, and then apologized for doing so. "Comes and goes."

"You cough as much as you need. It's fine."

"Even as old as I am now it feels like it all went so fast. It makes me wonder about Bloodbone. He has lived so much longer than anyone. When his end finally comes, do you think he'll feel the same? That all of his time here passed too quickly?"

"I don't know."

Ophelia's hand reached out with surprising speed and strength and encircled Adele's wrist. "Don't dare allow his words to make you into his own image. Stay true to yourself, young lady. No matter what, don't ever forget that your life, this wonderful and precious gift from God, is your own." Ophelia's hand dropped away, her head fell back, and her eyes closed.

Adele watched and waited, wondering if she had fallen asleep.

Ophelia grinned but her eyes remained closed. "Still here. Just resting."

They talked for some time until eventually Ophelia did fall into a deep slumber. Adele opened the door and called for Roland. He came in, sat down by the bed, and held Ophelia's hand for a few minutes before getting up. "We can go now."

"If you want to stay longer, I'm fine with that," Adele replied.

"No, that's not necessary. I'll be back to visit with her tomorrow."

"Can I tag along again?"

Roland took a deep breath, turned away, turned back, and then strode toward Adele, wrapped his arms around her tightly, and pressed his face against the side of her neck. It was then she fully realized just how fractured and lost he was. He wasn't merely hugging her—he was hanging on for dear life, drawing from her own strength in the hopes it might be enough to prevent him from losing himself completely into the deep abyss of despair.

"I thought I could handle this," he whispered. "That this pain was mine and mine alone, but I can't do it. I'm going to need your help to get through this, Adele."

She looked up into his eyes, pressed her palms against the sides of his face, and kissed his cheek. "Anything you need, Roland; anything I can do for you, I'm here."

A young nun with kind eyes and flawless, alabaster skin entered the room and applied ice chips to Ophelia's cracked lips and a damp cloth over her forehead.

Adele and Roland withdrew. They left the idyllic beauty of the monastery grounds and made the long walk hand in hand down to the shore where Adele's boat was tied up to the small and rickety public dock that was next to the Shaw Island ferry terminal. The sun was shining, the grass green and tall on either side of the road, and a chorus of birds could be heard singing within the surrounding brush. Neither said much to the other along the way, their hearts and minds full of sadness over Ophelia's condition. There was a moment when Adele thought she heard George the raven warbling in a tree behind her, but when she looked back, she saw nothing.

Across the water, sitting on the table inside of her sailboat at Roche Harbor, the Book of Bloodbone sat waiting for Adele's return even as Ophelia's warning whispered in her mind:

*"Don't dare allow his words to make you into his own image. Stay true to yourself, young lady. No matter what, don't ever forget that your life, this wonderful and precious gift from God, is your own."*

# 9.

*I really don't want to go in there.*

Adele stood near the cave entrance on the side of Turtleback Mountain. She had dropped Roland off at Shaw Island earlier that morning, crossed the water over to Orcas Island, tied her boat up at the public dock, and then made the long hike up the mountain. It took her nearly an hour to locate the entrance, which was hidden even more by overgrowth than the last time she had been there.

Roland was insistent she text him from time to time to let him know she was okay. Having just sent him a thumbs up emoji, Adele then took out Bloodbone's journal, sat cross-legged beside the cave, and started to reread the passage she had finished last night, wanting to make sure she didn't miss something important:

*I made certain to keep Asav in front of me as we made our way up the mountain together. He asked that he be allowed to accompany me into the cave. Again, I refused. He cursed. I ignored the tantrum.*

*When we arrived at the entrance, he tried yet again. "There could be danger inside. We should stick together. Safety in numbers and all that."*

*"No. I go alone."*

*"Why?"*

*I stepped past him. "Stay here."*

*"This isn't right."*

*"I doubt I will ever be interested in your peculiar version of right or wrong, Asav."*

*"But I am the one who found it. It's MY cave."*

*When I turned to walk into the entrance, he grabbed my arm. I pulled away and then shoved him backwards. "I don't wish to hurt you."*

*"If you weren't so big . . ."*

*"What?" I replied.*

*"Without me you would never have known this place was here. You took my knowledge and now cast me aside so that you can stake your own claim." Asav stood in front of me and jabbed a dirt-encrusted finger into my chest. "You're nothing more than a deceitful savage."*

*My hand instinctively went for my knife. Asav stepped back and grinned. "Do it. Do to me what you did to that white captain and his crew. You are Bloodbone—you were born to deal death to others."*

*"You would have me kill you?"*

*"I would have you return to what you were, not this thing named Karl."*

*I grew weary of Asav's contempt but then realized he was trying to goad me into an act of violence—the very thing*

*Old Raven's spirit had told me to avoid. It was as if Asav somehow knew of that warning even though it had been delivered to me in a vision while I slept.*

*"You still keep your weapon sharp, don't you?" Asav continued. "Why is that do you think? Out of habit or preparation?"*

*"Preparation for what?"*

*Asav's eyes narrowed. "You tell me."*

*I drew my blade and then held it out in front of me, the weight of the elk antler hilt so familiar in my hand. Asav was right about its fine edge. How easy it would be for me to plunge it into his chest, slice through flesh, and tear out his insides as I had so often done to others so many times before.*

*"Who is this who now stands before me?" Asav whispered as his fingers wrapped around the hilt of his own knife. "Is it to be Bloodbone or is it to be Karl?"*

*"I am both."*

*"Both?" Asav shook his head. "No, my friend, you must choose. It is to be one or the other."*

*"I will not kill you, Asav."*

*"You assume you can. How do you know for certain it isn't me who would walk down this mountain alone?"*

*"Not likely."*

*"But not impossible."*

*I straightened to my full height and looked down at the strange little Russian fur trapper and again wondered why he was pushing so hard for deadly conflict between us—a conflict he surely couldn't win. The mountain rose up behind me, seemingly waiting for a decision to a question I didn't understand. The knife suddenly felt heavy in my hand. I raised it further until it was directly in front of my face, the dark metal absorbing the sun's warm light.*

*Asav's mouth twitched as he watched and waited.*

*A passing cloud temporarily blocked out the sun, casting the mountainside in shadow. Wind blew across the valley below and carried with it the cries of all the lives I had cut short.*

*Men.*

*Women.*

*Even children.*

*None had been safe from my wrath.*

*The wind pushed its way up the mountain, swirling through the grass and trees until it reached the place where Asav and I stood facing each other. The screams of lost souls grew louder all around me. In my mind I begged them to stop, but if they somehow heard me, they didn't listen.*

*"C'mon then," Asav said. "Are you going to use that weapon of yours or not?"*

*I lowered the blade, began to turn away, and then heard Asav sliding his own knife from its sheath. Perhaps he was quick enough to reach me and bury it deep into my back before I could stop him or perhaps not. If so, it wouldn't kill me, at least not right away. What was more certain is that it would cost him his own life once I had my hands on him. I had never known Asav to take such a risk. He was too calculating, too conniving, too willing to sacrifice anyone and anything but himself.*

*Until now.*

*It made no sense, which meant his true motivations remained hidden from me. I continued to turn away, knowing that by doing so I would be fully exposing myself to attack from behind. The cave beckoned, but I was not yet ready to enter. There was something I decided I must do first.*

*I raised the knife high, stepped forward, and then brought it down with all of my strength, plunging it into the side of the mountain directly above the entrance to the cave. Sparks erupted as steel struck stone and the blade disappeared, leaving only the hilt visible. I kept my back to Asav as my arm dropped to my side.*

*"Why would you do that?" he asked.*

*"I have no more need for such weapons."*

*"But now you are unarmed."*

*I detected relief in Asav's voice. Whether that was because he thought it meant he had the advantage or because of some other reason I did not know.*

*Again, I waited.*

*Asav sighed. "I will remain here."*

*I entered the cave and then paused, allowing my eyes to adjust to the gloom.*

*"Goodbye friend," Asav said just loud enough for me to hear.*

*It was an odd choice of words. Why say goodbye to one who would soon be walking out of that cave? I thought to ask him, but the cave drew me in and soon I was deep inside the mountain, crouching as I walked to avoid hitting my head on the dark stones above me. The smell of bat grew stronger. Light pulsated from somewhere further within the cave's depths. I went as slowly and quietly as possible, not wanting to disturb the horde of leather-winged creatures that clung to the stone walls and ceiling, but I felt their dark eyes on me, watching.*

*Finally, I came to the source of light—an outcrop of crystals that appeared to have broken through the floor, their glow flaring and then receding like some great earthen heartbeat. The air here was warmer and the bats even more numerous. They shrieked angrily at my intrusion. I kept to the right as Asav had instructed and eventually came upon the second cave. The opening was lower and narrower, requiring me to crouch down further. My shoulders nearly scraped the sides as I shuffled forward, my eyes straining to see more than a few feet in front of me.*

*I stopped, looked down, and saw Asav's footprints in the dry earth. He had told me he barely went beyond the second cave's opening, but the tracks proved that to be a lie. I followed them further into the cave until I could no longer even see my hand as I held it in front of me. The smell of bats had receded but was replaced by something else equally wild, untamed, yet familiar.*

*A warm breeze caressed my face, but I knew that was impossible. There could be no wind in such a place so far beyond the reach of the outside world. The breeze continued to come and go like rhythmic breathing.*

*I froze, my back bent and my fingers digging into the earth.*

*Something was with me in that cave.*

*I reached down for a blade that was no longer there and then recalled Asav's strange goodbye. Was he aware of the presence within the second cave? Did he watch as I disarmed myself, knowing the increased danger I would face by doing so?*

*Movement—a scraping sound and then more air pushing against my skin. I crept backwards while keeping my gaze on whatever might be hiding in the blackness directly in front of me. The familiar scent was stronger now—like that of a dog that has come into the longhouse after a hard rain.*

*More movement.*

*I turned sideways, hoping to catch a glimpse of the crystalline light behind me, but there was still only darkness.*

*A low rumbling groan issued from inside the mountain depths. Whatever it was it was now following me as I retreated—something big.*

*The top of my head struck stone as I quickened my pace. My shoulders rubbed against the cave walls. I heard and felt the thrumming of the crystals.*

*The unknown thing continued to follow.*

*I fell backwards into the main cave and then sat up looking directly into the other cave as the bats screeched and fluttered around me. Another groan, this time louder, filled the space as the crystal heartbeat quickened.*

*I gasped when I realized that a pair of eyes was staring back at me. I sat there frozen, my throat tight, wanting to escape but unable to move. The eyes drew closer, encased in a massive head of light and dark. Its tufted ears tilted forward and then were pinned back as it unleashed a great roar that seemed to shake the entire mountain.*

*The bear lunged, pushing me back and then pinning me to the cave floor. Its fur was the same color as the crystals, while its long claws were as dark as raven feathers. I tried to push it away, but its strength was far greater than my own. It roared again, snorted, and then pressed its snout against my chest while inhaling deeply. When the black tip of its nose came into contact with the crystal around my neck the beast's head lifted as it continued to stare down at me. Then it rose up onto its hind legs and bellowed so long and loud I had to cover my ears with my hands.*

*Was it the white spirit bear spoken of by Old Raven—the one he said had discovered the islands when the world was still young? I recalled telling him how I did not believe in such things and his knowing reply that it didn't matter because such things believed in me.*

*I rolled to the side, stood, and then looked back as the bear dropped to all fours, moved toward the crystals, and gently nudged them while the white hairs of its body bristled in time to the pulsing stones.*

*When I moved sideways, the bear glanced at me and then continued nudging the crystals, seemingly no longer interested in my being there. I turned and ran, fearing the bear would decide to give chase so that it could drag me back to its lair. I emerged into sunlight, hands trembling and heart racing, grateful for the fresh air and open space.*

*"You're alive!" Asav shouted.*

*"Why wouldn't I be?"*

*Asav cocked his head. "Eh?"*

*"Is that why you told me goodbye when I entered the cave? You though I might not return?"*

*"What did you see?"*

*"The same as you."*

*"Nothing more?"*

*"No."*

*"I heard something."*

*"Did you?" I shrugged. "Perhaps it was the wind."*

*"The wind?" Asav grunted. "I think not." He looked me up and down. "You are not injured?"*

*"I'm fine."*

*"Did you see the crystals?"*

"Yes."

"And the other cave?"

"Yes."

"And?"

"And then I returned here."

"What will you do now?"

I looked up at the sun, noting how much lower it was in the sky than when I entered the cave. "Return to the village."

"Did you take anything?"

I gave Asav a thin smile. "Knowledge."

He glanced back at the opening. "The location of this place must remain a secret between us and us alone."

"I agree."

Asav nodded. "Good." He stuck out his hand. "Despite what you might think, I do consider you my friend."

When we shook, I noted a large tear in his sleeve and a fresh scratch that ran the length of his forearm. "What happened there?"

Asav's hand retreated. "My clothing caught on a limb."

"It left a wound."

Asav covered the scratch with his other hand. "It's nothing. I'm fine."

I began walking down the mountain and into the valley while Asav followed close behind. He was *uncharacteristically quiet, making me wonder what schemes might be swirling about in his head.*

*"Look!"*

*I turned around to find him pointing toward the sea beyond the trees. It was the largest ship I had ever seen. A flag with a red-and-white cross and blue background fluttered at the top of its mast and rows of cannons lined the sides of its hull.*

*"A British warship," Asav whispered, his eyes wide with wonder. "Fortunately for us it appears to be heading to San Juan Island."*

*I knew better. The warship would be the first of many more to come. It was just as Old Raven had said. The arrival of the white man was like the rising and falling of the tide—an unavoidable reality.*

*A great change was coming to the islands.*

Adele closed the journal, returned it to her backpack, and then stood looking up at the cave opening in front of her. She bent down, picked up a stick, and used it to push away the brush and vines that covered the top of the entrance. This proved to be more difficult than she thought it would be as some of the brush was growing directly out of the side of the mountain. After some time, though, she finally found what she was searching for. She reached up on her toes but was too short, so she went in search of something to stand on, returning with a rock cradled in her arms. She set it down, made sure it was stable enough, and then stood on top of it.

Her hand gripped the elk antler hilt left there long ago by Bloodbone as described in the journal passage she had just finished reading. She tried to pull the knife out, but it wouldn't budge. There would be no taking it with her; finding it would have to be enough.

Adele stepped off the rock, adjusted the straps of her backpack, and then stared into the cave, wondering if she would be able to find the second cave inside the mountain. *Only one way to find out,* she thought, grateful to feel the weight of the revolver given to her years earlier by Lucas that she had placed in one of the backpack's side pockets before leaving Roche Harbor with Roland that morning.

She knew the bats would be waiting inside the cave to greet her once again.

What was less certain was if someone, or something, would be waiting as well.

Adele went forward, leaving the world of light behind, and was soon swallowed by darkness.

# 10.

Sister Zhara Lowery, the young nun Adele had noticed earlier, was undeniably beautiful. Not yet thirty, tall and thin, with unusually bright blue-green eyes complemented by a backdrop of hair that was as dark as the nun's habit she wore that further emphasized her flawless white skin and prominent cheekbones. She greeted Adele at the monastery door.

"Good afternoon, Ms. Plank."

Adele crossed the threshold. "Please, call me Adele."

Sister Zhara nodded. "Adele." She extended her arm toward the great room. "Come inside. Can I get you something to drink?"

"No, thank you. Is Roland here?"

Zhara's features tightened and her voice lowered. "I'm afraid it's been an especially difficult day for Mother Mary Ophelia. She's had another stroke—a bad one."

"Is she okay?"

"I believe she's sleeping. Mr. Soros is in the room with her. You're welcome to join him there. He told us you'd be coming."

"Thank you," Adele replied. She turned away and then turned back. "Your accent."

Zhara's brows lifted. "Yes?"

"I can't quite place it."

"Ah, yes, I get that a lot. My parents were from Aruba. Their grandparents were from Spain. Growing up I spoke both Spanish and Dutch—Aruba has been governed by the Netherlands for hundreds of years. I left Aruba for college and received a bachelor's degree in early childhood education from the University of Mary in North Dakota. It was there my English became so much better. After that I spent nearly three years teaching at St. Benedict School in Seattle before applying for and then being accepted to transfer here."

"Why here?" Adele asked.

"Mother Mary Ophelia."

"You knew her already?"

"I knew *of* her and I had heard of this place as well. To be able to practice a more monastic life devoted to physical labor and self-reflection was very appealing to me."

"You've managed a lot of living for someone so young."

"As have you—I'm pretty sure we're close to the same age. Unlike you, though, I've never won a marathon."

"You heard about that?"

"It was all Ophelia could talk about the other day. She is so proud of you and wanted to make certain everyone here knew you two were close friends."

"She's a very special woman."

"Indeed." Zhara glanced down as she cleared her throat. "Ophelia wasn't the only reason I requested to be transferred to the monastery here on Shaw Island."

"Oh?"

"I've been reading your newspaper articles for some time. This place fascinated me largely because of those things that you wrote. I wanted to experience it for myself. The first story of yours I recall reading was the one that involved the sheriff and his former girlfriend from high school. What she did was so horrible, the murder of the poor young woman, and yet you still treated her with dignity and respect. I found that so admirable. Such genuine empathy is a rare quality these days. When I arrived here, Ophelia also shared some stories. I have to ask—when that sea lion was attacking you at Deadman Island, did you really punch it in the face?"

"In the eye, actually."

Zhara shook her head. "My goodness. That must have been unbelievably frightening."

"At the time it was just adrenaline and instinct; I didn't want to die so I reacted and did what I thought had to be done."

"Something tells me your levels of adrenaline and instinct are far beyond what the rest of us have."

"You'd be surprised at what one is capable of when a situation requires it."

Zhara lightly touched Adele's arm. "I apologize. You came here to be with Ophelia and Mr. Soros, not listen to me prattle on about how much I admire you."

Adele smiled. "Prattle away all you like." She was struck by how Zhara's admiration of her mirrored that of Sky's back at Roche Harbor—two young women who, because of her articles, looked up to her as some kind of role model. *I'm not too sure how I feel about that,* she thought. Being a role model had never been part of her life's to-do list. She didn't think of herself as being worthy of such a designation.

"I'll let you get to it," Zhara said. "Let me know if you need anything."

Adele told her thank you, went down the hallway to Ophelia's partially open door, and then paused just outside of it when she heard Roland's voice. She looked through the opening and saw him sitting next to the bed with his hand over Ophelia's.

"I know you're a fighter, but please don't think you have to put up with all of this suffering on my account. I'll be okay. I have Adele to help. She'll be here soon to say hi. She's over on Orcas right now looking in a cave for some clues as to where Bloodbone might be. I'd rather she not go off and do those kinds of things alone, but I've accepted that once she thinks there's something she needs to do there's no stopping her. I suppose that's why I love her so much. She's strong like you—so strong that it scares me sometimes. I can't imagine being with anyone else."

Feeling guilty about spying on the conversation, Adele raised her arm to knock on the door.

"Well, that's not entirely true," Roland continued. "There's this new barista at the coffee shop in town who is *really* something. I've never drank so much coffee in my life! Man, would I like to roast her beans."

*What the hell?* Adele thought as she prepared to yank the door open and storm into the room.

Roland started to whisper—but loudly. "I'm trying to work up the courage to ask her out. If she says yes, I suppose I'll have to find a way to let Adele down easy. Then again, maybe I can try to keep the both of them around. That could be fun. I might even be able to score free coffee out of the deal. I mean c'mon—fun *and* coffee? How does a guy pass that up?"

Adele walked in.

"Oh," Roland said as he turned his head toward her. "I didn't see you there." He tried hard not to smile while Ophelia started laughing.

"What is going on?" Adele asked.

"Don't blame him," Ophelia replied in a voice that was so weak and garbled Adele could hardly make out the words. "It was my idea. Some gallows humor at your expense to try to lighten the mood."

"I heard you speaking with Zhara," Roland added, "and then Ophelia here decided to play a joke on you."

Adele stood by the bed. "Zhara said you've had a rough day."

The fun in Roland's eyes immediately went out and his lips pressed tightly together. "Yeah."

"I'm dying," Ophelia said. "This isn't going to get any better." When she looked up, her eyes appeared to have trouble focusing. "I can hardly see you." Adele leaned in closer. Ophelia nodded. "That's better. These damn strokes are taking my vision from me as if killing me wasn't enough."

Adele glanced at Roland. He looked away.

Ophelia closed her eyes. "The cave," she murmured. "You were there?"

"Yes," Adele answered. "Earlier today."

"Find Bloodbone?"

"No—just the bats."

"Keep looking." Ophelia's voice lowered further. "He's out there somewhere," she said right before drifting off again.

Roland stood and then tipped his head toward the hall. Adele followed him out of the room. He closed Ophelia's door and then leaned his shoulder against the wall. "When you spoke with Zhara, did she tell you just how bad it really was?"

"She didn't go into any specifics."

"The nuns were amazing. They had her cleaned up in a few minutes."

"Cleaned up?"

Roland's hand partially covered his mouth and then moved down over his neck. "When the stroke hit, she lost control of her bowels. The worst part of it was she was aware enough to realize it was happening." He grimaced. "I saw the shame in her eyes. She was crying. It was terrible. The specialist I had look at her earlier told me this would happen. He said it's the body cleaning itself out in preparation for death. I thought I could handle it, but today. . ." Roland sighed. "It was rough. I wanted so badly to be anywhere but in that room."

"It's completely normal to feel that way, Roland."

"You think so? I bet you would have handled it better than I did."

Adele shook her head. "I doubt it."

"Do you mind if we go outside? I could really use the fresh air."

They walked out together and then stood in the grass under the branches of some nearby evergreen trees. Clouds gathered overhead and the wind was getting stronger, hinting at the rain that was forecast to arrive by late afternoon.

"The second cave," Roland said. "Did you find it?"

"There was nothing there."

"No legendary white bear with mystical powers?"

Adele grunted. "Hardly. The only thing I saw were bats."

"There was nothing different since the last time you were there?"

"Actually, there *was* something. The crystal structure that comes up out of the cave floor—it was hardly glowing and there was no humming or vibration, like somebody had pulled the plug on it."

"So now what?"

"I guess I keep reading the journal." Adele looked up. "What about you?"

"I'll be here as much as possible until..." Roland paused. "Until I don't have to be."

Adele turned toward the sound of the monastery door opening and watched as Zhara stepped out and then started walking toward them while holding something in her hand. The wind blew the bottom of her long black skirt out behind her and a silver crucifix bounced from side to side against her chest. Adele's mind snapped a mental picture of the nun confidently striding across the grounds with the monastery rising up behind her. It was an image that seemed to suggest the monastery itself was preparing for Ophelia's passing and considering Zhara as a suitable replacement.

"Apologies for the interruption," Zhara said.

"What is it?" Roland asked.

Zhara handed him a flash drive. "The song she chose. I didn't want to forget to give it to you. I also promise to do my best regarding getting approval for the other thing."

Roland took the device and placed it into the front pocket of his dress slacks. "Thank you."

Zhara nodded. "Of course, Mr. Soros." She turned away and then went back into the monastery.

"What song?" Adele asked.

"Ophelia wants it to be playing while I spread her ashes over the waters that run between Shaw and Orcas Islands."

"You mean around Blind Island State Park?"

"More to the west by Broken Point. Apparently, she and my grandfather used to walk out there all the time when they were together and look across those waters up at Turtleback Mountain. He was also the one who first introduced her to the song she wants played."

"Zhara also mentioned getting approval for something."

Roland squeezed the back of his neck as he rolled his head from one side to the other. "The Catholic Church doesn't allow the spreading of ashes."

"Why not?"

"Church doctrine mandates that remains are to be placed in a sacred place like a cemetery or church grounds."

"I can't think of anything more sacred than the waters that surround our islands."

"Funny—that's *exactly* what Zhara said as well. She intends to speak directly with the archbishop about it."

"And what happens if the church denies the request?"

"Ophelia says they'll be the ones to go to hell for refusing a dying nun her final wishes." Roland shrugged. "I'll do exactly what she asks of me regardless of what anyone else says."

"What's the song?"

"It's by some band called Cracker."

"Never heard of them."

"Me neither. The name of the song is 'Take Me Down to the Infirmary'."

"I guess the title is appropriate given the circumstances. Have you listened to it?"

"No. I'll do it later tonight. My plan is to take my yacht out on the day. . ." Roland's voice broke.

Adele rubbed his upper arm. "It's okay."

He clenched his jaw as he fought back tears. "I would like some of you with me when I spread the ashes—you, Lucas, Tilda, and whoever else wants to pay their respects."

"I'm sure everyone will be there."

"Except for him."

Adele knew Roland meant Bloodbone. "You never know. He might just show up at the last second. Has Ophelia been asking about him?"

"All the time. She was really hoping you'd find him in that cave, drag him out of there and then bring him here."

"I wonder why my finding him is so important to her."

"She's afraid. She does a good job of hiding it, but the fact is she's scared of what's coming. No one on these islands has helped more people make the transition from life to death than Bloodbone, including when my grandfather passed. I think she always assumed that he would be here for her as well when her own time came."

Hearing that made Adele even more determined to track Bloodbone down. "I'll keep looking."

"I know you will."

"When did you want to get going?"

"I'll be staying. I want to be sure I'm here when, you know, she goes. That could be tonight or tomorrow, or next week. All I know for sure is that it's coming fast. What about you?"

"Like I said—more reading of Bloodbone's journal. I have to check in at the newspaper office in Friday Harbor tomorrow, but then I can be back here around noon."

"You don't have to come."

"I know that, Roland—I want to." Adele looked up. The day's first drops of rain started to fall. "I should get going before the weather turns."

"When you're at Roche, can you pick up something for me and then bring it back here with you tomorrow?"

"Sure. What is it?"

"If you look through the right-side cabinet of the bar at my house, you'll find a bottle of Macallan's thirty-year Scotch that was part of my grandfather's personal collection. He had one last drink from it the day before he died. It was resealed shortly after that and hasn't been opened since. Ophelia asked that I bring it here for her."

"No problem. Do you need anything else?"

Roland smiled. "Just you."

The two embraced. Roland told Adele to be safe and then she started the long walk back to her boat. By the time she reached the water the rain was coming down hard and the sea was churning and getting worse by the minute.

It would be an especially slow and wet slog back to Roche Harbor.

# 11.

*I watched a pair of canoes paddle toward the shore. Each one carried six men.*

*"We must flee!" Asav shouted. The last of our warriors and their families had left a week earlier for what was by then known as Point Roberts, a common gathering place of various Salish Sea tribes. It was there they hoped to find strength in numbers against the white man's increasingly determined expansion into our lands. They made clear they had no intention of ever returning to Orcas Island.*

*Only Asav and I remained.*

*"We can hide in the woods," Asav continued. "Perhaps make our way to the other side of the island." He looked out at the approaching canoes. "First we spy a passing British warship and now this."*

*"No," I replied. "I shall wait here."*

*"That's madness."*

*I looked down at him. "Then go."*

*"And leave you here to face them alone? I prefer to grab some rifles and give them a proper greeting."*

*I clamped my hand onto Asav's shoulder. "No guns."*

*"Why not?"*

*"Because I wish to know what they want."*

*"And what if what they want is to kill you?"*

*"Then so be it."*

*Asav squinted up at me and then spit onto the ground. "You act like a fool with a death wish."*

*I ignored him, preferring to give my full attention to the arriving strangers.*

*"Did you hear me?" Asav asked.*

*"You can hide in the cave if you wish," I answered. "I doubt they would find you there."*

*"The cave? No, I don't think so."*

*"Why not?"*

*"Too many bats."*

*"And bears."*

*Asav frowned. "Eh? Did you say bears?"*

*His tone confirmed what I already suspected; he knew of the bear and had sent me into the cave alone, possibly hoping the creature might accomplish what he lacked the courage to—trying to kill me.*

*The canoes reached the shore. I noted one of the twelve men, the oldest among them, wore an ornate headdress. Short and lean with a weathered face and downturned mouth, he walked with the purposeful gait of one long accustomed to holding a position of authority. A revolver hung from his right hip.*

*"A chief," Asav whispered. "The others are all armed with knives."*

*The chief led the way while his warriors followed close behind in a V formation. He stopped in front of me and looked up. "You are Bloodbone."*

*"Do I know you?" I asked.*

*"The rumors are true then," he replied. "Old Raven is no more."*

*"You're a chief," Asav said.*

*The chief glanced at Asav and then looked back at me. "Why do you allow this thing to remain here with you in this sacred place?"*

*"Thing?" Asav growled as his hand drifted toward his knife. "Now hold on."*

*All eleven of the chief's warriors drew their weapons simultaneously. "What I have to say to you isn't intended for the ears of a white man."*

*I repeated my earlier question, which remained unanswered. "Do I know you?"*

*The chief nodded. "We have met."*

*"Where?"*

*"Years ago, you led a war party against my people. We are Semiahmoo."*

*My heart sank, heavy with the weight of terrible regret for the things I had done to his tribe. I bowed my head. "Apologies. I assure you I am no longer that man."*

*Asav stepped away from me. "Are you here to take revenge on him?"*

*"I am here," the chief replied, "to give counsel to Old Raven's successor."*

*"Counsel?" My eyes narrowed. "After what I did to you and your people why would you come here now to offer me counsel?"*

*"I have lived long enough, Bloodbone, to know that there are things in this world one must simply accept on faith because we lack the understanding to answer the unanswerable. The sun rises and falls each day. I know not how or why—it simply does. You murdered many in my tribe and took our lands from us. Yet now you are here, wearing Old Raven's crystal around your neck. I offer my counsel because I made an oath to Old Raven that I would do so if a great war was to threaten these islands."*

*"The British warship," Asav said.*

*The chief nodded. "Two powerful forces, one American, one British, now argue for control of the San Juans. For reasons known only to him, Old Raven chose you to be the one to navigate such troubled waters. You are now the protector of these islands, Bloodbone. Many will come and many will go, but like Old Raven was in his time, you will now remain the constant throughout all that will inevitably change here in your own time." He glared at Asav. "But this is not for the likes of you to hear, white man."*

Asav puffed out his chest. "I'm a free man. If I choose to stay nobody can tell me different."

"Go," I told him.

"The hell I will."

"Go now and return tomorrow."

"Where?"

I shrugged. "That is up to you."

"I wish to God that damn bear had—" Asav tried to look away.

"Bear?" I stared into his eyes. He had exposed his own deception and he knew it, but then he did what liars always do—he simply lied some more.

"It was you who mentioned a bear."

"No," I replied. "I said bears."

Asav threw up his hands. "Fine. I will leave here as you wish, but know this—I might never return."

It was another lie.

Asav followed the shore and then disappeared into the woods to the north.

"No good will come from your association with his kind," the chief said.

"You mean a white man?" I asked.

The chief shook his head. "An evil man." He pointed to the longhouse. "Let us now speak freely and in private. My men will remain on watch outside."

*I knew the risk I took in entering the longhouse with a man whose people I had decimated years earlier, but I also knew, or rather sensed, that no harm would come to me within that place for it was as it had been for Old Raven— a sanctuary for mind, body, and spirit from the chaotic world beyond the islands.*

*A fire was started after the chief complained of how the chill and pains of water travel had become worse with each passing year. We sat across from each other on the hard-packed earth floor looking through the flames that separated us.*

*The chief removed his headdress, revealing dark, shoulder-length hair streaked with strands of gray. I offered him chunks of salted deer meat, which he gratefully accepted. "I am Goliah, son of Yoikum." He looked around at the interior of the longhouse and smiled. "It has been so many years and yet it is just as I remember. Even the smell of the ancient fir walls and ceiling is the same. My father came here as well and his father before him. Beyond this place time moves so quickly while here it seems to hardly move at all." He swallowed the last of the deer meat and then sighed. "Do you know of the Treaty of Point Elliot?"*

*I shook my head.*

*"It was signed by the greatest chiefs from nearly all the tribes who inhabit these lands. Much will be taken from us while very little is to be given. Old Raven foretold of this long ago and now it has finally come to pass. I believe he took it as a sign, a confirmation, that he was to prepare for a new age and a new guardian of the islands. What is to*

*come won't be easy for you. Where Old Raven primarily dealt with our own kind you must now find a way to work with the same white interlopers who would make slaves of us all. The British warship you saw is but one of many that now regularly cross these waters. There is even talk of war."*

*"You journeyed all this way to tell me this?"*

*"THIS, as you put it, will mean everything to the survival of the islands. My oath to Old Raven was to deliver you this warning. Having done so I can now return home where I fight to restore my own people's place there. I did not sign the Treaty of Point Elliot. I owe no allegiance to the white man's agreement."*

*"What will you do?" I asked.*

*"Take what little is left of my tribe and flee further north into British territory, leaving the hostilities of the American government behind."*

*"Wouldn't you merely be trading the hostilities of one government for another?"*

*"It is said the British Empire is in decline. If given the choice of two enemies, why not choose the weaker and less aggressive one?" Goliah moved to get up.*

*I raised my hand. "Wait. Please tell me more of what you know of this place."*

*He stood behind the tendrils of smoke that swirled upward into the darkness of the high ceiling. "I likely do not know any more than you. My father and his father spoke of Old Raven with great reverence and neither of them were men* who gave their respect to another easily. Old Raven knew them as children, as warriors, and then as tribal elders. He existed before they were born and continued to exist long after they were gone."

"But how is such a thing possible? How can one man outlive all others?"

Goliah pointed at the crystal given to me by Old Raven. "He was chosen by the islands the same as you. It is a choosing that has been taking place long before our people first came to this place. These islands are in fact ancient mountains from when the world was young, separate from the mainland. The great ice came, covering everything, then retreated, but the surrounding waters remained. People arrived soon after, but they were not us."

"Us?"

"They were not Lummi, Semiahmoo, Nooksack, Skagit, or any of the other tribes that later called these lands their home."

"These people who were here before, what happened to them?"

"We happened," Goliah answered. "Over time more of us came. We took the land from them and made it our own, sometimes through agreement, other times through violence and slavery. They were absorbed until nothing of them remained."

"We did to them then what the white man would do to us now."

Goliah nodded and his tone was solemn. "Exactly."

*"So how am I to protect the islands as Old Raven and those chosen before him did?"*

*"I do not know. As I already explained, my purpose in coming here was to warn you of the impending war between the Americans and the British. Having done so my oath to Old Raven has been honored. How you act on that warning is up to you." Goliah paused, looked down at the fire, and then his head lifted. "What I am more certain of is this—your life must now be devoted entirely to the well-being of these islands. Everything you do from now until your last breath is to be toward that end."*

*"And will I have as many years as Old Raven did to accomplish this?"*

*Goliah shrugged. "Perhaps more. Perhaps less." When I stood, his eyes widened. "The day you attacked my people, I see it now so clearly as if it took place just yesterday. You were this monstrous force of dark nature come to take everything from me and I knew there would be no stopping you. Even the bravest of my warriors wailed your name like frightened children as they watched you descend the hill behind our village—Bloodbone." His hand gripped the handle of his revolver tightly enough it turned his knuckles white. "In the weeks and months that followed I yearned for the chance to one day have my revenge." The hand fell away and his shoulders slumped. "I wonder."*

*"What?" I asked.*

*"If our many tribes had not wasted so much time fighting amongst ourselves, if we had been fully united against the white man's intrusion from the beginning, how different*

*our futures might have been. Instead, we allowed our own pride, greed, and pettiness to divide us, and that division made us so much weaker, allowing the white man to conquer our people one by one by one."*

*"There will come a time when the same will happen to the white man. His own divisive nature will be his downfall."*

*Goliah's mouth remained a hard slash, but his eyes smiled. "You already sound so much like Old Raven. I won't be around to see such a thing, but you might, should the islands bless you with a life long enough to do so."*

*"To have to witness all those I care about die off while I continue on sounds as much like a curse as a blessing."*

*"That is true." Goliah turned toward the door. "My men and I will sleep near the water and be gone by morning."*

*"Why not enjoy the comfort of the longhouse as my guest?"*

*Goliah shook his head. "This place is not for us. It is now yours and yours alone."*

*He returned outside as I sat and stared into the fire and its curling and crackling flames, wondering what I was to do next while somewhere in the woods I knew that Asav watched and waited, but for what I did not yet know.*

Adele closed the journal. It was late. She went into the bathroom, brushed her teeth, and then slid under the soft covers of her bed, listening to the wind blow across the harbor and the waves splashing against the sailboat's hull. Even though her body was tired her mind raced with possibilities of where Bloodbone might be found before then turning to thoughts of what was happening to Ophelia and the impact her death would have on Roland.

Tomorrow was another day bringing with it the potential for answers to questions so numerous she was struggling to keep track. There was nothing to be done but to continue searching, to continue reading, in the hope that soon all would be revealed.

# 12.

It had been nearly two weeks since Adele had last stopped by her newspaper office that overlooked the Friday Harbor ferry terminal. The man she shared co-ownership of the paper with, Jose, continued to do a remarkable job of streamlining the publication process, which in turn allowed her the time to focus almost exclusively on her own articles that had accumulated an online readership which extended far beyond the borders of the San Juan Islands. She would sometimes ask him if he would prefer her to spend more time helping him out at the office, but his response remained a quick and decisive no. Nearly every corner of the paper was now monetized in some way, creating a steady increase in revenue and profits that afforded each of them comfortable livings. They had both come a long way since the days when Jose's only job was delivering physical copies of the paper to island residents and businesses and Adele was an anxious new college graduate trying to find her place in the world.

"Check it out," Jose proudly said as he tapped his laptop screen. "The paper's online local goods and services section is up and running. I basically took the Craigslist concept but made it specific to the islands only and because it's interactive all of the for-sale items, job offers, whatever, can be updated by the subscribers in real time. We have nearly three hundred paying subscribers already with an average of ten more sign-ups per day. At this rate we should have more than a thousand within a few more months.

Interestingly, about twenty percent of the new sign-ups are from the mainland—especially in and around the Anacortes area."

"A thousand registered users at five dollars per month—that's real money," Adele said.

Jose beamed. "I know and not only *real* money but *easy* money. The platform is self-directed with minimal upkeep requirements on our end. I've spent hundreds of hours getting this ready, but now we just sit back and watch the money roll in. I said a thousand users within a few months, but by the end of the year I bet we double that number."

"Ten grand a month coming into the business on this one application alone?"

"Exactly."

"Most of that should go to you."

"No," Jose said with a shake of his head. "We're partners."

It wasn't the first time Adele had suggested he take a bigger percentage of the newspaper's profits, but each time he adamantly refused. "You did all of the work on this, and we both know I don't spend nearly the same amount of time putting each issue together as you do."

"You're the face of the newspaper, Adele, and your articles are its heart and soul. Everything I do is built around that fact. Without you there'd be no me. I make a good living and, believe me, my wife and kids thank you for it. This business has allowed my family to experience the American dream. What more could a son of Mexican immigrants ask for than that?"

"I tell you what," Adele said. "Since the interactive goods and services section was your idea and your hard work that made it happen, you should get the majority of the income it generates.

We'll put fifty percent back into the company reserves and then you take the other fifty percent and add it to your monthly salary."

Jose frowned. "And you get none of it?"

"No, I'll eventually get my share of what goes back into the company, right? Look, I don't want to argue about money, especially when it's money that you earned. Besides, there's another subject I'd like to talk to you about."

"What is it?"

"Hiring another employee."

"Are you talking about Sky?"

"You know her?"

Jose nodded. "She emailed her resume to us yesterday. It said she's currently working up at Roche as part of their dock staff, so I figured you two had probably already met."

"I told her we'd be open to having her come back next summer as a paid intern."

"Her resume is pretty thin."

"As was ours at her age. Besides, isn't that what an internship is for? To give her some real-world experience?"

"True."

"So, you're on board with the idea?"

"How much were you thinking of paying her?"

Adele shrugged. "What do you think would be fair?"

"Will we be taking care of her living arrangements as well? You know how tough it is to find affordable housing on the islands during the summer months."

Adele pointed to the back part of the office where a hardly used storage room was located. "She could crash in there. It's private enough and she'd have the whole place to herself at night."

"There's no shower or washer and dryer."

"It's a two-minute walk to the Friday Harbor Marina. She can use the showers and laundry facilities there."

"Okay, so let's get back to the salary part. How much?"

"Four hundred a week?"

"And we give her a place to live. I'd say that's more than fair." Jose leaned back in his chair. "One more thing."

"Go ahead."

"If we invest an entire summer on her I think it would be wise for us to try to then keep her on as a permanent employee, which means we should find out if she would be open to that before we proceed."

Adele nodded. "I was thinking the exact same thing. The way the paper is growing there's no reason not to bring on some more help."

Jose wagged a finger. "Look at you, Ms. Business. I guess all that time you spend with Roland Soros is paying off."

"Huh?"

"You navigated this entire little negotiation between us like a pro. That's why you suggested we reinvest part of the new goods and services section proceeds back into the company. By doing that we're already more than covering the cost of bringing on a new employee, which made it much harder for me to argue against the idea, especially after you eliminated the concern over housing. You boxed me in without me even knowing it was happening—and you made it look so easy. That's some Soros-level skills right there."

"I don't think I had it all planned out nearly as well as you're suggesting."

"That's just it—you didn't have to plan it out. What you did was instinctive. You wanted our conversation to end up where it did and you made it happen. I'm not knocking it, Adele—just the opposite. I feel lucky to be a part of your growth as a businessperson."

"I feel the same about you. We make a good team."

"No," Jose replied. "We make a *great* team."

Adele left the office feeling good about locking down Sky's internship and the possibility of bringing her on permanently after she graduated college. She felt even better about her working relationship with Jose. He was right—they were a great team.

By then it was nearly noon. Adele thought of driving over to the Sheriff's Office to touch base with Lucas but then decided she'd prefer a casual stroll through town where she could literally stop and smell the flowers. It was the time of year when Friday Harbor's multitude of hanging baskets were in full bloom, giving the business district a welcome splash of color and scents that was so unique to their little corner of the world.

"Why hello there, Adele. How nice to catch you out and about. It sure is a beautiful day, isn't it?"

Adele turned around and then her mental rolodex matched the face and voice to that of Millie Harper, the owner and operator of one of the local real estate businesses that was among the newspaper's longest-running advertisers. "It sure is."

Millie was in her seventies but had the energy of a woman half her age. Smartly dressed in a light blouse and dark skirt, with short-cropped white hair atop a lean face, she exuded the casual confidence of someone who had managed to survive and thrive despite the often-challenging feast and famine nature of owning a business on the islands. "I want to give you some big kudos for the new goods and services section of the newspaper. I'm practically a technology illiterate but it's so easy to use and I love being able to post as many items as I want for one flat monthly fee. I created an ad for an old tractor that has been taking up space in my backyard and hasn't been run in at least ten years and had a cash buyer who showed up and then took it away the very next day. Sold it for almost my full asking price."

"I have to give Jose all the credit for that. It was his idea and he was the one who put it all together."

"Well then, kudos to him as well. And congratulations on your race. Jose can't take any credit for that. It was really something watching you cross that finish line first."

"Thanks."

"Did you hear the news about that other runner, the fella from Bellevue who came in second?"

"Jackson Ray?"

"That's the one. He pulled out of some marathon he was going to run up in Canada because of an online video that was posted of him trying to trip you during the race here. Apparently, he's losing sponsors over it and everything."

"I had no idea."

"You should check it out," Millie said. "Take it from someone who's had to deal with her share of male chauvinist pigs over the years—a man trying to trip a woman is never a good look. I don't know him personally, but I'm guessing he's a real piece of work. It made your beating him in that race that much more appreciated. You didn't just win that race for yourself—you won it for a lot of us."

Millie's phone started ringing. She took it out of her purse and held it up. "New listing client," she said. "You take care, Adele."

"You too," Adele replied as she started down the sidewalk, pausing every so often to smell another batch of flowers. When she reached the Sheriff's Office, she found Lucas already outside getting ready to get into his SUV.

"Are you here for me?" he asked.

"I was hoping you had something to report on Fin."

"Nothing definitive yet. I did touch base with an inspector over there who said he'll do a wellness check this week and then get back to me."

"Lucas—something isn't right about this. Fin wouldn't go silent for so long."

"There's nothing to be done about it except to keep checking in with the County Cork authorities. The inspector I spoke with said the Traveler population is notoriously tight-lipped with outsiders, especially when it comes to answering questions from the authorities.

"I could go over there myself."

"Will you?"

Adele thought of Ophelia and Roland and knew leaving now for Ireland wasn't an option. "I have things going on here that need to be taken care of first."

"I doubt you'll have to make a trip all the way over there. He'll show up soon."

"A vacation to Ireland doesn't sound so bad. I've always wanted to see it."

"And no luck finding Bloodbone?"

"Not yet."

"Where are you off to now?"

"Back over to Shaw." As soon as Adele said it, she knew Lucas would want to know why she had been going over there so often. He had let her off easy before, saying he'd give her time to decide when she was ready to tell him what was going on, but now she sensed his increasing interest. He initially gave her a hard look that then softened into one of concern.

"Ophelia is sick, isn't she? That's why I've hardly seen Roland around lately either."

Adele looked away. She wouldn't lie to Lucas, but she also didn't want to betray Ophelia's trust to keep her condition secret.

Lucas lowered his voice. "How bad is it?"

"Bad," Adele answered, relieved to finally be letting him know what was going on. "She's dying."

"Shit."

"She doesn't want anyone to know."

"How long does she have?"

Adele shook her head. "Not long."

"I'd like to see her before . . . before it's too late."

"I'll ask."

"How's Roland holding up?"

"He's hanging in there."

"The last of his family will be gone. That's tough."

"You know how that feels too, don't you?"

Lucas grimaced. "I do." Then he gave Adele a thin smile. "But we all still have each other."

"That's what I told Roland."

"Does Tilda know?"

"Not yet."

"I wouldn't keep her out of the loop for too much longer. She'll want a chance to say her goodbyes as well. Maybe we could come over to Shaw together."

"Maybe."

"Looking for Bloodbone, reading through his journal, worried about Fin, and now dealing with Ophelia and trying to be there for Roland—that's an awful lot on your plate right now, Adele."

"Tell me about it."

"I'm here for you both if you need me. Day or night—just let me know."

Adele turned around so Lucas wouldn't see her tears. *NO CRYING*, she told herself while clenching her jaw. She remembered how, years ago, it was Lucas who stood watch all night outside of her sailboat when she thought someone might be stalking her. He was exhausted the next morning but said not a word of complaint even though they hardly knew each other at the time. He was also the one who had saved her life when she was being attacked by

Visili Vasa on the hill above Rosario Resort. He was a good man who deserved the love of an equally good woman. Adele wiped the tears away, turned again, and looked up. "I'll get Ophelia to allow you to see her."

"Don't forget about Tilda."

"I won't." Adele paused. Lucas waited. She sniffed, started to speak, stopped, and then finally blurted out exactly how she felt. "I love you, Lucas. You're like family to me, and I want you to know that, okay? You've been such a big help over the years and I—" She felt the tears coming again. "I owe you so much."

Lucas stepped forward and wrapped his big arms around her. "I love you too." Even though she couldn't see his face Adele sensed he was smiling. "I always knew you would eventually come to your senses and leave Roland for me."

Adele tensed before realizing he was teasing. She laughed as she pressed her face against his muscular chest. "Dork."

"That's Sheriff Dork to you."

When they separated, Adele was surprised to see the glistening in Lucas's eyes. She wasn't the only one who had been overcome by emotion. "I should get going," she said.

Lucas nodded. "Me too. Have a safe trip over to Shaw and let me know when Tilda and I can come over there as well. Until then don't forget—you or Roland need anything, anything at all, let me know."

Adele watched him drive away and then headed back to her car, stopping to smell the flowers at nearly every hanging basket she came to.

It just felt like the right thing to do.

# 13.

Adele hugged Roland tightly after she entered the monastery. He stepped back and smiled, his eyes bright and cheerful. "Ophelia is having a *really* good day. She's been a chatterbox all morning. No strokes, her speech and eyesight are better, she's managed to keep some food and water down, and she even wants me to take her outside."

"Is that normal with this disease?"

Roland nodded. "In these kinds of end-of-life situations it's apparently common for the body to rally for a day or two toward the end, as if it wants to give you one last chance to experience life before what's coming next."

"Like a shot of eleventh-hour adrenaline."

"I guess so."

Adele held up the bottle of Scotch that Roland had asked her to get from his home and then bring back with her to the monastery. "As requested."

"Fantastic," he said as he took it. "Thank you."

"Will she be able to go outside?"

"That's the plan. Sister Zhara should be bringing a utility vehicle around soon. Ophelia wants to go out to Broken Point so she can show me exactly where she wants her ashes scattered."

"Can I see her?"

"Not yet. She's with a priest who flew in this morning from Seattle—Father Nick. He was sent personally by the archbishop to check in on her. He asked that he be allowed to speak with her in private."

"Is the church going to allow her ashes to be scattered?"

"Sister Zhara said she hasn't heard back on that yet, but I'm pretty sure the subject is being brought up now between Father Nick and Ophelia."

"What if they say no?"

"I'll make certain Ophelia's wishes are honored regardless of what the church says."

"And how are you doing?"

"Fine," Roland replied. "I know what's coming. I don't like it of course, but I accept it and watching Ophelia stare it down with so much courage makes me want to do the same. I can't be there for her if I'm a blubbering mess."

"Lucas knows."

"You told him?"

"He figured it out on his own. He's hoping to come here for a visit soon and he wants to bring Tilda with him."

"She knows too?"

"Not yet but Lucas thinks we should tell her, so she has a chance to say goodbye as well."

"I suppose he's right about that."

"Will you ask Ophelia for them?"

Roland rubbed his forehead. "Sure."

They both turned toward the sound of yelling coming from the hallway behind them.

"That sounds like Ophelia," Adele said.

Roland was already walking fast toward the room.

"I've had enough of you trying to dictate my own salvation to me," Ophelia shouted. "If the archbishop has a problem with having my ashes scattered, he can come here himself and tell me to my face, not send some fresh out of seminary school lackey to do it for him."

Father Nick bumped into Roland on his way out. He was around thirty years of age, of average height, with a round, boyish face, owlish eyes, large forehead, and thinning reddish hair. "I was told she was near death," he said while scowling.

"She's having a good day," Roland replied, "and feeling much more like her old self."

"Her behavior is unacceptable. She refuses to listen to reason."

"Unacceptable?" Roland's eyes narrowed. "That woman in there is dying. I think that allows her to act however she wants."

"Being ill does not excuse the absence of good manners and proper respect."

"Follow me, Father," Roland replied right before striding back into the monastery's great room. He whirled around and stuck a finger into the priest's chest. "Watch your tone. That's my grandmother in there and I won't hesitate to knock you on your ass."

Father Nick's cheeks burned red. "Are you threatening violence against me, Mr. Soros?"

"I'm defending a dying woman. If you want to call that violent, then be my guest."

"The archbishop will hear of this."

"So? I'm not Catholic. Your church has no power over me. And one more thing—if Ophelia wants her ashes scattered then that's exactly what is going to happen."

The priest's eyes flared. "It's a matter of her salvation, Mr. Soros. Don't you care enough to save her soul?"

"My grandmother's soul will be fine, Father. Now *yours* on the other hand. . ."

"Perhaps a dispensation is in order." Sister Zhara entered the room.

Father Nick shook his head. "No."

"What's a dispensation?" Adele asked.

"It doesn't matter," Father Nick answered.

Sister Zhara looked past the priest and directly at Adele. "A relaxing of the rules on a case-by-case basis. The archbishop could grant Mother Mary Ophelia one."

Father Nick raised his voice. "There is no hardship that would warrant such a consideration. Know your place, Sister."

Adele shot the priest a hard look. "Know your place? *Really?*"

"I will speak to the archbishop directly first thing tomorrow," Sister Zhara replied as she continued to ignore Father Nick.

The priest glared at the young nun. "You'll do no such thing."

"Father," Roland said, "would you mind stepping outside with me for a moment?"

"Is this where you plan to, how did you put it, *knock me on my ass,* Mr. Soros?"

Roland rolled his eyes. "Don't be an idiot. Noise carries in here. I just thought it would be more considerate of others if we took our conversation outside."

"I already planned to leave."

"Fine." Roland put an arm around the priest's shoulders. "I'll walk you out."

After the door closed behind them Adele turned toward Sister Zhara. "This dispensation thing—do you think you can make it happen for Ophelia?"

"I will certainly try."

"Thank you."

Sister Zhara nodded, mentioned that the utility vehicle was parked outside, and then left the room. Roland returned soon after, shaking his head. "That man suffers from a serious case of frustrated insecurity or what my grandfather would often call pinky dick."

"He's a misogynist."

"I thought that's what I said."

Adele grinned. "No—you said pinky dick."

Ophelia's laughter carried down the hall. "I remember that!" she shouted. "Charles loved that saying. Now get in here and take me outside."

Roland entered the room, gently picked Ophelia up out of the bed, cradled her body in his arms, and then carried her out into the daylight while she held tightly to his neck. She looked up at the sun, took a deep breath, and smiled. "That's better." She was placed in the middle of the utility vehicle's bench seat. Roland sat behind the wheel on her left while Adele sat on her right. From there they drove slowly away from the monastery on a dirt road that snaked through tall evergreen trees, heading north toward Shaw Island's Broken Point, a large outcrop of rock that extended like a big-knuckled finger across the water toward nearby Orcas Island.

"There weren't any houses here and the trees weren't so tall when your grandfather and I would walk together to this place back then," Ophelia said. "It often felt like the whole world faded away, leaving just the island and us." She closed her eyes. "Of course, it was an incredibly complicated time given he was married, and I was a nun. Part of me felt terrible, but the rest of me, most of me, couldn't resist. God forgive us, but it just felt right." She opened her eyes and pointed to a path that was nearly overgrown by grass and weeds. "There. That's the way to our spot."

Roland drove slowly down the path. Flashes of shimmering blue-green water could be seen in the gaps between trees filled with the sounds of birdsong. The three of them went quiet as the world beyond faded away just as Ophelia had described. Soon the trees were replaced by an expanse of sea and stone.

"Did you bring it?" Ophelia asked.

Roland held up the bottle of Scotch.

Ophelia took it from him and then stared down at the label. "The flat rock over there," she said. "That's where we sat, your grandfather and I." When Roland went to pick her up, she pushed him away. "No. I intend to walk it one last time." She required some help from Roland and Adele who supported her by her elbows as she took one careful and deliberate step followed by another and then another. When they reached the rock, they slowly lowered her onto it and then sat beside her. An especially large, lone bald eagle drifted down toward the water's surface, made a slow, graceful turn, and then, with a few powerful flaps of its wings, sped off toward Orcas Island.

"This is where Charles told me."

Both Adele and Roland looked at Ophelia. "Told you what?" Roland asked.

"That he was dying. We hadn't spoken for some time. By then he had his life and I had mine. I was quite surprised when he suddenly showed up at the monastery unannounced asking for me. As soon as I saw him, I knew something was wrong. He didn't look himself. He was nearly as old then as I am now, but it wasn't just his age. It's the eyes you know—the light starts to go out. When he said he wanted to take a walk, I sensed bad news was coming. He kept humming something to himself all the way here. When I asked what it was, he told me it had been playing in the hospital waiting room the day he received the diagnosis. I believe he saw it as a sign."

"The same song you want played when your ashes are scattered," Adele said. "'Take Me Down to the Infirmary.'"

Ophelia nodded. "It was a contemporary song back when he told me, something the young kids were listening to, and Charles wasn't what I would consider a contemporary man, but that was the song he kept humming to himself over and over. Perhaps it brought him comfort. I didn't understand it then, but I do now." She gave the bottle of Scotch back to Roland. "Please open this. We drank from that same bottle and looked out at the water after he told me he wasn't long for this world. I drank more than I cried because I knew that was what he wanted." Ophelia tapped the ground with the heel of her shoe. "Right here in this very spot." She took the bottle, pressed it to her lips, and then tilted it back, grimacing as she swallowed. "And I've missed him ever since."

The bottle was handed to Roland who drank from it and then handed to Adele who did the same. "What did you talk to Father Nick about when you went outside with him?" she asked.

"I told him he wasn't needed or wanted here and to never come back," Roland answered.

"That's it?"

"Pretty much."

"What did he say?"

"Nothing."

"He's a wretched little thing," Ophelia growled. "The church is full of his kind. Just a few years ago I would have marched him out of there by his ear."

Sister Zhara seems to think the archbishop might be open to granting you a dispensation," Adele said.

"Perhaps," Ophelia replied. "I wouldn't turn it down, but, in the end, does it really matter? My god is not one who obsesses over rules created long ago by men attempting to confine the blessings of His grace to those they approved while denying those they didn't."

Adele raised the bottle. "Amen to that."

Ophelia pointed down at the water. "That's the spot, Roland. Right there is where you will scatter my ashes." She looked up at him. "Will you do this for me?"

"Yes," Roland said in a voice that was soft yet still assertive. "I will."

"Thank you, my grandson." Ophelia grinned as she rested her head against his shoulder. "This truly is a good day."

They each drank more from the bottle but said little. Adele sensed that Roland and Ophelia were both lost in their own thoughts. Ophelia was especially pensive until eventually she started to hum again with her head raised and her eyes closed as the sun caressed her deeply lined face in its warm glow. She wrapped one arm around Roland's waist and her other arm around Adele's. A sailboat moved slowly and silently past the point, its bow gently lifting and falling as it cut through the small waves seemingly in time to the song Ophelia was humming.

Adele glanced out of the corner of her eye and first thought Ophelia had the faraway look of someone who had lost all hope, but then she realized that what she was actually seeing as the old nun gazed out beyond the limits of memory and recollection was a woman accepting her fate with quiet dignity despite the sad finality of the truth that now confronted her.

This was to be the last good day of Ophelia's long life.

# 14.

*I'm dreaming,* Adele thought. *I was already here.*

"Here" was the entrance to the Turtleback Mountain cave on Orcas Island. Adele stood looking into the gloom while listening for any clue as to what, besides thousands of bats, waited for her inside.

*Dream or not you have to go in,* she told herself, *because you're supposed to.*

She pulled away the brush and limbs that concealed much of the cave opening. She paused, afraid to go further. It wasn't the bats that she feared. No, it was something else—the unknown thing that had long waited so patiently inside for her arrival.

*The secondary cave—I didn't go far enough into it when I was here last time.*

When Adele crossed the threshold, leaving the day behind to enter the mountain's eternal night, the cave sighed. She heard and felt it and then had to fight the instinct to turn around and run out.

*None of this is real. I'm in my sailboat sleeping after coming back from Shaw Island with Roland. Nothing here can hurt me.*

She kept going, one cautious step after another. When the walls and ceiling began to shift and squeal as the bats cried out against her intrusion, she knew she was getting close to the outcrop of crystal that rose up from the cave floor. This time those crystals were pulsating again, pushing away the darkness and filling the cave with their primordial glow. Adele stood straight and pressed her hand over her chest.

Thump-thump-thump—the crystals pulsed perfectly in time with her heartbeat, the sound filling her ears as even the bats all around her went silent.

The other cave still waited, a dark patch in the wall that dared her to enter. Adele turned toward it, her hand falling away from her chest. The fetid scent of bat feces filled her nostrils as she crossed the floor and then stood in front of that second opening. The taste of fear was heavy on her tongue—sharp and metallic. Her heart beat faster as did the crystals behind her.

Thump-thump-thump.

The cave beckoned, seemingly hungry for her company. Adele crouched, her face a mask of determination. She ignored the rising fear within her, certain that this journey, regardless of its final destination, needed to be made.

She took out her phone to use it as a flashlight, but its battery was dead despite her having charged it that morning. She slipped it back into a pocket, waited for her eyes to adjust, and then stepped further into the unknown.

*Wait!* Adele's mind screamed. *There's something in there.* She stopped and leaned forward, her eyes and ears straining for confirmation that she wasn't alone. A gust of wind pushed the hair back from her forehead.

*Wind? I'm inside of a mountain. How is that possible?*

Another sigh came from deep within the cave, carrying with it the smell of rotting flesh. Adele covered her nose and mouth with her hand.

*Am I about to find Bloodbone's body?*

Adele knew she had to consider the possibility. Bracing for the worst, she continued moving deeper into the mountain until more wind struck her face, replacing the stench of decay with something entirely different. She had smelled it before but couldn't recall exactly what it was until finally it came to her.

*The top of a newborn's head.*

That memory was from a Fourth of July barbeque when Adele was a young girl. Their neighbors were the proud parents of a new child and they happily allowed Adele to cradle the infant in her lap. When she bent her face down to kiss the wispy soft strands of fine blonde hair atop the baby's head, she was fascinated by its slightly sweet, warm-soap smell. She brushed the bottom of her nose against the baby's hair and breathed it in over and over.

*That's it,* Adele thought. *That's what I'm smelling right now. Not bat shit. Not something dead. It's that new-baby scent.*

Then, just as quickly as the smell had arrived, it was gone.

Something stirred.

Something big.

Adele froze, watching and waiting for whatever it was to reveal itself.

A loud groan was followed by the scrape of clawed feet over dirt and stone. Another blast of air wrapped itself around Adele. *That's not wind,* she realized. *It's breathing.*

The thing remained hidden in darkness, groaning, huffing, yet creeping closer. Suddenly the walls were illuminated by light coming from behind Adele that then just as suddenly went out. The crystals in the main cave were blinking on and off as if God was playfully flicking a switch. When the light returned, Adele looked up at the wall and then gasped at the shadowy outline of some great beast lurching toward her. She nearly fell backwards when the cave went dark again.

*Could it be the white bear from Bloodbone's journal?* Adele wondered as she regained her balance, wishing she had brought her revolver with her.

More light filled the cave, creating another shadow on the wall that was different than the first. The slouching beast had been replaced by the outline of a very tall man whose long arm and hand stretched out toward Adele.

*Bloodbone!*

Adele tried to shout his name, but when she opened her mouth nothing came out. The shadow figure crept closer, its outstretched hand seeming to nearly touch her face.

The light blinked out.

The shadow disappeared.

Adele cocked her head and held her breath, listening for any movement coming from deeper in the cave. A pair of eyes stared back at her. She flinched and then blinked several times, wondering if her fear was making her see things that weren't really there.

The eyes remained.

A great roar shook the earth beneath Adele's feet followed by a flash of snapping fangs. She covered her ears. *This isn't real. This isn't real. This isn't real.*

The light returned; the eyes were gone, replaced by a new shadow that now moved across the cave wall. It was a person walking, much smaller than the Bloodbone shadow, yet also very familiar to Adele.

*It's me,* she thought.

This time the light remained. The shadow came closer and closer. Adele stood, wide-eyed, arms at her side, fists clenched, watching and waiting. "Hello?" she whispered.

The shadow stopped and a woman emerged from the darkness.

Adele's mouth hung open as she stared at what appeared to be an older version of herself. "Who are you?" she asked.

A crystal hung from the woman's neck. Adele's hand moved slowly up over her chest and then closed around her own crystal. *They're the same.*

When the woman smiled, deep lines encased the corners of her mouth. Her bright, intelligent eyes looked at Adele without fear or confusion.

"Tell me your name," Adele said.

The woman pointed.

"You're supposed to be me? How is that possible?"

The woman's head tilted slightly as she smiled again.

Adele stepped toward her. "Say something." Her frustration pushed aside her fear. "Where is Bloodbone?" The woman came forward as well until they were nearly eye to eye with only a few feet separating them. Adele saw strands of gray running the length of the woman's shoulder-length brown hair. *My hair,* she thought.

"Your decision. Your choice. Your way."

"What?" Adele replied in a voice that, though lacking the deep-throated edges put there by the passage of time, was nearly an exact match to the woman's.

"Your decision," the woman repeated. "Your choice. Your way."

"*What* decision? *What* choice? *What* way?"

The woman reached up and caressed the side of Adele's face with fingers that were warm and rough. She smelled strongly of the islands—the combination of sun, sea, and pine. And then she was gone, silently striding past Adele toward the waiting world outside.

"Hold on," Adele said as she turned her head to watch the woman go.

The cave went dark.

Adele put her hand against the wall and retraced her steps until she emerged back into the main cave. The cluster of crystals appeared to be dormant again, absent light or heartbeat. What that meant she didn't know. The bats stirred, shrieking at her to leave. She reached out to touch the crystals but then stopped, her hand hovering over them. The smell of rotting flesh had returned, as did the sound of heavy movement from the other cave.

The bats fluttered about, their cries and movements suddenly more chaotic. Adele looked up and then wondered if the creatures weren't merely angry at her for being there but were also warning her to flee.

The white bear was coming.

Its snorting rage echoed against the cave walls. Adele turned to run but her feet wouldn't budge. A bat struck the top of her head and then another and another.

Adele screamed.

The bear burst into the main cave, its jaws stretched wide, a white mass of muscle, claws, and teeth. It saw Adele, growled loudly, and then charged.

Adele glared down at her feet, ordered them to move, and was then running as fast as she could toward the light outside. She glanced back. The bear was right behind her, its ears pinned back tight against its massive head and its jaws snapping shut mere inches from her heels.

The cave exit was straight ahead. Adele gritted her teeth, pumped her arms and legs, and prepared to leap into the light. She cried out when her toe struck something hard, sending her flailing forward with her arms out in front of her. Her knee struck the earth. She knew if she fell completely the bear would have her. Sunlight hit her face. With a final push she jumped from the cave opening and onto a large rock, which she then promptly slid off of, grunting as she landed on her side and then slamming her elbow into another stone, sending painful electric shivers up her entire arm. She rolled over onto her back, bracing for an attack.

The bear was gone.

Adele sat up, feeling a stabbing pain in her side each time she took a breath. She winced as she felt around her ribs. *Bruised, not broken,* she thought. With a loud groan she got back onto her feet and then stood just outside the cave trying to see or hear for any sign that the bear was close.

The cave remained dark and silent. Nothing moved inside the mountain.

"Your decision. Your choice. Your way."

Adele whirled around toward the sound of her own voice coming from directly behind her, but no one was there. The valley spread out below Turtleback Mountain and to the surrounding waters beyond. The sun had started its slow descent into late afternoon.

It was time to go.

———

Adele opened her eyes, pulled the covers up toward her neck, and waited for the images from the dream to recede, relieved to be tucked away inside the safe cocoon of her sailboat. She grimaced after taking a deep breath because her side hurt. She sat up, lifted her shirt, and gingerly felt around her ribs.

*Bruised, not broken.*

Thinking she must have somehow hurt herself while sleeping and then the pain manifested in her dream, Adele started to lie back down but stopped when something bumped the side of the sailboat with enough force she felt it in the bed.

Someone coughed outside.

Adele checked the time on her phone—2:30 a.m.

The dock creaked, followed by the sound of shuffling and then footsteps.

Adele opened the top drawer near the bed, took out her revolver, slid her feet into her slippers, and counted down: *One, two, three...*

She moved quickly toward the hatch, ignoring the sharp pain in her side, and flung it open. The fresh air hit her face and cleared her mind, helping her to focus. She stepped out holding the gun in front of her. The dock finger that ran the length of her boat was empty, but she sensed movement further away. Someone wearing a dark hoodie and sweatpants was running up the main dock ramp toward the parking lot.

Adele lowered the gun and started to turn back when she discovered that the person who had just been outside her boat had left something behind for her to find. Spelled out in black spray paint in big bold letters across the side of the hull was a single word:

**BITCH.**

# 15.

Adele didn't bother trying to get back to sleep. With her adrenaline up and her mind racing to figure out who sprayed profanity on her boat, she turned on the coffee machine and waited. Three in the morning was too early to bother Lucas with a case of vandalism, which left another four or five hours to pass the time until she would call him about it.

Bloodbone's journal sat on the table waiting for her return. She had devoured several pages of it the night before, fascinated by the descriptions of the tensions between the Americans and the British that continued to escalate throughout the islands in the 1850s. Bloodbone was at first a somewhat distant observer of these events, but that changed when he personally met with a Captain George Pickett, commander of the American forces on San Juan Island. Pickett had summoned him three days earlier, making it clear Bloodbone could either come to him voluntarily or, if need be, soldiers would be dispatched to retrieve him by force.

Pickett's interest in Bloodbone originated from his recently deceased second wife, a woman named Morning Mist who, like Bloodbone, was once a member of the Haida tribe to the north in Canada. Pickett met and then married her while he was stationed nearby on the mainland overseeing the construction of Fort Bellingham on Bellingham Bay. Morning Mist had shared with him stories of this mythical warrior figure in the San Juan Islands who was said to possess great power and influence there.

Bloodbone traveled from Orcas Island to San Juan Island by canoe, following the shoreline until he came to what would later be known as Grandma's Cove which was located just below the American military camp on the island's southern tip. Nearly one hundred soldiers were stationed there by then. Ten of them, all armed, escorted Bloodbone up the hill where he was greeted by Pickett himself.

Adele, wanting to be certain she didn't miss something, sat at the table and opened the journal, deciding to reread Bloodbone's description of that first meeting between himself and Captain Pickett.

*He was a slight man with narrow shoulders, a lean, partially bearded face, and smallish hands. He crackled with the caged energy of one who is convinced they are meant for greater things—a too common affliction of men of his kind. When he saw me, his eyes widened greatly as he looked up.*

*"Good God! Are you man or mountain?" He spoke slowly in a reedy voice that slithered in one's ears. We shook hands. "Captain George Pickett." He tilted his head to one side and then to the other side. "Everything you see here is under my command. The damnable English would have it all for themselves, but I've seen to it that won't happen."*

*"Karl Bloodbone," I replied.*

*Pickett's eyes had an unusual silver hue to them—cold, predatory, taking everything in while giving nothing back. I sensed he was a man who had come to know death often and no longer recoiled from it as nearly all others did. "You're Haida," he said.*

*"I was."*

*"My wife Morning Mist, God rest her savage soul, was Haida as well. I've heard the stories."*

*"Stories?"*

*"About you." Pickett's mouth smiled but his eyes hardened further. "You've done a lot of killing around these parts, feared by red and white man alike."*

*When I went to speak, he cut me off, holding his hand up high. "I don't give two small shits about any of that. We're warriors, you and I—killing is what we do best. My concern at this moment is your willingness to keep doing it."*

*"Captain Pickett, all due respect to the memory of your wife, but what she shared with you are stories, most likely exaggerations, of long ago. I am no longer what I was before."*

*"Do I strike you as someone who wastes time on what was then, Mr. Bloodbone?"*

*"I don't know you well enough to answer that."*

*"Sure you do." Pickett withdrew a flask from the inside of his jacket, staring at me intently as he unscrewed the top. "Men like us, warriors, regardless of the color of our skin, we're all cut from the same cloth."*

*"What cloth would that be?"*

Pickett sipped from the flask, turned his head, and stared out at the wide swath of water that was the Strait of Juan de Fuca. "Don't play coy with me. It isn't likely you were given your name by accident. No, you earned it." He turned and looked up at me. "Let me be clear—I'm not someone you would wish to disappoint."

"Why did you summon me here, Captain Pickett?"

He motioned for his men to leave us, then pointed at a path through the tall grass that cut across the sheep-covered hillside. "Shall we?" We walked the path for some time before Pickett abruptly stopped. "One hundred and twelve," he said. "That's how many we counted of your people on this island."

I hoped my silence spoke to my confusion.

Pickett took another sip from his flask. "By people I mean Indians of course. Not giant versions like you unfortunately, but they'll do."

"Do what?"

"I need to start a war, Mr. Bloodbone, and I require your help to make that happen."

"Between you and the British."

"That's right."

"But why?"

"To save this country from tearing itself apart." Pickett rested his hands on his narrow hips. "I'm a son of the South—Richmond, Virginia. Heard of it?"

"No."

*Pickett sighed. "I miss it so."*

*"Then why not return there?"*

*"That's not how military service works."*

*"Then why not quit the military?"*

*"Mr. Bloodbone, if the world were half as simple as you make it out to be I'd likely be more inclined to follow that advice."*

*"You are proposing I attack the British camp to the north of here."*

*Pickett grinned. "I knew you were a quick study. Round up as many as possible from that one hundred and twelve of your kind and then go out and slit as many British throats as you can. It needs to happen soon because time is short, understood?"*

*I shook my head. "That isn't going to happen."*

*"If it's a matter of compensation I assure you that'll be handled. You and your people will receive a fair sum for your services."*

*"I won't kill British soldiers for you."*

*"Why the hell not?"*

*"Your fight is not my fight."*

*"Your fight is what I tell you it is, Mr. Bloodbone. We start a war with the British here or another war is certain to break out on the other side of the country. Tens of thousands or more will die. I don't wish to see that happen. I want to keep us united not broken apart—*

divided between the North and the South, family against family, brother against brother, parent against child."

"You mean to save America from itself."

"I do. The winds of a most uncivil conflict blow strongly across these lands and don't for a second think they won't reach here. I'll be leaving this island soon, but more like me will follow. Instead of you being forced to deal with them why not allow me to help you make it so they will be forced to deal with you? I have friends in high places who could make certain your standing around here not only remains intact but is further strengthened."

"I would much rather that none on these islands be forced to do anything that is not their choice. These islands are to be a sanctuary from such abusive coercion."

Pickett drew the gun that hung from his side. "Are you telling me no?"

"I am."

"And you're willing to die right here and now for that decision?"

"I would rather not, but you're the one with the weapon, so it seems the decision is actually yours to make, Captain Pickett."

"You're nothing like I thought you'd be."

"I am sorry to disappoint you."

"It's not so much disappointment as it is surprise. I figured a red savage like yourself would gladly accept a chance to kill some white men."

*"You figured wrong."*

*"I guess I did." Pickett holstered the gun. "Well shit." He grunted. "You didn't even flinch when I pointed my weapon at you. If I had more of your kind among my men, I'd chase the British from here for good."*

*"Perhaps you will have to kill another pig to create the conflict you desire."*

*Pickett chuckled as he rolled a cigarette and then lit it. "How'd you hear about that?"*

*"The islands told me."*

*Pungent tobacco smoke swirled around Pickett's head. "The islands, huh? Is that a reference to that mystical Indian bullshit some around here are so keen to believe in? I'm a Christian man, Mr. Bloodbone. I have little regard and even less patience for such heathen nonsense and I told my wife as much prior to our getting married. She was converted soon after, which does bring me great comfort knowing she was welcomed into Heaven's embrace upon her passing."*

*"It must be nice knowing YOUR version of faith is the truly righteous one while all other versions are, as you say, heathen nonsense."*

*Pickett blew out another cloud of smoke. "Careful now—I might just shoot you yet."*

*He didn't. I was allowed to leave the American encampment and return to Orcas Island. As promised, Captain Pickett left the islands soon after. War with the British had been avoided and an agreement struck that officially handed complete control of the islands to the United States, thus opening the floodgates for further settlement by yet more whites from the mainland, some who had come west to escape the horrors of the "most uncivil conflict" Pickett had warned was coming.*

*Years later, I received a letter from him that didn't arrive until four months after his death. This was early in 1876. That letter stated the following:*

*Dear Mr. Bloodbone,*

*I do hope this communication finds you well. As for me I am afraid my body has abandoned all hope of serving me further. The doctors tell me it is my liver. Too many years of negligent drinking perhaps, but I do believe they are wrong about that. No, what ails me now, as it has since the War Between the States ended, is a heart cleaved by so much loss and regret.*

*To lose a war is one thing, but to lose so many men who were under your command . . . I am haunted by their many names and faces and cannot help but wonder how many families were left fractured and broken by my inability to see them returned home safely.*

*Shortly after our one and only meeting together at the Cattle Point encampment I urgently departed for the East Coast and was made a colonel and then a general of the First Corps Army of Northern Virginia fighting on the side of the Confederacy, confident then that the fame and accolades I had yearned for were finally to be mine. There's a fine line between fame and infamy, though, and it wasn't long before I accumulated ample servings of both during those horrific years of near constant bloodshed that at times likely made me more animal than man.*

*With the war lost and my reputation and finances in tatters, I fled for a time into Canada, fearing I would face charges for war crimes. Only the assurances from my old friend President Grant allowed me to return once again to my beloved Richmond where I lived somewhat unhappily with my third wife as a farmer and insurance agent, lost in the fog of drink and debilitating recollection. My nights remain filled with the screams of men whose limbs were torn from them on the battlefield and the empty eyes of lost souls who physically survived but would never recover their spent spirits, their lives devoid of even the simplest of pleasure.*

*War is likely to be humankind's greatest evil. Knowing that, I cannot escape the realization that must make me, and the things I mistakenly did in the name of duty and honor, to be evil incarnate. Oh, for the happy innocence of youth before my choices put me so firmly upon the path of eternal damnation.*

*I have often wondered what my life might have been like had I chosen to remain a resident of those faraway islands of yours that were to provide, as you said to me on that gently sloping hill that overlooked the sea, a sanctuary from the abusive coercion of society's darker motivations. It was such a wild place unencumbered by the false burdens of the civilized world. I do hope you have managed to keep its true nature intact and to further protect it from those who would see it changed as I arrogantly attempted to do all those years ago. We need such places to exist so that we can be reminded of how things were and might be again if only we would allow ourselves the time and consideration to make it so.*

*May the future remain yours, Mr. Bloodbone, and a life that is long enough to better secure and appreciate its many wondrous blessings.*

*Respectfully,*

*-G.E. Pickett*

# 16.

"You have no idea who would want to do this?" Lucas asked.

"If I did, I'd be confronting them about it right now," Adele answered.

"I'll pull the security footage from the marina entrance and see if we can get a look at their face. Until then there's not much else we can do."

"I can remove it, right?"

Lucas took a picture of the graffiti with his phone. "Sure. I can help."

"I'll take care of it."

"Speaking of taking care of things, have you told Tilda about Ophelia yet?"

"No."

"How about now?"

Adele looked up at the hotel. "The both of us?"

"I don't need to be anywhere for a while."

"Okay. Give me ten minutes to clean up."

"I'm going to do a quick check of that security footage and then I'll meet you outside the hotel."

"One more thing."

"There's been no word yet on Fin," Lucas replied. "I planned on following up with the Irish authorities later today."

"I've texted him several times, tried to call—he isn't getting back to me. Something is wrong. I know it."

"Don't get yourself worked up, Adele. Fin can take care of himself."

"I'm not getting *worked up,* but I also know when something doesn't feel right. He wouldn't ignore my messages like this. Are you saying we *shouldn't* be worried?"

"That's not what I meant." Lucas stuck his hands into his front pockets. "It's just that I know how full your plate is right now so I'm trying my best not to add any more to it."

"I'm asking for your help, Lucas, not your protection. If Fin is in trouble, or worse, I want to know and I want to know as soon as you know. Will you do that for me?"

"Of course."

"I mean it."

"I know you do."

Adele stared at him for a second or two and then nodded. "Thanks."

"Did Roland give the okay to let Tilda know about Ophelia?"

"I'll text him now."

"Okay, see you up at the hotel."

Once she was back inside the sailboat Adele sent the text, washed her face, brushed her teeth, dressed in a clean T-shirt and shorts, and then checked her phone. Roland hadn't replied so she decided to call. A phone started ringing outside.

"Good morning," Roland said.

Adele looked through a porthole and saw him standing on the dock with his phone to his ear. "What are you doing?"

"Answering my phone."

"Did you get my text?"

"I did."

"And?"

"I agree that it's time Tilda knows."

"I'm meeting Lucas at the hotel in a few to tell her. I was hoping you could be there with us when we do."

"I have to finish this phone call first."

"Who are you talking to?"

"A very sexy woman." Roland paused and then continued. "Who are *you* talking to?"

"Just some pervert. I have to deal with that kind of crap all the time."

"Do you need me to take care of him for you?"

"Nah—he's harmless. Besides, he's kind of cute."

"I thought he was a pervert?"

"I don't mind. My standards are pretty low when it comes to that sort of thing."

"Hmm."

"What?"

"He sounds like trouble."

"I like trouble," Adele replied. "Trouble is *good*."

"I have some bad news."

"Oh?"

"I'm afraid you might be a pervert as well."

Adele looked the porthole again and caught Roland grinning into his phone. *"Might be?"*

Roland chuckled. "Thanks for the laugh—and that's no joke. I needed it."

"I figured you might. Are you going to walk with me to the hotel?"

"Sure. Does that mean you want me to hang up the phone?"

"That's probably a good idea."

Roland greeted Adele with a light kiss on the cheek when she stepped off the sailboat and onto the dock. Then he scowled as he pointed at the graffiti on the hull. "Who did that?"

"Not sure yet."

"Does Lucas know?"

"He was just here. He's checking the security footage and then meeting me at the hotel to speak with Tilda about Ophelia."

"Do you want some help cleaning it off?"

Adele shook her head. "No need."

Roland turned and scanned the marina. "A weird thing for someone to do don't you think?"

"Definitely but let's not worry about it right now."

"Okay—your call."

Adele tugged on the back of Roland's light blue dress shirt. "You're looking more like your usual self."

"I slept well last night."

"Good. At least one of us did."

"Trouble sleeping?"

Adele tapped the painted vandalism on the side of her boat with the toe of her shoe. "This got me out of bed and then I couldn't get back to sleep so I stayed up and read more of Bloodbone's journal."

"Anything interesting?"

"You wouldn't believe it if I told you."

"Try me."

"Not now. Lucas will be waiting for us."

Adele was right. By the time they reached the top of the marina ramp Lucas was standing near the hotel entrance. He nodded to Roland and her as they got closer. "I was told by the desk clerk that Tilda was out here taking care of her roses," he said.

"Did you find anything in the security footage?" Adele asked.

"I saw the figure you described running away from the marina, but it was too dark and grainy to tell if it was male or female. They were definitely heading toward the parking lot. Do you recall hearing a vehicle pulling away?"

"No."

Lucas's eyes narrowed. "Huh."

"What?"

"He's thinking it could have been someone here," Roland said.

Adele looked back at the marina. "One of the staff?"

Lucas nodded. "That's where we should start looking. Until then, do you have any idea which batch of roses Tilda might be working on because I have no idea. There are roses all over this place."

"Follow me," Adele answered. She led them to the other side of the hotel where they found Tilda on her hands and knees carefully placing protective netting over two red rose bushes.

Adele cleared her throat. "What?" Tilda said gruffly without looking behind her.

"It's me."

"Oh, Adele, just a moment." In the few seconds it took for Tilda to stand she was transformed from a simple gardener to the imposing matriarch of the Roche Harbor Hotel. She pulled off her gloves, straightened her long, cream-colored summer dress, and then gave Roland and Lucas a long look. "What brings all three of you here?"

"Can we talk inside?" Adele replied.

"Certainly, but could you lend a hand first? I need to finish covering these roses. The damn deer really did a number on them last night. I'll be lucky to save even half the blooms. Here, take that side of the netting and hold it there while I pull the other side."

Adele stepped forward and grabbed the netting. "These are the roses you planted when you were a girl."

Tilda smiled. "That's right. I forgot I told you about that. My mother and I planted them together. When I saw what the deer had done to them, I could have chewed through a box of nails I was so upset. These bushes might very well be the oldest flowering plants we have at the resort." She secured the netting and then turned around. "There, now we can go inside."

They each took a chair around one of the hotel lobby tables. Tilda had ice water brought to them. She looked at the others over the brim of her glass while sipping from it. "How sick is she?"

Adele and Roland shared a quick glance. "You know?" Adele said.

"Given how many times Roland has been going over to Shaw recently and the serious looks on all of your faces it wasn't too difficult to figure out. Is she dying?"

"Yes," Roland answered. "She doesn't have long."

Tilda put her glass down, leaned forward, and took his hand. "Oh, Roland, I'm so very sorry."

"We thought you should know," Lucas said.

Tilda let go of Roland's hand and sat back in her chair. "I appreciate that. Will I be able to visit with her?"

Roland nodded. "I was hoping you and Lucas could come over to Shaw tomorrow."

"So soon?" Tilda's face tightened.

Roland explained the nature of the disease, Ophelia's worsening symptoms, and the strong possibility she could be gone within a week or two.

"Dammit," Tilda whispered. "She was one of those people you think might go on living forever. I remember the first time I saw her like it was yesterday. She was marching down the hill toward the hotel, black robe flying out behind her and a crucifix bouncing against her chest. I was actually tending to the very same rose bushes you found me at. I waved to her. She stopped and looked at me—I mean she *really* looked at me. I was around sixteen or seventeen then, not lacking in confidence to be sure, but nothing like the kind of confidence Mother Mary Ophelia possessed. Her eyes were so fierce. And she was beautiful—a stunning woman even when covered by all of the nun garb. She asked if those were my roses. When I said yes, she tilted her head up just a little, appeared to almost smile, and said that tending to nature is as close to God's grace as we might get while bound to this earthly realm and that it pleased her greatly to see someone so young participating in that act. Then she told me to carry on and was off again to the marina where she hopped onto a little skiff and took off out of here like she stole something. I wasn't the only one who was watching her leave either."

"My grandfather?" Roland asked.

"That's right," Tilda answered. "I noticed him standing in the shadows under a tree and he was actually smiling, which surprised me because everyone my age assumed that Charles Soros *never* smiled. Then he saw me as well and I nearly swallowed my tongue out of fear. I've never known a man to be so handsome and so scary at the same time. I pretended to work on my roses for a while and when I turned to spy on him again, he was gone."

"I'll be going back to Shaw this afternoon," Roland said. "I'll tell Ophelia to be expecting all of you tomorrow. Will noon work?"

"Sure," Lucas answered. "I'll ask some questions of the staff around here before I leave today so that I don't have to worry about it tomorrow."

Tilda cocked her head. "What questions for the staff?"

"Someone spray-painted the word bitch on the side of my boat," Adele said.

"Spray painted. . ." Tilda's voice trailed off and then her eyes flared. "Someone among our staff did it? That's unacceptable!" She looked at Lucas. "I'll be happy to help with the investigation. Have you already reviewed the resort's security footage?"

Lucas nodded. "It didn't show a face."

"You be sure to tell me what you find out."

"I will."

Tilda stood. "Okay then, that's more than enough bad news for one day. Will we be meeting at Adele's sailboat tomorrow at noon?"

"If you prefer, I can have a chopper available for you instead," Roland replied. "I hired a pilot to be on standby for the next couple of weeks. He takes off from Roche and can land in a field right by the monastery. That's how I'll be getting there today. It only takes a few minutes from here."

"That sounds perfect," Tilda said. Adele and Lucas both agreed as well. Tilda gave Roland a quick hug, said they were all there for him, and then went upstairs.

Lucas was next to leave, explaining he was going to interview some of the resort dock staff before heading back to Friday Harbor. That left Adele and Roland sitting together in the hotel lobby. "What time are you leaving for Shaw?" Adele asked.

"One o'clock."

"You'll be staying the night there?"

"Yes. You're welcome to join me if you like."

"I'll wait until tomorrow and come over with the others."

"At least let me help you clean off the graffiti before I go."

Adele was about to tell Roland no but then changed her mind, sensing his need for company. He was outwardly far more stoic toward his grandmother's sickness than before, but she knew he was still hurting. "When was the last time you picked up a scrub brush?"

Roland looked up and squinted with one eye as he pretended to think long and hard. "It's been a while."

"I don't know if I have time to train an apprentice brush scrubber."

"I'm a hard worker and a fast learner."

"Is that right?"

"Scout's honor."

"Roland Soros, you were never a Boy Scout."

"That's true, but in my defense, I told you I was a hard worker and a fast learner—I never said I wasn't a liar."

Adele laughed.

Roland smiled. "So, do I get the job?"

"Are you willing to roll up those fancy sleeves?"

Roland promptly rolled his sleeves back and then held up his arms. "Done." He leaned forward and lowered his voice. "And I don't mind dropping my trousers if, you know, the job requires."

"That won't be necessary," Adele deadpanned.

"I was really kind of hoping it would be."

"I'll take it under consideration."

Roland pursed his lips and furrowed his brow. "What's the job pay?"

"It doesn't."

"Intriguing."

"Not really."

"Will I be allowed to hold the hose?"

"I can guarantee there will be some hose holding so long as you have adequate hose-holding skills."

Roland folded his hands in front of him. "My hose-holding skills are excellent. You won't be disappointed."

"Didn't you just admit to being a liar?"

"I lied about that."

"You lied about being a liar."

"That's true."

"What's true?"

Roland arched a brow as he pointed at Adele. *"Exactly."*

"As much as I'm enjoying this Abbot and Costello routine we should probably get going."

After stepping into the sun outside together Roland turned toward Adele, placed his hands on her shoulders and then leaned down and kissed her fully on the mouth.

"Get a room you two," Tilda shouted from the balcony above them. "And you're in luck. I still have a few available."

"We're off to wash my boat," Adele said.

Tilda smiled. "Boat washing? How romantic."

*Actually*, Adele thought, *it is.* She couldn't really explain why and as Roland took her hand and they started walking toward the marina she didn't care to try.

It simply was and that was good enough.

# 17.

Adele continued getting through Bloodbone's journal at a stop and start pace. She reviewed the sections that covered the decades following the 'Pig War' era, which saw the steady increase of white settlers to the islands and the resulting creation of the first and only incorporated town, Friday Harbor. Bloodbone described how he largely kept to himself during those years, choosing to remain at the ancestral Orcas Island longhouse, which he viewed as his sanctuary from the increasing troubles of the white man's world. Eventually, one century gave way to the next, and with this new century arrived two prominent figures whom Bloodbone determined he must get to know better. The first was Roche Harbor founder John McMillin and the second would be Rosario's Robert Moran.

It was during a dream that Old Raven first emphasized to Bloodbone the importance of the two men to the future of the islands. While reading these passages Adele noted how she too had experienced especially vivid conversational dreams since first arriving at the islands and wondered if that was yet another connection between Bloodbone and herself.

With Roland already having left for Shaw and the graffiti successfully removed from the side of her boat, Adele settled into a long night of reading, beginning with Bloodbone's first meeting with John McMillin.

*I was summoned by Roche Harbor royalty late in the summer of 1904. His name was John S. McMillin, a transplant from the state of Indiana who had traveled west seeking, and then finding, his fortune. He had been an attorney in Tacoma prior to his discovery of rich deposits of lime in and around the northwestern tip of San Juan Island. The Tacoma and Roche Harbor Lime Company was formed soon after, with McMillin moving full-time to Roche Harbor where he oversaw a significant expansion of the mining outpost including a marina, his family residence, and the jewel of his harbor empire, the twenty-four-room Roche Harbor Hotel.*

*With McMillin's guidance, Roche Harbor became the single greatest producer of lime west of the Mississippi and Mr. McMillin became a very wealthy man whose influence extended far beyond the San Juan Islands. If I was to be successful in my charge to protect and secure the future of the islands, he was clearly someone that fate required I get to know better.*

*John McMillin was a large, middle-aged man with an equally large appetite for success. His hawk-like eyes sat behind a pair of wire rim glasses perched atop a somewhat prominent nose made more so by a bristly white swath of mustache. Wide in both the shoulders and hips, with thinning hair that he kept oiled down and combed tightly across his scalp, he had an air of considerable seriousness about him. His deep gravelly voice would sometimes rise with his mood, be it cheerful or churlish, carrying across* the Roche Harbor grounds where his orders were unquestioned law for all who worked and resided there.

"You're the big Indian I've heard so much about." Those were McMillin's first words to me when I entered the lobby of his Roche Harbor Hotel. He didn't get up from the table he sat at, instead motioning for me to come closer. "Tell me something," he said. "Are you saved?"

"Do you speak of spiritual matters?" I replied.

McMillin sat up in his chair and tossed a cloth napkin onto the plate in front of him. "I'm speaking of the state of your soul, Mr. Bloodbone. Do I have your name right? It is Karl Bloodbone?"

"Yes."

"Well? Are you saved?"

"From what?"

McMillin scowled. "I don't play games. I asked you a direct question and I expect a direct answer. Are you a good Christian man?"

"Christian? No."

"A heathen then? A non-believer."

"I believe in a great many things, Mr. McMillin."

He pushed one of the chairs around the table out with his foot. "Sit." When I did, he grunted. "Even when you sit, you're taller than most men." He tilted his head. "What do you think of my hotel?"

"Very impressive."

"President Roosevelt was my guest here a few months back. We sat together at this very table. I consider him a friend."

"As I said, very impressive."

"And what do you think of my Roche Harbor?"

"I miss all of the trees that were once here."

"Trees?" McMillin removed his glasses and started cleaning the lenses with the same cloth he had earlier tossed onto his plate. "Those trees helped to build this hotel, the cabins, the docks—everything I take I put to use. It's the way of the world, Mr. Bloodbone."

"Yes, it is—the white man's world."

"I have a few of your kind working for me you know. That's how I learned of you. They whisper your name like you're more devil than man. My curiosity demanded I meet you and now here you are."

"Here I am."

"Most of my workers are Orientals. Many of them are heathens as well, but I'll forgive them that because they work so hard and don't demand more than a fair wage—a wonderful people who have made my success possible." McMillin leaned forward. "Is it true you met with General Pickett himself during that ridiculous Pig War nonsense?"

"It is."

"What was he like?"

"Ambitious."

*"You speak that word like it's a sin."*

*"Ambition can consume a man like wood to the fire, burning them up until nothing but ash remains."*

*McMillin stared at me for some time from across the table before resuming our discussion. "Do you enjoy mathematics, Mr. Bloodbone? I don't mean anything too complicated—just basic one plus one equals two kind of math."*

*He didn't allow me to answer before continuing.*

*"Let me get to my point. The man known to the world as General Pickett died nearly thirty years ago. The dispute between the Unites States and Great Britain for control of the islands is practically ancient history, having taken place more than forty years ago. Do you deny these facts?"*

*"I do not."*

*"And yet you would have me believe you knew General Pickett personally despite you and I appearing to be close to the same age, which would mean you could have been no more than ten years old when you met the general." McMillin's eyes narrowed. "Basic math, Mr. Bloodbone, but in this case, it doesn't add up. Either you're lying or something else is going on and I'd appreciate you telling me which it is."*

*"I don't lie, Mr. McMillin."*

*"How old are you?"*

*"I'm not really sure."*

McMillin shook his head. *"That's not an answer. What kind of man doesn't know his own age?"*

*"One who doesn't see time as being terribly important,"* I replied.

McMillin sat there staring at me until I looked down at my hands resting on the table. *"Is it okay if I call you Karl?"* he asked.

I nodded.

*"Okay, Karl, you have my attention. I can see why your people speak of you in such hushed tones—you're a rather frightening enigma."*

*"I am just a man, Mr. McMillin."*

*"There's more to you than that."* McMillin rubbed the ends of his mustache with the tips of his thick fingers. *"No matter. I have a task for you."*

*"I am not your servant."*

*"Then consider it a favor between friendly acquaintances—one that I'm willing to pay you well for. It involves an important individual who I have been told is making his way to Orcas Island."*

I knew the man's name already, having been told it during a dream vision by Old Raven, but didn't think it necessary to let McMillin know that. *"Go on."*

*"He's the former mayor of Seattle and a shipbuilder of some repute—Robert Moran. It is my understanding he has purchased a significant amount of land on the island to build a permanent residence there."*

"Why does this interest you?"

"Anyone who comes to this place with that much coin and influence will be of interest to me. Perhaps he intends to chop down every tree on Orcas so that he might build more ships to sell to the U.S. military. You don't wish to see more of your precious trees lost, do you?"

McMillin was right about that. Watching so many island trees cut and torn from the earth pained my soul. "When do you wish for me to meet with this Mr. Moran?"

"As soon as possible. He might be on the island already. Find out what his true purpose is here and then report back to me."

"Is that it?"

"For now."

When I stood McMillin did as well. He extended his hand across the table. We briefly shook. He chuckled and his eyes twinkled. "That's the largest hand I've ever seen. Most men disappoint me—they fall far short of expectation. Not you, though, and for that I am truly pleased. We are to be good friends you and I—good friends indeed. What do you think of that?"

"There was a time when I preferred enemies to friends."

McMillin frowned. "Why would anyone prefer that?"

"Far fewer immediate complications. The choices are more direct and simpler—I live and they die."

"But those simpler times as you call them, are no more?"

"I am no longer a source of such violence, Mr. McMillin."

"Thank goodness. I would not wish to be on the wrong side of the violence I'm certain you're capable of inflicting." He pushed his glasses higher onto his nose. "One last thing before you go."

"Yes?"

"Your Russian friend Asav."

"I know him well, but he is no friend."

"That's not what he says."

"Asav says a great many things that are his own version of truth."

McMillin grunted. "Own version of truth—isn't that just a nicer way of calling him a liar?"

"Perhaps."

"Anyways, he shows up around here regularly, mainly to gamble with my Orientals."

"And?"

"I don't condone such gambling—it's immoral. I've told him as much, but he keeps returning and taking my workers' wages from them. If I were a betting man myself, I'd wager Asav is cheating them."

"And you would likely win that bet."

"I was hoping you'd have a talk with him given your shared history. He says you two go way back. Is that true?"

"Yes."

*"How far back?"*

*I thought of the many decades that had passed since first coming down from the north with Asav to make war against the island tribes. "Far enough," I answered. "If I see him, I will mention your concerns, but he's not likely to listen. Asav is very much his own man."*

*McMillin pointed to the crystal that hung from my neck. "He wears one of those too. Where'd you get them?"*

*"Mine was given to me. His was taken by him."*

*"Was he around here during the time of General Pickett as well?"*

*"Captain Pickett."*

*"Pardon?"*

*"He was Captain Pickett when he commanded the American forces here."*

*"I don't care about that. I'm asking about Asav. Was he on the islands then as well?"*

*"Yes."*

*McMillin stared at the crystal. "Might I hold it?"*

*"No."*

*"Why not?"*

*I straightened to my full height. "Because that is my answer."*

*McMillin continued to stare before his brows arched and then he shrugged. "Very well. Please get back to me regarding what you learn regarding why Robert Moran is staking such a significant claim on Orcas."*

*"I will. You have my word."*

*"What's that worth? Your word that is."*

*"A man's word is everything."*

*McMillin nodded his approval. "Agreed." Just then a large orange cat jumped onto the table and proceeded to clean its face with its paw. "This thing," McMillin huffed. "My wife left a saucer of cream out for it one time and it has remained ever since, wandering around here like it owns the place. She named it Tilda."*

*When the cat turned its head to look at me, I smiled down at it and then held out my hand. It walked to the edge of the table and snugged the tips of my fingers with the top of its head. "Tilda," I whispered.*

*"Huh," McMillin said. "Normally that cat can't stand strangers. Why just the other day it hissed and growled at your friend Asav so much I was certain it was about to claw his eyes out."*

*I scratched the soft tuft behind Tilda's ears. "It seems she's a good judge of character."*

*McMillin looked like he was preparing to brush the creature off the table but when the cat's tail started to twitch, he apparently changed his mind. "I look forward to speaking with you again soon, Karl," he said. "Safe travels back to Orcas."*

*I nodded, turned away, and then stepped outside. The air was heavy with the smell of the fiery stone kilns that melted the limestone down into what the white men called "quicklime", which makes the product much more easily transportable to far-off locations where it is used as a valuable construction and farming material. Supervisors shouted orders to workers who shouted yet more orders to other workers while ships sat waiting in the harbor for the next load of valuable cargo.*

*The waters were calm, but a glance up at darkening skies indicated troubled weather was fast approaching. I strode toward my canoe that sat on the beach to the east away from the noise of McMillin's commercial operation. Soon I was paddling toward Spieden Channel and then Orcas Island, wondering what kind of man Robert Moran might be. Was he another example of driven ambition like John McMillin or perhaps something else?*

*I continued to wonder as I paddled, taking in the slow-passing scenery of Spieden Island's gently sloping, sun-browned grass hillsides. With the wind at my back and the tide running with me, the return trip to Orcas proved enjoyably uneventful.*

*These were my islands, my waters, my home.*

*I could not ask for more.*

# 18.

"Ms. Plank."

Adele turned and saw a nervous looking Sky standing at the end of the dock. It was late morning, and she was on her way to the Roche Harbor airport to catch the helicopter ride with Roland, Lucas, and Tilda to the monastery on Shaw Island. "I'm in a hurry, Sky. What do you want?"

"I need to tell you something."

"Go ahead."

Sky fidgeted with the hems of her shorts. "It's about what happened to your sailboat."

"Uh-huh."

"I know who did it."

"Who?"

"I can't say."

"Why not?"

"I don't want to snitch on a friend."

*"She's* a friend?"

Sky nodded. Then her brows lifted. "That was pretty slick."

"You caught that did you?" Adele replied.

"You just got me to confirm the person who did it was female."

Adele quickly checked the time on her phone and then looked up. "What's her name?"

"I can't—"

"Say. Yeah, got it. Then why are you bothering to tell me anything about this?"

"First, I wanted you to know that as soon as I heard what happened I went to work finding out who did it because it really pissed me off."

"And second?"

"She won't ever do something like that again."

"Why did she do it in the first place?"

"A lot of alcohol and pot were involved."

Adele rolled her eyes. "You're actually going with the *drunk and stoned* excuse? What was the *real* reason she did it?"

"Jealousy, I suppose."

"Over what?"

"A guy."

"Roland?"

"No, not Mr. Soros."

"Then who?"

"She saw you with Sheriff Pine in Friday Harbor."

"So?"

"You two were hugging."

"And this mystery friend of yours had a problem with that."

"I guess so," Sky answered. "I suspected it was her right away because a few of us were hanging out the night before and the subject of the sheriff came up and she really seemed obsessed over him and then she mentioned seeing you two together and I could tell it bothered her. I never thought she'd actually spray-paint your sailboat though. When I confronted her, she eventually broke down and admitted what she did. She feels awful, Adele—awful and scared."

"Why is she scared?"

"She can't afford to get fired."

"Then she shouldn't have vandalized my boat."

"I know. Losing her job isn't the only reason she's afraid though."

"No?"

"She thinks you'll kick her ass. We've all heard the stories of what you're capable of."

"I *should* kick her ass." Adele took a deep breath and let it out slowly. "But I won't."

Sky's face broke out into a big smile. "Thank you."

"I'm not finished."

The smile vanished. "Oh."

"Your friend needs to come talk to me. I'll give her three days. If she can't do that then she *will* be fired, and I'll likely press charges as well. What she did was low-class stupid and that kind of thing has no place here in Roche Harbor."

"How can she be fired and have charges against her if you don't know who she is?"

Adele's head lowered slightly. "Sky, do you *really* think I won't be able to find out who it is? Making me waste even one second of time having to figure it out will place your position here at the resort in jeopardy as well and you can also forget about the paid internship with my newspaper next summer."

Sky's mouth dropped open. "You would do that?"

"Do you want to take a chance on finding out?"

Sky shook her head. "No."

"Good." Adele's thin smile let it be known she was in no mood for any more nonsense. "Then we understand each other. You go tell your friend about our talk. I'll be gone today but should be around most of the day tomorrow. I strongly suggest she make her way here so we can get this hashed out between us. The longer I have to wait the more likely I am to change my mind."

"I'll let her know. And I really am sorry for what she did."

"That apology shouldn't come from you, Sky. It needs to come from her."

"I'm going to try to make that happen."

"If she was any kind of real friend you wouldn't have to. Now, I need to get going."

"Okay. I'll talk to her as soon as I see her."

"Good luck."

"Thank you."

Adele watched Sky leave while wondering what would possess her friend to do something so stupid over a man she didn't even know, but then she recalled her own bouts of terrible jealousy that had made her act in ways she wasn't proud of. Her phone vibrated. It was a text from Roland telling her the chopper was ready. She texted back that she was on her way. When she reached the nearby airport, she found Roland, Lucas, and Tilda waiting.

"Busy morning?" Tilda asked.

"Something like that," Adele replied.

Roland opened the helicopter door. "Time to go."

The others nodded and then took a seat inside. The whine of the chopper engine intensified as it slowly lifted off the ground, hovered over the resort, and then flew across land and water in the direction of Shaw Island where they landed in a field next to the monastery less than five minutes later.

After Roland and Tilda exited Lucas turned in his seat and faced Adele. "Did you find out who vandalized your boat?"

"I have a lead."

"Will you be pressing charges?"

"I haven't decided that yet."

Lucas nodded. "Okay, let me know when you do." He stepped out and Adele followed behind him, grateful that he didn't try to push her for more information. The group walked together to the monastery's main entrance where they were greeted by Sister Zhara who invited them inside.

"Sister Zhara," Adele said, "these are my friends Tilda Ashland and Sheriff Lucas Pine."

Tilda smiled. "Nice to meet you, Sister."

Lucas looked down at the floor before repeating the exact same greeting Tilda had used. "Nice to meet you, Sister."

"You own the Roche Harbor Hotel," Zhara said.

"For many years," Tilda replied.

"And you're the sheriff." Zhara's eyes were as bright as her smile. "Thank you for your service to our islands."

Adele stifled a laugh when she caught Lucas blushing badly as he mumbled a thank you.

"She had a difficult night," Zhara told Roland. "But she's awake at the moment and looking forward to seeing you again."

"Is she comfortable?" Roland asked.

"As much as possible. We bathed her early this morning, tried to give her some broth, but I'm afraid her ability to swallow has worsened considerably over the past twelve hours." Zhara placed her hand on Roland's forearm. "Be prepared—your grandmother is very weak." She faced the others. "I think it best that Mr. Soros see her alone for now and then we can decide if Ophelia is up for more visitors after that."

"She will be," Tilda said. "When she learns we're all here, Ophelia will want to see us."

"As I said," Zhara replied, "we shall see."

The two women locked eyes. It was Tilda who looked away first. "Tough nun," she remarked after Zhara and Roland left the room together.

"And beautiful," Adele replied while sneaking a glance at Lucas out of the corner of her eye.

"She is indeed," Tilda said.

"What do you think, Lucas?"

"Huh?" Lucas was still staring at the space where Zhara had just been standing. "About what?"

"About Sister Zhara."

"She seems nice. How well do you know her?"

Adele shrugged. "We talked a bit. She's originally from Aruba. Went to college in North Dakota, landed a teaching job in Seattle, and then requested to be transferred here in part so she could work with Ophelia. Oh—and she's about the same age as you by the way."

Lucas frowned. "Stop it."

"Stop what? I have no idea what you're talking about."

"She's a *nun*."

"I saw how you were looking at her."

"Drop it. We're here to see Ophelia."

Adele backed off, but she also knew Ophelia would have delighted in seeing Lucas squirm a little after having been so clearly smitten by the attractive nun.

Roland came back into the room. "She wants to see everyone."

"Now?" Tilda asked. "All at once?"

"Yes."

They followed Roland down the hall and then into Ophelia's private chamber where they found her in bed propped up by some pillows. The room was clean and tidy but also smelled of impending death.

"Look at this," Ophelia croaked. "My own personal parade."

Tilda stepped toward the bed and took Ophelia's hand. "Hello, old friend."

"Old is right." Ophelia's eyes were wet with tears. "I didn't want anyone to see me like this," she whispered. "But I'm glad you're here." She smiled. "Do you remember the first time we saw each other?"

"The roses at Roche Harbor. I recently shared the story with Adele."

"Even then, when you were still so young, I sensed your strength and potential."

"And I yours. You were very intimidating."

Ophelia's laughter rattled inside of her chest. "I was a foolish thing chasing something I could never have—at least not completely." She paused, gasped for air, and then turned her head slightly to look at Lucas. "Sheriff Pine, thank you for coming."

Lucas stood on the opposite side of the bed and took Ophelia's other hand. "Thank you for inviting me."

"I didn't invite you."

"I know." Lucas grinned. "I came anyway."

Ophelia laughed again but then shut her eyes and grimaced. "It hurts. Give me a second." She groaned. "Roland—my drawer."

"So soon?" Roland asked. "Sister Zhara said you already had some earlier."

Ophelia's cracked lips drew back in a snarl. "Sister Zhara isn't the one in pain."

Roland opened the top drawer of the dresser nearest the bed and withdrew a finger-sized vial with a dropper on the end of it. Lucas stepped aside so Roland could stand next to Ophelia. She opened her mouth and then he administered two drops of liquid onto her tongue. After that he carefully returned the vial to the drawer and closed it.

"That's better." Ophelia sighed with her eyes closed.

"Morphine," Roland said to the others. "She started taking it yesterday."

"It helps a great deal." Ophelia's voice was already noticeably stronger. "Especially with the headaches and my breathing." She turned her head to look at Adele. "Hey, there's no need for that."

Adele was wiping her eyes with the back of her hand.

"I'm not going anywhere just yet," Ophelia said. "Let us fill this room with the sound of our laughter. Tilda, tell us a joke—preferably a dirty one."

The request alone was enough to make everyone chuckle. Tilda once again gripped Ophelia's hand and nodded. "Thanks a lot. A joke for a dying woman is a lot of pressure."

Ophelia gave Tilda's hand a squeeze. "Get to it."

"Okay," Tilda replied, "but I better not be going to hell for this."

"For a dirty joke?" Ophelia winked. "At worst it'll just be purgatory."

Tilda cleared her throat. "Four Catholic men and a woman are seated around a table having coffee. The first man says that his son is a priest and when he walks into a room everyone calls him Father. The second man says that his son is a bishop and when he walks into a room everyone calls him Your Grace. The third man says that his son is a cardinal and when he walks into a room everyone calls him Your Eminence. The fourth man says his son is the Pope and when he walks into a room everyone calls him Your Holiness. All four men then look at the woman seated with them and wait for her to say something. She smiles and explains that she only has a daughter who is tall and slim with very large breasts, a narrow waist, long legs, and a perfectly sculpted backside. When she walks into a room all the men say, 'Oh, My God.'"

Ophelia shrugged. "Not bad. Not great mind you but not bad. I do appreciate the effort."

"        I have one," Lucas said. "My dad told it to me once."

"Ah," Ophelia replied. "Doctor Pine was such a kind and considerate man. I wasn't aware he was much of a joke teller though."

"He loved making my mother laugh."

"As all good men do. Go on then—let's hear it."

Lucas silently mouthed some words as he concentrated; then he nodded. "I think I remember it right."

Just then Zhara knocked on the door before entering the room. "Does anyone need anything?"

"The sheriff is about to tell us a joke," Ophelia answered and then she scowled. "Are you blushing?"

"No," Lucas answered, far more loudly than he needed to.

Zhara grinned. "I love a good joke. Is it okay if I stick around to hear it?"

"You don't mind, *right* Lucas?" Adele said. He sent her a quick *I'm going to kill you for this* look.

"If your father told it then it must be good," Tilda added. "He was so intelligent."

Lucas held his hands up in front of him. "Alright, I'll tell the joke." He scratched at the stubble on his cheek while avoiding looking directly at Zhara. "A drunk stumbles into a church, opens the confessional booth, sits down, but doesn't say anything. The priest waits and then coughs, trying to get the man's attention. When that doesn't work the priest bangs three times against the wall. 'It's no use knocking, buddy.' the drunk man mumbles. 'I can't help you out. There's no toilet paper in this stall either.'"

Ophelia and the others all laughed but the one who laughed loudest was Zhara. She patted Lucas's shoulder. "That was very funny, Sheriff Pine." Lucas's satisfied gaze followed her as she left.

"That *was* funny," Roland said. "I didn't think you could pull it off. You seemed a little, oh, I don't know, distracted."

"What about you?" Lucas asked.

"What about me?" Roland answered.

"You able to tell a decent joke?"

"I'm pretty sure I could manage something."

"Okay—we're all ears."

"There's a few my grandfather told me a time or two when I was growing up."

"You know some Charles jokes?" Ophelia smiled. "Please tell them to us."

"Alright," Roland said. "Where does a waitress with only one leg work?"

"Where?" Ophelia asked.

"IHOP," Roland answered.

Lucas rolled his eyes. "Oh geez."

"This next one is for you, Sheriff," Roland said. "What happens when a police officer goes to bed?"

Lucas shrugged.

"He becomes an undercover cop."

Tilda pointed to Ophelia. "She's not laughing. You better step it up."

Roland sighed as he ran a hand through his hair. "Tough crowd, huh? Okay, one more."

"Thank God," Lucas muttered.

Roland continued. "What's the biggest difference between a woman with PMS and a terrorist?"

Adele's eyes narrowed. *"What?"*

Roland snickered as he delivered the punch line. "You can negotiate with a terrorist."

This time Lucas laughed hard and gave Roland an appreciative slap on the back.

"Sheriff Pine," Tilda said with mock seriousness. "What do you find so funny about that joke?"

"It's funny because it's true."

Adele, Tilda, and Ophelia all shook their heads at him as Roland stepped away. "Sorry buddy," he whispered. "You're on your own."

The next hour was spent retelling old stories and sharing thoughts on past and current events. The subject of Ophelia's condition wasn't brought up, but it hovered over the conversation like a dark, heavy cloud. Eventually she apologized for feeling very tired in a voice weak from exhaustion. Tilda leaned down over the bed and hugged her. Their hands touched, lingered, and then Tilda retreated, saying goodbye not with words but her eyes, two women of the islands who had experienced so much and survived it all, knowing and accepting that soon one of them would be gone for good.

Lucas was next to step to the bed. He kissed Ophelia on the forehead as she smiled up at him. Then he too retreated, leaving the room along with Tilda.

"And now it's just us," Ophelia said to Roland and Adele. She opened one hand and Roland took it. She then opened her other hand and Adele took that, each of them standing on opposite sides of the bed. "Nothing else matters but this."

Roland cocked his head. "What?"

A faint grin etched Ophelia's sunken face. She closed her eyes. "The love between you two. Time will pass, the world will change all around you, but your love must always remain because that is what will sustain you both no matter what comes." Her eyes opened wide, suddenly sharp and clear. "Promise me."

Adele and Roland shared a quick glance. "What do you want us to promise?" Adele asked.

"To never give up on each other. There is nothing so debilitating in this life as deep regret. Don't ever stop trying to find new ways of making each other happy."

"We won't give up," Roland said. "We promise."

Ophelia's face tightened as she took in a ragged breath. She nodded. "Good." Her eyes closed. "My turn." She paused and then continued. "Knock-knock."

Adele clasped Ophelia's hand between both of hers. "Who's there?"

"Tank."

"Tank who?"

Ophelia smiled. "You're welcome."

Roland used his finger to brush a wisp of hair back from Ophelia's forehead. Soon she was asleep. He looked over at Adele. "I meant it."

"Meant what?"

"You and me and the promise to never give up. She's right. Nothing else matters but the time we have together and how we choose to spend it."

"I know," Adele said while simultaneously feeling the silent tug of Bloodbone's journal and the implications the history it outlined would have on her future. Even as she stood next to a dying Ophelia while sharing that important moment with Roland, she was drawn back to Bloodbone's words, sensing how his story was becoming her own.

It felt like a betrayal on so many levels but mostly against Roland. He deserved better. He deserved more. Adele was being pulled in too many disparate directions and losing herself in the process. *No,* she thought. *I won't let that happen. I made a promise to Ophelia. I won't give up on what Roland and I have.*

"Hey."

Adele flinched.

Roland appeared concerned. "Are you okay? You looked like you were a million miles away just now."

"I guess I was." Adele forced a smile, hoping to reassure him. "I'm back."

*But for how long?*

# 19.

Adele poured the herbal tea into her cup, wrapped the blanket around her shoulders, turned on the table light, and then pulled Bloodbone's journal toward her. It was nearly dark outside and the Roche Harbor marina had already settled into evening-quiet mode.

Roland had chosen to stay on Shaw Island with Ophelia, indicating to Adele and the others that he would likely remain there until she passed. Both Tilda and Lucas said little during the short helicopter flight back. Once they landed Tilda retreated to the hotel, remarking that she planned on turning in early that night. Lucas would be going straight home to Friday Harbor as well. They said their goodbyes to one other knowing that soon, perhaps in the next day or two, and certainly by the end of the week, they would be informed of Ophelia's death.

The leather-bound journal felt heavy in Adele's hands as she pulled back the cover and opened it to the last page she had read. She sipped her tea, looked down at the handwritten words, and started to read once again.

*"This is a special place."*

*"It is," I replied to Robert Moran, a somewhat waifish man with unusually dark eyes who proudly showed me*

around the seaside Orcas Island grounds where his mansion was being constructed. His suit and shoes, like his eyes, were dark. He spoke in soft tones, the volume rising and falling like a gently sloping hill as he pointed to various rooms-in-the-making, explaining with some enthusiasm the purpose of each one.

"Years ago, when I was mayor of Seattle, your name was first spoken to me by a woman named Angeline, a daughter of Chief Seattle. She remarked that you and her father knew each other."

"Chief Seattle?" I replied. "Not personally, no. My people and his did engage in warfare from time to time. He was noted for having the single largest collection of slaves in the region—slaves we desired to take from him."

Moran stopped walking and looked up at me. "Chief Seattle was a slave trader? I didn't know that."

"A very prolific one," I said. "And when required, he was also a bloodthirsty warrior who went so far as to wipe out an entire people—the Chemakum of Port Townsend. He later brought hundreds among neighboring tribes to the white man settlements of Olympia and Seattle where they were compelled to work for wages so low they represented yet another form of slavery."

"So, he was a bad man?"

"Chief Seattle wasn't bad so much as he was deeply flawed with great ambition and greed who was also highly capable and uniquely successful in making himself critical to the white man's success throughout these lands—a *success that ultimately also proved to be his own undoing."*

*"His was the most important Indian chief signature on the 1855 Treaty of Elliot Bay that eventually forced his people onto reservations."*

*I nodded. "History will likely record it as his most debilitating act against our kind—the entrapment of generations not yet born."*

*Moran turned away and looked out at the choppy waters of East Sound. The wind blew the tips of his dark mustache upward toward his nose. "Chief Seattle was a politician like me," he said. "I lived in that world for far too long. Politics is no place for a man of conscience. It eats you alive until nothing remains of who you once were. Do you know you're talking to a dead man, Mr. Bloodbone?"*

*"You don't appear to be dead."*

*"But I'm supposed to be. My personal physician gave me no more than a year to live. My body was spent. My hands shook; my legs could barely take me from one room to the next; my breathing was always labored and getting worse—he said my heart was failing, that my time was short, and I had no reason to think he was wrong."*

*"What happened?"*

*Moran pointed to the water. "This place happened. Last year, I took a pleasure cruise through the San Juan Islands and knew from the moment I stepped ashore that I must find a way to make it mine. I purchased thousands of acres here and then personally began to design what will be my lasting legacy—a home that will withstand the ever-changing world beyond these islands."*

*"And what of your impending death?" I asked.*

*"I'm now fit as a fiddle. I don't understand the how or the why of it, but the more time I spend on this island the more my health improves. It's as if these islands now demand I have a new purpose to somehow serve them and so have generously given my life back to me."*

*"Do you really believe that, Mr. Moran? That the islands have the power to alter the course of a man's destiny?"*

*Moran itched his nose and sniffed. "I'll only speak for myself. A doctor delivered to me an irrevocable death sentence. I arrived at Rosario a dying man who only hoped to create a place that could be a happy home to the family I would be leaving behind. Yet now I look forward to watching my children grow and prosper and who will then give me grandchildren to fill the many rooms of the Moran Mansion with laughter."*

*"If the islands gave you this second chance, then do you not owe them a debt of gratitude?"*

*Moran nodded. "I most certainly do and I intend to pay that debt in full when the time comes."*

*"How?"*

*"I don't know yet, but I'm sure the answer will visit me eventually. But what of you, Mr. Bloodbone? How is it that you stand here with me now while also admitting you fought against Chief Seattle? He was nearly eighty when he died forty years ago. Perhaps it is you who owes an*

*even greater debt to the islands." Moran started walking. "Let us go from the clatter of construction to the top of the hill over there so I can tell you of my most recent dream— that is if you wish to hear of it."*

*I told him I did and then followed, impressed by his quick pace. For a man who was supposed to be dead he scampered up the hill like one half his age.*

*"The dream took place here," Moran said. "Along the cliffs. There was a man and a young woman. The man was a big, mean-looking fella who spoke with an accent that sounded vaguely familiar to me and then I heard it again when some stonework was being done down on the new house by a worker named Asav whom people around here call the Russian. He speaks exactly like the man in the dream did. Do you know this Asav?"*

*"Yes."*

*"I thought you might. Anyways, the man I dreamt about, he was hanging from the cliffside right here in this very spot, desperate to climb back up, and the woman was doing all she could to make him fall. I was going to try to help him but there was this voice in my head telling me not to. It took me a few seconds to realize that voice was my own."*

*"Did she succeed?"*

*"In kicking the man off the cliff?"*

*I nodded.*

*"She did. He was broken against the rocks below. I remember standing at the edge here and looking down at*

*the body, knowing that he deserved to die but not knowing the reasons why."*

*"Was the woman still there?"*

*"Yes and no. I could see her, but I don't think she saw me. It's as if I wasn't really there—she seemed to look right through me."*

*"Did she have an accent like Asav?"*

*"I don't know. She didn't say a word and then I woke up."*

*"Why are you telling me this?"*

*"Because, Mr. Bloodbone, I believe you have dreams as well."*

*"Most people do."*

*"No, around here, for some, these dreams are unlike any we've had before."*

*"And why do you think that is?"*

*Moran looked into my eyes. "I believe it's the islands trying to communicate to us. Do you believe I've lost my mind for thinking that?"*

*"I do not."*

*Moran smiled. "You do understand far more about this place than you are letting on, don't you?" He held up a hand. "No need to attempt to explain the unexplainable to me. There is something I would like to know though."*

*I asked what that was. Moran bent down, snapped off a long blade of dry brown grass and stuck it in between his teeth and then went over to a Madrone tree and leaned against its trunk, somehow looking both relaxed and intensely curious at the same time.*

*"Was it McMillin who told you to come here today?"*

*"I am no errand boy, Mr. Moran. He requested and I agreed in part because I was curious to meet you as well."*

*"Worried I'll be overshadowing his influence around here is he?"*

*I shrugged. "Perhaps."*

*"I have already been to where he is and have no interest in going back to that place because it nearly killed me. McMillin is a man obsessed with more while I am a man now content to make do with less."*

*"The size of the home you are building and the thousands of acres you have purchased on the island would appear to say otherwise."*

*Moran chuckled as he folded his arms over his chest. "You make a fair point, but I assure you, should I have chosen to buy up this entire island I could have. I am a very wealthy man, Mr. Bloodbone—wealthier than even McMillin and he knows it. As for the thousands of acres you speak of, it is my intent to see it remain as it is today in perpetuity so that future generations will be free to enjoy its splendor. Where McMillin tears into the earth to extract his limestone, I would see the land left intact, free from the ugly scars of commerce."*

*"It would seem," I said, "that you two are different sides of the same coin."*

*"Eh?" Moran flicked the stock of grass away.*

"McMillin's side of the coin is commerce while your side is conservation. Both are necessary for the long-term survival of the islands."

"A balance you mean—like the sun and the moon or light and dark."

"Yes." The concept of light and dark made me think of Asav and myself. I wondered if the islands meant for each of us to represent a similar dynamic in order to maintain such an essential balance.

"Or good and evil," Moran continued.

"I do not believe Mr. McMillin to be evil," I replied.

"Just nosey?"

"Among other things."

"You let him know that I have no intention of buying up any more land or exerting undue influence over any of the other islands," Moran said. "Rosario is now my family's home and that is more than enough to keep me content for the remainder of my days, God willing." He stepped away from the tree and stuck out his hand. "I sincerely hope this isn't your last visit to Rosario, Mr. Bloodbone. You are welcome to stop by here anytime."

After we shook, I thanked Moran for the invitation and then turned to leave. "One more thing," he said.

"What is it?" I asked.

"There was something else Chief Seattle's daughter Angeline told me about the islands." Moran paused. "Have you heard of a Truthing Tree?"

"It's an ancient term—a belief that certain trees possess powerful magic."

"Angeline was convinced that Truthing Trees exist on these islands. She said they were used as meeting places among the great Salish chiefs of long ago to help ensure honest agreements between tribes."

"I do not know if the islands have such trees."

Moran appeared mildly disappointed. "Pity. I would love to see one of those trees in person."

"You believe in old Indian folk tales?"

"Why not? I'm supposed to be dead, remember? There was some kind of mystical intervention on my behalf, of that I'm certain. Any who deny the possibility of wondrous things beyond our understanding are arrogant fools."

"You are an interesting man, Mr. Moran."

"From where I'm standing it's you who is the interesting one, Mr. Bloodbone. Will you now be returning to your longhouse on Eastsound?"

"Yes."

"That's a long walk."

"And a pleasant one."

Moran bent down to inspect a wildflower growing near the edge of the cliffside. He lightly touched the petals, careful not to harm it. Then he straightened, looked at me, and tipped his head. "Until next time, Mr. Bloodbone. When the construction of my Rosario home is completed, you must stop by. I'll be happy to give you the tour."

*"I look forward to it."*

*Moran smiled. "As do I. And let McMillin know he is welcome to visit as well. It only makes sense that he and I would eventually meet in person. You could also go out and find one of those Truthing Trees and then we could hold a meeting under its branches if that's something he would prefer."*

*"Like the great chiefs of old."*

*"Exactly."*

*I left Rosario, disappearing into the surrounding woods while wondering what impact powerful men like Moran and McMillin would have on the future of the islands and what my role would be in trying to manage that influence.*

*Time would tell.*


Adele sat up, yawned, and then flipped the pages back to the part where Moran told Bloodbone about his dream:


*"The dream took place here," Moran said. "Along the cliffs. There was a man and a young woman. The man was a big, mean-looking fella who spoke with an accent that sounded vaguely familiar to me and then I heard it again when some stonework was being done down on the new house by a worker named Asav whom people around here call the Russian. He speaks exactly like the man in the dream did. Do you know this Asav?"*

*"Yes."*

*"I thought you might. Anyways, the man I dreamt about, he was hanging from the cliffside right here in this very spot, desperate to climb back up, and the woman was doing all she could to make him fall. I was going to try to help him but there was this voice in my head telling me not to. It took me a few seconds to realize that voice was my own."*

*"Did she succeed?"*

*"In kicking the man off the cliff?"*

*I nodded.*

*"She did. He was broken against the rocks below. I remember standing at the edge here and looking down at the body, knowing that he deserved to die but not knowing the reasons why."*

*"Was the woman still there?"*

*"Yes and no. I could see her, but I don't think she saw me. It's as if I wasn't really there—she seemed to look right through me."*

Adele recalled the fight with Visili Vasa, brother to Liya and son of Vlad Vasa, on the day he tried to rape her and murder Lucas. She was the woman Robert Moran had dreamt about nearly a century before she was even born. How such a thing was possible didn't really concern her. She had long ago stopped trying to disprove the many mystical eccentricities of the islands. *But why did Moran dream of my future?* Adele thought. Were they all somehow connected—Moran, McMillin, Bloodbone, and Asav, who would later become the Russian oligarch Vlad Vasa?

"Bloodbone and Asav," Adele whispered to herself, "two different sides of the same coin, both living extraordinarily long lives." She grabbed a pen and paper and wrote down the name Asav and then spelled it backwards which gave her the name Vasa—the very link she had uncovered during her earlier search for the Truthing Tree that had led her to finding the Book of Bloodbone.

Adele was too tired to continue reading. She closed the journal, put down the pen, and turned out the light, wondering what dreams might visit her that night. The last thought she had before heavy sleep dragged her down into its deep subconscious waters was about Roland. She pictured him seated next to Ophelia's bed watching over her, the one remaining blood relative he had in this world who was now quickly fading into the beyond.

What a sad thing it must be for him, knowing that he was so soon to be the last of his kind.

# 20.

The next day, Adele returned from an early morning run to find Sky waiting next to her sailboat. She asked her what she wanted and Sky replied that the girl who had vandalized the boat would be there soon to apologize in person.

"How much convincing did it take to get her to come?" Adele asked.

"A lot," Sky admitted. "She really wanted me to let it be, but I told her that either she shows up here or I would tell the sheriff what happened. We basically had an argument over it but in the end, I think she finally figured out I wasn't going to let it go."

"I appreciate that. Do you still consider her a friend?"

Sky shrugged. "I guess. Why?"

"You might want to reconsider that situation."

"What do you mean?"

"Ultimately it's your business who you decide to associate with, but having said that, it seems that your generation places way too much emphasis on trying to convince others and themselves that everyone is a friend when in fact few if any of those relationships resemble anything close to actual friendship."

"*My* generation? You and I are only about ten years apart in age."

"True but social media seems to have accelerated the age gap so that a difference of ten years could be measured in dog years these days. How I grew up when I was your age is vastly different than how you are growing up now."

"Do you think that difference is better or worse?"

"Worse—much worse. People seem to be a lot slower to mature than they used to be. So much of what they place value on is superficial crap that changes from one day to the next so that words like friendship or love lose all meaning. Honestly, I have to wonder how many people your age actually know what a real friend is."

"I take it you don't do social media."

"None," Adele said emphatically. "I want nothing to do with that soul-rotting garbage. It's one thing to promote a business, but this obsession of people constantly wanting to promote themselves—no thank you."

Sky smiled, likely trying to lighten the mood. "Gee, tell me how you really feel."

"I know I'm coming off like some grumpy old lady, but you know what? That's just it—*I don't care.* Way too many people are running around pretending they care about everything and it's all just so phony because the fact is they don't really care about anything other than themselves and how they hope the world sees them. They're so self-absorbed they have no idea of what genuine caring feels like."

"I like to think that I really care," Sky said.

"And maybe you do," Adele replied, "which makes who you choose to call a friend even more important because I'll let you in on a little secret—misery loves company and people instinctively will want to drag you down to their level. If you have potential, *real* potential, they'll want to take it away because they can't stand the idea of someone being better or having more than them."

Sky turned toward the sound of footsteps. A tall, college-aged woman with naturally curly, shoulder-length blonde hair streaked in colors of pink and blue was coming toward them wearing a pair of shorts that were at least a size too small. She was heavyset, with a round face, pouty lips, and arms covered in tattoos. She stopped next to an especially large and beautiful yacht, took out her phone, and then took several selfies in front of it.

"Is that her?" Adele asked.

"Yeah," Sky answered. "Her name is Zuby."

"Zuby?" Adele sighed. "Of course it is."

"Hey," Zuby mumbled to Sky as she stood next to her.

"This is Adele Plank," Sky said.

Zuby rolled her eyes. "Duh. I know who she is."

"You need to apologize to her for what you did to her boat."

More eye rolling followed. "Whatever. This is some seriously patriarchal bullshit."

Adele scowled. "Say what now?"

"Look," Zuby replied, "I get that you're mad about me tagging your boat and I know I shouldn't have done it, but there are a lot more important things going on in the world that we all need to be working together to solve."

"Back up," Adele said. "What did you mean by *patriarchal bullshit* and what does that have to do with you vandalizing my property?"

"I really don't have time to explain to you how the world works."

Adele felt a headache coming on as she clenched her fists. "You know how the world works but I don't?"

Zuby snorted. "Whatever."

Adele raised her voice. "Not whatever. I was expecting an apology from you not an attempted lecture with the emotional depth of a parking lot puddle."

"It's not my fault you don't have the brains to understand where I'm coming from."

"Zuby," Sky hissed, "don't talk to her like that. You promised me you would apologize."

"I *did* apologize. What's your problem?"

"You apologized?" Adele said. "*Really?* I must have missed it."

Zuby gave yet another roll of the eyes. "You are like the most annoying person in the world right now."

Sky faced her alleged friend. "Shut up. You are being a total bitch to her and she doesn't deserve that."

"You don't tell me to shut up," Zuby shouted back. "That is not okay. Seriously, I'm looking at you right now and it's like I'm literally looking at Hitler."

Adele watched and waited, wanting to see how Sky handled the situation but also ready to step in if required.

"You apologize to her," Sky demanded.

"Or what?" Zuby replied. "You think you can make me? I didn't even want to come here—it was your stupid idea. And look at her boat—it's already cleaned up. Probably took her, like, all of ten minutes to wash the paint off. This is so stupid. You're making a big deal out of nothing."

"What an immature brat you are."

Zuby pushed Sky hard in the chest. "Say that again. I dare you."

"Immature—" Sky leaned forward "—brat."

Zuby raised her hand. Her fist clenched tight and then accelerated toward Sky's face but was suddenly stopped mere inches before impact.

"I don't think so," Adele said, her fingers digging into Zuby's wrist.

"That's assault!" Zuby cried. "Let me go."

"No, this is *me* stopping *you* from assaulting *her*. Now back off."

Instead of stepping away from Sky, Zuby tried to yank her arm free from Adele's grip. She was taller than Adele by four inches and likely outweighed her by at least fifty pounds, but Adele easily maintained her hold.

"Help!" Zuby shouted. "She's hurting me."

"Back off," Adele repeated.

Zuby, her face red and sweaty, spit out a long litany of curse words and then swung at Adele's head with her other hand. "Let me go, you psycho."

Instead of letting go Adele calmly sidestepped the clumsy attempt at a punch and then shifted her grip on Zuby's wrist so that her thumb could press hard into the soft flesh between the top of

Zuby's thumb and forefinger. "I'll let you go when you stop trying to hit people. I don't want to hurt you, but I will if I have to."

"I'm going to sue your ass for this."

Adele's smile was cold and confident. "No, you won't." Zuby tried to throw another punch but again missed wildly. Adele dug her thumb into Zuby's hand, causing her to cry out and drop to one knee. "Hurts, don't it? I warned you."

"I'm sorry," Zuby gasped.

Adele let her go and then looked up to find Lucas striding down the dock toward them.

Zuby rubbed her hand. She was on the verge of tears, her lower lip trembling. "She attacked me. I think my hand is broken or something. It hurts really bad."

"She's the one who vandalized Ms. Plank's boat," Sky said while pointing at Zuby.

"Is that true?" Lucas asked.

Zuby continued to cradle her hand as she started to sob. "It's true that she attacked me."

"That's not what I asked. Were you the one who damaged the boat?"

"Look at it," Zuby whined. "You can't even tell. It's just like it was before."

"Because I cleaned it off," Adele said, "and it took a lot longer than ten minutes."

"Zuby was also the one who tried to attack me first," Sky added. "Ms. Plank was protecting me and I'm willing to sign a statement to that fact."

"Some friend you are!" Zuby shouted.

"We're not friends," Sky replied as she glanced at Adele. "I think I just realized we never were."

Lucas turned toward Adele. "Do you want to press charges?"

"Why are you asking her that?" Zuby held up her hand to show the red mark by her thumb. "I'm the one who was hurt."

"I'm sure your hand will be fine if you just stop rubbing it so much," Lucas said.

Zuby's face scrunched up, making her look like an enraged, red-faced pig. "Oh, I get it. You're one of those badge-wearing assholes we've all been warned about—a fascist cop goose-stepping for the machine. I'll have you know I spent nearly an hour at a 'defund the police' rally last summer because, unlike privileged scum like you, I actually care about trying to make the world a better place. And to think I thought you were one of the good ones. Boy, was I dumb. Now that I see you up close, you're not even that hot."

"Sorry to disappoint." Lucas looked at Adele again. "Well?"

"I won't be pressing charges," Adele replied.

"Are you sure?"

"She said it herself—she's dumb. I don't see any need to make her already miserable life any worse."

"Who are you calling dumb?" Zuby bellowed.

Sky shut her eyes and shook her head. "Oh my gosh, Zuby, you just called yourself dumb not ten seconds ago."

"No, I didn't."

"Yes, you..." Sky sighed. "Never mind."

"Is everything okay over here, Sheriff Pine?"

Lucas grimaced and then shook his head at Zuby. "Now you've done it." He turned around. "It's fine, Tilda. Apologies for the disturbance."

"I could hear yelling all the way from the hotel." Tilda stood tall and glared down at Zuby. "Coming from *you,* young lady."

"That's impressive." Zuby smirked. "Who would have thought someone so old could still hear so well?"

Adele and Lucas both stepped back at the same time.

"What's your name?" Tilda asked.

"Zuby Jackson."

"You work here at the resort?"

"Yeah."

Tilda's lips pressed tightly together as she arched a brow and her chin tilted up. "Not anymore."

"Wait, that's not fair. This isn't my fault. I was assaulted and then the sheriff shows up and he doesn't care and—"

"Hush," Tilda said. "No more talking. You will march your way back to employee housing right now, gather your belongings, and leave. Failure to do that will result in you being charged with trespassing."

"But—"

Tilda shook her head. "You. Are. Done."

"I'm recording all of you. This is some human rights level violations going on right here." Zuby took out her phone. "You can't treat people like—"

Tilda snatched the phone away and then tossed it into the water. "Your comprehension skills appear to be lacking so I'll try this just one more time in terms I hope you can understand: move your ass, pack your shit, and go. If I see you here again, I promise that phone won't be the only thing I drop into the water."

Zuby's mouth shut. She swallowed hard, wiped away tears with a trembling hand, and then walked off without looking back.

"Poor thing," Tilda said. "Nobody drowning under the weight of that much manufactured entitlement will ever know true happiness." She turned and faced Sky. "Were you a part of this as well?"

"She was trying to help," Adele replied. "I'll vouch for her."

"Okay, then I suggest you return to doing the job you're being paid to do." As Sky quickly walked away Tilda looked out at the water. "Any word on Ophelia?" she asked.

Both Adele and Lucas shook their heads.

"I imagine it won't be long now. Please let me know as soon as you hear anything." Tilda said goodbye and then returned to the hotel as the resort staff, desperate to avoid her wrath, scurried away in front of her like the Red Sea parting before Moses.

"Sorry about you having to deal with that idiot girl," Adele said to Lucas.

He shrugged. "Dealing with those kinds of people comes with the badge. I just wish there weren't so many of them. Back when I was a kid there were people like her, but they were far and few between and were ignored by the rest of us, but now it seems they are the majority. I swear sometimes it feels like society is just falling apart all around us. We're losing our sense of basic decency. I'm all for fighting the good fight and trying to make this a better world but in my experience most people are doing just the opposite these days despite what their social media profiles would have us believe."

Adele stifled a laugh. "I can't believe Tilda actually grabbed her phone and threw it into the water."

"Man, I can't tell you how many times I've wanted to do that to someone, but I didn't have the guts." Lucas stared across the marina at the Roche Harbor Hotel. "You got to love Tilda. She just does what she does. I knew as soon as I saw her walking this way that girl had a hard lesson coming to her."

"Good riddance."

"Yes indeed."

"Were you on your way here to talk to me about something?"

"Actually, I was already in the area and someone called about a disturbance at the resort."

"Tell the truth—did you assume I was involved?"

Lucas grinned. "It appears you're still capable of raising a little hell."

Adele poked his bicep. "A *lot* of hell and don't you doubt it for a second."

"No ma'am."

"*Ma'am?* How dare you."

Lucas's grin turned into full-throated laughter. "*What?* It's a show of respect toward your elders."

"Need I remind you that you're older than me?"

"Only by a few years."

"Old man."

"Actually, I did find a few gray hairs on my head recently to say nothing of the crow's feet that are making a permanent home around my eyes. A lot of time has passed since I was running plays on a football field. When I look in the mirror these days, I'm really starting to see my dad's face staring back at me."

"There's nothing wrong with that. Your father was a very handsome man."

"Can I ask you something?"

Adele sensed the discussion was about to take a more serious turn. "Sure."

"That nun at the monastery—Sister Zhara."

"Uh-huh."

"Ever since I saw her, I can't stop thinking about her. I know that having these kinds of feelings is nuts. I mean you can't date a nun because, well, she's a nun. But damn if I can't get her out of my mind."

"Are you asking me for advice or giving a confession?"

"I want to ask her out, but I know she'll probably say no because—"

"She's a nun."

"Right."

"Go with your heart, Lucas. Life is short. Even if it can't be a romantic relationship, I'm sure Sister Zhara would be open to getting to know you better. There's nothing wrong with having lunch or dinner together sometime."

"That's the thing, I want more than just lunch and dinner—I want it all."

"You might want to tap the brakes there. You hardly know each other."

"I didn't necessarily mean Sister Zhara specifically. It's just that by this time in my life I always figured I'd be settling down with someone, you know? I even bought an old four-bedroom homestead property with these amazing three-sixty views near Mount Grant a few months back. I've been working on remodeling it whenever I get some free time but I'm no carpenter, so it's been slow going. It'll be nice someday—the kind of place to raise a family."

"Lucas Pine, you've been holding out on us. I had no idea you were remodeling a home. Good for you. I mean it. That's great."

"It's a lot of rooms for just one person though."

"You'll fill those rooms eventually."

"Yeah?"

"Absolutely."

"I'm going to hold you to that."

The conversation paused again as the morning sun warmed the thick wood dock planks under their feet. Lucas squinted when he looked up at the sky. "I'll be checking in with the Irish authorities again this afternoon. If they have anything new to report on Fin, I'll be sure to update you."

"Thanks."

"I should probably get going."

"How about some coffee first? We can drink it on the bow of the boat."

Lucas nodded. "I'd like that." He sounded both surprised and grateful for the offer.

For the next hour Adele sat with Lucas outside sipping coffee in lawn chairs on the bow of her sailboat, making small talk, enjoying how the light above danced upon the water's surface below, until eventually he got up, gave her a quick side hug, and said he had an appointment back in Friday Harbor. She watched him walking away, contemplating the contradiction of a man who was so big and strong looking so lonely and lost. Adele knew that feeling well, having been there many times herself.

*He'll be okay,* she thought, *because he has friends—real ones.*

# 21.

*"Okay, you got us out here standing under this damn tree,"* McMillin huffed as he looked around at the grass clearing that was surrounded by evergreens. *"Now what?"*

*"Was the trip over from Orcas uneventful?"* I asked Moran.

He nodded. *"Water like glass the entire way here. And thank you, John, for allowing me to drop anchor in your harbor. It truly is a lovely place."*

*"Better than your Rosario?"* McMillin wondered.

Moran's dark eyes twinkled. Though a quieter and more contemplative personality, he was every bit as competitive as McMillin. *"We are both blessed to call such places home."* He looked up at the tree. *"Is this it?"*

*"I believe so,"* I answered. *"You can see the dark marks within its branches left by the lightning strike from long ago."*

Moran ran his hand over the tree's rough bark. *"A Truthing Tree."*

*"You don't actually believe in that heathen nonsense, do you?"* McMillin wiped the sweat from his brow with a handkerchief. *"I really don't mind the effort it took to climb this hill to get to this place, but let's not kid ourselves—it's just a tree the same as all the others."*

*"Come now, John, surely you are capable of consideration of things not so easily understood. Who is to say there are not certain trees imbued with powers beyond our knowing?"*

*McMillin puffed out his barrel-sized chest. "Me, that's who."*

*"You are not so closed minded as that."*

*"How would you know what I am or am not?"*

*"Because you were drawn to these islands the same as me,"* Moran replied.

*"I came here because I recognized ample opportunity to turn something into something more."*

*"Ah, but why then do you stay? You've made your fortune. You could live anywhere in the country or even the world and yet you have chosen to remain here in this watery wilderness that remains blissfully beyond the reach of mainland civilization."*

McMillin opened his mouth but then abruptly closed it. His brow furrowed as he frowned. He kicked at the earth beneath the tree with the toe of his boot. *"I suppose, if I'm being completely honest, I do like it here,"* he finally muttered as much to himself as the others.

"Of course you do," Moran said. "You are building a legacy in this remarkable place—a legacy that will outlast all of us."

"Would such a legacy outlast even him?" McMillin replied as he stared up at me.

"You speak of our Indian friend's unusually long life."

"I do."

"Does it trouble you?"

"Troubling? No. Confounding? Yes. I prefer to know the how and why of things, but the condition of his longevity remains a mystery—one that he doesn't seem too keen on explaining to us."

"Perhaps because he doesn't understand it any more than we do. Look around. What do you see?"

McMillin's frown deepened. "What do you mean?"

"You already said it yourself—mystery. It's all around us in these islands, as undeniable as the dark waters that surround us. You were drawn to this place the same as I was, John. While economic opportunity might have been your precursor for coming, it is something far deeper than that which now keeps you here."

"And what might that be?"

"Love."

"Hah!" McMillin clamped a meaty hand over Moran's shoulder. "I never would have taken you for such a silly romantic, Robert. You are nothing like I expected."

*"Do you not love this place? Isn't your Roche Harbor an undeniable testament to God's presence here? How could one look out at the scenery from a home such as yours and deny the part divine intervention played that made such natural beauty possible?"*

*"I would never deny God's presence." McMilllin gave me a hard look. "Or the devil's."*

*"Mr. Bloodbone is no more a devil than you are," Moran said.*

*"Nor is he my equal."*

*Moran's thin smile let it be known how much he was enjoying the back and forth with his San Juan Islands contemporary. "Or you his."*

*McMillin's mouth twitched and for a moment I feared he might strike the smaller Moran, but then he chuckled. "Fair enough." He looked at me as he pointed at the base of the tree. "How do you know this is actually a Truthing Tree?"*

*"Because it told me," I replied.*

*"You speak to trees now do you?"*

*"No, I listen to them the same as I try to listen to all things that I share this world with."*

*"Is that right?"*

*I nodded. "It is."*

*"Why did you bring us up here?"*

*"So that we might all meet together."*

*"But why here to this particular tree?"*

*"I thought it appropriate that we meet in a place previous great chiefs met to discuss issues openly and honestly that are important to the islands."*

*McMillin appeared pleased by my reply. "You believe we three represent the newest of the great chiefs of the San Juans?"*

*"I hadn't thought of it quite like that, but, yes, your interpretation could be considered appropriate."*

*"An agreement of cooperation." Moran nodded. "I like it."*

*"So, if I have a concern," McMillin said, "this would be the place to share it—under the branches of what you call a Truthing Tree."*

*"Yes," I replied.*

*Moran casually hooked his thumbs into the front pockets of his wool trousers. "What's your concern, John?"*

*"That damnable Russian. I've already spoken about him to Karl."*

*"What has he done now?" I asked.*

*"More like what hasn't he done. People are complaining from all over. As if the gambling and whoring weren't enough, it was recently brought to my attention that he's been paying pennies on the dollar for goods on one island and then reselling them at a significant upcharge to settlers on other islands. I'm all for making a profit,*

believe you me, but what this Asav has been doing borders on the criminal."

"If the quality of his stonework is any indication, he does possess some valuable talent," Moran said.

"Talent?" McMillin looked horrified. "No talent is worth the corruption of an entire community and that is exactly what he seems so hell-bent on doing. I say we run him off for good."

"No," Moran replied. "I have yet to see evidence that would support such an action against him."

"You need evidence? I just told you what the man has been up to. What more do you need?"

"What you shared was as much personal opinion as anything. People come to these islands to be free, not dominated by those who happen to already own more than them."

McMillin glared at me. "Are you going to just stand there like the world's tallest mute or do you have something to contribute?"

"The issue of Asav is complicated," I answered.

"Why is it complicated?" McMillin shrugged. "Just run him off and be done with it. I have plenty of men in my employ who would gladly do it for a reasonable sum."

"Perhaps there is another option," Moran said. "We invite him to join our Truthing Tree group."

"Are you mad?" McMillin growled.

*"Go on," I told Moran. He then explained how including Asav instead of isolating him might make him far more likely to listen to our concerns regarding his behavior.*

*"No, no, no." McMillin wiped his brow again. "Clearly the man's true nature is only dedicated to his own self-interest. He simply cannot be trusted in any capacity no matter how much someone might wish him to be."*

*"I believe it is worth a try," Moran said. "Asav is talented. I have seen his stonework first-hand and others have spoken of his carpentry skills as well. The islands need men who can build responsibly."*

*"Exactly," McMillin countered while pointing at Moran. "They key word there being **responsibly.** Asav is the opposite of responsible. We would be choosing to associate ourselves with a known degenerate. How are we to provide leadership and direction to the islands going into this new century when we allow someone like him to be a part of this group?"*

*"Because being part of this group might appeal to Asav's better nature," Moran replied.*

*"I already told you that his true nature is his own self-interest. There is nothing more to him than that."*

*Both men turned their heads and looked up at me, waiting for my response as I contemplated their divergent opinions on how best to deal with Asav. I knew forcing him from the islands would be difficult if not impossible. He would inevitably return, even when faced with the potential for violence against him by some of McMillin's workers. Then again, allowing him to continue corrupting the islands* with his appetite for easy-profit pursuits might also seriously compromise the greater good.

"Well?" McMillin asked.

"I side with Robert," I answered. "We give Asav a chance to be part of our group. With that will come opportunities for honest commerce for him. The current construction projects in both Friday Harbor and Eastsound alone could make him a wealthy man should he prove capable of conducting himself with greater integrity than he has in the past."

"Agreed," Moran declared. "Asav stays and will be a part of our group. If anything, it will make it far easier for us to keep an eye on him."

"How can we believe he'll actually live up to any promise of better behavior he might make?" McMillin shook his head. "This is a mistake."

"We bring him here," I said. "He will be in the presence of the Truthing Tree when he gives us his word."

"His word?" McMillin looked up at the ancient, lightning-singed branches that stretched out above him. "You actually believe a tree will compel a known liar to suddenly speak truth?"

"I believe it is worth a try," Moran said. "Who among us at some point in our lives has not needed a second chance?"

"Your idealism scares the hell out of me," McMillin replied. "I fear it could be our undoing. No promise made *under a tree can make someone like Asav suddenly want to walk the more righteous path."*

*"Asav is but one man. The fault of our undoing, should it come, will be ours not his."*

*"I hope you're right."*

*Moran stuck out his hand. "Then it is settled?"*

*The two men shook. "God help us," McMillin said. "Will you be staying overnight at Roche?"*

*"No," Moran answered. "I appreciate the invitation, but I will be returning to Rosario this afternoon. When my home is completed, you must come for a visit though."*

*"I'll do that." McMillin started walking down the hill. "Until then you're welcome to catch a ride back to Roche on my carriage." He stopped and turned around. "And what of you, Karl?"*

*"I hope to locate Asav as soon as possible so that I might tell him of our decision to have him to join our group."*

*"Very well. And when will our next meeting under the Truthing Tree take place?"*

*"I will let you know."*

*Moran gripped my hand with both of his and gave it a firm shake. "Well done, Karl. I appreciate you supporting my decision regarding what should be done with Asav."*

*"I supported that decision because I believe it to be the right one."*

*"Until next time then."*

*The sight of McMillin and Moran walking down the hill together pleased me greatly. While they likely did not yet consider themselves friends, some form of partnership between the two business titans had been achieved by the conclusion of that first gathering under the Truthing Tree, one that I knew would help to secure the future of the islands.*

*It was progress—slow, steady, and necessary.*

Adele looked up from the pages of the journal, breathed deeply, and yawned. It was nearly midnight. Roland's last message earlier that evening described Ophelia's worsening condition. He was certain she wouldn't last the week but was grateful for those few brief moments when she would awaken and be able to communicate and listen if only for a few minutes before again returning into a deep sleep.

The Book of Bloodbone lay open in front of her. She thought of the long-lasting implications of the decision to allow Asav not only to remain on the islands but also to be given a position of influence as part of the Truthing Tree group. So much wrong would come from that one attempt to do right. Adele wondered if others would later voice the same concerns as John McMillin did regarding Asav. Did Roland's grandfather, Charles Soros, consider the Russian a friend or foe?

*The answers are likely inside these pages,* Adele thought, ignoring the fatigue that was by then pressing down over her mind and body.

The reading continued.

# 22.

"Please look at me when I talk to you."

Adele rubbed her eyes as she sat up in bed. It was too dark to see where the deep male voice was coming from.

"Over here. You need not fear me. Knowing how much my grandson cares for your well-being, the thought of hurting you is inconceivable."

The outline of a tall, thin figure in a black suit and tie could be seen standing near the galley table ten feet from Adele's bed. The moonlight that filtered in through the sailboat's portholes illuminated the slicked back white hair on his head. His narrow, clean-shaven face had deep lines that ran the length of a strong, square jaw. He looked both old and young, masculine yet delicate, cautious but formidable—a disjointed mix of seamless contradictions that all came together almost perfectly. His voice had the rough edge of a longtime smoker and each word spoken was perfectly enunciated. When he lightly rubbed the side of his forehead, Adele noted the long fingers and manicured nails as well as the metallic flash from the gold watch around his wrist.

Charles Soros was a remarkably attractive older man.

"Given how you will soon be reading the part I played in Karl's long tenure as protector of the islands I thought it appropriate that I finally and formally introduce myself to you."

"This is another dream," Adele said. "My subconscious talking to itself."

"A figment of your imagination?" Charles sounded slightly offended.

"Something like that."

*"Something more* I assure you." He pointed down at the journal that Adele had left closed on the galley table after she finished Bloodbone's descriptions of the first half of the twentieth century on the islands, which included the far-reaching influences of John McMillin and Robert Moran who both lived well into their eighties and then died within a handful of years of each other. "What do you think of it so far?"

"It's fascinating reading."

"Karl is a fascinating man."

"He's gone missing. I don't suppose you know where I might find him?"

"Karl always had a knack for disappearing when he wanted to and then suddenly reappearing as if he had never left."

"That's not much help."

"My point is that he shows up or he doesn't. Either way you need to continue on your own path, Adele."

"I'm not sure what that path is supposed to be."

"Sure you do—you're the new Karl, the protector of the islands."

"I'm not Bloodbone. This is my decision. My choice. My way."

"Your particular way or his doesn't concern me so long as what needs to get done is done."

"And what is that?"

Charles shrugged. "My time came and went. Your time is now, which makes the future yours to know."

"Ophelia is dying." Adele stared hard at Charles, wanting to see every nuance of his reaction to that message.

"Yes."

"Will you visit her the same as you're visiting me now?"

"I already have."

"She loved you."

"And I her." Charles looked down at his shoes. "Very much," he whispered. His head lifted. "You make Roland very happy."

"He's a good man."

"And an imperfect one."

"The same as you were."

Charles's lower lip stuck out slightly. "Indeed." His eyes narrowed. "Might I give you some advice?"

"There's no guarantee I'll take it." Adele noticed Charles's shoulders shaking slightly and then she realized he was chuckling.

"It pleases me greatly to know that Roland chose such a strong woman."

"I'm not so strong—I've just gotten better at faking it."

"Should you ever be blessed to find someone who truly makes you content, hold on to them and don't let go," Charles continued. "Few things are as painful as having something so valuable as that and then losing it."

"Like how you lost Ophelia when you chose to end your relationship with her?"

Charles stepped toward Adele. "Careful the tone you take with me."

Adele wanted to look away but didn't, determined not to show fear. "I meant no disrespect, but at the same time I have to ask why you chose to leave her like you did."

"You know the complications—she was a nun; I was married, it was a terribly messy and uncomfortable situation for the both of us. I assure you hurting her was the last thing I wanted to do."

"But you did—you hurt her terribly."

"I know," Charles said through clenched teeth.

"Why?"

"Because I was told that was my only option."

"Bloodbone?"

Charles nodded. "After she became pregnant, I sought his counsel. Ophelia demanded the decision be our own, but I respected Karl's considerable knowledge and wisdom that was the byproduct of his long life. His words carried a great deal of weight with me and he made it very clear that the best decision, the only real decision, was that Ophelia and I permanently end our relationship. A divorce would have greatly weakened my financial standing, which in turn would have endangered the islands and that couldn't be allowed to happen. For him the islands always came first."

Adele sat up straight. *"That's* why Ophelia hated Bloodbone so much when I first met her. She blamed him for convincing you to leave her."

"Yes. It wasn't entirely fair of course, but I think she found it easier to hate him than it was for her to hate me."

"Because she never stopped loving you."

Charles grimaced. "Though we were no longer lovers we remained close. Ophelia was my most trusted friend and I hope she felt the same about me. Since my death I have waited for her so that we might be together again."

"I hope that happens—for the both of you."

"Dark times are coming to the islands, Adele. You must prepare."

"I have been."

"Asav will stop at nothing to take that which he believes to have always been his."

"How well did you know him?"

"I knew the Russian well enough to order him gone from here."

"You were the one to make him leave?"

Charles nodded. "I demanded it and Edmund Pine, Lucas's father, and Delroy Hicks, Fin's father, both agreed. We voted in the presence of the Truthing Tree to banish Asav from the islands. He fled to Russia with the considerable wealth he had accumulated over his long life, took the name of Vlad Vasa, and set out to become the billionaire Russian oligarch he is known as today. Before he left, he promised to return, saying he would outlive us all until none were left to stop him. I am certain that time is now. Do you believe yourself strong enough to survive his challenge?"

"He sent his son and daughter to the islands. They're both gone and I'm still here. I'd like to think that means something."

"It likely means Asav, Vlad, is more determined than ever to see you, Roland, Lucas, and Tilda all punished."

"And Fin."

"Yes, and Fin as well."

"Is he okay?" Adele asked. "Like Bloodbone, he also seems to have gone missing."

"I don't know. My knowledge doesn't extend beyond the islands."

"How is it that Asav has lived as long as Bloodbone?"

"I posed that very question many times during my own life as I watched the rest of us grow old while time seemed to hardly touch those two. It had something to do with the crystals around their necks, that much I was sure of."

Adele rubbed her own crystal that rested against her chest.

"Karl gave you that," Charles said.

"Yes," Adele replied. "It was years ago, shortly after I moved into this sailboat."

"The sailboat that Delroy gifted to you after he died."

"That's right."

"You were being directed to the islands at every turn."

"It often felt that way."

"It felt that way because it *was* that way."

"I'm here because I want to be."

"Because my grandson is here as well?"

Adele nodded. "Roland is certainly a big reason why."

"There is no better reason than love. I am very proud of my grandson."

"Did you ever tell him that?"

Charles pinched the tip of his chin. "Not nearly as much as I should have." He pointed at Adele. "You could tell him for me."

"Tell him that his dead grandfather visited me in a dream to say he was proud of him?"

"Why not?"

"Roland is a pretty open-minded guy, but I'm not sure he'd believe it."

Charles lowered his head, tilted it to the side, and then pulled some hair back from his scalp. "Do you see it?" A faint one-inch scar ran just below the hairline. "He gave this to me when he was a boy not long after his grandmother and I adopted him following the car accident in Florida that killed his parents. Roland was acting out. He was understandably very emotional at the time, especially being so young. He threw that rock and split my head open. He didn't really mean to hurt me and I'm sure he thought I was going to kill him after he did it, but, instead, I hugged him tight and said it was okay. You see, I wasn't a particularly good father to my son, Roland's father. Business matters consumed me often at the expense of those around me and I was determined to do better with my grandson. By hugging him so tightly I hoped to let him know that I wasn't going anywhere. He would be loved and cared for and receive all the advantages my wealth could afford to give to him. You mention this scar and he'll know you heard it from me."

The smell of smoke filtered into the cabin. Adele hopped off the bed and looked around. "Something is burning."

"I believe you're right," Charles replied.

Adele moved toward the bow looking for the source of the smoke. When she turned around, Charles was gone. A quick peek out one of the porthole windows revealed orange flames climbing up the side of the hull.

The sailboat was on fire.

Adele jumped out onto the dock and stood there in her sweatshirt and underwear. The fire was already spreading quickly over the top of the bow as the smell of gasoline hung heavy on the night air. Suddenly the flames erupted, covering the front half the boat in seconds. There was movement further down on the main dock. Someone was running away. Adele started to sprint after them, but then she stopped and turned around. Bloodbone's journal remained inside the sailboat. Adele gulped air, held her breath, and then walked through a wall of pungent smoke. She dropped into the cabin, grabbed the journal, and then ran back outside where she placed the journal into a nearby dock bin. Then she snatched up a hose, turned on the water, and started spraying down the top of her boat.

For a few panic-stricken moments the flames appeared to grow even stronger, but finally they began to recede as more and more water was poured over them until, eventually, they were fully extinguished. The front of the sailboat was deeply charred with burn streaks where the flame had eaten through the gelcoat and into the top layer of fiberglass. Five minutes more and her boat might have been completely lost to the fire. As it was, the exterior damage was significant, though likely not structural, while inside, the smell of smoke would take several days to get out.

*Someone poured gas over my boat and tried to burn me alive,* Adele thought. *Who would do such a thing?* The list of possibilities was much longer than she cared to admit, but the recently fired Zuby was the most obvious suspect.

Adele took out her phone. She felt guilty about calling 911 which would lead to Lucas being woken up in the middle of the night and then having to drive out to Roche, but this most recent attack was far more serious than some spray-painted vandalism—she could have been killed and the entire marina put in danger of going up in flames as well. Whoever did this had to be caught as soon as possible.

The call was made.

# 23.

"You didn't get a good look at the individual who was running away after the fire was started?"

Adele shook her head. "No, not their face."

"Do you think physically, height and build-wise, it could have been Zuby?" Lucas asked.

"It's possible but it was also dark, and I was most concerned with stopping the fire from spreading, so I just can't say for sure. Following up with Zuby would definitely be where I'd start looking though."

"I'm on it. If she's unable to provide an adequate alibi, she'll be arrested. As soon as I'm done here, I'll put in a call to the Port of Friday Harbor and have them cross-check the ferry records to see if she was a recent passenger. That way I'll know where to start first— here on the islands or put out an APB with the mainland law enforcement agencies. This is a serious situation—you could have been killed."

"Believe me, I know."

"Whoever did this could be charged with attempted murder."

"That's fine by me." Adele handed Lucas the cup of coffee that she had brought down from the hotel while she waited for him to show up. The sun was just starting to come up over the horizon and, judging by his stubble-covered face and mish-mash hair, he hadn't even had time to take a shower before responding to the 911 call.

"Thank you," he said as he took the cup and then sipped from it.

"I'm sorry this got you out of bed so early."

"I wasn't sleeping much anyways."

"Why is that?"

Lucas lowered the cup. "I was planning on coming out here first thing this morning to talk to you about Fin."

Adele's stomach tightened with worry. She had felt for days that something was wrong with him. "Is he alive?" she blurted out.

"The Irish authorities have been unable to locate him. For the first time since I've been checking in with them, they seem genuinely concerned by what might have happened."

"Is he alive?" Adele repeated.

"No one knows."

"Shit," Adele hissed. "Have they brought in Arthur Olegovich for questioning?"

"I suggested that to them, but they believe Olegovich has already returned to Russia."

"But they're not certain?"

Lucas shrugged. "The conversation we had was brief. I'm sure there are aspects of the investigation they aren't sharing with me, which I completely understand given I'm a nobody small county island sheriff on the other side of the world. They did say it's possible Fin has gone to ground."

*"Gone to ground*—what's that?"

"Something the Irish Travellers are quite good at apparently. It means he intentionally disappeared. If a Traveler doesn't want to be found, their community has a real knack for helping out to make that happen. If Vlad Vasa's henchmen suddenly showed up asking around for Fin's whereabouts, they would be quick to smell trouble and work to keep him safe."

"But then why isn't he returning our messages to him?"

"Maybe he lost his phone or threw it away, thinking it could be used to track his location."

Adele hadn't considered that possibility. She nodded, hoping that was the reason for Fin's prolonged silence. "Maybe."

"The good news is that the Irish investigators are now taking Fin's disappearance much more seriously than they were before."

"We should be there," Adele said.

Lucas's eyes widened. "Ireland?"

"Yes."

"Adele, no, that's not a good idea."

"Why not? Fin would do it for us."

"Give the authorities more time to locate him."

"They won't."

"You don't know that."

Adele's crystal felt warm against her chest. She reached up and pressed its smooth surface between her fingers. "Yes, I do."

"Are you seriously considering going to Ireland to search for Fin?"

"I'm not one to say things I don't mean, Lucas."

"You shouldn't go there alone, but there is no way I can leave work right now to jump on a plane with you to Ireland."

"I *can* go by myself if that's what I decide, but maybe Roland will want to come with me."

"He's not going anywhere until after Ophelia passes."

*That's right,* Adele thought, *and neither am I.*

"It won't be long," Lucas continued. "Be patient." He brought his coffee up to his lips again but then stopped when he saw Tilda walking down the dock toward them, her eyes ablaze and her long yellow summer dress billowing out behind her.

"Good morning, Tilda," Adele said while bracing for the impact of her apparent foul mood.

"Nothing good about this," Tilda seethed as she looked at the damage done to Adele's boat. "Was it that damn Zuby?"

"I'm looking into it," Lucas replied.

Tilda pointed at the fire-scorched boat. "This is priority number one, Sheriff. Adele could have been burned alive and the whole marina might have gone up in flames as well."

"I know."

Adele detected the annoyance in Lucas's tone. "He'll do everything he can to find out who did this," she said, hoping to avoid conflict between him and Tilda.

Tilda looked Lucas up and down and then nodded. "I know he will." She put her hands on her hips. "We haven't had something like this happen here since the Russians burned Roland's family yacht to a crisp. That made me sick to my stomach then and I have that same feeling now. Whoever did this needs to be caught and punished."

"To the fullest extent of the law," Lucas replied.

"The law?" Tilda scowled. "Sure—*the law.* But know this, if it was up to me, I would take them out into deep water with a big rock chained around their feet and throw them overboard."

"That would be murder."

"No, Sheriff, that would be justice."

Adele could almost see the wheels spinning in Lucas's head. He wanted to respond but also knew that when Tilda was in a mood like this the best option was often to simply allow her to vent. He handed Adele her coffee cup back and then said he should get to work on confirming Zuby's whereabouts so that he could interview her about the fire.

"I hope he didn't think I was questioning his competence," Tilda said as she and Adele watched him walking away. "It's just that seeing what was done to your boat, your home, and knowing that the person or persons responsible are out there somewhere walking free, I want to scream."

"We're in good hands with Lucas. He's an excellent sheriff."

"Yes, he is." Tilda straightened the sides of her dress. "Perhaps I should apologize to him."

"That's probably not necessary. I doubt he took anything you said personally. He totally understands your anger because he's as upset about all of this as you are."

Adele's phone vibrated. It was a text from Roland asking if she would be coming to Shaw today. She replied yes and that she should be there no later than noon. He offered to send the chopper. She answered that she wanted to come over on her boat.

"Was that Roland?" Tilda asked.

"Yeah."

"Did you tell him about the fire?"

"I'll wait until I see him. I don't want him to worry. His plate is plenty full already."

"You should leave out a bowl of vinegar inside of your boat while you're gone."

"Vinegar?"

"It's an old boater's trick. It'll help to remove the smell of smoke."

"Or leave it smelling like a burnt Caesar salad."

Tilda smiled. "Burnt Caesar—that sounds like a potential menu item." Her smile faded. "How are you for clothes and whatnot?"

"All of my belongings are fine, but they probably stink like an ashtray."

"You can come over to the hotel to take a shower and I'll have someone on the staff wash your clothes for you while you're cleaning up."

"Thank you."

Tilda put her arm around Adele's shoulders. "I'm just so relieved you're okay. If something had happened to you. . ." She shook her head. "I don't want to even think about it."

"You don't have to because I'm fine."

"I'll also have the staff get you some breakfast ready so you can fill up before you head out for Shaw. Did Roland say anything about how Ophelia is doing?"

"No, but I don't think she has too much longer."

"Please update me when you find out."

Adele promised she would and then spent the next hour showering, waiting for her freshly washed clothes, and wolfing down a welcome breakfast of scrambled eggs and toast. She drove her power boat out of the marina a few minutes after ten o'clock under clear skies and calm waters. Bloodbone's journal lay in the passenger seat beside her. Instead of accelerating up to twenty knots or faster speeds she decided to go at a much quieter pace, enjoying the shoreline scenery of nearby Spieden Island and the northeast side of San Juan Island that included a slow cruise through Rocky Bay where she watched a bald eagle swoop down and then grab up a small fish from the water before flying off toward the island's interior. Next came the southern tip of Jones Island, followed by North Pass and the small but densely wooded Reef Island that was located on the outer edges of Deer Harbor. Adele then aimed for the narrow opening that was Pole Pass. From there it was a straight shot across the water to the rocky outcrop of Shaw Island's Broken Point, the place where Ophelia had instructed Roland to spread her ashes.

The sea's glass surface was the perfect complement to the near silent solitude that enveloped Adele. She took the boat out of gear and looked around her, marveling at the beautifully rugged surroundings. A flash of bright color caught her eye. It was a pair of tufted puffins diving together under the water in search of the small bait fish that sustained them. Seeing puffins was rare as the large saltwater birds were generally quite shy and avoided the company of humans. Adele smiled as she watched the dark-feathered, orange-beaked creatures paddle in slow circles before they momentarily disappeared into their world beneath the world until, eventually, perhaps after sensing her presence, they called out to each other, flapped their wings, and then flew south toward the Strait of Juan de Fuca.

Adele continued to sit at the helm while the boat drifted, breathing in the land and sea air and wondering how long it would be until Ophelia's remains would become part of this special place. She got up, leaned over the side of the boat, closed her eyes, and then let the tips of her fingers cut tiny ripples across the cold water.

A shift in the islands was currently underway—big changes were coming. Adele wasn't exactly sure what those changes were, but she felt the shifting deep inside of her, like a faint electrical current coursing through her soul and connecting her in some way she did not yet fully understand to the beating heart of the islands themselves. It both scared and thrilled her and left her wondering if she would be strong enough to meet the coming challenges.

Shaw Island rose up in front of her. Beyond its shores, through the woods, was the monastery where Ophelia would breathe her last. Adele returned to her place at the helm, gripping the steering wheel with one hand and pushing the throttle forward with the other. The boat jumped out of the water, settled, and then skipped across its smooth surface.

*I'm strong enough,* Adele thought.

*Because I have to be—for all of us.*

# 24.

"She hasn't spoken since yesterday," Roland said. "And that was for just a few minutes. Pretty much all she does now is sleep."

Adele held Ophelia's withered hand while listening to her shallow and ragged breathing. Roland hadn't shaved in days, leaving his face covered by a thick layer of stubble. The bags under his eyes were so dark it almost looked like he had recently been punched in the face.

"You should get some rest," Adele suggested. "I'll watch over her for a while."

Roland started to object, but then his shoulders slumped as he hung his head. "Rest sounds really good right now and I wouldn't say no to a hot shower either." He looked up. "Are you sure?"

Adele nodded. "I'll be fine."

"Okay—thanks." Roland gave her a quick hug. "I'll be in the cabin outside if you need me."

"Rest up," Adele said. After Roland left, she grabbed the journal, settled into her chair, and began reading the part where Bloodbone described his first encounter with a very young Charles Soros.

*Some walk with destiny while others run from it. Even when he was a boy I could tell Charles Soros was not one to run from anything. He was barely ten when he came up to me as I stood on the docks of Friday Harbor and asked why I was so tall. "This is the view of the world God chose to give to me," I answered.*

*"God?" Charles squinted as he looked up. "My pa says that God stopped caring about us a long time ago because we aren't worthy of His attention and so it's up to us to make our own way in this world. Do you think that's true?"*

*The elder Soros had made a reasonable fortune as a bootlegger, using the islands as a midway point between alcohol shipped in from Canada and then distributed along the coast primarily through an agreement he had with a man of allegedly ill repute on the mainland named Levi Bowman. It was a relationship facilitated by Samantha Ashland, a young woman whose family would soon own the increasingly popular Roche Harbor Hotel. Samantha had fallen in love with one of Levi Bowman's four sons, a twenty-something named Dylan who lost his life during a dispute with a powerful and dangerous Chinese criminal enterprise located along the shores of Lake Union in Seattle. Because of Samantha's love for him, and his sacrifice for her and thus for the islands as well, I made certain that Dylan's spirit would become a permanent fixture throughout the islands in the form of a large raven I named George who would help to be my eyes and ears in places I could not be. If that sounds fantastically complicated it should because it was just that—complicated but also quite necessary.*

*I smiled down at Charles, impressed by how he never looked away. Most people, especially those in my presence for the first time, feared me but not Charles. "I don't think I'm nearly wise enough to even try to explain God's intent."*

*"My pa also says that you're the oldest man on the islands, but you don't look that old."*

*"I might be."*

*"How old are you?"*

*"Old enough."*

*"Old enough for what?"*

*"For whatever the islands require of me."*

*"You talk like they're alive or something."*

*"I believe they are."*

*Charles propped his skinny forearms up onto the dock rail and then rested his chin on them. "I think that too," he said very seriously. "They talk to me."*

*My eyes widened. "The islands?"*

*Charles nodded. "Uh-huh. The rocks and the wind and the trees, they all do sometimes."*

*"What do they say to you?"*

*"It's kind of hard to explain." Charles scowled while he concentrated. "They let me know that I'm here for a reason and that I need to be tough and ready to fight because there are things that want to hurt this place."*

"Does any of that scare you?"

"No." Charles pursed his lips. "I don't get scared." He looked up at me. "Do you?"

"Sometimes."

"Really? But you're so big and you're probably really strong too."

"Being scared doesn't mean you're weak."

"It doesn't?"

"No."

"Then what does?"

"Giving up," I answered. "You won't give up will you, Charles?"

The scowl and pursed lips returned as he shook his head. "Never."

I put my hand on his little shoulder and gave it a gentle squeeze. "Good."

"And when I say never, I mean it because I don't lie."

"I believe you."

"You should because it's true."

The conversation paused as we stood side by side looking out at the sea. I could sense the wheels furiously turning inside the unusually contemplative boy's head. "What do you want to be when you grow up?" I asked him.

"You answer my question first and then I'll answer yours."

*I barely stifled a grin when I realized he was instinctively negotiating with the respectful assurance of one much older and more experienced than he actually was. I knew then that Charles Soros would grow up to be a formidable presence on the islands. "Ask your question of me."*

*"My pa calls you Karl, but I've heard others call you Bloodbone. Why is that?"*

*"It's my name from another time in my life."*

*"Were you a monster or something?"*

*"To some I suppose I was."*

*"Does it bother you when people use that name?"*

*I took some time to consider the question. Did it bother me? "No," I eventually replied. "That name is part of who I am because it represents who I once was. We can no more run from our past than we can our future no matter how we might try."*

*"You talk funny. It's kind of hard to understand, but I think I get it."*

*I tipped my head. "Good."*

*"An orca."*

*"Eh?"*

*"An orca whale," Charles said again. "That's what I want to be when I grow up because they're not scared of anything. I saw one coming back on a boat from the mainland with my pa. It was huge. Its fin was bigger than me! Pa says they're the kings of the sea around here so I*

*figure that's what I should be if I'm to protect this place like the islands want me to."*

*"Qwe 'lhol mechen."*

*Charles laughed. "Those aren't real words."*

*"I assure you they are."*

*"What does it mean?"*

*"In my native tongue it roughly translates to, 'family under the waves', which is what my people called the great orcas that inhabit these waters.*

*"Family under the waves, huh?"*

*"That's right."*

*"I like that."*

*"As do I."*

*Charles turned away from the dock railing. "I should get going. I don't want my mother to start to worry."*

*"Keeping mothers happy is very important."*

*"I'm going to call you Karl like my pa does on account you don't seem so scary to me anymore. You know what **does** scare me?"*

*"What?"*

*Charles glanced to his left and then to his right before answering. "Nuns," he whispered. "But do you know what's strange about that?"*

*I shook my head.*

*"They wear the same outfit as an orca whale does. Pretty weird huh?"*

*There have been very few times in my long life when I was caught by surprise by a fit of laughter, but on that warm sunny day standing on the docks of Friday Harbor, laughter had its way with me until tears left tracks on my cheeks. As I watched Charles scamper away up the hill on Spring Street I wondered if his island legacy might even surpass that of John McMillin and Robert Moran. He would likely be just as strong-willed and economically capable, but more importantly I already sensed in him an unyielding devotion to duty, letting me know that when the islands chose Charles they chose wisely. Where once they had the commerce of McMillin and the conservationism of Moran, in Charles Soros the islands would have both.*

*In the land of nuns and orcas it seemed all things were possible.*


"Charles."

Adele looked up to find Ophelia awake, clear-eyed, strong-voiced, and staring intently at something in the corner of the room. She closed the journal and put it down next to the chair.

"Charles," Ophelia repeated. She glanced at Adele. "Do you see him?"

Adele looked into the corner and then shook her head. "No."

"He's right there—such a beautiful man."

Adele looked again. The only thing she saw was shadow.

"He's waiting for me. I knew he would be. Charles wasn't perfect but he was always a man of his word." Ophelia sighed. "Soon," she said with a hint of impatience. "Very soon." Her trembling hand reached out toward something that wasn't there. "My love." She smiled as she sighed again. Then the smile fell away and the hand dropped.

"What is it?" Adele asked. "Do you need something? A glass of water?"

"He has a message for you." Ophelia's voice was already weaker. She moaned softly and her eyes closed. "A warning."

Adele crouched over the side of the bed. "It's okay. You can rest."

Ophelia's eyes flew open. "No, all of you are in terrible danger." She grimaced as her dry, cracked lips drew back against her teeth. "He's the bait."

"Who?"

"Delroy's son."

"Fin?"

Ophelia nodded. "Don't go. To leave the safety of the islands is to die. Please listen. Charles knows things. He always has." Her hand clamped down over Adele's wrist with surprising strength. "Charles wants you to know he's sorry. This should have been taken care of long ago, but Bloodbone talked him out of it and now the beast is preparing for its eventual return as it promised it would."

"What beast?"

"Asav. Vlad. Whatever name it chooses to call itself now." Ophelia's brow furrowed, further deepening the many lines across her forehead. "And don't forget to tell Roland his grandfather is proud of him. It is important he has the required confidence to survive the darkness that is to come."

How Ophelia could possibly know about Adele's recent dream of Charles Soros didn't really matter. She accepted the fact of that knowledge and simply nodded. It was like Bloodbone had said in his journal—in the land of nuns and orcas it seemed all things were possible. "I'll tell him."

"Adele."

"Yes?"

Ophelia started to cry. "The devil is real. He wants to take me. I can feel him tugging at my soul."

"That won't happen."

"No?" Ophelia's tears stopped as quickly as they had started. Her jaw clenched. "No." She turned her head and locked eyes with Adele. "That sonofabitch has no power here."

Ophelia's use of such profanity first shocked Adele and then made her smile. The old nun still had some fight in her yet. "No, he doesn't."

"Charles will protect me. In his own way he always did even when he couldn't protect himself." Ophelia's eyes closed and the back of her head sunk into the pillow behind it. "I'm so tired," she murmured. "So tired and so ready for this to end."

Adele sat in silence as Ophelia fell into a deep sleep within a room that suddenly felt very much like a tomb. She looked up and then over at the shadowy corner where Ophelia was so convinced Charles stood watching over her.

The shadow was no longer there.

# 25.

"That sounds like some dream."

"It was more than a dream."

Roland arched a brow. "How so?"

"Ever since I came to these islands, more specifically ever since I met Bloodbone, I've experienced dreams that are so clear, so real, they're unlike any dreams I ever had before. They're more like visions."

"Hold on," Roland said as he poured more whiskey into Adele's glass where they sat at the large dining table inside of the monastery's great room. It was ten in the evening and they had recently finished a simple meal of soup and sandwiches given to them by the nuns who had since retired to bed. "You're talking real-deal visions?"

Adele nodded. "Your grandfather showed me something so that you would know the message really came from him."

Roland sipped his whiskey and waited.

"You don't believe it's possible?" Adele asked.

"Having conversations with the dead?" Roland frowned. "I don't know. There's a lot going on right now and you reading all the time from that journal—"

"The scar on his forehead."

"My grandfather's forehead?"

"You put it there when you were a boy."

Roland's frown deepened as he leaned back. "How did you know about that?"

"He showed the scar to me and told me it was you who threw the rock that put it there."

"Wow." Roland exhaled loudly as he ran a hand over his stubble-covered face.

"He's proud of you, Roland. He made it clear how important it was for you to know that. Do you believe me?"

"I want to."

"But?"

"Why is he choosing to speak through you? No offense, but why aren't I the one to have that dream or vision or whatever?"

Adele gripped the sides of her glass with both hands. "I don't know."

"But you're absolutely convinced the dream was real?"

"The message of the dream—yes. How else would I know about the scar on his forehead?"

"You wouldn't."

"Exactly."

"And you've dreamt of other people?"

"Over the years."

"Does it scare you?"

"It used to," Adele replied, "but not anymore."

"You also mentioned you wanted to talk to me about Fin."

Adele worried this particular subject might start a fight she would much rather avoid. She stared at the whiskey in her glass and then looked up. "After Ophelia is gone, I plan to go to Ireland to find him."

*"What?"*

"He's missing, Roland. I'm worried he's in trouble."

"Absolutely not."

*Don't,* Adele thought. *Don't try to tell me what I can and can't do. You know how much I hate that.* The last thing she wanted was to argue with Roland while Ophelia was dying in the other room.

"Is your mind made up?"

Adele nodded. "If I don't hear from him beforehand then, yes, I'm going."

"Alone?"

"If I have to. You're welcome to come with me though."

"I can't. The bank is already low-staffed and is barely handling its day-to-day obligations as it is, especially with me spending so much time here. There's no way I can drop everything to take off to Ireland with you right now. I would if I could."

"That's fine, Roland. I'll be okay."

"You don't know that. What if Vlad is using Fin as bait to draw you out? I don't want to argue with you about this, but I also have to say I think it's a terrible idea."

"Duly noted."

"I couldn't handle losing you, Adele."

"You won't."

Roland looked up at the ceiling while rolling his head from side to side. Despite the nap earlier he still looked tired. "This waiting around is really starting to wear me down. I feel terrible for saying that but. . ." His voice trailed off.

Adele placed her hand over his. "It's okay."

"It's like there's hardly anything left of the old Ophelia in that room." He sighed and then poured more whiskey. "I'm getting drunk tonight. I hope you don't mind."

Adele pushed her glass toward him. "I'm right there with you." She cleared her throat. "Something happened at the marina before I came over here."

Roland stopped mid-pour. "Oh?"

"Someone set fire to my boat."

"Seriously? How bad?"

"Cosmetic damage to the outside mostly. I managed to put it out before it spread too far."

"Do you know who did it? Was it that Zuby girl?"

"That's where Lucas is looking first. He should have an update for me by tomorrow."

"People who would do something like that. . ." Roland continued to pour and then set the bottle down hard enough Adele worried it might break. "I bet Tilda is pissed."

"And then some."

"Are you still able to stay in your boat?"

"I'll see when I go back tomorrow. When I left, the smoke smell was pretty bad."

"Use my yacht for as long as you need to." When Adele started to object, Roland raised his hand. "I insist. I'll keep quiet for now about your trip to Ireland as long as you agree to use the yacht. Let me do this one thing for you."

"You do *plenty* for me, Roland." Adele sipped from her glass, enjoying the warm whiskey buzz that was working its way through her.

"So, you agree to camp out on the yacht until your boat is ready to move back into?"

"Sure."

When Roland smiled, his eyes twinkled happily, letting Adele know she wasn't the only one feeling the effects of the whiskey. "Then we have a deal." He raised his glass. "A toast."

"To what?" Adele asked as she raised her own glass.

"To anything and everything that's still good."

The two glasses clinked together. Roland drank from his and then stood. "How about we continue with our drinks under the stars?"

"You want to go outside?"

Roland stepped toward the door. "That way we don't have to worry about being too loud and waking the nuns."

"How loud were you planning on getting?"

Roland looked back at Adele and winked at her. "The night is still young, Ms. Plank. Who knows where the rest of this bottle will take us."

"Uh-oh—you're calling me Ms. Plank. Now I *know* I'm in trouble." Adele followed Roland outside. The evening air had a slightly cold bite to it, which helped to partially clear her head and wake her up. Roland walked toward the tree line and then eased himself into one of four chairs that sat around a stone fire pit. An opening in the tree canopy above them allowed for glimpses of the moon and stars.

"Let's have us a nice sit and talk," Roland said. "The way people did before the world got so busy."

Adele took the chair next to his. "What's on the agenda, Mr. Soros?"

Roland stared into his whiskey glass and then looked up. "Where do you see yourself in the next five years?"

"Here on the islands," Adele quickly answered.

"Will you be the same person then as you are now?"

"Probably not. Should I be?"

"That's not up to me to say. How do you think you'll be different?"

Adele let the whiskey linger on the top of her tongue as she considered the question. "Hopefully wiser and more patient."

Roland leaned forward until a ray of moonlight illuminated his face. "What about us?"

"Oh," Adele said with a shrug, "I'm sure I will have dumped you long before then."

"Yeah?" Roland nudged Adele's shin with his toe. "Why is that?"

"Boredom most likely."

"Boredom?" Roland scratched the back of his head. "Ouch. I never took myself for the boring type."

Adele shrugged again while trying not to smile. "It happens."

Roland refilled both their glasses and then let out an exaggerated sigh. "That's a shame. I really thought we'd make it."

"Feeling pretty confident, were you?"

"Good looks, plenty of money, and charming as hell—why *wouldn't* I be confident?"

"Don't forget humble."

When Roland reached over and rubbed Adele's shoulder it sent an electric shiver down her spine. He chuckled. "That's right—humble."

"What about you?" Adele asked. "Where do you see yourself in five years?"

He glanced up at the night sky and then his head lowered slowly as he locked eyes with her. "With you," he said very seriously. "It'll be us against the world until you put me in the ground."

"Maybe you'll be the one to put *me* in the ground."

Roland shook his head. "No, I'll be gone long before you will."

"Why is that?"

"You know why. I've been sensing it for a while. I wasn't totally sure before, but now I am. You're becoming the new version of Bloodbone, which means you'll have a whole lot more living to do before the last chapter of your story is written. Think of the people who were here on the islands when you first arrived: Decklan and Calista Stone, Tilda, Lucas, me—we all look older now than we did then. But you. . ."

"Me what?"

"You're leaner, certainly tougher, but you hardly look any older. It's like your internal clock is running a lot slower than everyone else's."

An owl's forlorn call carried through the trees. Adele suddenly felt very cold and wished there was a fire to sit around. It was then she better understood the terrible burden of long life that Bloodbone had been suffering under. To watch powerless as those you called friend withered and died over and over again was a slow-moving tragedy uniquely his own—one that now was seemingly being passed on to her. She imagined Roland growing older, weaker, until he was no more, leaving a gaping wound in her life that would never fully heal. *Tilda and Lucas and so many others,* she thought. *Everything important to me now would be taken away. That isn't life—that's a horror.*

"Adele."

"Huh?" she said, startled.

"You're crying."

"Because I'm sad. I like my life as it is. I don't want it to change. I don't want to lose the people I care about." She swallowed hard, battling the sobs that now gathered at the back of her throat that were trying to pour out of her. "I don't want to lose you."

Roland got out of his chair, knelt in front of her, and hugged her tight. "It's you and me, kid—for a long time yet. I promise."

His kindness and understanding only made Adele want to cry even more. She nuzzled his ear and then bit down on the lobe. "Damn your *'in five years'* hypothetical questions."

The owl's lonely serenade continued.

"Let's dance."

Adele leaned back. "There's no music."

Roland held up his phone. "There's a song I want you to hear. I think it pretty much sums up how I feel about my life these days."

"Really?" Adele replied, genuinely intrigued.

"It's called 'Something in the Orange.'" He stood, scrolled through his phone, and then set it on the chair behind him as the sound of a strumming guitar and harmonica started to play. "Since you've met me, I've been a selfish mess at times, but I like to think I'm finally starting to get this life thing figured out."

"Let me know when you do." Adele stood. "Lord knows I could use the help."

"I'll lead."

Adele pressed her cheek into Roland's neck, enjoying the warmth and smell of his skin. "And I'll follow—no matter what." Her arms wrapped around his shoulders while he pulled her hips against his. A lone voice joined the guitar, speaking of dusk light and the weightlessness of true love as they both swayed in time to the music underneath a San Juan canopy of moon and stars.

"Roland."

"Yes?"

"I love you."

He stopped dancing, cradled Adele's face, and silently stared at her while the song continued to play around them. His lips brushed against hers. They kissed briefly before he began to pull away. Adele wrapped her arms tighter around the back of his neck and kept him close, hungry for the kiss to continue. At first his body tensed; then it relaxed, and he kissed her again and again and again.

Adele felt Roland's heart beating madly against her chest.

The song played on.

The dance resumed.

She wished that it would never end.

# 26.

"The request for a dispensation has been denied."

Sister Zhara loomed over the shorter Father Nick. "I'll be contacting the archbishop directly later today to ask that he reconsider."

Father Nick's cheeks reddened. He was clearly unhappy over being challenged by the younger nun. "He won't. The matter is settled. Mother Mary Ophelia's remains will *not* be scattered over water—it is forbidden."

"Ophelia made it very clear to me that is what she wants." Roland stepped forward, his voice even but his narrowed eyes hinting at his just-beneath-the-surface anger toward the priest. "You have no say in the matter."

"I am here representing the Church, Mr. Soros, which means I *very much* have a say."

"Nah." Roland shook his head. "I don't think so."

"With all due respect, Mr. Soros—"

"Shut up," Roland nearly shouted.

Father Nick's myopic eyes widened behind his glasses. "Excuse me?"

"I said shut up—and I mean it. March out of here, get in your helicopter, and go back to Seattle."

"We are talking about Mother Mary Ophelia's eternal salvation. Surely you don't wish to endanger that with this appalling display of selfish immaturity."

Adele stepped in between the two men, sensing how close Roland was to taking a swing at the priest. She figured the hangover he was likely suffering from due to the heavy drinking the night before wasn't helping either. When he started to shoulder past her to get to Father Nick, she gently but firmly pushed him back. "Don't do it," she whispered. "It'll only make things worse."

Roland strained against her hands for a second before relenting. "He has no business being here," he whispered back.

"He'll be leaving soon," Adele replied. "How's your head?"

"I don't have much of a headache, but my stomach is churning pretty bad. You?"

"Thanks to some aspirin the headache I woke up with is almost gone." Adele leaned in closer. "You're still a fun date, Mr. Soros. I really enjoyed the dance last night."

"I will be informing the archbishop of this," Father Nick said as he straightened his shoulders, attempting to look tough but failing miserably. He glared at Sister Zhara. "You would do well not to deviate from the Church's decision regarding this matter."

Sister Zhara stared back at the priest until he looked away. "You do what you must, Father, and I will do the same."

Father Nick clicked his tongue. "Such a disappointment."

"Yes," Sister Zhara replied. "You are."

"How dare you."

"I thought I told you to shut up," Roland said.

"What is wrong with you people?" Father Nick looked like he wanted to spit in Roland's face. "You treat me as if I am the cause of your grandmother's demise. Let me be clear—*I am not*. She instructed you to spread her ashes in the sea. The Church has made it clear that is not allowed. Her remains are to be placed in consecrated ground."

"There is no more consecrated a place than these island waters," Roland replied. "Ophelia's ashes will be spread per her wishes, with or without the Church's approval."

Father Nick wagged a finger at Sister Zhara. "Should you and the other sisters go along with this grievous offense in any way, there will be serious repercussions against you and the monastery."

Zhara remained indifferent to the priest's attempt to assert his authority over her. "As I already told you, Father Nick, you do what you must and I'll do the same."

"What you must do is obey!" Father Nick shouted, red-faced and wide-eyed.

"Father," Zhara said, "I think it best you go."

"That sounds like good advice," Roland added. "You should take it."

The priest puffed out his chest and stared at Zhara, Roland, and then Adele, before turning and leaving the room.

"Thank you," Roland said to Zhara. "I hope sticking up for Ophelia doesn't land you in trouble with your superiors though."

Zhara shrugged. "No worries. Often the right choice isn't the easy one. I'll demand the archbishop hear our side and try to get him to reconsider granting the request for a dispensation."

"And if he doesn't?" Adele asked.

"The nuns here won't do anything to prevent you from carrying out Mother Mary Ophelia's final wishes."

Adele's phone rang. She apologized for the interruption and then stepped outside holding it to her ear. "Good morning, Lucas. Did you locate Zuby?"

"I did. She was staying at the hostel in Friday Harbor. I missed her there by just a few minutes but then intercepted her trying to walk on the ferry to Anacortes."

"Was she the one who set fire to my boat?"

"She's not admitting to anything and the public defender is already pushing for her release."

"How long can you hold her for?"

"I could push for forty-eight hours but I won't because we don't have anything specific on her yet besides speculation based on a prior incident. She'll most likely be allowed to leave the station this afternoon."

"Can I see her?"

"I'm not sure that's a good idea, Adele."

"Why not? I'm the victim of a crime and she's the most likely suspect."

"With the public defender involved we really have to be by the book on this from the outset."

"It's not illegal for me to see her, is it?"

"Not really but I worry it could be construed as a form of intimidation or coercion if you were to meet with her while she's in my custody."

"Then just let me know what time you'll be releasing her."

"Like I said—this afternoon."

"Can you be more specific? I don't want to spend the rest of the day standing outside the station waiting."

"Adele. . ."

"I promise I'm not going to hurt her. I just want a chance to look in her eyes when we're talking to gauge if she's the one who started the fire or not."

"Zuby Jackson gives off a very bad vibe."

"You think she could be violent?"

"Yes, I do. She suffers from the entitled narcissism that is so common to her generation, but with her it's far worse. Frankly I think she might be psychotic and certainly not the kind of person you'd want to confront alone."

"We'll be standing right out in front of the station. I doubt she'd want to start something there."

Lucas sighed into his phone. "Mark my words—if she thinks she can push you into a physical confrontation she will."

"I won't let that happen. I'm not the easily provoked hothead I used to be."

"You're not exactly what I'd call mellow."

"Well, that's good because mellow is boring. Look, I just want to talk to her for a minute. If she tries to escalate the situation, I'll walk away—I promise."

There was a long pause before Lucas spoke next. "Zuby will be released at three o'clock."

"Thanks. I'll be there."

"Please don't have this blow up in my face, Adele."

"I'll be a good girl."

"I'm having a hard time picturing that."

"Hah-hah. Seriously, though, don't worry. I'll come into the station and touch base with you after I speak with her."

"Okay, see you then."

Adele went back into the monastery and explained to Roland she would be leaving for Roche Harbor soon. Her plan was to shower and grab a bite on Roland's yacht and then head into Friday Harbor for the planned run-in with Zuby.

"Thanks for coming over," Roland said. "It was really nice having someone to drink and laugh with last night to take my mind off of what's going on with Ophelia. Whatever you need on the yacht is yours—use it for as long as you want to. I mean that."

"I know you do," Adele said as she brushed the tips of her fingers over the whiskers on Roland's cheek. "You're a good man." She straightened, gripped his sinewy upper arms, and then pulled him close. "I'll be back tomorrow afternoon."

Roland offered to walk her down to the dock next to the ferry terminal, but Adele said that wasn't necessary and that he should stay with Ophelia. She enjoyed the long walk through the trees and past the open fields of Shaw Island that marked the way back to her boat and was then equally grateful to see water conditions that promised a smooth and quick return to Roche Harbor. Once there she did a brief smell test of the inside of her sailboat and found it still reminded her of the spent remains of a recent campfire, though it wasn't as bad as before. After that she walked to the end of the dock, stepped onto Roland's beautiful Burger yacht, input the security code, and then opened the door into the dark teak wood-drenched main salon.

The large leather couch that sat against one of the walls beckoned. Adele plopped down into it, thinking she would rest for just a minute or two before jumping into the shower.

She woke up two hours later.

"Shit," Adele hissed as she sat up and looked around, trying to clear her head. Three o'clock was fast approaching. She crossed the salon, went down the stairs that led to the multiple cabin quarters, and opened the door into the master stateroom. She put Bloodbone's journal on the bedside table and then opened a hanging locker where she found several changes of her clothes that she had left on the yacht after her trip with Roland years earlier up into the pristine waters of Canada's Desolation Sound.

After grabbing some jeans and a T-shirt, Adele started what she intended to be a quick shower, but it turned into a much longer one because of the water pressure that was so much more intense than the barely-better-than-a-dribble version on her sailboat. *I could really get used to this yacht life,* she thought as she tilted her head and let the shower's spray lightly sting her face. Once dried and dressed she located a box of granola bars in the galley and washed one down with a bottle of orange juice from the stainless-steel fridge.

A quick-paced walk took her to her Mini in the Roche Harbor parking lot. She had just over twenty minutes to reach Friday Harbor before three o'clock arrived—plenty of time for someone who had become well-known throughout the island for her record-setting Roche to Friday Harbor driving speeds. When she pulled into a parking spot in front of the Sheriff's Station there was still time to spare.

Adele leaned against the Mini's hood and waited, watching the entrance. At two minutes past three the door opened, and Zuby Jackson walked out staring down at her phone and presumably scrolling through her text messages.

"Hey," Adele said.

Zuby's head snapped up and then she went down the steps while glaring at Adele. "What do you want?"

"How were the accommodations?"

Zuby's clothes were badly wrinkled and her hair multi-colored hair hung dirty and limp over her shiny forehead. "How's your boat?" she sneered back.

"Smoky. I don't suppose you'd know anything about how it got like that would you?"

"The sheriff says someone set it on fire. That's just awful. You sure seem to have a lot of enemies."

"Or just one. Did you do it?"

"If I didn't answer the sheriff's questions, why would I answer yours?"

"Because I'm *not* the sheriff. This isn't a formal interview. It's just the two of us standing outside having a talk."

"Like you wouldn't go to him as soon as I said something and try to frame me regardless."

"If you were the one responsible, I wouldn't be framing you. You might want to look up what the word framing actually means."

Zuby's nostrils flared. "You think you're so smart."

"Admit it—you set fire to my boat."

"I'm not admitting anything and if you keep harassing me, I'm going to file a complaint. I have a lawyer now and everything."

"You have a public defender—big difference."

Zuby started walking past Adele. "Whatever. Just leave me alone."

"You did it. I know you did."

Zuby spun toward Adele, fists clenched and eyes blazing. "Prove it. You don't know shit."

"I know. I might not be able to prove it, but I know."

Zuby leaned in close until Adele could smell her sour breath on her face. "So?"

"Why?" Adele asked.

"Why not?"

"I'm serious," Adele continued. "Why do you hate somebody you don't even know? That boat is my home. I could have been killed."

Zuby leaned back and rolled her eyes. "Whatever."

"Tell me."

"People like you make me sick."

"Sick?" Adele scowled.

Zuby nodded. "Yeah, sick. Everybody thinks you're so special, but you're not. You go around with men like Sheriff Pine and Roland Soros hanging on your every word. Why you and not me? Do you know how many friends and followers I have on my social media pages? It's almost a thousand."

Adele wanted to scream. This was a level of stupidity she wasn't prepared to deal with. "I wouldn't know anything about that because I don't do social media."

"Do you think that makes you better than me? Little Ms. Perfect doesn't do social media, huh? Well, good for you."

"I hate to break it to you, Zuby, but you don't really have nearly a thousand friends. None of that is real. It's all pretend and it's clearly making you miserable."

Zuby bit down on her lower lip as her eyes welled with tears. "You don't know anything." She held up her phone. "I have friends. I have *lots* of friends—a lot more than you."

"Please get that out of my face. That is unless you want me to throw it into the water like Tilda did to your other phone."

"Good luck with that." Zuby looked around. "I don't see any water."

A headache arrived as the levels of stupid somehow managed to get even worse. Adele pushed the phone away.

"Don't touch me!" Zuby bellowed. "Assault! Assault!" She turned toward the Sheriff's Station. "Help! Help!" Up until then her behavior, however mind-numbingly stupid, was about what Adele had expected it would be but then Zuby somehow managed to descend even further into the abyss of moronic madness. She collapsed onto the sidewalk and started to moan loudly, rolling from side to side while holding her hands to her face.

Lucas came outside, saw Zuby's performance, and shook his head. He walked up to her and looked down as she continued to roll and moan. "Ms. Jackson?"

"She hit me," Zuby whimpered.

"Where?" Lucas asked.

"My head."

Lucas gave Adele a quick sideways glance to let her know he wasn't buying it. "If you were hit in the head, why are you covering your face?"

"It was the side of my head, which is basically the side of my face."

"Ms. Jackson, that didn't happen. Sit up."

Zuby lowered her hands and looked up. "What do you mean it didn't happen?"

Lucas pointed up at the red brick county courthouse building. "We have cameras there, there, and there. I saw you speaking to Ms. Plank. She didn't hit you—not even close."

"She didn't?" Zuby sat up. "Are you sure?"

Lucas helped her back onto her feet. "Yes, Ms. Jackson, I'm sure."

"Well, she verbally assaulted me then. Isn't that a crime or something? Shouldn't you be arresting her?"

"No."

Zuby repeatedly clenched and unclenched her fists. "You're an asshole and a dirty cop. I'm just lucky I'm not a minority or you probably would have shot me by now."

Lucas's voice took on a dangerous edge. "Do you want to spend another night in jail?"

"That's *exactly* the kind of threat a dirty cop would make." Zuby put her hands together and held them in front of her. "Go ahead, Sheriff—march me back into your station and strip search me and everything. I know you want to, and I promise not to resist. You are one seriously fine hunk of a man."

"Two seconds ago, you said I was a dirty racist cop."

Zuby giggled. "Nobody's perfect but that body of yours sure is." She swayed her wide hips from side to side. "Do we have a deal? Are you going to lock me up or what?"

*She's real-deal crazy,* Adele thought. *The poor thing needs help.*

Lucas turned toward Adele. "Are you done talking to her?"

"Yeah."

He turned back toward Zuby. "The ferry to Anacortes is about to leave. You should get going if you're going to catch it."

Zuby kept swaying her hips. "Maybe I want to stay." She gave Lucas a big smile. "Maybe *you* want me to stay."

Lucas shook his head. "I don't."

Zuby's smile was replaced by a snarling mask of loathing. "Do you even like women?"

"I can escort you to the ferry terminal myself," Lucas replied, ignoring the taunt.

"No, I'll walk. Now that I know you're a useless fag I won't waste any more time hanging around you."

"Self-obsessed, stupid, *and* homophobic," Adele said. "You really are quite the catch."

Zuby pointed at Adele. "I am NOT homophobic. I volunteered for an LBGTQIA fundraiser last month. If you bothered to check out my social media, you'd know that."

"I noticed you didn't deny being self-obsessed and stupid."

Lucas stepped in between the two women. "Ladies, that's enough. Ms. Jackson, please start making your way to the ferry terminal."

Zuby shrugged. "Fine. I can't wait to get the stink of this island off of me."

Adele and Lucas watched her walking down the sidewalk, face in her phone, oblivious to the world around her.

"If we're lucky she'll do the world a favor and walk right into the water and sink to the bottom," Adele joked.

Lucas didn't quite smile. He hung his head and rubbed his temples. "That young lady needs professional help."

"I was thinking the exact same thing."

"I'm worried we haven't seen the last of her."

"Why is that?"

"Just a hunch."

"Lucas, are you holding out on me?"

"I ran a background check on her."

"And?"

"Nothing came up on her adult record, but she had some juvenile records that were sealed."

"You can't see them?"

"Not without a court order. People like her are often very troubled kids who then become dangerous adults. I know I'm repeating myself here, but you need to stay away from her. Was she the one who set your boat on fire? Most likely. Can I arrest her for it? Not without actual proof. I'm sorry I couldn't get a confession from her. I know how badly you wanted to see her pay for what she did."

"Actually," Adele said, "I don't care so much about that anymore. Not after seeing how pathetic she is. It's like you said— she's in need of some serious help."

"I submitted an alert with the ferry system. If she returns to the islands, they'll give me a heads-up."

"Smart."

Lucas grunted. "We'll see." He sighed. "What do you have on the agenda for the rest of the day?"

"I'll be checking in with Jose at the newspaper office and then heading back to Roche. Roland is letting me stay on his yacht while my boat continues to air out."

"The yacht, huh? That's a nice upgrade."

"Tell me about it."

"Are you still reading Bloodbone's journal?"

"I'll start up again as soon as I get back."

The ferry horn blasted, announcing its departure. Adele hoped that Zuby had made it there on time and was at that very moment pulling away from the dock, never to be seen on the islands again. She knew Lucas was likely wishing for the same thing.

From somewhere in the trees near the courthouse a raven called out. Adele turned to look, thinking it might be George, but nothing was there.

The ferry horn blew once more and then Friday Harbor went quiet.

Adele turned again, feeling like she was being watched. She scanned the trees, but the raven was nowhere to be found.

It was as if it had never been there at all.

# 27.

*"From now on I am to be known as Vlad Vasa."*

*"Vasa, that is your name Asav spelled backwards," I replied as I sat on a stone beneath the ancient madrone tree that overlooked the narrow pebble-strewn East Sound beach close to where my now hidden longhouse was still located. The sun hung low in the sky, its gradual departure painting the sea in shimmering hues of gold and silver.*

*Asav's teeth flashed white in between the dark whiskers of his beard when he smiled. "I do this not to forget who I was but rather to reimagine who I might be."*

*"Why?"*

*"Why not? Are these islands not a place of perpetual new beginnings?"*

*"Or sudden ends."*

*"Don't be so pessimistic, Karl."*

*"You have made enemies here."*

*"That is of little concern when I can still count you as a friend."*

"You have no friends, Asav—only those who know of you and those who don't."

"Is that what your new prodigy Charles Soros tells you?"

"We speak of a great many things, but you are rarely among them."

"I doubt that; Soros despises me."

"Only because you give him so many reasons to."

"His dislike is fueled by jealousy. He fears his own island empire will pale in comparison to the one I intend to build starting with the purchase of the Rosario mansion."

"The Moran Mansion?"

Asav nodded. "That's right. I have been negotiating with the owners for the past few weeks and we are now very close to agreeing to terms. I was hired to help build that place long ago. Why should I now not make it my own?"

The thought of Asav owning such an important island landmark made my stomach churn. "Does Charles know of this intended deal?"

"Not likely. I swore the sellers to secrecy. I don't want Soros meddling and then trying to take for himself what is rightfully mine."

"I cannot allow this."

Asav looked at me stone-faced. "Allow? Who are you to think you can allow me anything? I have been on these islands for as long as you. We go way back, Karl, as far back as when you were the bloodthirsty savage known as Bloodbone." He held up the crystal that hung from his *neck that was so similar to my own. "We share a bond. The islands chose us, and in that time, we have watched other lives come and go while we somehow remain. There cannot be you without me. Search your heart and mind and you'll know this to be true."*

*He was right about that. I had stopped questioning the mysterious joining of Asav's path with my own. The islands had linked us in some way and my lack of understanding regarding how or why did not make it any less so. "Rosario is not to be yours."*

*"I intend to make it my home just as Robert Moran once did and remain there for as long as the islands will allow it."*

*"No," I said firmly. "This cannot be."*

*"It will be, friend, and there is nothing you or anyone else can do to stop it, including that pompous, preening little ass of a man Charles Soros."*

*"You should not be so quick to make an enemy of one so formidable as him."*

*"Formidable?" Asav snorted. "Soros is nothing to me."* *He grinned like a clever child who thought he had gotten away with stealing cookies from the jar. "I know of his plans for a bank so that he can then dominate the economy of our islands—a bank built upon the ill-gotten gains his family accumulated during Prohibition."*

*"Asav—"*

*"My name is Vlad," Asav said, nearly shouting. "Vlad Vasa."*

*"Going by a different name won't change the fact that you won't be allowed to purchase the Rosario mansion."*

*"Who will stop me? You?" Asav wagged a finger. "We both know that is truly what isn't allowed—personal intervention. You cannot stop me just as I cannot stop you. Those are the islands' rules—the only rules that I must follow."*

*Again, Asav was right. Regardless of the lack of a definitive answer as to how or why, neither of us was allowed to directly alter the future of the islands. That had to be done via intermediaries such as George Pickett, Robert Moran, John McMillin, Samantha Ashland, and, more recently, Charles Soros. For me to do any harm to Asav would be to do harm to myself, and vise-versa. Why the islands had made it so all those years ago I did not know.*

*It was infuriating.*

*"I have a proposition," I said.*

*"For me?" Asav replied in a high-pitched, mocking tone.*

*"Yes."*

*"Go on."*

*"That you be allowed to join our Truthing Tree group. This would give you access moving forward into the most critical decisions impacting the islands."*

*"Soros would never allow it."*

*"I believe he will."*

Asav snatched up a pebble, tossed it into the water, and then shook his head. "He's too threatened by me."

"Give me just a little time to discuss it with him before proceeding further on the purchase of Rosario."

"You have one week," Asav replied.

I nodded. "Thank you."

Asav's grin was almost manic as it etched across his face. "Your proposal will drive Soros mad. That alone is worth a brief wait."

"I do this for the good of the islands, not to further your petty personal war against Charles Soros."

"And make sure he knows to call me Mr. Vasa."

I sighed. "I will try."

Asav slapped me on the shoulder. "Very good. I shall be going now."

"Where?"

"None of your business, friend. On these islands I answer to no one—not even you." Asav flinched when an unusually large raven landed on a branch near him. "Is that thing your pet or what? I see it around you all the time these days."

"That is George," I answered.

"George the raven, huh? I swear it's been spying on me. It seems no matter what island I happen to be on he makes a brief appearance before flying off."

"He is an especially inquisitive bird."

*Asav's coal-black eyes narrowed. "Inquisitive? I'd call it nosey."*

*"Perhaps."*

*"It better stay out of my way." Asav bent down and picked up a stone. "Or find its wing broken and its head smashed in." He raised his hand. George hopped onto another branch further away. I didn't mean to grab hold of Asav's wrist as hard as I did, but seeing him acting as if he might throw the stone at George, my instincts took over. Asav cried out, dropping the rock and falling to a knee. "I wasn't going to hurt him," he gasped. "It was just a bit of pretend is all."*

*I released him and then helped him up. "My apologies."*

*Asav rubbed his wrist. "You damn near broke it."*

*George's entire body shook as he cackled laughter before flying off.*

*"A giant Indian and his pet raven." Asav chuckled. "What an interesting world these islands are." The knife he was suddenly waving in his other hand gave off a metallic flash in front of my face. "I'd have cut you deep before allowing you to harm me," he said. "Don't you doubt it."*

*"We both know that is not allowed."*

*Asav jammed the blade into the leather sheath that hung against his hip. "I know we both feel that's the unspoken rule—feel it in our bones, but I'd be lying if I said I wasn't curious to know what would **really** happen if I decided to slit your throat and watch you bleed out at my feet."*

*"The punishment delivered to you by the islands would likely be both swift and irrevocable."*

*Asav's hand hovered over the hilt of his knife. "Would it?"*

*"Yes," I replied. "Without a doubt."*

*Asav shrugged. "Not that it matters. I would never do so much harm to such a good friend as you, Karl." He turned and started to walk away. "Don't forget to tell Soros my new name." He laughed. "I only wish I could be there to hear him rage when you do."*

The tide was coming in, covering what little remained of the beach. I looked out across the water toward neighboring San Juan Island where Charles Soros resided at his hillside Friday Harbor home.

It was time to pay him a visit.

———

*"Are you mad?" Charles bellowed. "Absolutely not!" He smashed a cigarette out in the ashtray on his study desk and then promptly lit another one. "How many times must I tell you that scoundrel is a perpetual threat to the safety of this place?" His voice lowered to a near whisper. "Things are in motion, Karl—important things. I might very well be hosting a man who will be this nation's next president and I don't want that damn Russian within a thousand miles of him."*

*"What man is this?" I asked.*

"His name is Kennedy," Charles replied, "John Kennedy." He turned toward the sound of knocking on the other side of his closed study door. "Yes?"

The door opened and in walked Donatella Soros. Charles had married her two years earlier. She was tall and thin with delicate features, a slightly downturned nose, and short blonde hair with the bangs combed down straight over her forehead just above a pair of especially expressive blue eyes. A white wool Chanel suit complimented her lean, aristocratic figure. "I wondered if I might bring you and your guest something to drink?" she said. "Iced tea perhaps?"

Charles took a long drag from his cigarette and then unleashed tendrils of smoke out through his nose that swirled around his head. "We're fine. Thank you."

"Mrs. Soros," I said with a nod.

"Mr. Bloodbone," she replied before looking over at her husband. "Then I will leave you men to your island schemes." The door closed behind her with a click.

"Don't let the cool exterior fool you," Charles said. "She's excited to the point of hysterics over the possible visit by Mr. and Mrs. Kennedy. Apparently, Jacqueline Kennedy has become something of a sensation among the East Coast elites. She's a pretty thing, I'll give her that, and represents the kind of social status Donatella wants so badly to be a part of."

"What do you hope to achieve from meeting with this Mr. Kennedy?"

*"Access to power and influence, Karl. That's it. Unlike Donatella I care little for status. What I really want, what I know we both want, is control of our islands. Having the ear of a president will help us to achieve that. I say keep the federal government as far away from here as possible. Let us continue to be a world unto ourselves. Kennedy, as well as my ongoing friendship with Senator Jackson, can help to make that happen, but allowing someone like Asav to be a part of that is madness. He will only threaten everything I've worked so hard to achieve."*

*"He intends to purchase the Moran Mansion and its accompanying property at Rosario."*

*Charles's cigarette nearly fell from his mouth. "Tell me that's an attempt at a very bad joke."*

*"It's true."*

*"My God." Charles put his back to me and stared out through the window at the waters of Friday Harbor below. "There is simply no way I can allow such a thing to happen."*

*"He is willing to reconsider under one condition."*

*"Go on."*

*"As I suggested to you earlier—we allow him to be part of our Truthing Tree group."*

*Charles laughed. "Now I know you **are** joking."*

*"If you refuse then he will proceed with the purchase."*

*"Asav will never own Rosario." Charles turned around. "Never—do you understand?"*

"Then we invite him to join the group."

"And give him direct access to our plans—access he will no doubt use to profit from at our expense? Karl, please, I beg you to reconsider."

"By keeping him close we can better control him."

"There is no controlling that animal disguised as a man. He should have been run off long ago. He has been scheming and taking from islanders for as long as I can remember. Why have you put up with his presence here for so long?"

"It's complicated."

Charles smashed out another cigarette as he gave me a sideways glance. "Complicated, eh? Glutton for punishment is more like it."

"The islands, for reasons I don't understand, chose Asav the same as they chose me."

"Don't waste your breath telling me about your magical horseshit beliefs. I'm not interested. I deal in reality and the reality regarding Asav is that he's an unrepentant sonofabitch."

"Would you have him be the new owner of the Moran Mansion then?"

Charles slapped the top of his desk. "Hell no!"

"Then we invite him to join—"

"The Truthing Tree group. I heard you the first time and my answer remains the same—NO."

"It has to be one or the other, Charles."

"I'm not someone who easily accepts being backed into a corner."

"It's not a corner but a solution. Asav is willing to drop his plans to purchase Rosario in exchange for a seat at the decision-making table."

"Exactly, that scum wants a seat at **my table** and you seem oddly motivated to give it to him."

"We do this for the good of the islands. I don't wish to see him as the new owner of Rosario any more than you do."

"How in the hell could he possibly afford to buy the mansion?"

"His long life has afforded him ample time to accumulate wealth."

"By ill-gotten gains no doubt. Theft, perhaps even murder, who knows?"

I straightened to my full height and looked down at the young magnate. "I have plenty to account for myself."

Charles grunted. "I bet you do."

"And your own family is not without sin."

"What? The bootlegging my father did? Hell, that was a stupid law that was begging to be ignored."

"I need your answer, Charles."

"There's that corner you're backing me into again."

I waited.

*"Fine."* Charles sighed. *"He can attend our Truthing Tree meetings for now so long as he forgets this nonsense about purchasing Rosario."* He pointed at me. *"You make that very clear to him."*

*"Of course."*

*"You're a man of your word, Karl, so this falls entirely on those big shoulders of yours because Asav is anything but trustworthy."*

*"There is just one more thing."*

*Charles grimaced. "What?"*

*"He is to be known as Vlad Vasa from now on."*

*"Asav?"*

*"Yes."*

*"Wants to be called Vlad Vasa?"*

*"Correct."*

*"Why in the hell does he want that?"*

*I shrugged. "It seems he believes it represents some kind of new beginning for him."*

*"It's idiotic is what it is."*

*"It's what he wants."*

*"And there you are again so willing to give him what he wants."* Charles rolled his eyes. *"Vlad Vasa it is. I don't care. There are so many more important things I have to deal with right now."*

*"Like meeting with a future president."*

*"Exactly." Charles went to the window and looked out it again. "I'm going over to Shaw Island this afternoon to meet with some nuns who want to build a monastery there." He turned around. "Do you know much about them?"*

*"No. Why do you wish to meet them?"*

*"I figured they could use a donation and I could use the tax write-off."*

*"A simple matter of commerce then?"*

*"Sure, but also an opportunity to help build something that I believe will add value to the islands. A group of nuns living out in the wilderness of Shaw Island—it just somehow seems appropriate to this place don't you think?"*

*"I suppose."*

*Charles smiled, which was something he didn't do often. He also stuck out his hand. "Regarding Asav, I mean Vlad, it's a deal then." We shook. He reached up and slapped me on the shoulder. "You're not a bad negotiator, Karl. I respect that. Everything in life is a negotiation."*

*"Even love?"*

*"Most definitely love, not that I would know much about that."*

*It was an odd reply given Charles was so recently married. I ignored the urge to ask him further about it, grateful for having secured his agreement to include Asav in our Truthing Tree group, which in turn would keep him from pursuing ownership of Rosario. Charles walked me to the door. Once outside I came upon Donatella who sat on a bench reading a book on their front porch.*

*"Leaving so soon, Mr. Bloodbone?" she said.*

*"Our business is concluded."*

*Donatella closed her book and placed it next to her. "Tell me something." She stood. "Have you ever felt like you were waiting for your real life to begin?"*

*I struggled to answer.*

*She smiled. "I didn't mean to make you uncomfortable."*

*"It's not that," I said. "I'm not entirely sure I understand the meaning."*

*"Of the question? Oh, it's just that sometimes I can feel the future tugging at me and I grow impatient to find out what it wants. Charles will always have his work, his ambition, his hunger for more, but I can't help but wonder what my role in all of that will be. Perhaps it is to be no role at all."*

*"You're here in this place for a reason, Mrs. Soros."*

*"You say that with such confidence."*

*"Because I know what I know."*

*"I envy your certainty." She smiled again. "There are those who consider me to be a cold, unfeeling woman. Given that you know what you know, as you say, are they right to think that?"*

*"No."*

*Donatella looked me up and down. "I tend to agree." She straightened her shoulders and pulled her jacket tight. "You're good for Charles because you help to keep him from being swallowed up entirely by his ambitions." I sensed she was saying more than the literal meaning of her words and wondered if her marriage was already facing strong headwinds. "Please continue to help him, Mr. Bloodbone. You are among the very few whose approval he values." She crossed the porch, reached up, and placed her hand behind my neck. After I bent down, she kissed me on the cheek. "You might very well be the most honorable among us all."*

*I stepped off the porch in a daze, hardly aware of where my feet were taking me next. It had been so long since I had experienced such feelings for another.*

*"Safe travels, Mr. Bloodbone."*

*I kept walking, too confused to turn around and too afraid to understand why.*

Adele closed the journal, set it down, and picked up her glass. She could see the midnight stars through the salon windows of Roland's yacht. The bottle of wine that sat on the coffee table in front of her was nearly empty. The first glass had been enjoyed while soaking in the tub. The next few were consumed while reading and snacking on some chips. The time had passed so quickly Adele could hardly believe it was already so late. She got up, laughing a little when her wine-drenched head made her stumble to the side.

*"Vasa, that is your name Asav spelled backwards,"* I replied as I sat on a stone beneath the ancient madrone tree that overlooked the narrow pebble-strewn East Sound beach close to where my now hidden longhouse was still located. The sun hung low in the sky, its departure painting the sea in shimmering hues of gold and silver.*

With a phrase repeating in her head, Adele turned and stared down at the Book of Bloodbone. The half-full glass of wine was placed next to the bottle.

*...the narrow pebble-strewn East Sound beach close to where my now hidden longhouse was still located.*

Adele's heart beat faster. She picked up the journal and opened it to the page where those words were found. "My now hidden longhouse was still located," she whispered slowly while her mind raced to process and fully understand the just-discovered clue.

*That's where he's been all this time—hiding in plain sight.*

# 28.

The sun had been up for just over an hour when Adele steered her boat toward the small Eastsound guest dock. Her excitement over finally finding Bloodbone had kept her up for much of the night, but two cups of strong early morning coffee were enough to get her moving and back out onto the water. The shoreline was quiet and still and draped in shadow due to the heavy, slow-moving clouds overhead that blocked out the sun and threatened rain at any moment.

*There's the madrone tree,* Adele thought. It was where she had met with Bloodbone many times before. After securing her boat to the dock she walked a narrow dirt path that took her to the clearing. At the back of that clearing was an unusually thick cluster of trees and underbrush and at the center of that cluster was a slightly darker space in front of which the grass had been repeatedly trampled down, forming the beginning of what she hoped was a trail that she had failed to notice before. The damp grass made the toes of her shoes wet as she strode across the clearing and then stood in front of the trees and underbrush.

*I was right. That is definitely a trail, but apparently, it's a trail to nowhere.*

The trampled grass path disappeared into a natural wall of brush and tree limbs. Adele reached up and pulled one of the limbs closer to her. *The leaves have fallen off in just this one spot,* she thought. *Not fallen off—rubbed away by someone or something coming and going.* She pushed her way further into the underbrush, walking slowly, carefully, while noting how some of the smaller limbs were broken in places. Ten feet turned to twenty and then forty. Adele was about to give up and turn around when she glimpsed a change in color behind a dried-out pile of cedar branches. She looked around and saw no sign of any nearby cedar trees. *Which means those branches were gathered up and placed here to hide something.*

Rain began to fall. Adele looked up and waited to see if any managed to seep through the trees and brush. None did. The ground around her remained dry. She crouched in front of the mass of cedar branches and discovered it had been bound together by twine.

*Is that it?*

Adele pulled away the stack of limbs and then stood in front of an ancient door made of partially rotted wood planks marked heavily by the passage of time. "Hello?" she said, her voice cracking. She cleared her throat and called out again, but no one answered.

The door was heavy, requiring that Adele use her shoulder to push it open. A rush of air from inside the structure blew the hair away from her forehead. She stood just inside the threshold and waited for her eyes to adjust to the darkness. The space was as much as twenty feet wide and at least four times as long. Her nostrils flared as she inhaled the smell of ash from a recent fire. She looked down to find her crystal pulsing brightly against her chest, allowing her to see further into the longhouse.

"Is anyone here?"

Again, no answer.

Adele stepped further into the gloom.

"Bloodbone—it's me."

The longhouse was empty. The earthen floor and wood walls were dry and dusty. Adele crept forward, guided by the crystal's light, until she came to a bed of blankets and firs piled next to a small fire pit. She knelt low and put her hand over the ashes, detecting a hint of warmth, meaning that a fire had likely been burning there as recently as yesterday.

Directly above the fire pit was a small opening in the roof where a narrow cylinder of daylight shined down onto Adele's face. She scooped up some dirt, closed her eyes and felt it fall between her fingers. Her stomach churned and sweat broke out over her face. *I think I'm going to be sick.* She gulped air, got down on all fours, and waited for the waves of dizziness to pass. *Bloodbone, where are you?*

"He is where he needs to be in this moment."

Adele gasped as she sat up and then spun around in the direction of the voice. The longhouse door closed and a figure emerged from the surrounding darkness. He was old, bent, and leaned heavily on a walking stick. Strands of long white hair hung nearly to his waist. His eyes sparked like midnight emeralds as he drew closer. "Greetings, child."

"Who are you?"

The old man gave Adele a toothless grin. "You already know that." He continued to shuffle forward. "Tell me who I am."

"Old Raven."

He nodded. "Yes."

"You're dead. They buried you long ago down at the beach. Bloodbone said so in his journal."

"I remember."

"That means you're not really here. This is another dream or vision."

"Perhaps."

"What do you want?"

"If this is your dream or your vision, then you should be asking what it is that *you* want."

"I want answers. I want to know where Bloodbone is."

Old Raven's eyes darted from side to side. "He doesn't appear to be here."

"Do you know where he is?"

"He is where he needs to be—"

"In this moment. I got it."

"Bloodbone's friend is very near death."

"If you're talking about Ophelia, then yes, she is."

"This saddens him greatly." Old Raven bowed his head and his voice lowered. "To have to endure the loss of so many is perhaps the greatest burden of our path."

"You speak of your path and his path, but that doesn't mean any of this will be *my* path."

"But you have been chosen. There is no refusing it now. You are me and him and us."

"I didn't say I was refusing anything, but at the same time, this thing, the protector of the islands or whatever, isn't going to replace who I am. I won't let it. Whatever changes are coming I'll be doing it my way."

"Such a strong-willed little thing you are. I can see why Bloodbone has placed so much trust in you."

"You're the one who first gave him my name, among others, remember? I read that in his journal as well."

"The islands spoke those names to me." Old Raven held out a trembling hand. "Help me to sit in front of the fire, child." Adele guided him to the fire pit and then let him down slowly, his bones cracking like ice in spring. He looked up at her. "Thank you. It has been so long since I last enjoyed the warmth of this place."

Adele considered pointing out that the fire had long gone out but decided against it when she saw Old Raven rubbing his hands together and then holding them up as if flames crackled in front of him. She thought that perhaps somehow the memory of that fire was enough for him.

"So, you are reading from the Book of Bloodbone are you?"

"I am," Adele answered. "I believe he wanted me to find it."

Old Raven tilted his head back. "I believe you're right. There are very few accidents when it comes to him but his time, like mine before him, is coming to an end while your own time is now underway."

"Where is he?"

"Bloodbone?" Old Raven shrugged. "As I said—where he is meant to be."

"He was here."

"Here, there, then, now, and everywhere in between."

"How did you know about Ophelia?"

"The islands have whispered of her demise."

"He should be here to tell her goodbye."

"If Bloodbone wished for you to find him then you would have by now. He knows the moment to come and is likely waiting for its arrival. There are plans within plans, child. My advice to you is simple—trust the plan."

"What do you know of Vlad Vasa?"

Old Raven's expression soured. "You speak of the Russian trapper called Asav. I remember him and all those like him. They came to our lands, and we cared for them, showed them our ways, only to have them return to their own people, bring more of them back, and then take and take and take until there was nothing more for us to give."

"Why did Bloodbone allow him to stay on the islands for so long?"

"I cannot speak to another's motivations. What was done is done."

"Asav intends to return."

Old Raven picked up a stick and used the end of it to poke at the ashes in the fire pit. Adele looked away for a moment. When she turned her head back, she saw flames flickering within the pit, illuminating Old Raven's deeply weathered face from below. "Yes, Asav is coming," he said, "and he is likely to bring death with him."

"He has to be stopped."

"It will be up to you to do so—not Bloodbone. This is your time now."

Adele wiped the sweat from her forehead with the back of her hand. "Why me?"

Old Raven chuckled as he continued to poke at the fire. "That's always the lasting question, isn't it? No matter how great or small the one asking it, we all look to God and ask, "Why me?"'

"I'd really like to know the answer."

"Wouldn't we all, but it is within the absence of total understanding where we find the mystery that binds us: the earth to the sky, land to the sea, fire to water, light to darkness—"

"And good to evil," Adele said.

Old Raven nodded. "Indeed."

A single ember broke from the fire and rose up from the pit, carried upon a wave of swirling smoke. Adele watched its glowing retreat until it reached the opening in the ceiling and was then extinguished by a flash of shadow that moved across that same opening, blocking out the sky for just a second.

Adele lowered her head slowly, realizing she was once again alone in the longhouse. Old Raven was gone and the fire no longer burned.

The door to the longhouse opened and another man walked in, giving Adele a reassuring smile as he did so. He was about six-foot, young, clean-shaved, with hazel-green eyes that were nearly the same color as the tie he wore. He stopped in front of the fire pit and then motioned toward the space where Old Raven had been sitting.

"May I?"

Adele nodded, more curious than concerned over the stranger's sudden arrival. He smiled again, sat down, and then brushed some of the dust off of the tops of his dark leather shoes. "Who are you?" she asked.

The man picked up the same stick Old Raven had used to poke at the ashes in the fire pit. "A friend." His voice was pleasant enough but also hinted at a familiarity with things of a more violent nature. When he adjusted the wool cap on his head, tilting it further to the side, Adele caught a whiff of Vetiver aftershave, an earthy dry grass and tobacco scent familiar to her, having first smelled it on her grandfather when she was very young.

"Do I know you?"

"The world knew me once as Dylan—Dylan Bowman."

A shiver ran down Adele's spine. "The same Dylan Bowman who was part of a family of bootleggers from the mainland who knew Tilda's great aunt, Samantha Ashland?"

*"Knew her?"* Dylan replied. "I loved her—with all my heart."

"You died for her."

"Yes."

"A sacrifice for her and for the islands."

"To be fair, at the time I was just doing it for her. I didn't understand how the islands were involved. That was Bloodbone's doing."

"Can you please tell me where he is?"

Dylan jammed the stick into the middle of the fire pit and left it there. "He's a tough one to pin down, isn't he?"

"The islands are in danger."

"He knows."

"I need his help. I can't do this alone."

Dylan sat straight, folded his arms over his chest, and stared into Adele's eyes. "He wants you to understand that at the turning of the tide he'll be there to do what must be done. You must believe this. Don't lose faith, Adele. Don't ever lose faith."

"The turning of the tide? I don't understand."

"You will." Dylan got up and then straightened his suit. "I must be going now."

"Where?"

"Here, there, then, now, and everywhere in between."

"That's exactly what Old Raven said."

"He's rather clever, that one." Dylan started walking toward the door.

Adele wanted to get up and follow but her body refused. "George!" she cried out.

Dylan stopped, turned around, and then smiled as he tipped his cap at her. "Adele."

And then he was gone.

---

Adele lay on the ground inside of the longhouse staring up at the opening in the roof. She wasn't sure how much time had passed. The dizziness and nausea that had gripped her earlier were now almost gone. *Old Raven and Dylan Bowman—was any of that real?* she wondered. *Did it actually happen or was I imagining it all?*

She strained to rise but for some reason remained unable to move anything other than her arms. From somewhere outside came the call of a raven. Adele watched another shadow pass over the opening above her and then saw something slowly falling into the longhouse. It flittered and spun, inching closer and closer toward her outstretched hand. She watched and waited. Each second that passed felt like hours. Down it came, a thing almost as light as air until finally it rested in her palm. Only then was she allowed to sit up. She brought her hand toward her face, looked down, and saw a single black feather that was so dark it seemed to almost glow.

*It is within the absence of total understanding where we find the mystery that binds us,* Adele thought, recalling Old Raven's real or imagined words to her. *The earth to the sky, land to the sea, fire to water, light to darkness—and good to evil.*

She smiled faintly as she closed her hand around the feather.

It smelled of Vetiver aftershave.

# 29.

Adele struggled to get back to Roche safely due to an unusually powerful summer storm sweeping across the islands that afternoon. Winds on the water reached forty knots, creating confused seas and a churning three-foot chop. She had never been more grateful for her boat's commercial-rated aluminum hull as she fought to track straight while being pummeled by waves repeatedly smacking up against her port side. Twice she buried the bow, sending a column of seawater slamming into the windshield as the wipers worked furiously to clear the glass.

What normally would have been a short run took over an hour of white-knuckled determination, especially when she reached the especially rough waters of Spieden Channel where the fast-moving northern currents did battle with the equally powerful currents coming from the south. Adele would accelerate in the trough, slow down when she reached the crest, and then accelerate again before reaching the next big wave as she fought to keep the vessel pointed toward home.

Grateful to finally be in the protected waters of Roche Harbor, Adele tied off at the dock and sprinted to Roland's yacht with her head down in an effort to keep her face and eyes from being stung by the sideways rain. Once inside the yacht she shed her soaked clothes, threw them in the dryer, and then put on a soft cotton bathrobe with Roland's initials **RS** monogrammed in gold across the lapel.

The next twenty minutes were spent on the phone with Jose about the next issue of the newspaper. He indicated several more people had contacted him regarding the rumor Mother Mary Ophelia was dead or dying. He continued to inform them that the newspaper had nothing to report at this time, but an official statement would likely be forthcoming soon. Adele told him to keep space available for the obituary, which she would be writing when the time came to do so. She then texted both Roland and Lucas that she was safely back at Roche. Roland messaged that Ophelia remained in a coma-like state. A physician had checked in on her earlier that day and indicated she was likely to pass within the next forty-eight hours. Adele promised to return to the monastery soon, though, she wasn't yet sure exactly when.

After that she settled into the couch and continued reading from Bloodbone's journal, going from the early years of Charles Soros's growing island empire to the introduction of a young Doctor Edmund Pine, Lucas's father, into the Truthing Tree group. Soon after, Delroy Hicks, Fin's father, also became a fixture of Bloodbone's world. The addition of both men served to further undermine Asav's influence, which Adele was certain had been Bloodbone's intention all along.

Adele eventually came to a moment in the journal she knew was critical to the era the islands were about to enter then—a private meeting between Bloodbone and Charles Soros that involved the fate of a young and beautiful nun named Ophelia. As the wind and rain shook the windows of Roland's yacht, she allowed Bloodbone's words to pull her back in time:

*"She's pregnant."*

*The sudden declaration left me sitting inside the rich teak wood interior of Charles's yacht silently contemplating how I should respond to such a delicate subject.*

*"Say something," he barked.*

*I sighed. "Are you certain the child is yours?"*

*Charles poured himself a whiskey. "Of course I'm sure— she's a goddamn nun." He turned and faced me, holding the drink in one hand while stuffing his other hand into the front pocket of his slacks. "What do I do?"*

*"You're a married man, Charles."*

*"I didn't invite you here to state the obvious to me, Karl. I'm in need of some advice."*

*"Any advice I give you would just as likely be advice you chose not to follow."*

*Charles sipped his whiskey, gave me a hard look, and then shook his head. "I love her."*

*"The nun?"*

*"Yes."*

*"What about your wife, Donatella?"*

*"I care for her as well."*

*"But you don't love her?"*

*"It's different. I respect her."*

*"You created life with another woman. How is that respecting Donatella?"*

*Charles stared out through a window at the darkness surrounding the Roche Harbor resort. His shoulders slumped. He was in that moment as confused, weak, and uncertain as I had ever seen him. "You don't understand."*

*I thought of that recent and all too brief kiss given to me on the cheek by Donatella and how it had awakened in me something I had believed was long dead. Despite the many years of my life there remained a whisper of my prior savage inclinations that had once ravaged villages and taken whatever I desired, including those things of a more carnal nature. Feeling Donatella's lips on my skin that day, I had very much desired to have her fully and completely. Those were my personal needs, though, needs that were inconsequential when compared to the needs of the islands and so I buried those feelings deep where they could do no harm.*

*"I understand more than you might think, Charles."*

*"Oh?" Charles tipped his glass back, emptying what remained in a single gulp. "Is that right?" He refilled the glass again and then offered me some, which I declined.*

*"Does Ophelia intend to have the child?"*

*Charles's eyes widened. "Are you suggesting she have an abortion?"*

*"I'm not suggesting anything. I was merely asking—"*

*"That's not an option."*

*"What of her position in the Church?"*

"Who the hell knows what that self-righteous rabble will say about any of this? It's not like it hasn't happened before. Ophelia loves being a nun. It's her life's calling."

"Does Donatella know?"

"Not yet."

"When will you tell her?"

"Soon, but I fear what she'll do—lawyer up quick most likely. Everything I've built here on the islands will be at risk, including the bank that is to be the foundation for the islands' independent economic future." Charles grimaced. "The thing of it is, as much as this could end up costing me, I don't think I would have done it differently. When I'm around Ophelia, there's something about her that I can't refuse. She's the flame and I'm the moth. I know I'll be burned, but I can't help myself and I'm certain she feels the same about me."

"We cannot allow your indiscretions to endanger the islands, Charles."

"Please, just tell me what you think I should do."

"Will you listen? Will you follow the advice I give?"

Charles stood in front of me thinking it over. It took longer than I would have liked, but eventually he nodded. "Yes."

"Ophelia will give up the child to be raised by Donatella and you."

"Geez, I don't know. . ."

"This is how it must be to keep your marriage intact. Donatella would not turn her back on a child."

"I'm not so sure about that."

"But I am. Your task in the coming days is to get Ophelia to agree."

"To have her child raised by another woman? That's a mighty big ask."

"There is no other way. It will allow her to continue as a nun while the child is afforded the full privileges of growing up a Soros on the islands."

"But what if Ophelia wants to be part of the child's life?" Charles asked. "I mean why wouldn't she?"

"Do you believe Donatella would allow that?"

"No. She wouldn't want anyone else to know the truth."

"Then that is our answer."

"Ophelia would give birth and then be forced to watch in secret from a distance as her child grows up knowing nothing about his biological mother." Charles closed his eyes and hung his head. "She's going to feel like I'm punishing her, but she's done nothing wrong except allow me to love her."

"Charles, Ophelia is a grown woman, a nun, who should have known better than to allow her physical needs to overcome good sense."

"Don't talk about her like that." Charles pointed up at my chest. "Not to me. Not ever. I told you that I love her and I meant it."

"I believe you do, but this must be the way forward."

"Truth be told, I'd rather go back."

"Unfortunately, we can't do that."

"Not even you?"

"Not even me."

"I'll speak to Donatella first," Charles said. "Once I get her to agree I'll go over it all with Ophelia."

"If you wish, I can speak to Father Ifan Thomas about the situation. He isn't directly affiliated with the new monastery but I'm sure he would be willing to help keep Ophelia's condition a private matter within the Church and ensure she is allowed to maintain her position there after giving birth."

"Isn't he the young priest who oversaw the remodel of the little church here in Roche Harbor?"

"He is."

"And why do you think he'd be willing to help Ophelia?"

"Father Thomas is a good man, Charles. He'll do what he can."

"Which means the rest of this is up to me."

"And Ophelia," I added.

Charles finished his drink. "Yes, Ophelia." He set the glass down. "I'm not going to lie—there's a part of me that doesn't care if I lose everything for the chance to be with her."

"That choice could truly leave you with nothing and the damage to the islands—"

*"Would be significant." Charles nodded. "I get it. I don't like it, but I understand what you're saying." He poured himself yet more whiskey even as a dull alcohol sheen had settled over his normally sharp, penetrating eyes. "Tell me something—do you miss it?"*

*"Miss what?" I replied.*

*Charles straightened and then lifted his glass high. "Life. You're a man, right? The biggest damn man I ever saw. This burden you accepted to be the protector of the islands, it has come at the expense of living a normal life— a wife, children, grandchildren, all that shit. There has to be a part of you that wonders how different, how better, it might have been had you chosen to walk a more normal path."*

*"Is that what you have done, Charles, walked a more normal path? You are married but fathered a child with a woman who is not your wife—a woman who also happens to be a nun. You are the son of a bootlegger who now counts senators and presidents among your acquaintances. That hardly sounds like one who has chosen a more normal path."*

*"Point taken." Charles stared into his glass at something only he could see. "But still, to have to watch everyone you know grow old and die around you, I don't think I could do it." He looked up. "I stand here still a relatively young man in the prime of life, but the years will continue to pass; I will age, tire, weaken, and then eventually expire while you remain much like you are now, left alone in a world that resembles so little of the world you came from."*

*His words struck me hard as they spoke to a pain I had long felt but had grown accustomed to ignoring. Charles was right. The burden of my choice weighed more heavily with each passing year, increasing the sense of displacement I had long felt. I thought again of Donatella's kiss, wondering what it would be like to spend a lifetime with such a woman, while also knowing that was impossible.*

*"Or is it?"*

*Charles frowned. "Eh?"*

*I hadn't meant to ask the question out loud. "Nothing," I murmured. "Just lost in my own thoughts."*

*Little was said between us after that. Charles drank. I sulked. More time passed. I eventually left after he assured me that he would speak with Donatella the following day about the plan to raise Ophelia's child as her own. He was far less confident than I regarding the potential for Donatella to agree but I knew her heart. Beyond the hard exterior was a woman who cared deeply for the well-being of others. She would not deny a child the chance to grow up safe and cared for. Ophelia was another matter. My certainty that she would agree to the plan was precarious at best, but I hoped having Father Thomas working behind the scenes to ensure she would be allowed to remain a nun at the monastery would be enough to convince her.*

*None of this would be easy on any involved. I walked from Charles's yacht that night enveloped in darkness. The future was as uncertain as it had ever been to me despite my attempts to listen for any hint from the islands about how best to proceed, but up to then no such hint had come.*

*A gust of wind struck my face, both cold and warm at the same time, a brief collision of past, present, and future. I stopped and turned, looking up at the evergreen-covered hillside that stood watch over the Roche Harbor resort while the wind whispered a name to me.*

**Roland.**

*The islands had finally spoken on the matter. I did not yet know the meaning of the name but was certain that eventually I would.*

*Having delivered its message, the wind departed as quickly as it had arrived.*

*I walked on.*


Adele put down the journal, leaned back in the couch, and rubbed her eyes. The storm outside had gathered even more strength, gently rocking the big yacht from side to side against the dock as a downpour drenched the entire resort. She was fascinated over having just read the genesis of Roland's beginning. There were so many ways things could have turned out differently, but clearly Ophelia had agreed to the plan originated by Charles and Bloodbone. She gave birth to her son, Roland's father, remained a nun, and then lived out her days at the monastery while watching her son, and later her grandson, from afar. Roland's parents died in a car crash in Florida and Roland was sent to the islands to be raised by his grandparents. If Lucas Pine was the islands' golden boy as Roland so often liked to joke, then Roland Soros had been the islands' crown prince, a young man made so very different by an upbringing shrouded within a secret agreement between Ophelia, Charles, Donatella, and Bloodbone.

*If not for that meeting all those years ago,* Adele thought, *Roland might never have been born and my own life right now would be vastly different. The ripples of a single action continue to push out further and further into an unknown future.*

The ropes holding the yacht in place groaned from the pressure exerted by the wind and waves. Adele picked up the journal and held it in her lap under the soft glow of a nearby lamp. She caught herself picking at her lower lip, a bad habit made worse when she was engrossed in something. She turned the pages until she came to the place she had left off, traveling again with Bloodbone through time and events that included the banishment of Asav from the islands just six months after Roland's birth.

The brief affair between Donatella and Asav stunned even Bloodbone. Donatella would later explain how Asav began to show up at the house when Charles wasn't around, hinting that he knew about Ophelia and promising a way for the both of them to hurt Charles for having fallen in love with what he called "the godless nun." Soon after, while Charles was away on business and Donatella was deep into self-medication via a late-night bottle of gin, Asav arrived at the back door, urging that now was the time to get back at the man who had done so much wrong to the both of them. When she initially refused his demands, he decided then to simply take from her what she wasn't yet ready to give to him willingly. Donatella never called it rape, despite the bruises to her face and the cut lip, perhaps not wanting to admit she was capable of such weakness. Regardless, she then chose to lie with Asav three more times. It was during that third time when Charles, returning home unexpectedly, caught them together in his bed, resulting in a confrontation that had Charles pushing the barrel of a gun against Asav's head while Donatella stood to the side silent and stoic, waiting for the violence to escalate to a final conclusion that would leave Asav dead and her husband guilty of murder. She eventually intervened, begging Charles not to do it even as Asav dared him to pull the trigger. Charles lowered the gun and backed away. Asav mocked him for his cowardice while also threatening Donatella that he would let all of the islands know she was not the true mother of the child she was raising.

Charles again pointed his weapon. Bloodbone had arrived by then and promptly stepped in between the two men and demanded Charles put down the gun. Charles in turn demanded Asav leave the islands never to return. Bloodbone explained he did not have the power to do that on his own but should the others from the Truthing Tree group vote to do so, he would support their decision. A call was made. Doctor Edmund Pine and Delroy Hicks arrived at the Soros home a short time later, listening intently as the situation was explained to them.

There was a brief deliberation. The vote was unanimous—Asav was to be banished immediately. He raged at first, made more threats, but then eventually grew quiet and accepted his fate with one caveat—a promise to one day return and take what he claimed to have always been his. He was gone by morning, leaving no clue as to where he intended to go.

The rift between Donatella and Charles was never fully mended after that, made worse in fact by the shame she felt over having allowed herself to be so easily manipulated and used by a thing like Asav. Charles made more and more frequent trips to Shaw Island, staying at a small guest cabin he had paid to have constructed near the monastery.

Ophelia would eventually learn of the role Bloodbone played in the decision to have her child given over to Charles and Donatella. She was understandably upset, thinking he was a negative or even dangerous influence. Bloodbone hoped her feelings toward him would improve over time, describing her as a remarkable woman and potentially powerful ally.

As more time passed Donatella withdrew further into herself, rarely leaving the house. That is until Roland arrived many years later from Florida following the death of his parents in a car accident. His presence gave her life a sense of renewed purpose. It pleased Bloodbone greatly to see her acting more and more like her old self. Unfortunately, those better days were short-lived. Her death left an elderly Charles to continue raising Roland alone.

According to Bloodbone's journal, Charles seemed to fair only marginally better than Donatella did. He was not one to grow old gracefully and he grew increasingly abrupt and short-tempered toward those around him with the exception of Ophelia. It was her company he sought more and more of as it became clear his own time was running out. Toward the end even Bloodbone, Edmund Pine, and Delroy Hicks became, at best, distant acquaintances. All that Charles had built was to be left to Roland who, by the time he graduated from Friday Harbor High School, was the sole heir to a multimillion-dollar banking business and property portfolio, a situation Bloodbone described in the following way:

*I understood why the islands whispered the name Roland to me years earlier for it would be Roland who would not only carry on his grandfather's legacy but in time potentially forge an even greater legacy of his own. He is a far more complex young man than most yet realize—as intelligent and driven as Charles but also more considerate and earnest in his intentions. And he has a friend, a local football star named Lucas, the son of Edmund and Katarina Pine, who shows equal promise in helping to usher in this next long chapter in the storied history of our islands.*

Adele then came to the journal's final passage, reading it over several times:

*There remained one mentioned to me first by Old Raven almost two centuries earlier whom I had not yet discovered until very recently. I noticed the name in a news article for a mainland university newspaper—Adele Plank. She was a reporter and, according to the attached bio, a fan of a famous/infamous island author named Decklan Stone. Though having never met Mr. Stone I knew the tragic story of his wife Calista's mysterious disappearance some years earlier. When I later learned that Adele had not only visited the islands for an interview with the notoriously reclusive writer but also managed to reunite the long-missing Calista with her husband, I realized the islands were preparing the way for a new protector. My primary task now is to see her safely arrived and given the tools to reach her true potential.*

*To that end I intend to hide this journal from the world. Like the islands, it too will await Adele's arrival. Should she find it, as I believe she will because the islands wish her to, the transition from my time to hers will be nearly complete.*

*I do hope to have the privilege of calling her friend before my own days here are finally concluded.*

*We shall see.*

Adele looked up and then glanced outside, thinking there was lightning but finding it odd that it wasn't accompanied by the usual roiling growl of thunder. She put down the journal, stood up, and then walked to a window that faced the marina, watching the golden glow coming from a very familiar place further down the dock.

*What the hell?*

Her sailboat was once again on fire.

# 30.

"Stop!"

The only other person on the dock with Adele was still holding the gas can they used to start the fire—a fire that was already nearly out due to the torrential downpour that continued to fall.

"Why?" Adele shouted.

The person turned around. Though their face was partially hidden within a dark hoodie, Adele recognized the strands of wet, pink and blue-colored hair poking out from the sides.

"Why?" Adele repeated, her fists clenched and her lips pulled back from her teeth like a feral wolf. "Why do you keep doing this to me?"

"Why not?" Zuby answered, her tone both mocking and dismissive. "I heard this sailboat was given to you like pretty much everything else you have: the newspaper, your friends, Roland Soros. The question I keep asking myself is why you and not me?"

Adele struggled to respond to such incoherent stupidity. When she looked at Zuby, it felt like she wasn't looking at a human being but something so diminished, so selfish, so absent self-awareness that she couldn't find the right words to make someone like her understand that what she was doing was so wrong. What eventually came out might not have been the best choice, but it was likely the most accurate. "You're insane."

Zuby's disjointed cackle unnerved Adele even more. "That's what they keep telling me."

The sideways rain pelted Adele's face. She wrapped Roland's robe more tightly around her and then looked down, realizing she wasn't wearing any shoes.

"Nice outfit," Zuby said.

Adele fought the urge to roundhouse kick her into the water. Zuby represented so much of what was so wrong with modern society—the manic self-obsession and belief that their own feelings and interests were always more important than basic right and wrong and that their actions, regardless of how harmful they might be to others, should never have real consequences—it was all an increasingly dangerous state of constant dysphoria that would inevitably lead to widespread cultural collapse. "You're going to jail. You know that, right?"

"I doubt it. They'll hold me for a psych evaluation, put me back on my meds, force me to do some stupid counseling sessions or whatever, and then I'll be back to doing what I want when I want, which is putting privileged little bitches like you in their place."

"That might have been how things were handled when you were a minor, but you're an adult now. Things won't go nearly so easy for you."

Zuby's eyes narrowed. "How do you know about when I was a minor? Those records were sealed."

Adele wanted to keep Zuby talking. She figured the ferry service would have alerted Lucas about her arrival on the island by now, so he was likely already on his way to Roche. She had left her phone on the yacht, though, so there was no way at the moment for her to find out for sure. And then another thought struck her nearly as hard as the sideways rain was doing. *The fire earlier in the year in Friday Harbor,* she thought. *The authorities were convinced it was arson.* She stepped toward Zuby. "You burned those buildings down, didn't you?"

"Sounds like you're the crazy one." Zuby lifted the gas can and used it to point at Adele. "You keep away from me." She started to turn.

"Wait," Adele said. "We can get out of this rain and talk about it."

"Talk about *what*? I have nothing to say to you. Besides, all you'd be doing is stalling me until your sheriff friend gets here to hassle me even more than he already has."

"Zuby, you're holding the gas can you used to light my boat on fire for the second time. You've been caught. There's no getting out of this now."

"Since when is holding a can of gas illegal? You really are a fascist, aren't you?"

"First, it's obvious you have no idea what the word fascist actually means. Second, I said it already but apparently you didn't hear me, so I'll say it again—you're going to jail for arson. There won't be any juvenile courts or sealed records for you this time around."

"Those buildings were old."

It was almost a confession to a much bigger crime than merely damaging a small sailboat. Adele took a step toward Zuby, hoping she wouldn't panic and try to run. "Are you talking about the buildings in Friday Harbor that you burnt down?"

Zuby wiped the rain from her face and then rolled her eyes. "Nice try."

"I bet Sheriff Pine has already started to look into your involvement."

"No witnesses means no suspect. He can look all he wants, but he'll never prove it."

"I'm a witness to what you did here. That will go a long way toward linking you to what happened to those buildings. The question I still have though is *why*? You mentioned you were supposed to be on medication. Are you struggling with some kind of mental illness?"

"I'm not a freak!" Zuby cried out over the sound of the wind and rain. "It's perfect little people like you who need to stop judging me. I'm sick of it." She raised the gas can again. "Now leave me alone or else."

"Or else *what*, Zuby? What are you going to do?"

"I mean it." Zuby reached into her pocket with her other hand and then withdrew a lighter. Her head lowered slightly as she looked at Adele from under heavy eyelids. "I'll burn you bad." She tipped the gas can and watched fuel dribble out onto the dock. A gust of wind blew some of it onto her shoes as well.

"Put the lighter away," Adele said. "You're going to hurt yourself."

Zuby poured more gas as she walked toward Adele. "Stay right there you bitch." Her thumb clicked the lighter, creating a spark that the wind quickly extinguished.

"The gas is all over your shoes," Adele warned.

Zuby laughed. "What's the matter? You afraid of a little fire?" She flicked the lighter again.

"I don't want to see you hurt." Adele held up her hands. "Let me get you some help, okay?"

"Help? From you? I don't think so." Zuby poured out even more fuel while continually flicking the lighter. "People like you have been telling me I'm crazy my whole life. People like you always seem to get what you want without getting what you really deserve. Well, now that's going to end. I'm giving you what you deserve."

"Zuby, you don't even know me."

"Sure, I do—Little Ms. Perfect who everybody adores while I'm just the crazy fat girl who can't even get more than a few replies to her social media posts. Someone like you has no idea how lonely it is for people like me. It's like I don't even exist."

"Except when you're setting things on fire."

Zuby's soulless smile frightened Adele even more than the gas she continued to pour out onto the dock. "I learned a long time ago that fire has a way of getting everyone's attention."

The lighter in her hand went flick-flick-flick.

The storm seemed to hold its breath for a moment when the fuel first ignited. Adele stood frozen, locking eyes with Zuby between the flames that separated them. Zuby's smile widened. "All that warmth—it feels so good."

And then she screamed.

Fire erupted all around her before racing over her shoes and up her legs. She dropped the gas can and covered her face while backing away and then into the fire that was growing behind her.

Adele launched herself at Zuby, wrapping her arms around her upper body and pushing with all her strength to the side. They fell into the water together in a slip that was home to a Bayliner

Motoryacht, drifting beneath its hull as Zuby fought to break free from Adele's grasp by kicking her away.

The cold water quickly sapped Adele's strength and she was already desperate for air, but when she tried to swim to the surface the top of her head struck one of the Bayliner's prop shafts. Zuby was in a full panic by then, disoriented and flailing, unable to swim out from under the big boat's hull. Adele tried to reach out to her to help, but as soon as she touched her arm Zuby turned and clawed at Adele's shoulders and back. She was no longer on fire but now she was drowning—they both were.

*Death by Bayliner,* Adele thought, knowing she couldn't continue to hold her breath for much longer before the same panic that had already taken Zuby would overcome her as well. She grabbed hold of one of the shafts to anchor herself, knowing that to follow it to the prop and rudder would take her to the boat's stern and then into open water where she could more easily reach the surface. Zuby nearly elbowed her in the face as she continued to thrash around, her terror-filled eyes rolling within their sockets. It took all of Adele's remaining strength to try to push her away and out from under the hull.

Zuby's flailing slowed. She spasmed a few more times and then her eyes closed.

*I need to get her out of the water now.* Adele's fingers dug into Zuby's multi-colored hair so that she wouldn't be taken by the current and pulled out into the channel where there would be no saving her and the body might never be found. The first attempt to hoist her up onto the dock failed, leaving Adele fighting the urge to take a breath, which would only fill her lungs with water. She tried hoisting Zuby a second time, but she was far too heavy.

Adele was weakening and knew she was seconds away from drowning. A choice had to be made—continue trying to save Zuby or save herself.

Zuby's eyes opened wide. She unleashed an underwater scream that sent a line of bubbles swirling toward the surface as her hands clawed at Adele's face and neck. One of her knees struck Adele's stomach, her chest, and then the top of her shoulders. Zuby was using Adele's body like a ladder to push herself up to the side of the dock.

Deeper and deeper Adele went down until she could hardly see the outline of the boat's hull above her. Her lower body tilted outward as the current grabbed at her. She kicked hard, straightening out, and then felt her feet touch the muddy bottom. Looking up she saw the bottom of Zuby's shoes still in the water and then they disappeared. Adele's brain was too starved of oxygen by then to consider where she might have gone. Drawing a breath was the only thing she could think of. She used her arms and hands to steady herself, crouched low, and then pushed off against the bottom, hoping her momentum would get her to the surface.

It didn't.

Adele floated between the worlds of land and sea, her hand reaching up one last time before she began to descend once again. Her heart slammed against her chest, pumping blood starved for oxygen. The water surrounding her seemed to darken as her eyes began to close.

*Open your mouth, fill your lungs, and float away into the abyss.*

It would be so simple yet also so disappointing. Adele had spent the last several days reading through the Book of Bloodbone. He had lived lifetimes while her own story was now about to come to an abrupt and incomplete conclusion.

*Roland will be devastated. He's losing Ophelia and now me.*

It wasn't fair—but life and death rarely are.

Adele's body twitched and stiffened and her starved lungs burned fire.

She opened her mouth.

*I'm so sorry, Roland. I'm sorry I couldn't be there for you.*

An unusually long arm plunged into the water above Adele's head. She vaguely felt a hand grabbing at the robe's collar behind her neck. Water rushed against both sides of her body, forcing her chin against the top of her chest. Up and up she went, limp and nearly lifeless, but just aware enough to realize someone was gently placing her onto her back and pulling the saltwater-soaked robe closed over her breasts as the storm crashed all around the marina. She couldn't make out the shadowy face hovering over hers. She couldn't move. She couldn't speak.

*But I can breathe!*

Adele coughed and gasped while crying and laughing at the same time.

*I'm alive. I'm alive. I'm alive.*

She tried to sit up. The same hand that had just pulled her out of the water forced her to stay down. "Not yet." The voice was deep and soothing. "Rest."

"Zuby?" Adele mumbled.

"She's fine," the voice replied.

"Roland?"

"Waiting to see you again. There is much work that remains to be done by all of you."

Adele tried to open her eyes, but the lids felt like they weighed a thousand pounds. "Bloodbone," she whispered. "Is this the turning of the tide? Is that why you're finally here?"

No answer.

"Bloodbone," Adele repeated. Her eyes opened. The voice and the shadowy face it belonged to were gone. She heard heavy footsteps but couldn't tell if they were coming or going. *Is someone shouting my name?* she wondered. *Or is it just the wind?*

Adele smiled again because, for the moment, those things weren't important. She was exhausted. Her lungs still ached. Her body felt like lead. Her heart and head were pounding.

But she was alive and would see Roland again.

Nothing else mattered.

# 31.

"There you are," Tilda said while smiling down at Adele. "You gave us quite a scare, young lady." Last night's storm had passed. Sunlight now filtered in through the windows.

"What happened?"

"We found you and that Zuby girl lying next to each other on the dock."

"We?"

"Sheriff Pine was there first."

"He saved me."

"No," Lucas replied. Adele turned her head until she could see him standing at the end of the bed. "You were both already out of the water by the time I arrived on scene."

Adele looked up at the ceiling, realizing she was in one of Tilda's hotel rooms. She blinked, trying to push the fog from her mind. "You didn't pull me out of the water?"

Lucas shook his head.

"Then who did?"

"No idea," Lucas answered. "There was no one else there but you and Ms. Jackson."

"Where is she?"

"Back at the station. The medics looked her over—she's fine. They said the same about you. You've been asleep here for hours."

"I'll have a plate made up for you when you're ready," Tilda added. "Toast, eggs, sausage, juice, coffee, all of the above—whatever you want."

"It's morning?"

Tilda nodded. "Like the sheriff said—you've been sleeping for some time."

Adele looked at Lucas. "The fire in Friday Harbor—Zuby did it."

"I was thinking the same thing," Lucas replied. "I've actually been looking into her possible involvement for the last few days."

"She all but admitted it to me."

"Can I get you to fill out a statement to that fact?"

"Of course. She needs to pay for what she's done."

"I agree." Lucas paused. "There's one other thing."

Adele scowled as she propped herself up onto her elbows. "What is it?"

"After they made sure the fire was completely out and there was no danger to the other vessels in the marina the fire marshal looked over the damage done to your sailboat and concluded it's pretty extensive."

"And?"

"He tagged it as uninhabitable."

"*Uninhabitable?* But that's my home."

"I'm sorry, Adele. There's nothing I can do."

"All of my things are in there."

"You can get them out—you just can't live there. If the marina were to allow it, they would be in violation of their own insurance requirements."

"You're always welcome to stay here at the hotel," Tilda said.

"I was already staying on Roland's yacht."

Tilda nodded. "Good. I'm sure he has no problem letting you use it for as long as you need."

"I suppose." Adele shook her head. "I don't like handouts though."

"*Handout?* Don't be silly. After all of the good you have done for so many others, staying here at the hotel or on Roland's yacht isn't charity, Adele. It's friends helping friends."

"Will I ever be able to move back into my sailboat?"

"That'll most likely be between you and your insurance adjuster," Lucas replied. "Fair warning, though, the fire marshal was pretty sure that, given the age of the boat, your insurance will call it a total loss as the cost to restore it will be far greater than the actual value."

"It's only insured for about thirty grand. How am I supposed to replace my home with that?"

Tilda reached down and squeezed Adele's forearm. "Anything you need we're here for you and of course Roland will help out as well."

"I'm not a charity case."

"It's not charity."

"No? What would you call it?"

Tilda's chin jutted upward just a bit. "As I already told you—friends helping friends."

Adele realized she was overreacting—there wasn't anything inside of the sailboat that couldn't easily be replaced because the most valued things were the memories of her time spent inside its cozy interior and those memories would remain with her for the rest of her life. "You're right," she said. "I should be more grateful that nobody was hurt. Thank you for the offer to let me stay."

"Are you accepting?"

"No. I'll be staying on Roland's yacht for now."

Tilda's eyes warmed with kindness as she patted the top of Adele's hand. "Very well, but should you change your mind there will always be a room for you here should you need it."

"I know." Adele returned Tilda's smile. "You're a good friend."

Lucas shifted on his feet. "Uh, if you don't mind, I'd like to ask you more about who you think fished you out of the water last night."

"This sounds like official law enforcement business," Tilda said. "That's my cue to let you two talk alone." She closed the door behind her on her way out.

"Did you see who it was?" Lucas asked as he took out a pad and pen.

"If it wasn't you then it had to be Bloodbone," Adele answered. "The voice." she paused. "I think the voice was his, but there was so much wind and rain it was hard to hear it clearly."

"I already reviewed the marina's security footage. There were no cameras on that part of the dock though."

"The way I was pulled out of the water, it had to be someone very strong. That's why I thought it was you."

"Let's assume for now that it was Bloodbone. What did he say?"

"That we all have work to do."

Lucas looked up from his notepad. "What kind of work?"

"I don't know for sure, but if I had to put money on it, I'd guess it's something to do with Vlad Vasa."

"The damn Russians."

Adele nodded. "The damn Russians." She pushed herself up further into a sitting position. "Anything new from the Irish authorities on Fin's whereabouts?"

"Sorry, not a word. I'll be sure to follow up with them again soon. Are you still planning on traveling to Ireland to search for him?"

"If he's still missing after Ophelia passes then yes, I am."

"Did you tell Roland?"

"I did."

"Will he be coming with you?"

"No, I'll be going alone and don't you go trying to talk me out of it. My mind is made up." When Lucas started to reply, Adele cut him off. "I know I've mentioned it before but apparently it needs to be repeated. When I was being held captive in the basement of the Turn Point Lighthouse by Liya Vasa and her father's men, Fin dropped everything, no questions asked, to fly out here to help you and the others save me. A trip to Ireland to find out if he's okay is the very least I can do for him."

"Perhaps when the time comes for you to leave, Roland will be able to come with you."

"That would be wonderful, but it isn't required. Alone or not, I'm going."

"I really wish you would reconsider. If Vlad Vasa is responsible for Fin's apparent disappearance, then you going to Ireland alone is exactly what he wants to happen."

"For Fin that is a risk I'm willing to take—one that I would take for any of you."

"I would never doubt your courage or loyalty, Adele."

"That sure sounds like a nice way of questioning my intelligence though."

"You know better than to accuse me of saying something like that."

"I was trying to be funny."

"I'm not laughing."

"I see that."

As Lucas sat his oversized frame on the edge of the bed it creaked loudly in protest. "I'm worried about you making a trip like that by yourself is all."

"Life without risk isn't much of a life at all. It has never been my plan to just sit around waiting to get old. I still consider myself young, but I'm also more than old enough to realize how precious time is. None of us can afford to let days go to waste while telling ourselves we'll do it later and then later never comes."

"You won't be able to take the revolver I gave you."

"I know." Adele held up her tightly clenched fists and grinned. "I have all the guns I need right here."

"As impressive as those are I sure hope to hear from Fin before you fly off to try to find him."

"For now, I think it best you focus on building the case against Zuby. That girl is a serious menace. I saw the crazy in her eyes—the kind of crazy that runs deep."

"I'm working on it. She's not getting away with anything. Not this time."

Adele glanced down at the robe she was wearing, realizing it was different than the one from Roland's yacht. "Hey, I don't remember changing into this."

Lucas grimaced. "Yeah, about that, uh, your other robe was soaked, and after the medics looked you over and confirmed you were okay Tilda demanded we get you into something dry, so we put you into one from the hotel."

*"We?"*

"I hardly looked."

Adele tried not to smile but couldn't help it. *"Hardly?"*

"You don't remember us changing you into the new robe?"

"I guess so—vaguely."

"Now we're finally even for the bathtub situation."

"I *do* remember that. I also remember how you kept telling me how cold the water was."

"That water *was* cold."

Adele started to laugh. "Like a frightened turtle hiding in its shell."

"Geez, not this again. How much longer am I going to have to put up with your giggling over that memory?"

"Until the good Lord takes me away."

Lucas went quiet for a moment and then he straightened his wide shoulders. "Let's hope that won't be for a very long time."

A light rap on the door was followed by Tilda's return. She carried a silver tray with a steaming cup of coffee and a small plate of buttered toast. "I hope I'm not interrupting. I thought it best we get something in you before you get up. After what you've been through an empty stomach might make you dizzy." She set the tray down on the bed.

"Thank you," Adele said right before nibbling off a corner of toast and then bringing the cup of rich dark coffee to her lips.

"Can I get you anything, Sheriff?" Tilda asked.

Lucas stood. "I should be getting back to the station. There's a meeting with the prosecutor later this morning regarding the case we're building against Zuby." His phone started to ring. He glanced down at the number and then looked at Adele. "It's Roland." He put the phone to his ear. "Hello? Yeah, she's here. Just a second." He covered the phone with his hand, whispered to Adele that Roland didn't yet know about what happened last night with Zuby, and then handed the phone to her.

"Can you come to the monastery?" Roland asked. "Ophelia is begging to see you. She's so weak, Adele, but seems to be hanging on so she can speak with you one last time."

"Of course," Adele replied. "I'll come over on my boat."

"No, I'm sending the chopper." Roland's voice cracked. "I think this is it—she won't see another day. I need you with me. I can't do this alone. The chopper will be there in ten minutes."

"Okay, I'm on my way." Adele ended the call and handed the phone back to Lucas. "It's Ophelia." Now her voice was the one that cracked. "She's almost gone."

Tilda shook her head as she wiped away a tear. "Dammit," she whispered.

"He's sending the chopper," Adele said. "I need to go. I have some clothes on Roland's yacht that I'll change into first."

Lucas reached down and took Adele's hand. "I'll walk you there."

"No, you're busy. You don't have to do that."

"I know I don't have to—I want to."

Adele made sure her robe was wrapped tightly around her before pushing away the covers and getting out of the bed. "We should hurry."

They said little during the short walk to Roland's yacht. It was still early so thankfully there were few others on the docks. Adele threw on a pair of jeans, a light sweater, and some old tennis shoes she had forgotten about and then grabbed her phone and saw the multiple times Roland had tried to call her earlier. She texted him that she was on her way. Lucas stood waiting for her outside. When they reached the hotel, Tilda was there and indicated she wanted to join them on their way to the chopper.

"Please let us know as soon as Ophelia passes," Tilda said. "People all over the islands are wondering. She was far more loved and respected than she likely ever knew."

Adele just nodded, afraid that if she tried to talk she might start crying. The chopper sat ready and waiting. She turned and hugged both Lucas and Tilda, thanking them for their help and promising to update them soon. They stood side by side watching as the chopper hovered and then lifted up into the sky. It turned toward the resort and made a wide circle over it. Right before it headed toward Shaw Island Adele looked down and saw the fire-charred exterior of her sailboat, realizing that she hadn't even noticed it when she walked by it on her way to and from Roland's yacht.

*It's just a thing*, she thought. *Unlike Ophelia it can easily be replaced.*

The waters beneath her reflected the bright and hopeful calm of that day's morning sun.

Adele refused to cry. There would be time for tears later. During their brief phone conversation, she had sensed how close to a breakdown Roland was as the full impact and finality of Ophelia's imminent death was now hitting him very hard. He needed her strength, not her sadness, and that is what she would give him because he deserved nothing less.

As the chopper completed its turn Adele looked down at all of Roche Harbor—the multitude of sailboat masts and various colored yacht hulls, the rustic wood plank docks, Tilda's white-and-green hotel, and Roland's hillside mansion. The resort had never before seemed so small, so fragile, and so in need of protection as it did that morning. And so she would work to see that it, and all of the islands, remained protected, just as Bloodbone had done before her and Old Raven before Bloodbone.

*But first I must travel to Ireland to find Fin and if Vlad Vasa really is waiting for me there then so be it.*

# 32.

Adele was escorted into the monastery by Roland who was there to greet her outside when the chopper landed. He explained how Ophelia had suddenly awakened that morning and was calling out to speak to her. Another series of especially violent seizures the night before had left her completely blind and her speech was little more than a series of gasps, grunts, and garbled words, but Roland was able to make out Adele's name being repeated over and over.

"Father Thomas," Adele said after walking into the monastery's great room. "What are you doing here?"

"It's just Ifan, remember?" The retired priest Ifan Thomas still reminded Adele very much of the actor Clint Eastwood. His back was perhaps a little more bent than when she saw him last during her search to uncover the mystery of the Truthing Tree, and she noted a slight tremble in his right hand, but the flinty eyes were still sharp, the jaw strong, and the voice a low, gravelly whisper that hinted at an underlying toughness that remained within his nearly ninety-year-old body. The scar on one side of his face was there as well—the one he had told Adele was put there by Vlad Vasa after Ifan had sided with Charles Soros and Bloodbone to see the Russian banished from the islands. "I heard Ophelia was having a bit of trouble with the machine."

Adele cocked her head. "The machine?"

"That's my term for the Church's never-ending bureaucracy—old men in big hats sitting about making up rules to justify their positions."

Sister Zhara, who had been standing behind Ifan, stepped forward. "Father Thomas was kind enough to contact a cardinal he knew who then granted Ophelia a dispensation."

"The Church gave its approval to spread her ashes on the water?" Adele asked.

Sister Zhara nodded. "Thanks to Father Thomas."

Ifan shrugged. "If one man in a big hat tells you no, you need only find another in an even bigger hat to tell you yes. In this case a cardinal outranks an archbishop and that, as they say, was that—Ophelia's final wishes will be allowed to proceed as planned."

"That's wonderful," Adele replied. "Thank you."

Roland stuck out his hand. "Yes, thank you so much for helping my grandmother."

As Ifan shook Roland's hand his eyes narrowed. "You are indeed the spitting image of your grandfather. It's fascinating how things appear to change on these islands when in fact so much actually remains the same. He was a good man, Charles. Complicated to be sure, but his intentions and loyalty to the islands remained true throughout his life, there can be no denying that." Ifan leaned in closer and his voice lowered. "But I sense some of Ophelia in you as well and that is a good thing. She has long been a much-needed blessing to this place."

"I hope to do both their memories proud," Roland said.

Ifan held on to Roland's hand and silently stared at him for a moment before replying. "Yes, I believe you will." He glanced at

Adele and then winked at Roland. "And when it comes to her don't you dare blow it, young man."

Zhara cleared her throat. "Adele, I think it best we take you into Ophelia's room now. There may not be much time."

"Perhaps I could have a moment alone with Adele first?" Ifan asked. "We won't be long."

Zhara nodded. "Of course, Father."

Ifan extended his hand toward the door. "Some fresh air?"

"Sure," Adele answered. She followed him outside while wondering what it was that he wanted to tell her.

Ifan picked one of the many paths that led away from the monastery, remarking how nice it was to enjoy the sun's return after the recent and unusually powerful summer storm. His hands were clasped behind his back as they walked side by side through a field of tall grass. "You must be curious as to why I asked to speak with you in private," he said.

"Yes."

"I understand you uncovered Bloodbone's journal in the church tower at Roche Harbor."

"Did you know it was there?"

Ifan stopped, closed his eyes, and tilted his weathered face upward toward the sky. "You have been chosen to be his replacement."

"I know."

"It is a great privilege but also a terrible burden." Ifan turned toward Adele and looked down at her. "You are free to refuse it."

"Should I?"

"That is not for me to say."

"What would you do?"

"I can't even conceive of being in the position you are now. Karl never shared more than he thought necessary. The one individual he seemed most willing to be a part of his machinations was Charles Soros and Charles hasn't been an active part of the islands for some time now. I do find it interesting though."

"What?" Adele asked.

"That Karl's closest confidant was Charles and now yours is Charles's grandson, Roland."

"It's like you said— things appear to change on these islands when in fact so much actually remains the same."

Ifan grunted. "Indeed." His brow furrowed. "Karl is leaving you with a very dangerous complication."

"Asav."

"Yes. I believe the Russian intends to return sooner rather than later."

"How do you know?"

"Call it a very old priest's intuition." Ifan reached into the front pocket of his jeans and withdrew a pack of cigarettes and a lighter. He was soon inhaling his nicotine fix while staring out at the water in the distance. "Do you believe in the principle of yin and yang?" he asked between puffs.

"Like hot and cold, light and dark, that sort of thing?"

"Yes."

"I suppose."

Ifan flicked ash onto the ground. "Opposing forces that are inextricably connected. You mentioned hot and cold and light and dark. I would also include good and evil as part of that universal truth."

"Bloodbone and Asav," Adele said.

"Exactly—each is connected to the other."

"Bloodbone described something very similar in his journal when comparing John McMillin and Robert Moran. He said they were two sides of the same coin."

"Even I sometimes forget the breadth of Karl's longevity. To have known those two men during his lifetime is nothing less than remarkable." Ifan paused. "But McMillin and Moran were not comparable to the bond that links Karl to Asav. No, that is a link I feel more easily aligns to that between God and the devil."

"So, if I'm to be the one who replaces Bloodbone as the protector of the islands who does that align me with—God or the devil?"

Ifan put his cigarette out by pinching the end of it between his fingers and then flicking it onto the ground. "That will be up to you, Adele, or least until Asav shows up here to make that choice for you."

"I make my own choices and that won't change no matter what."

Ifan stared into Adele's eyes. "Are you willing to do to Asav what Karl would not?"

"What would that be?"

"Kill him."

Adele didn't hesitate. "If I have to, yes."

The crystal around Ifan's neck appeared to glow when the sunlight struck it. "You will," he replied with a hint of sadness. "And from that moment on nothing within you will ever be the same."

A gust of wind whipped the tops of the tall grass from side to side and created ripples across the water below. Adele turned toward the sound of a voice, deep and calm—the same voice that had whispered to her as she lay on her back on the Roche Harbor dock after saving Zuby from being burnt alive.

*The turning of the tide.*

The words swirled inside of Adele's head much like the windswept grass that surrounded her. She scanned the field for any sign of Bloodbone, but he wasn't there, or, if he was, he wasn't yet willing to be seen. She turned toward Ifan. "Did you hear that?"

"The wind?"

"A voice."

The breeze abruptly stopped and the world went still and silent until Ifan coughed into his hand and shook his head. "I only heard the wind, but that doesn't mean you didn't hear something. Did you recognize the voice?"

"It was Bloodbone."

Ifan's eyes widened. "Are you sure?"

"I don't understand why he's hiding from us. We need him."

"Tell me something, Adele. Why do you run? Why are you always pushing your body's physical limits? Why do you train and fight?"

"To be stronger."

"That's right—you are preparing for something, aren't you? Even though you might not yet know what it is, this preparation for what is coming is now so deeply part of your essence that you do these things instinctively—it's who you are."

"What does that have to do with Bloodbone?"

Ifan squinted into the sun. "Perhaps he knew how important it was to give you the space to prepare fully and on your own, only intervening directly when absolutely required. Hiding is not necessarily cowardice. Even Jesus was known to disappear into the wilderness for long periods of time as a means of preparing himself for the ultimate sacrifice he was destined to make for all of humankind. Later, arguably the greatest of the apostles, Paul, walked alone in the desert for many years while he too prepared himself for the considerable and dangerous task of building Christ's Church."

"All due respect, Father Ifan, but Bloodbone isn't Jesus and I'm certainly no apostle."

"And yet the parallels are there for those willing to see and learn from. God provides the tools, but it is up to each of us to find the courage within ourselves to properly use them."

Both Adele and Ifan turned toward the sound of approaching footsteps. Sister Zhara was walking quickly toward them, her face flushed and her features strained. "I apologize for the interruption, but Mother Mary Ophelia grows more restless and is demanding to see Adele now. The other sisters fear she is going to suffer another attack."

Adele started walking back toward the monastery and then paused and turned around. "Is it okay that I go, Father Thomas?"

Ifan waved her on. "Of course. I'll catch up." He started to light another cigarette.

"Roland tried to calm her down," Sister Zhara said as she and Adele walked together, "but she's having none of it. It's hard to believe someone so near death could remain so determined. Whatever she wants to say to you must be very important." She glanced behind her at Ifan who now stood alone in the field looking more than a little like a withered old leafless tree in winter with tobacco smoke swirling around its head. "He's a very interesting man, isn't he?"

"That he is." Adele looked up to find George the raven perched atop the entrance to the monastery, his midnight feathers shining brightly under the sun. He appeared to be following her approach intently. When she was about to walk beneath him, he nodded to her and she instinctively nodded back.

Zhara stopped inside the great room. "I'll let the other sisters know you wish to speak with Ophelia alone."

Adele waited there until Zhara reappeared and motioned for her to come into Ophelia's room where Roland stood beside her bed.

"Is she here?" Ophelia gasped, her voice weak and barely recognizable, the words garbled as if her tongue was too big for her mouth.

Roland bent down. "Yes," he whispered.

Ophelia's head turned toward Adele, her eyes ricocheting from side to side. "I can't see you. I can't see anything."

"I'm right here," Adele said as she came to the bed and took Ophelia's hand. The old nun's skin felt unusually cool and thin, like a piece of parchment left outside during winter.

Ophelia let out a grateful sigh. What little was left of her body sunk into the pillow that propped up her head. The smell of impending death hung heavy throughout the small space.

"I was told you needed to speak to me."

"I'm so tired," Ophelia murmured. "Is that you holding my hand?"

"It is," Adele answered.

"And Roland?"

"He's here as well, standing on the other side of the bed."

Roland looked away for a moment, clenching his jaw and taking a deep breath.

"Good." Ophelia closed her eyes and smiled. "You two must listen carefully."

"We're listening, Grandmother," Roland said. "Go on."

"Don't let anything come between you. Love, real love, is so rare, so precious; others would destroy it out of jealousy, insecurity, or just ill intent. The future is both blessed and cursed and navigating it requires great strength and determination. Make each other stronger and you will succeed. Allow them to break you apart and you both will fail. Do you understand?"

Roland looked at Adele and then nodded. "We do."

Ophelia's body stiffened as she grimaced. Her breathing was no more than short and increasingly shallow gasps. "Now I must speak to Adele alone," she muttered. "Leave us."

"Okay," Roland replied, the corners of his mouth trembling. He kissed Ophelia's forehead. "I'll be right outside."

Ophelia's unseeing eyes stared up at the ceiling. "How do I look?"

"Dead," Adele blurted, instantly horrified that she had said it out loud. "I'm sorry, I didn't mean it like that."

Ophelia laughed, groaned, and then laughed again. "Yes, you did and I love you for it." She struggled to sit up. "Would you mind putting another pillow behind me?"

"Of course." Adele easily pulled Ophelia forward, shocked by how little she weighed. *She's literally nothing more than skin and bones.* "How's that?"

"Better, thank you."

"Can I get you something? Some water?"

Ophelia's breathing seemed to improve a little. "No, I'm afraid I'm long past the need for food and drink. The next round of seizures is certain to take me."

"You don't know that. There's still some fight left in you yet."

"I'm old, I'm blind, I can barely speak, and my body is shutting down. Dear girl, I'm done for. Let's not waste time pretending otherwise. I need to tell you something."

"Okay."

"I dreamt of Bloodbone last night. He was agitated, angry even. It frightened me seeing him like that. It was a glimpse of the warrior he once was—a terrifyingly powerful thing of destruction and mayhem. But then the Bloodbone we know, the more mysterious and gentler version, emerged. His anger was replaced by concern and sadness."

"For you," Adele said.

Ophelia's cracked lips pressed together when she shook her head. "No, not for me. He kept repeating a message over and over, one that I knew was meant to be given to you. It was just two words. He spoke them more loudly and with greater urgency each time. When I awoke, I was alone in this room. I couldn't see, but I felt the sheets on my skin and heard the storm raging outside my window. I was awake—I'm certain of it. And then, somehow, I heard those two words one final time, spoken in Bloodbone's voice coming from the end of the bed, as if he was somehow here in the room with me."

"Maybe he was."

"He's like me, Adele, caught between the world of the living and the world beyond, desperate to finalize the path upon which you will soon be walking with what little time he now has left."

"What was the message?"

"Get up."

"That's it?"

"Perhaps that is everything. You will be tested Adele, far more than you might now realize. Bloodbone carried the great weight of his responsibility to the islands upon those giant shoulders of his, year after year, decade after decade. Will you be able to do the same? Will you, when that weight feels unbearable, when it presses down on you so that even the taking of a single breath seems impossible, find in yourself the courage, the grit, the sheer force of will to GET UP and do what must be done?"

"I hope so."

"Hope won't be enough—you must know. I told you the devil was real. Do you believe me?"

"Yes."

"I also told you he was tugging at my soul. Now I believe different. It isn't me he wants—*it's you.* Since your arrival here all those years ago he has been watching and waiting."

"For what?"

"For the turning of the tide when he thinks he will be allowed to safely return to these islands."

*The turning of the tide*—it was the very same message first delivered to Adele when she had a vision of Dylan Bowman inside of Bloodbone's hidden longhouse near the shores of East Sound. It was either an impossible coincidence or an actual warning of an increasingly precarious future. Adele chose to believe the latter. "You mean Vlad Vasa," she said.

"Vlad Vasa or Asav Dalv," Ophelia muttered. "The devil goes by many names, wears many faces, but he remains the same foul creature." Her eyes shut tightly as she groaned loudly and her fingers curled inward like claws. She began to pant. "One more thing," she whimpered. "One more request."

Adele was crying. She didn't care. Her friend was dying right in front of her. "Anything."

"I told you the song to be played when my ashes are being spread over the water."

"Yes, 'Take Me Down to the Infirmary', I remember."

"I chose that as much for the memory of Charles as for myself." Adele waited for Ophelia to continue. It took some time as she struggled to catch her breath. "I would also like another song played as you return to Roche Harbor with Roland," she finally said. "Consider it something for the both of you to remember me by." She smiled. "If Fin were here, I'm certain he would approve." She motioned for Adele to come closer and then whispered the name of the song into her ear. When Adele sat up, tears streamed down her cheeks.

Ophelia's head tilted back against the pillow and her mouth opened slightly. Her eyes suddenly cleared and then focused on something above her. She let out a long sigh. When she spoke, the voice was that of a much younger woman, the woman she had once been—clear, strong, and vibrant.

"It is time."

Adele was stunned by how quickly the seizure came on as it grabbed hold of Ophelia's entire body and shook it violently. She cried out for help. Roland, Sister Zhara, and Ifan entered the room as Ophelia arched her back, her eyes wide, mouth opening and closing like a fish out of water as she struggled to take another breath. More nuns followed, circling the bed, laying hands on Ophelia, and then stepping aside as Ifan approached, making the sign of the cross while solemnly reciting the last rites.

"Stop that!" Roland shouted. "She just needs to rest." He strode toward the bed and grabbed hold of Ophelia's hand. "She just needs rest," he repeated while looking over at Adele, his eyes pleading for help. "She's so cold." He stroked the top of Ophelia's head, pursed his trembling lips, and exhaled. "It's okay, Grandmother," he whispered to her. "You're free now—no more suffering." His chin dropped toward his chest. "I'll never forget you."

Ifan continued the last rites. When he finished, Ophelia lay unmoving on her back, her eyes and mouth open, her head turned slightly to the side and her body no longer convulsing.

Roland let go of Ophelia's hand, stood up straight, and then moved toward Ifan. Adele feared he might strike him, but instead Roland reached out, gripped Ifan's shoulder, nodded, and then told him thank you before walking out of the room.

Some of the nuns stood silently around the bed with their heads bowed while others tried but failed to muffle their sobs. Sister Zhara reached down and used the tips of her fingers to close Ophelia's eyes. Watching her do that reminded Adele of a door slamming shut—one that could never be opened again. She flinched as the lids were pulled down, the finality of what it represented feeling like a punch to the stomach.

Outside, George the raven's wailing warble echoed against the monastery's roof and throughout the surrounding trees. Adele wondered if the cry might somehow carry to every corner of the islands, delivering the message of the beloved nun's passing.

Mother Mary Ophelia was gone.

# 33.

# The Island Gazette

## San Juan Islands Mourn Passing of Mother Mary Ophelia

By Adele Plank

Last week, following a brief illness, longtime Shaw Island resident and spiritual leader Mother Mary Ophelia passed away surrounded by close friends and monastery colleagues.

Ophelia was an inspiration to many over the course of her long life. As a devoted nun, she was greatly respected. As a loyal friend, she knew no equal. For island business leader Roland Soros, she had become a precious member of his family, a woman he was so grateful to have come to know as Grandmother.

It was my honor to meet Ophelia some years ago and I was instantly fascinated by her intelligence, consideration, and inner strength. She was both simple and complicated, a seeming contradiction that, in fact, wasn't. For others who knew her you likely understand exactly what I mean. Ophelia loved tending to the monastery grounds and the many creatures that lived there with her and if needed she would protect that place with the tenacity of a mother bear as I personally witnessed on one occasion when an unwanted visitor arrived and it was Ophelia who, with shotgun in hand, made it very clear he had a choice to make—leave on his own two feet or in a body bag. Thankfully he chose to make a hasty retreat.

She embraced a holistic approach to living, feeding both mind and spirit with food and drink that she produced with her own hands and then shared with others. I was blessed to be a guest at her table a number of times. She was always such a gracious host, quick to laugh, slow to judge, and one who understood the importance of listening first and speaking second.

When her time came, Ophelia died as she had always lived—on her own terms.

We will all miss her terribly.

"It's a wonderful obituary," Tilda said as she folded the latest edition of the newspaper and placed it on a table next to the helm of Roland's yacht which was pushing its way through the storm-churned waters between Orcas Island and Shaw Island. A forty-knot wind was blowing from the north, bringing torrents of rain and the occasional explosion of lightning followed by booming thunder. Adele stood with Tilda and Lucas as they all peered out through the pilothouse glass at Roland who, despite the horrible conditions, stood alone statue-like at the end of the long bow leaning into the wind and rain while holding tight to the urn that contained Ophelia's ashes.

The waves crashed against the yacht's hull, lifting it up and then dropping it down, drenching the windows in saltwater spray. Roland gripped the stainless-steel railing with one hand and the urn with the other, seemingly indifferent to the storm. When Adele had suggested earlier that morning that they could delay the spreading of the ashes until the weather improved, he refused, saying his yacht could handle anything the inland waters might throw at it. So far it appeared he was right—the ride was rough but remained manageable as the yacht's autopilot system constantly adjusted to the challenging conditions.

"We're coming up to Broken Point," Lucas announced while pointing to the familiar outcrop of rock that extended out from Shaw Island that was to be Ophelia's final resting place where she had recently shared a bottle of whiskey with Roland and Adele and where, years earlier, she had spent so much time with Charles Soros looking out at the sea.

Adele reached down and picked up the sound system remote as Roland had instructed her prior to their leaving Roche Harbor and pushed play, making certain that both the interior and exterior speakers were turned up loud enough to be heard over the storm. When the music started seconds later, Roland glanced back at the pilothouse and nodded. "Take Me Down to the Infirmary" filtered throughout the yacht and was carried on the wind outside. Both Tilda and Lucas were silently mouthing the words while staring out through the windshield.

The yacht's bow continued to rise and fall as it cut through the tumultuous waters. When they reached the tip of Broken Point off of their port side, Roland opened the urn, held it up high, and then tipped it backwards. Ophelia's ashes poured out, swirling upward like a shadowy vortex before falling down into the sea as the music played on. At the very moment the remains touched the water multiple electrified fingers of lightning erupted across the sky, seemingly stretching out to simultaneously connect each of the surrounding islands of San Juan, Orcas, Lopez, and Shaw.

Roland turned and faced the pilothouse. He appeared leaner, almost gaunt, his hair completely white, and his eyes even more piercing than usual. Tilda gasped.

"What?" Adele asked.

Tilda scowled as she blinked several times. "I think I just saw a ghost."

"Charles Soros," Lucas said. "I saw it too. He looked just like him."

"Perhaps a trick of the light from the storm," Tilda replied.

Adele looked out onto the bow. Roland was there staring back at her. The wind had suddenly died down and the dark storm clouds were now pushing farther south toward the Strait of Juan de Fuca and the Olympic Mountains beyond. A sad smile accompanied the exhaustion that enveloped him like a torn and tattered coat. He straightened his shoulders and took a deep breath, his hair no longer white, his features softer, his eyes reflecting their usual friendly intelligence. He motioned for Adele to join him.

*Such a beautiful man,* she thought.

"Go," Tilda said. "He needs you now more than ever."

"Here." Adele handed her the stereo remote. She had already queued up the next song. "Right before we reach Roche, push play. Think of it as Ophelia's last gift to Roland."

Tilda's eyes twinkled with a bit of mischief. "I have something for him as well."

"What is it?" Adele asked.

Tilda smiled. "You'll see."

Adele looked up at Lucas. "Are you good to bring us into Roche?"

"Between the autopilot and the thrusters this thing pretty much drives itself," he answered. "No worries."

Tilda gave Adele a gentle nudge. "Go on. He's waiting for you."

Adele zipped up her windbreaker, opened the sliding pilothouse door, and stepped outside. The earlier hard wind was now merely a gentle breeze and the raging rain no more than a light drizzle. The storm was passing as quickly as it had arrived. "You did good," she told Roland. "It was exactly like Ophelia wanted."

"I hope so." He tipped his head toward the pilothouse. "Is Lucas okay behind the helm?"

"He says this thing practically drives itself." Adele's eyes widened. "Check that out."

Roland turned. A massive rainbow arced across the water between San Juan Island's Limestone Point and Spieden Island's Green Point. When Adele came up to him, he reached around her shoulders and pulled her close. "Did you order that up?"

"Something tells me that might be Ophelia's doing."

"I'd like to believe that. It sure is beautiful."

"Yes, it is." Adele paused, her mind searching for the right words. "Are you okay?"

Roland stuffed the urn into the side pocket of his jacket. "I will be." His damp hair lay flat against his forehead. "What about you?"

"I'm glad we were all here together for this."

"Me too—I really appreciate it."

Adele sensed Roland wanted to say more so she waited. When he finally cleared his throat, she knew he was about to.

"In the final days, there were times when, uh, when I wanted it to be over. I hated seeing her like that, but then, at the very end, I didn't want her to go."

"That's natural," Adele replied. "You have nothing to feel guilty about."

Roland massaged his forehead and then ran his hand over his face. "I know. It's just, well, I always thought I'd handle that sort of thing better than I did."

"There's no right or wrong way in that situation. You just react as best you can. In the end the most important thing is that you were there for Ophelia. She knew how blessed she was to have you in her life and I know you felt the same about her."

Roland's lower lip quivered. "I did." He squeezed Adele tighter. "Thank God I still have you."

Adele rested the side of her face against the space between his collar and jaw and breathed in the heavy mix of sea and storm as Roche Harbor's hillside backdrop rose up to greet them in the distance and another song started to play. She smiled hearing the soft growl of Van Morrison's delivery as the opening verse to "Into the Mystic" carried across the surrounding waters.

"Did you pick this?" Roland asked.

Adele looked up at him. "No, Ophelia did. She said the first song was for her and Charles and their past and this song was to be for you and me and our future."

"Our future." Roland's eyes threatened tears. He looked back and then nudged Adele. Lucas and Tilda were slow dancing inside the wheelhouse. "Shall we?" Roland asked as he took Adele's hand.

"I'd be disappointed if we didn't," Adele said.

Roland kissed her on the lips. "I know better than to do that." He twirled her around, dipped her low, brought her back up, and then kissed her again. A whoosh of wings startled them both. Roland chuckled. "That damn bird."

George the raven had landed on the bow pulpit railing. His head tilted from side to side as he looked at Adele and Roland before he turned to face the misty sea as Van Morrison sang of letting your soul and spirit fly into the mystic.

"What's going on?" Roland's mouth fell open as he looked out at two long rows of vessels that lined the saltwater path back to Roche Harbor like silent floating sentinels. It was a diverse collection of watercraft, from gleaming multimillion-dollar yachts to little skiffs that bobbed up and down in the waves.

Tilda wrapped her long coat tightly around herself as she stepped out onto the bow to join Roland and Adele. "From every island great and small they have come to pay their respects, and not just to Ophelia," she said. "They're here for you as well and the lasting legacy your last name represents."

"Soros," Roland said softly.

Tilda nodded. "Soros." She glanced back at Lucas, who remained inside carefully steering the vessel into the harbor, and nodded again. Lucas blasted the yacht's horn for several seconds, its sepulchral cry announcing their return. The sound was greeted by a multitude of other horns going off on both sides of them as they idled slowly between the two rows of boats. Figures emerged, walking out onto their bows and raising their hands in greeting as Roland's yacht passed in front of them.

"We love you, Roland," someone called out from the mist. This was repeated by another and then another and then another.

"You lost your grandmother, the last of your biological family," Tilda said, "but you will always have a family here on these islands. We take care of our own—don't ever forget that."

George launched himself from the pulpit and flew in front of the yacht like a feathered pilot ship guiding the way back home. The horns had stopped. The only sound was that of the song playing, the yacht's hull pushing through the water, and the rhythmic rumble of the big Detroit Diesel engines. Even the wind had gone still.

"Thank you for this, Tilda," Roland said. "It was very kind."

"How did you get them all to show up like this?" Adele asked. "Especially given how rough the weather was."

"All I had to do was ask," Tilda replied. "The respect and appreciation they have for Roland and Ophelia did the rest." She stared at Roland. "Young man, you are far more loved than you likely know."

Roland looked out at the rows of boats. "I think I'm finally starting to realize that."

"Now, if you don't mind," Tilda said, "I'll leave you two alone and go back inside to get warm."

Roland and Adele both turned to face the resort. George flew higher over the marina, up the hillside, and then disappeared directly over the gothic stone and bronze spires of Roland's residence. Sunlight cut through the mist, promising that blue skies and warmer temperatures would soon follow.

Adele snuck a peek at Roland. His eyes were closed and his face tilted up toward the sky. "Penny for your thoughts," she said.

"Big changes are coming," he answered.

"Does that worry you?"

"Nah." He squeezed her hand. "U.A.T.W."

"Huh?"

Roland gave her a sheepish grin. "Us against the world."

Adele squeezed his hand back. She liked the sound of that. Not because it was silly or quaint or funny but because it was so very true.

*Us against the world.*

Van Morrison's voice faded out as he sang of it being too late to stop now.


Indeed.

# Epilogue

"This time will be different." Jackson Ray continued stretching in his designer tracksuit as Adele, dressed in an old pair of shorts and a sweatshirt, did the same a few yards from him. He appeared even more supremely confident in himself than she remembered—a tall, sinewy-bodied combination of spa-treated skin, manicured nails, whitened teeth, and perfect hair.

"Maybe—maybe not," she replied.

"I won't be underestimating you today."

"But if you lose—"

"I donate twenty grand toward the reconstruction of those buildings that burned down in Friday Harbor."

"And if you win?" Adele asked.

"*When* I win, that'll be reward enough."

"It really means that much to you to beat me, huh? Is it because I'm a woman?"

Jackson bent down and touched his toes. "I don't like losing to anyone."

"Neither do I."

"Prepare to be disappointed because on this run, unlike last time, you're getting your ass kicked."

"Good luck."

"Don't say it unless you mean it."

Adele shrugged. "I do mean it."

"Why is that?"

"Because you're going to need it."

Jackson smirked. "We'll see." He pointed at the paved road that was directly under the "Welcome to Roche Harbor" sign. "This here is the starting point, right?"

"Yeah, it's the main road from Roche to Friday Harbor."

"Almost ten miles to the roundabout in front of the ferry terminal?"

"Correct. The first one to reach the two big trees in the middle of that roundabout wins."

Jackson took off his tracksuit pants to reveal his long and lean runner's legs. He adjusted the waistband on his shorts and then took a knee and retied his shoes. "I studied the route on my phone," he said as he stood. "I know where to go and ten miles is nothing."

"It'll be more than enough," Adele replied as she did a final few stretches and then made sure her hair was pulled back tightly from her forehead.

"More than enough for what?"

"To prove to you that the last time was no fluke because I'm the better runner. It'll sure be nice seeing more of your money going to a good cause."

"Have you always been this confident?"

Adele looked up and locked eyes with the older man. "No."

"What changed you?"

"Life."

Jackson gave Adele a long look. "Yeah, there's some grit to you that's for sure."

Adele started running in place. "You ready?"

"You don't want to talk more?"

"I'm here to race. This was *your* idea, remember?"

Jackson's invitation for a rematch came just a day after the spreading of Ophelia's ashes. Only when he also included the donation did Adele agree. "Fair enough," he said. "I'm ready when you are."

"Just one thing." Adele pointed at him. "You try any crap like last time and I swear I'll knock you into the dirt."

"I believe you'd try." Jackson grinned. "Don't worry—I'll be so far ahead I couldn't mess with you even if I wanted to." He took some deep breaths, rolled his shoulders, and then stared straight ahead. "Say when."

Adele shook out any remaining tension in her arms and legs. Unlike the last time they had raced, there would be no spectators—it was just Jackson and her and a ten-mile stretch of winding road through the island's interior. Not even Roland knew she was running today's race because Jackson insisted on it being done in secret. Adele figured that was because underneath all of the bravado and repeated promises of a decisive victory, there remained doubt that he could actually beat her. She knew that after a few miles, when he realized he was unable to pull away, that doubt would grow until it overcame him and that was when she would have the race won because he would push too hard too soon and wear himself out prematurely. Ten miles wasn't a marathon, but it was still more than enough time and distance to break a runner's spirit if they didn't run smart.

"Before we start, I need you to be honest."

"I wasn't aware I hadn't been," Jackson replied.

"You went through all the trouble of contacting me, setting this up, flying out here, just because I beat you last time?"

"I told you I don't like losing."

"But you've lost races before."

"What's your point?"

"My point is that you're doing this because I'm a woman. That's also why you demanded our little rematch remain a secret in case I win again. Your ego couldn't handle another dose of humiliation."

Jackson sighed. "Fine, I'll admit that you being a woman might have played a part in my wanting a second shot at you."

"I appreciate you telling me the truth."

"Here's some more truth—you won't win this time. I've been training hard."

Adele's smile was as cool as it was confident. "We'll see." She crouched forward with her arms hanging loosely at her sides. "Ready?"

"On three." Jackson counted down.

The race started.

Jackson sprinted the first mile, quickly putting nearly a hundred yards between himself and Adele. She knew his initial pace wasn't sustainable, though, and by the third mile he proved her right, slowing considerably as they reached a long and gradual incline in the road that took them past a number of large farm properties to their right and wooded hillsides to their left. By the fourth mile his initial lead had been cut in half—close enough that she could hear the soles of his running shoes hitting the asphalt surface, which meant he likely heard her behind him as well.

Clusters of cows munching on field grass looked up as they ran past them on the side of the road. The early morning traffic was minimal with only a handful of cars having driven by them since they started running. The air was still cool enough that Adele could see her breath in front of her face. By the time they reached what she knew to be the halfway point marked by a lone dilapidated barn in the middle of a field that dated back to the time of the original island homesteaders, she was pleased at how strong her body felt despite what remained an unusually fast pace. She had to admit that Jackson's effort was impressive and wondered if she could actually overtake him with just five more miles to go. He remained at least fifty yards ahead and was possibly pulling away a little as he seemed to be catching a second wind.

*Stick to the gameplan,* Adele thought. *If he can keep up that pace, then he deserves to beat me.* Her legs started to feel heavy and a metallic taste filled her mouth. She figured her own second wind was bound to come as well but it was a matter of when. If it didn't arrive soon then she would have little chance of overtaking Jackson before he reached the waterfront roundabout in Friday Harbor. *Don't force it. Let It happen. Trust the plan.*

Adele's "plan" was simple—don't allow Jackson to get too far ahead before they reached the Friday Harbor city limits and then unleash an all-out one-mile sprint to the ferry terminal roundabout. It was the significant descent from the top of Spring Street to the bottom of the hill that Adele hoped would give her the advantage. Where some favored running uphill, she had found over the years that she was able to run much faster than most while going downhill. Going uphill took more energy but going downhill for an extended period created pain and uncertainty as the impact on the feet, legs, and back, as well as the chances of falling and getting injured, were far greater. She found that people instinctively fought the pull of gravity when racing downhill, but she embraced it by leaning forward and running faster and faster until she was on the brink of losing control and wiping out.

*But you have to catch him first.*

Though several years older, Jackson remained an undeniably great runner. He had been doing it for far longer than Adele and was at that moment literally finding his stride as he raced along the paved road with his arms and legs all moving as a single, well-balanced machine. Merely trying to keep up was proving more difficult than she had thought it would be and there were just a few more miles to Friday Harbor.

*Run faster.*

That was easier said than done. Adele's lungs burned. She pushed through the pain, focused on her breathing, and willed herself to quicken the pace. She had never before run so fast for so long.

The road started to rise up again. Jackson slowed. Adele didn't. Once again, the distance between them shortened considerably. When she caught him glancing back at her, it suggested he could be faltering and getting worried that she might catch him.

*Faster.*

The city limits sign was now straight ahead. The road leveled out. Jackson quickened his pace. Adele did the same after taking in a big gulp of air and then breathing it out slowly while her arms and legs churned. Her second wind had finally arrived. She stared at the back of Jackson, estimating that he was no more than thirty yards in front of her. A little over a mile remained. Soon they would reach the top of Spring Street, turn left, and begin the final downhill stretch toward the ferry landing roundabout.

When Jackson looked back again, Adele clearly saw his shock at seeing her so close behind him. He was entering that zone of self-doubt as the full impact of running several hard miles pushes mental motivation and physical ability to the brink when, as the great Olympian Jesse Owens once said, all that remained was the strength of your feet and the courage in your lungs.

They reached Spring Street. Jackson turned left. Adele followed.

The road began its long descent.

For Adele the real race had now started.

Jackson began to slow just as she had predicted. He leaned back slightly while she leaned forward, her arms and legs moving faster and faster.

Halfway down the Spring Street hill she caught up to him and then seconds later she passed him. The business district was waking up to greet another beautiful island day. Parked vehicles lined both sides of the road. Some stopped to watch the two runners racing down the hill. One of them was Lucas who stood next to a pickup truck writing a parking ticket. He did a double take as Adele sped by. He called out her name, but she didn't look back or slow down. All that mattered now was reaching the roundabout first but not because beating Jackson was all that important. Even the donation to the town rebuilding effort was secondary. No, what motivated Adele to win went far deeper than either of those things. She had come to realize that a comfortable life was not for her. She wanted adventure—the kind of adventure where the seemingly impossible was made possible through sheer force of will that it be so. Ophelia's passing was a strong reminder of the fragility and briefness of our time and place in this world and Adele didn't want to see a single second wasted on negativity like fear and insecurity because in the end those things didn't matter.

Jackson cried out behind her. She heard him fall hard and then tumble forward. His lack of experience with running so fast downhill had doomed his chances of winning. Adele's plan had worked perfectly.

*He might be hurt.*

Adele slowed and then stopped and turned around. Jackson sat in the middle of the street. Both of his knees were scraped and bloody. He used his forearm to wipe the sweat out of his eyes.

"Are you okay?" she asked.

"You win," he answered dejectedly. "Go on and make it official—finish the race."

"You're bleeding."

"I'll be fine. It's not my first wipeout and it won't be the last."

Adele walked up to him and stuck out her hand. "C'mon." She suddenly felt a great deal of sympathy for the aging runner who had to know he was well beyond his competitive prime. With no wife, no kids, and now being less and less likely to ever win another marathon, perhaps he was without any sense of real purpose either. It had to be difficult trying to come to terms with all of that at once.

Jackson stared at Adele's hand like it was covered in excrement and then looked away. "You beat me—*again.*"

"I had home road advantage."

"This damn hill. You were practically flying down it."

"I picked this route for a reason."

"You're crafty." Jackson took Adele's hand and let her help pull him up onto his feet. "And you're also one hell of a runner."

"Thanks." Adele looked down at his scraped knees. "That looks like it hurts."

"Not nearly as bad as my pride."

"Do you want to finish?"

"The race?"

"Yeah—if you're up to it."

"Together?"

"Why not?"

"I didn't think we liked each other all that much."

"I *don't* like you," Adele replied, "but I respect your ability to run and I believe everyone should try to finish what they started."

"Me too."

"Then let's go—it's just a hundred yards more."

"If you're worried about the donation—"

"I'm not."

"I'll make good on our deal."

"I know you will."

Jackson dabbed at the blood on his knees with the tips of his fingers and then wiped them off on his shorts. "Ready when you are."

They jogged together toward the roundabout. After they reached it, Jackson turned toward Adele. "I still can't believe you never ran competitively."

"I don't run to compete."

"No?"

"I run to prepare."

"For what?"

Adele grinned. "If I told you I'd have to kill you."

Jackson looked at her as if he was really seeing her for the first time. "How about you celebrate your win by letting me buy you dinner tonight in Bellevue? I'm happy to fly you there and back."

"Thanks for the offer but I'm with someone."

"The local banker, right?"

Adele nodded.

"You ever consider trying something different?"

"Not a chance."

Jackson laughed. "Geez, you didn't even take a second to think it over." He pointed down at his legs. "Is it the bloody knees?"

"The knees will heal. To be honest it's the personality that could use some work."

"Ouch."

Adele stuck out her hand. "Good race."

"You too," Jackson said as they shook. "I'll have my bank transfer the funds as soon as I'm back in Bellevue."

"Do you need a ride to the airport?"

"No, a nice long walk sounds good about now. I figure it might give me some time to work on my personality."

"Can I give you a little advice?"

Jackson shrugged. "Sure."

"Don't try so hard to convince people to see you the way you want them to. You'll never experience a real relationship that way because you will always be running from who you really are."

"And who am I really?"

"I actually think you have the makings of a decent man if you'd only stop letting your ego and constant need for approval get in the way."

"That's some unusual wisdom coming from someone as young as you."

"I'm not wise so much as observant. In this world we're all alone together screaming in silence."

"Did you just come up with that?"

"It's from a book called *Manitoba,*" Adele replied. "I'm friends with the writer. Have you read it?"

"No."

"You should."

"What's it about?"

"Everything and nothing—just like life."

Jackson grunted. "I'm really glad I came back here again."

"Why is that?"

"Because it gave me a chance to get to know you better and I have to say, Adele, you are a fascinating mix of contradictions." Jackson flashed his big white smile—the old dog couldn't help himself. "Are you sure I can't convince you to have dinner with me?"

"Sorry."

"The banker?"

Adele nodded. "The banker. Besides, I have somewhere I need to be."

"Where's that?"

"Ireland."

"Oh? Business or pleasure?"

"Not sure. I think a friend there might be in some trouble."

"And if they are then you hope to help them."

"I intend to try."

"It must be nice having a friend like you."

"Thank you for the compliment."

Jackson bent down and dabbed at the blood on his knees again. "I meant it." He looked up. "Maybe *we* could be friends." His eyes betrayed just how lonely he really was.

"Maybe," Adele said, not wanting to break his spirit any further.

Jackson turned to go. "Take care of yourself."

"You too." Adele watched him go while standing under the branches of the roundabout trees. The early morning calm had been replaced by another buzzing summer day in Friday Harbor. Lucas stood further up the hill by his SUV staring down at her, likely making sure that she was okay. He waved. She waved back. Another ferry was arriving to unload yet more tourists eager to discover for themselves the magic of the islands. The historic buildings that lined both sides of the street waited patiently to greet them all as they had done for more than a century.

Adele wondered how long it would be until she saw Friday Harbor and the San Juan Islands again. She would be flying out first thing tomorrow to a much larger island halfway across the world.

It was to be another adventure.

Ireland awaited.

―――――――

# Book #10 of the San Juan Islands Mysteries

is coming in 2024: *The Walking Ones*

Until then you are encouraged to check out these other series

by D.W. Ulsterman available now at Amazon.com:

## The Montana Adventures Collection

## The Bowman Boys

Made in United States
Troutdale, OR
07/23/2023

11482672R00236